BENEATH A CRESCENT SHADOW

THE BALKAN LEGENDS

OTHER BOOKS BY A. L. SOWARDS

THE BALKAN LEGENDS SERIES

After the Crescent Strike (ebook prequel)
Beneath a Crescent Shadow
Beyond the Crescent Sky (coming January 2025)

DUCHY OF ATHENS SERIES

Of Sword and Shadow
Of Daggers and Deception

FALCON POINT SERIES

Heirs of Falcon Point
Codes of Courage

STAND-ALONES

A Waltz with Traitors
Before the Fortress Falls

BENEATH A CRESCENT SHADOW

THE BALKAN LEGENDS

A. L. SOWARDS

SHADOW
MOUNTAIN
PUBLISHING

This novel is a work of historical fiction and depicts a time and place with widespread violence, which includes references to off-page sexual assault. Characters and events in this book are products of the author's imagination or are represented fictitiously.

Visit us at shadowmountain.com

Library of Congress Cataloging-in-Publication Data

Names: Sowards, A. L., author. | Sowards, A. L. Balkan legends ; v. 1.
Title: Beneath a crescent shadow / A. L. Sowards.
Description: Salt Lake City : Shadow Mountain, [2024] | Series: The Balkan legends; v. 1 | Summary: "A devastating battle has claimed the lives of his father, uncle, and most of their army. Now Konstantin finds himself thrust into an inheritance he isn't prepared for, ruling as a vassal of the Ottoman sultan. After an arranged marriage, Konstantin and Suzana must shoulder the burdens of an Ottoman overlord amid a torrent of dangers much closer to home."—Provided by publisher.
Identifiers: LCCN 2023050706 (print) | LCCN 2023050707 (ebook) | ISBN 9781639932467 (hardback) | ISBN 9781649332714 (ebook)
Subjects: LCSH: Balkan Peninsula—Civilization—14th century—Fiction. | Turkey—History—14th century—Fiction. | BISAC: FICTION / Historical / Medieval | FICTION / Romance / Historical / Medieval | LCGFT: Historical fiction. | Romance fiction.
Classification: LCC PS3619.0945 B46 2024 (print) | LCC PS3619.0945 (ebook) | DDC 813/.6—dc23/eng/20231226
LC record available at https://lccn.loc.gov/2023050706
LC ebook record available at https://lccn.loc.gov/2023050707

Printed in the United States of America
Lake Book Manufacturing, LLC, Melrose Park, IL

10 9 8 7 6 5 4 3 2 1

For Elizabeth

I am so impressed by your compassion,
your diligence, and your intelligence.
Thank you for being a beautiful person inside and out.
You are a priceless part of our family.
I know you would probably rather read a book about dragons,
but this series has a character named Dragomir.
That's close, right?

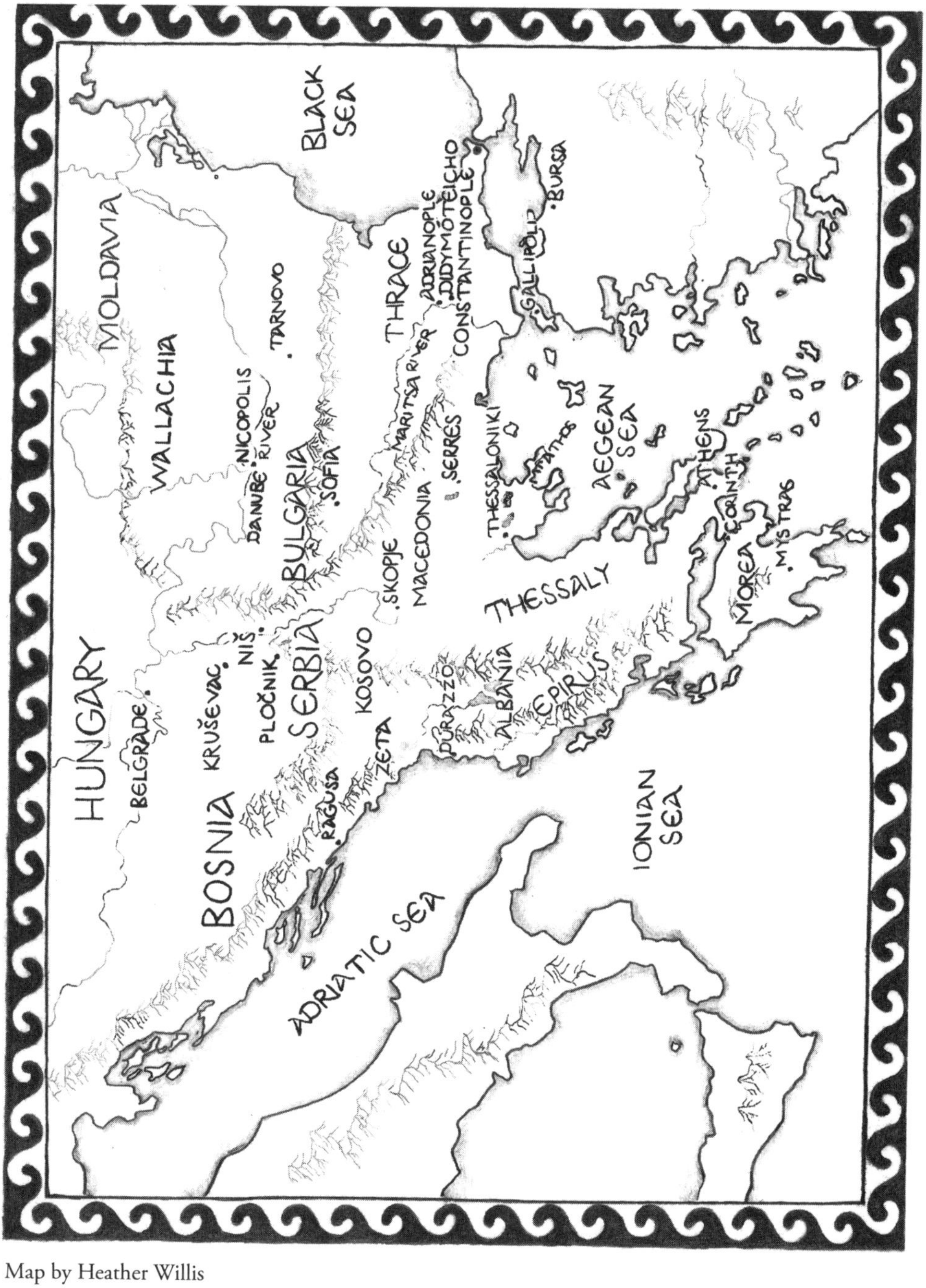

Map by Heather Willis

Glossary and Historical Background

Akincis: Ottoman irregular light cavalry, often serving as scouts or a vanguard to the regular army.

Bey: Originally a term for a Turkish tribal chieftain but also used as an Ottoman title for a local representative of the sultan's authority.

Boukellaton: A dense, ring-shaped loaf of bread baked twice and dried to give it a long shelf life. Normally eaten after being soaked in oil or wine.

Byzantine Empire: The Byzantine Empire was the eastern half of the Roman Empire, though contemporaries did not use the term. The Byzantines referred to themselves as Romans, and their neighbors often referred to them as Greeks. Their capital was Constantinople. For centuries, the Byzantine Empire controlled the Mediterranean world, but by the 1370s, their borders had shrunk significantly. The empire still included much of Thrace, the Peloponnese, and lands around Thessaloniki. Though their military and political power was on the wane, their cultural influence remained strong. Their religion was Orthodox Christian.

Caravansary: An inn with a central courtyard, rooms, and an outer wall to shelter travelers, merchants, and their goods and animals. Normally situated along trade routes.

Corselet: A piece of armor meant to protect the torso. It was normally hip length, with or without sleeves. Often made of lamellar in this novel's setting.

Courser: A warhorse known for strength and speed.

Dalmatica: A garment with wide, three-quarters-length sleeves and a roughly knee-length skirt, generally layered over a tunic. Could be worn by men or women.

Dama: Term of respect for a Serbian noblewoman.

Desetnik: Commander over a military unit of ten men.

Destrier: The most valuable type of warhorse, trained for battle and tournaments.

Dinar: A silver coin minted in Serbia and used there for several centuries. Originally, its value was roughly equal to the Venetian grosso, or one-eighth of a Byzantine hyperpyron, but at the time of this book, its relative value was decreasing.

Ducat: A gold coin primarily minted in Venice at the time of this book, worth roughly one florin, three hyperpyra, twenty-four grossi, or twenty-four dinars.

Florin: A gold coin minted in Florence, worth roughly one ducat, three hyperpyra, twenty-four grossi, or twenty-four dinars.

Ghazi: For the purposes of this novel, the term refers to an Ottoman raider who depended on plunder for his pay. The word has a more expansive definition outside the setting of the fourteenth-century Balkan Peninsula, but the more limited definition is used for clarity and accuracy in this book's historical setting.

Grad: A fortified Slavic town.

Great Mortality: The term contemporary people used to refer to the plague now known as the Black Death, which swept through Europe and peaked in the late 1340s and early 1350s.

Grody: A fortified area of a town or village.

Grosso: A silver coin minted in Venice, one-eighth the value of a hyperpyron or one-twenty-fourth the value of a ducat or florin. (plural *grossi*)

Gusle: A single-stringed musical instrument held in the lap and played with a bow.

Hauberk: A shirt of mail armor, usually with sleeves and reaching to the midthigh.

Hyperpyron: A gold coin minted by the Byzantine Empire, worth roughly eight grossi or dinars or one-third of a ducat or florin. (plural *hyperpyra*)

Karamanid: A Turkish emirate in south-central Anatolia. At the time of this novel, they were rivals to the Ottomans. They were Muslims.

Kephale: Leader with civic and military responsibilities in Byzantine or former Byzantine lands.

Kontarion: A type of cavalry lance with a wooden shaft and iron blade, normally eight to twelve feet in length.

Kral: Serbian term for king.

Lamellar: A type of body armor made from laced plates of leather, horn, or metal.

Meroph: A serf. Merophs owed labor and/or tribute to their feudal lord and to the church.

Narthex: The entrance area, antechamber, or court of an Orthodox church.

Nave: The main part of an Orthodox church between the narthex and the sanctuary.

Ottoman Empire: A Turkish empire that was established in Asia Minor, then expanded into Europe. Murad I, the founder's grandson, is sultan during this story. By the 1370s, many Balkan Christian rulers were vassals to the Ottomans, but Turkish control was not yet complete, nor were their rival Turkish tribes in Anatolia vanquished. The Ottomans were Muslims. They saw Europe as a new frontier—a land of opportunity and destiny.

Palfrey: A horse valued for its smooth gait, ideal for riding long distances.

Pasha: Ottoman title for a high-ranking military or civic leader.

Protovastar: A Serb official with financial duties.

Satnik: Serbian official, subordinate to the župan, with military and civil responsibilities.

Scimitar: A sword with a curved blade.

Serbian Empire: The Medieval Serbian Empire reached its zenith in the middle of the fourteenth century and included much of the Balkan Peninsula. It suffered serious setbacks with the death of Emperor Stefan Dušan in 1355 and a devastating loss at the Battle of Maritsa in 1371. The Serb religion was largely Christian Orthodox, and their culture was heavily affected by both Byzantine and Italian influences.

Sipahi: Ottoman cavalryman, compensated by salary or land grant.

Spathion: Type of sword common in the late Byzantine era, about three feet long with a double-edged blade.

Surcoat: A long, loose outer garment worn over armor.

Vila: Women of legend who play a prominent role in Serb song and stories in guardian-angel-type roles. Their qualities include beauty and speed.

Župa: A geographic area ruled by a župan.

Župan: Serb lord, comparable to a count.

*Relative values of coinage are included for curious readers, but it should be noted that values fluctuated with time and location, and sources often disagree on precise values.

Character List

Konstantin's Family

Župan Konstantin Miroslavević: Župan of Rivak

Župan Miroslav: Konstantin's father, former župan of Rivak who perished at Maritsa prior to the time of this novel

Dama Yaroslava: Konstantin's mother, wife of Miroslav, daughter of Župan Đurad Lukarević, who died of camp fever prior to the time of this novel

Lidija: Konstantin's sister

Ivan: Konstantin's brother

Militsa: Konstantin's sister who died as an infant prior to the time of this novel

Bogdana: Konstantin's sister who died of camp fever prior to the time of this novel

Dama Zorica: Konstantin's aunt, sister to Župan Miroslav

Darras: Zorica's husband, who died at Maritsa prior to the time of this novel

Danilo: Konstantin's cousin, son of Darras and Dama Zorica

Cedozar: Župan Miroslav's cousin who perished prior to the time of this novel

Other Serbs from Rivak

Miladin: Member of the Rivak garrison

Magdalena: Miladin's wife

Svetlana (Sveta): Magdalena's niece

Grigorii: Rivak's satnik

Vasilija: Grigorii's sister

Viktor: Vasilija's betrothed, who died at Maritsa prior to the time of this novel

Father Vlatko: Rivak's priest, tutor to Ivan and Danilo

Kuzman: Member of the Rivak garrison, weapons instructor

Bojan: Member of the Rivak garrison, riding instructor

Jasmina: Bojan's daughter, who works in the grody

Čučimir: Rivak's protovastar

Zoran: Member of the Rivak garrison

Akinin: Member of the Rivak garrison

Predislav: Member of the Rivak garrison

Ljubomir: Member of the Rivak garrison

Risto: Konstantin's manservant

Nevena: A cook

Jakov: A stableboy

Serbs from Sivi Gora

Župan Đurad Lukarević: Leader of Sivi Gora, Konstantin's maternal grandfather

Aleksander Igorević: Sivi Gora's satnik

Adamu: Member of the Sivi Gora garrison

Cyril: Member of the Sivi Gora garrison

Other Serbs

Suzana: Konstantin's betrothed, daughter of Baldovin

Baldovin: Suzana's father, a prosperous merchant

Župan Dragomir: Župan in lands that border Rivak to the east

Dama Isidora: Župan Dragomir's wife

Decimir: Župan Dragomir's oldest grandson and heir

Divna: Isidora's maid

Ilija: Member of Župan Dragomir's garrison

Josif: Member of Župan Dragomir's garrison

Radomir: Župan Dragomir's estranged brother

Župan Nikola: Župan in lands that border Rivak to the southwest

Dama Violeta: Župan Nikola's wife

Župan Teodore: Župan in lands that border Rivak to the northwest

Dama Emilija: Župan Teodore's wife

Ottoman Turks

Sultan Murad: Ottoman ruler, later known as Murad I

Lala Şahin Pasha: One of Sultan Murad's military leaders

Arslan: Turkish envoy sent to Serb lands

Esel: Translator for Arslan

Hamdi: Member of Arslan's diplomatic team

Kasim bin Yazid: Sipahi leader, who serves Sultan Murad

German Mercenaries

Ulrich: Captain of a band of mercenaries

Otto: Member of Ulrich's band, second in command

Erasmus: Member of Ulrich's band

Ludolf: Member of Ulrich's band

Chapter One
Sparks of Arson, Sparks of Hope

The Balkans, 1373

THE WOODEN DOOR SWUNG ON a squeaky hinge, moving with the wind as flames licked along the roof and brought down the home's last rafter. Only the stone hearth remained upright, singed and smoldering with heat from the inferno. Mere hours before, the house had sheltered nine people.

Konstantin Miroslavević dismounted and led his bay palfrey upwind of the smoke. "Did everyone make it to safety?"

"Yes, lord." The middle-aged man, one of the home's former inhabitants, kept his voice firm, but firelight showed tear trails cutting across the soot that clung to his cheeks.

"The other homes?" Konstantin glanced around the village.

"We were able to save them."

No deaths. Only one home destroyed. Small mercies to mitigate a massive disaster. The home could be rebuilt, but the burned fields couldn't produce another crop before winter. The entire village's harvest had been consumed in the blaze. Lookouts at the grad had spotted the fire in the middle of the fourth watch, and now the predawn light revealed destruction as far as Konstantin could see.

Upon the merophs fell the task of growing food for the župa. If they had no crops, they would be unable to pay their taxes. If they couldn't pay their taxes, Konstantin's coffers would remain empty. And if he had no money for tribute to the Ottoman sultan, Konstantin would lose his lands and his ability to protect the people from both Christian and Muslim raiders.

The fire seemed one more proof of his failure as župan. Defending the people of Rivak was his sacred duty. If he couldn't protect them from arson, why should they owe him loyalty or a hearth tax? But he had so few men.

Battle against the Ottomans had devastated Konstantin's family, taking his father, his uncle, and most of Rivak's garrison. The battle had done the same to most of Serbia. The kral had been slain, and new royalty was unlikely to be crowned while the sultan held power. Tribute payments to their Ottoman overlords left Konstantin with no way to afford mercenaries, and every year the financial strain grew. Famine had followed the war, but this year's crop had seemed so promising. Now that promise and its accompanying hope had gone up in flames.

He forced all emotion from his face. When he had been made župan at seventeen after his father had been taken in battle, he'd known he could show no weakness, not when his age and inexperience were plain for all to see. That hadn't changed in the last two years—he was still unproven. Now he was also on the brink of impoverishment, but he couldn't show the panic he felt. "Did anyone see how the fires began?"

The meroph whose home had been burned kept his eyes downcast. "We were sleeping."

Konstantin clasped the man's shoulder, hoping the gesture contained comfort. "Take your family to the grad. Father Vlatko will find somewhere for you to sleep until your home can be repaired."

"And the crops?" A lean man with bushy eyebrows pushed through the growing crowd of villagers. "What will we eat all winter?"

"I'll make sure you don't starve." Konstantin prayed his promise wouldn't turn into a lie. After two lean winters, there wasn't sufficient grain stored in Rivak to feed each inhabitant, but he'd make inquiries at nearby monasteries. The monks had granaries. Konstantin might have to barter some of his land in exchange for food, but fields were worthless if the merophs tending them all starved.

Miladin rode across the burned field and dismounted beside Konstantin. In the seven years since Miladin had been assigned to be Konstantin's bodyguard, Konstantin had closed the gap in their heights, but Miladin was still taller and brawnier. He held out the remnants of a torch. "The fire was no accident."

Konstantin hadn't expected a different verdict, but the proof of arson in Miladin's hands made Konstantin's throat, already feeling the bite of smoke, burn with rage.

Miladin looked over the destroyed home. The sorrow showed on his face in a way Konstantin hoped wasn't mirrored in his own. His friend could afford to show emotion. He wasn't a župan on the brink of failure, he was clearly past the cusp of manhood, and the scar that cut across the side of his face clearly proclaimed that he had faced danger and survived. "Bojan and Grigorii also found torches. I suggested they keep searching while I informed you."

What would Konstantin's father have done? Župan Miroslav would have sent his army of a hundred men to scour the countryside in search of the arsonist, and he would have fed the merophs with his plentiful stores of wheat, barely, millet, and rye.

Konstantin bit his tongue, hoping the pain would help hide his growing frustration at his own impotence. Few would have dared attack Rivak when his father was župan. Now Konstantin had a mere twenty-five men-at-arms and no money to hire more. "Did you find any clues about who's behind it?"

Miladin shook his head. "No, lord."

Konstantin gritted his teeth. Someone had destroyed his people's crops, and they were likely to get away with it. "Help me question the villagers."

Konstantin spoke with the man who'd lost his home, with the man's wife, and with his elderly mother. Then he asked a few children, who told stories of flames lighting their windows in the pitch black of night, but they'd seen nothing that revealed who was responsible. Nor had any of the other villagers.

The sun rose and grew ever higher, casting its stark, revealing light on the destruction. Grigorii, Konstantin's satnik, rode over with a half dozen retrieved torches. A frown creased his narrow face, and perspiration dampened his dark, lank hair. "The timing was cruel. Too soon for harvest but dry enough to burn with a vengeance."

Konstantin nodded his agreement. "Any idea who did it?"

Grigorii looked down. "I can guess neither who nor why. You?"

Konstantin didn't like to admit weakness, not even to his satnik, but honesty would serve them best. "No. Whoever did this has vanished as completely as the harvest."

When they finished speaking to the villagers, they headed back to the grad. Konstantin rode next to Miladin, but neither of them spoke. When they passed destroyed farmland, Konstantin wondered how he would keep his people from starving. When they rode through a stretch of woods, he tried calculating how much selling the timber might bring in. It wouldn't be enough to replace the harvest and raise the tribute money.

He would consult his aunt Zorica on how the family and the župa might survive the winter. She had been daughter of a župan, then sister to one, and now aunt to one—and Konstantin often leaned on her advice. If a solution existed, Aunt Zorica would find it, but not even she could solve the impossible.

The župa's largest settlement, Rivakgrad, came into view at midmorning. The fortified grody, built on a rise, towered over the small town that had grown around it. A moat and a palisade wall surrounded the grad—though the palisade needed repair. At least that problem was one he could fix with a few staves and a few men.

When they reached the grad, he led his company through the main gate. Two score homes made up the lower grad, and the inhabitants went about their business as usual. A scrawny lad carried water. The brawny blacksmith pounded on a long piece of red-hot metal. A gray-haired woman delivered a fragrant loaf of bread. Those closest to the road lowered their heads in respect as Konstantin and his group rode past. Respect for his position as župan, because they remembered better times, when the previous župan had been their protector in a way his son was not.

They rode past the last home of the lower grad and urged their horses along the causeway that led across a second moat and into the grody, where his family and men lived. The upper portion was more secure than the lower portion, and its elevation gave a better view of the surrounding lands. If only the view could have warned them against arson instead of merely revealing the fires once they'd begun.

Kuzman waited with the guards at the gate. He had taught Konstantin's father how to fight, as well as Konstantin and most of the garrison. His gray hair and weathered cheeks revealed his age, but his muscles and reflexes remained strong and sharp. "Is it as bad as it looks from here?" he asked.

Konstantin kept his answer brief. "Yes."

Kuzman's face fell. He was experienced enough to know that another failed harvest would lead to ruin. He had seen firsthand the destruction an uncontrolled Ottoman army could cause. Kuzman adjusted his stance and gestured to the extra horses outside the stables. "Župan Dragomir has arrived."

Konstantin nodded. He wished his father's friend had come another day. Their lands shared a border, and they frequently hunted together, but leisure after the tragedy of a burned harvest felt callous. Konstantin was in no mood for a hunt today. Regardless, he would play the gracious host. Dragomir was a trusted ally, and Konstantin had precious few of those.

"Aleksander Igorević traveled with him."

His grandfather's closest adviser. "Do you know the purpose of his visit?"

"No, lord."

"Very well." The last time Konstantin had spoken with the župan of Sivi Gora, their words had grown harsh, but perhaps dealing with the messenger would be easier than dealing with the župan.

Konstantin's maternal grandfather held lands made rich by a silver mine, and they had escaped the ravages of the battle of Maritsa and the Ottoman suzerainty that had followed. Unlike Serbian lands to the south and east, Sivi Gora was free. It wasn't, however, without its hardships. A generation ago, Župan Đurad Lukarević had lost all his children, save Konstantin's mother, to the plague. The marriage agreement between Konstantin's parents had arranged for the first son to inherit Rivak and the second son to inherit Sivi Gora, and Grandfather wanted his heir, Konstantin's younger brother, Ivan, to be raised and trained in Sivi Gora. Konstantin had refused to send away a boy of six, not when Ivan had already lost Mother and Father and a pair of sisters. He wouldn't deprive the boy of his brother, his last sister, his beloved aunt, and the cousin who was like a twin and give him over to a grandfather who frightened him. Konstantin had gained his grandfather's wrath, but he'd saved his brother's childhood, at least for a while.

Konstantin hadn't been quite so desperate a year ago. Would he be forced to pay his grandfather's price now? He could think of no other options. Sacrifice Ivan to save the people of Rivak? His brother would be provided for and honored in Sivi Gora, but he'd also be homesick. Their grandfather might feel affection, but he never showed it, and Ivan still needed the tenderness of a family.

When he reached the stables, Konstantin dismounted and handed his palfrey, Perun, off to the groom. Selling a few horses might supply some of the tribute money, but he needed his destrier for war and his palfrey for riding. It would be like selling his weapons—in the short term, it would gain him coin, but in the long term, it would make him even feebler, even more unable to protect his lands and his people.

Dragomir's freckle-specked fourteen-year-old grandson stood on the other side of the courtyard next to Konstantin's sister, showing her a composite bow. Lidija looked suitably impressed. The breeze swept her rich brown hair back, and her lips curved into a wide smile. Decimir said something to her, and the resulting giggle carried across the yard. Konstantin allowed himself a bit of peace. Lidija's future was secure, even if Konstantin failed to save

Rivak. She and Decimir weren't betrothed, but both families had expected their eventual marriage since they'd been respectively seven and nine.

Lidija spotted Konstantin and rushed over to him, looking back to make sure her gangly companion followed. "How did the fires start?"

"Arson."

Lidija's face fell. "Why would someone burn our crops?"

Decimir placed a hand on Lidija's elbow. "Someone must want to weaken Rivak. If the harvest disappears, poverty and unrest follow." Decimir glanced at Konstantin. "I am sorry, Župan Konstantin. I'm certain I speak for my grandfather when I say we will do all we can to support you."

"Thank you, Decimir." Having a neighbor he could trust was a blessing Konstantin did not take for granted, but unless Decimir or Dragomir was capable of miracles, there was little they could do to help. War and famine had ravished their lands too.

Konstantin left Decimir and Lidija in the courtyard and went into the keep.

As he reached the top step, his cousin, Danilo, nearly ran into him. The boy's head reached the level of Konstantin's ribs, and his dark eyes, almost black, held pleading. "Kostya, can Ivan and I stay up late for the wedding feast?"

"What are you talking about?" Konstantin liked Decimir, but he wasn't ready to marry Lidija off to him quite yet—not unless they were very desperate indeed. Canon law allowed brides as young as twelve, Lidija's age, and she was fond of Decimir, but she deserved a few more years of childhood before she left Rivak.

Ivan arrived only a moment after Danilo, trailing after him much as he had since he'd taken his first step. "You'll let us stay up, won't you? Aunt Zorica said the feast will go well into the night. But you're the župan. She can't send us to bed if you say we can stay awake."

Konstantin had no intention of overriding his aunt when it came to bedtimes, but confusion swirled around him almost as swiftly as the boys jumped from foot to foot. "What feast?"

A smile lit Ivan's face. If Konstantin accepted money from his grandfather and sent Ivan to live in Sivi Gora, would he ever smile like that again? "Your wedding feast, Kostya."

"*My* wedding feast?" Konstantin had no marriage plans. Other matters took priority—like determining how to feed the merophs and keep whoever had burned the harvest from attacking again. Danilo had seen all of eight winters, and Ivan but seven. They were no doubt mistaken.

Aunt Zorica met Konstantin in the great hall. "Danilo, Ivan, go ask Father Vlatko to join us. The župans have matters to discuss."

"Like the wedding?" Ivan's frail face seemed pleased. Only a fortnight before, he'd been so ill he couldn't get out of bed, but now a rambunctious expression played on his lips.

"That has yet to be settled. Now go." Aunt Zorica shooed them along. Danilo whistled for their dog, and the boys disappeared into the corridor.

Suspicion and curiosity tugged at Konstantin as he studied his aunt. "It sounds to me as if you've been keeping secrets." He pushed down irritation that no one had bothered to inform him of wedding plans that placed him in the role of bridegroom.

"I knew nothing of it the last time we spoke." Aunt Zorica glanced over her shoulder, where Dragomir, his wife, and Sivi Gora's satnik sat near the hearth. "Your grandfather's idea. I heard it only when they arrived, but I think it's a wise one."

"Marriage? Now? I don't have time or the means to take a bride." He kept his voice quiet but firm.

Aunt Zorica motioned him toward the others, her movements more lighthearted than he'd seen from her in some time. "Listen to his reasoning before you reject it."

Konstantin normally trusted his aunt's experience, but her expression held more indulgence than wisdom at the moment. Regardless, he followed her to the table to greet his guests. He needed answers, and since he'd eaten nothing before riding off to see the cause of the fires, he also needed food.

Župan Dragomir stood, still spry despite outward signs of age, and grabbed Konstantin's wrist in a firm greeting. His pale eyes met Konstantin's. "I am sorry we arrived on a morning of ill news for you."

"At times like these, it is comforting to know I have friends." Konstantin turned to Dama Isidora. Gray streaked the small portion of her hair not covered by a veil, and wrinkles had crept into the corners of her eyes, but frailty still seemed decades away. "How was your journey?"

"Pleasant, until we saw the fires," she said. "How bad is the destruction?"

"One home lost. The village's entire harvest gone." There were other villages in Rivak, but the blow was a mortal one. For the present, he would focus not on the approaching doom but on his duties as host. "Welcome, Aleksander. I assume you bring news from Sivi Gora?"

The probing eyes of his grandfather's satnik surveyed Konstantin from beneath thick eyebrows. "Your grandfather sends his regards. He will be pleased to hear that Ivan is in good health. You and Lidija as well, though that's more expected."

Aleksander hadn't been present at the dispute between Konstantin and his grandfather, but it sounded as though he'd been told at least part of Konstantin's arguments. Family tenderness aside, Ivan was sickly, and Konstantin didn't trust anyone other than Aunt Zorica to keep him alive when his fevers came.

Konstantin murmured his thanks when one of the servants brought a bowl for him to wash in, then the group sat around the long table to eat. How soon would he need to ration food at the grody? After the company left, perhaps, but not before. They might be friends and representatives of family, but it was dangerous to reveal how desperate Rivak had grown.

Father Vlatko and Miladin joined them at the table. Miladin remained quiet.

The priest said his greetings to Župan Dragomir, Dama Isidora, and Aleksander, then cast twinkling eyes at Konstantin. "The boys tell me you are to be married."

"They told me the same rumor." Konstantin turned from Father Vlatko to his guests. "But I have received no information beyond their word."

Aleksander spoke first. "You're of age. Your grandfather has found you a match."

"I do not think the timing is right."

Aleksander lifted an eyebrow. "Given what I've seen this morning, I would think the timing is perfect."

Konstantin shook his head. "My largest village has lost its harvest. They won't be able to survive the winter without help, let alone pay their hearth taxes, and our granaries are already depleted. It will be a harsh winter. And in the spring, I'll owe tribute to the sultan."

"And how do you intend to survive the winter and raise your tribute?" Aleksander asked.

Konstantin didn't know how he could pay the sultan and keep custody of his lands, but he wouldn't give up. Rivak had belonged to his family for too long. He couldn't surrender. "I suppose I will ride to Sivi Gora and ask my grandfather for advice."

Perhaps he and his grandfather could reach a compromise. Ivan would have to go to Sivi Gora when he came of age, but perhaps until then, he could divide his time between the land of his father and the land of his mother.

"Will you ask for advice or for coin?" Aleksander ran his fingers along his cup.

Konstantin didn't answer.

"Rivak is blessed with friendly neighbors." Aleksander turned to acknowledge Župan Dragomir and Dama Isidora. "Sivi Gora has not been so fortunate. We've spent much fighting the Hungarians this past year. We've no coin to spare for tribute to the Turks. Nor does the župan wish to give a potential enemy strength that might one day be turned against him."

Konstantin understood. Even if the money had been available, his grandfather would have objected on principle. "Then, perhaps a journey to Sivi Gora would be unwise when I have pressing matters at home."

"No, a journey to Sivi Gora is unneeded at present," Aleksander said. "Your grandfather plans to meet you for the betrothal ceremony. He departed Sivi Gora on Saint Vitus Day. So unless you plan to keep him waiting, we ought to leave today. Župan Dragomir and Dama Isidora have agreed to accompany you."

His grandfather and his closest ally had conspired to see him married off? He met his aunt's eyes. Surely she, at least, would recognize the folly in leaving his lands when the situation was so desperate.

She reached out a hand and laid it on his wrist. "You carry a heavy load, Kostya. A wife could help."

Župan Dragomir cleared his throat. "Sentiment aside, the bride comes with a dowry. One large enough to pay your tribute, fill your granaries, and hire mercenaries."

Konstantin considered that new information. Rivak's biggest problems could all be solved with enough coin. It sounded so easy . . . until he tried to summon an image of the woman he was supposed to bind himself to. Marry a stranger? That was not so easy. "So, you concur with my grandfather and think I should marry away my problems?"

Dama Isidora spoke next. "You are old enough to marry. A wife with a dowry is the perfect solution."

Konstantin looked at his hands. He didn't like revealing weakness, but better to lay it out now, before he traveled to wherever Aleksander planned to lead him. "Why would anyone want to marry a župan who is vassal to the Turks and whose coffers are almost empty?"

"Because her father doesn't need money." Dragomir tapped his fingers on the tabletop. "He's a successful merchant, thirsty for prestige. He can't buy nobility for himself, but he can arrange a noble husband for his daughter."

"The woman isn't noble?" Konstantin could live with that, but he was surprised his grandfather had agreed to it.

Dragomir shook his head. "No, but she is young and prosperous."

"How young?" Konstantin didn't want a twelve-year-old bride.

"She just turned seventeen."

Seventeen. That was reasonable. "Grandfather approved?"

Aleksander nodded. "It's not an ideal match, but given the circumstances, it is a necessary one. Fortune has not favored Rivak these past years. That prevents the best of matches. Other options run the risk of consanguinity, and you need a dowry more than you need noble blood. The bride gift is to match the worth of the dowry, so your grandfather suggests a portion of your lands. While married, you'll retain their use, and as long as you have an heir, they will pass to the next župan of Rivak."

A dowry could save Rivak without weakening or dismembering it. But what would the bride be like? He could endure a homely wife, but he didn't want to endure a stupid or an evil wife. Konstantin glanced to Miladin. He was happily married, but he'd loved Magdalena before they'd been betrothed. Likewise, his Aunt Zorica and Uncle Darras had been a love match. That would not be his fate. "It seems that if I wish to fulfill my duty to Rivak, I must marry a stranger."

Dama Isidora gave him a smile, an expression that showed understanding and compassion. "Her name is Suzana."

Chapter Two
Betrothed

Suzana Baldovinević peered from the balcony into the garden below and recognized the man she'd seen yesterday, Župan Đurad Lukarević. He'd been speaking to her father then about her marriage to the man's grandson. She'd been forced to leave before the conversation had ended, but it had sounded as if the deal had been settled already through letters and messengers. The tie to nobility would suit her father's pride. Having a daughter like her out of his sight would suit his indigestion.

Today, the grandfather stood with a different man. Rumors of the bridegroom's arrival had flown around the villa that morning. If the man below was the grandson, he was young, much younger than the middle-aged bridegroom she'd expected prior to yesterday. His deferential posture could be because he spoke with his grandfather . . . or he could be a man-at-arms reporting to a master.

The walls of the villa surrounded three sides of the garden. Suzana watched from the upper-level balcony on the east, and the men stood on the west. Their voices did not carry over the sounds of the river. She pulled back from the balcony to make her way around the villa to where the men stood, but then she hesitated. Whatever they said to each other, it wasn't meant for her. Her father would not approve of eavesdropping. She did not wish to earn his wrath, but she would soon leave his household and join her husband's. Learning to survive in a household was no easy task—and she was tired of merely surviving. Perhaps with the right knowledge, she might not only survive but also find contentment.

Which was the greater risk? Going ignorant into a marriage or learning more and angering her father or her husband-to-be if she were caught?

Suzana tiptoed around the north side of the garden and stayed near the inner wall, where shadows would make her nearly invisible. The men passed out of sight as she rounded the corner and walked along the west side of the covered hallway, but their voices became clear. They spoke Slavonic, so at least she and her husband-to-be would have a common language.

"Is it lawful to use her dowry that way? Dowries are supposed to provide security for the bride, not pay off the husband's debts." That voice was new to her. The bridegroom?

"It's not a debt; it's a tribute to the sultan." The grandfather's voice, with a deep timbre and words clipped in strict precision. "Baldovin knows your situation and expects you to do exactly as I advise. He has no qualms. He doesn't want his daughter married to a deposed noble. He wants her married to a župan, so it's in his interests that you keep Rivak."

"But will she mind?"

Suzana held her breath. Did he ask because he genuinely cared about her wishes? Doubtful. He probably wished to ensure he did nothing unlawful.

"She's seventeen. I doubt she knows what she wants."

Suzana bristled but remained quiet in the shadows.

"Seventeen is not so very young." The other voice again.

"Not for you, perhaps. Your destiny called you early. And your brother's destiny calls him. Aleksander reports he is in good health."

"His health comes and goes. Aunt Zorica works miracles with him."

A grunt from the grandfather. "Sivi Gora has a physician trained at the University of Salerno."

"Ivan is too young to be parted from his family."

"I am also his family. How is he to learn his role if he does not grow up in the land he will rule?"

"He can go when he is older." Silence ran for several long moments, then the younger voice spoke again. "When is the betrothal to take place?"

"Today."

"But I haven't even met her!"

"Will that matter? You can marry and use your wife's dowry to save your lands, or you can reject the offer and lose everything. We've been over all this. You ought to be pleased. Wealth and youth—what more do you want in a wife?"

"I am not displeased. I am grateful to you for arranging it. The timing just feels . . . rushed."

Suzana agreed with the young voice—it was rushed, but if their marriage was inevitable, postponement offered no benefit to her. The bridegroom couldn't be any worse than the men she already knew, so maybe a new start would offer an improvement.

"The timing is not negotiable, I'm afraid," the grandfather said. "Baldovin insists on the betrothal taking place at once. A previous betrothal was canceled, but if a betrothal still occurs at the planned time, Baldovin hopes to escape any hint of scandal."

Suzana felt her face heat. The pain in her past was not of her making, but in her father's eyes, the slight over the canceled betrothal was all Suzana's fault. Best to marry her off as soon as possible, and if the marriage could bring him a bit of prestige, so much the better.

"Was there a scandal?" The young voice again. She wanted to see him. Her view from across the courtyard hadn't been close enough to determine eye color or if his face showed any hint of kindness.

"It doesn't matter. This is your only viable option if you wish to remain župan of Rivak."

"So, I'm trapped?"

Suzana felt the sting of those words and tucked her hand into a fist to keep it from trembling. She had no choice save to marry the man her father picked for her, but if he, too, felt forced into the marriage, would that frustration turn against her?

The grandfather's voice changed so it was softer, less stern. "Marriage can be a source of joy, Konstantin."

"Was it like that between you and Grandmother?"

"It took some time to find our way together, but yes, we had joy. While she lived. Losing a wife and six children to plague changes a person. No doubt the losses in your family have changed you. But tragedy does not make happiness impossible. You're at the beginning of your story, Konstantin. The beginning of your reign, the beginning of your marriage. Don't be so gloomy."

Footsteps sounded on the paving stones, and Suzana crept closer to the edge of the upper walkway, hoping for a glimpse of her soon-to-be betrothed. Would his worry over scandal taint their marriage, or would he follow his grandfather's advice?

The older župan walked around a corner and disappeared behind a fountain and a wall of vines. She scanned the garden for the younger župan, and when she located him, she froze.

He stood below and to the left of her, and his eyes had found her. His face was pleasant. A short, well-tended beard, not yet full, sad gray eyes, dark-brown hair.

She hadn't meant to be caught, and the jeweled circlet atop her hair veil was too fine for her to be mistaken for a servant. Maybe he'd think she was only passing through rather than intentionally listening to his conversation with his grandfather. He wore mail under a lamellar corselet, with a sword strapped about his waist—a shorter Greek-style spathion rather than the longer swords the Italians favored. Her father's keen eyes had shown her the value of observing and discerning what a group of people might be interested in trading for. She evaluated clothing and weapons out of habit, but trade was not her concern now. She searched his face for signs of anger or signs of forgiveness, signs of surprise or signs of interest. Whatever emotions he felt, they were hidden away, unreadable.

His eyes held her, and she stood unmoving, unsure what to do. Speaking first would be too bold, at least for a woman. Even if she were brave enough to speak, what would she say? Offer greeting or apology? Express her hope that the marriage soon to be forced on them would not turn to misery?

His lips parted, and his head tilted, as if he had a question. "A fair morning to you, lady."

She managed a nod, and then someone called from across the garden to Konstantin, and the moment his attention was diverted, Suzana ducked into the shadows.

Grigorii was invaluable when it came to protecting Rivak and offering counsel, but Konstantin wished he wouldn't have interrupted. Something about that woman had mesmerized him. "What is it?"

"I saw your grandfather leave and thought you might wish to know that Perun has settled well."

Of course Perun had settled. It was Svarog that didn't like unfamiliar stables, but Konstantin had left his warhorse at home. He glanced at the upper level again. The woman had disappeared. "Do you know what Suzana looks like?" The woman he'd seen was either Suzana or one of the legendary vila, because he felt an unexplained connection with her. He'd been praying for years for ways to save Rivak. He'd been praying for days that he would be able to love the woman he was to marry. God seemed to be granting both pleas at exactly the same time through the same person. He couldn't call it love, what he'd felt when he'd seen the woman with the large eyes and exquisite mouth. It was more a hope that love was possible and this marriage was part of God's plan.

"I hear she is seventeen and plain."

Disappointment bore into Konstantin's chest. The woman he'd seen had been the correct age, but he would not call her plain. He would use words like *intriguing* and *superb*. Or perhaps he wouldn't, if the woman weren't Suzana. But why would God allow such an intense longing for a woman other than the one he was to marry when he'd been praying so hard to become a good husband?

Only a while ago, he'd wanted to delay the betrothal ceremony as long as he reasonably could. Now he wanted it to happen at once because he needed to know if the woman in the garden was Suzana. "My grandfather said something about a previous betrothal, one that was broken, I assume, before any vows were made. Will you ask around, discreetly, and tell me what you find?" Konstantin meant to leave it in the past, whatever it was, but he wanted to know *what* he was leaving in the past. Probably a misunderstanding over the dowry. "I don't plan on avoiding the marriage . . ."

Grigorii plucked a dead leaf from one of the vines. "But all the same, you'd rather know than be blindsided. Arranged marriages are difficult enough without unpleasant surprises."

"Yes." Konstantin had felt occasional mirth at some of the stories Grigorii and Čučimir had told on the ride from Rivak about arranged marriages that had gone poorly, but mostly, he'd felt dread.

"I'll make a few inquiries, lord."

"Thank you."

They left the garden, and Miladin joined Konstantin as Grigorii left. Miladin, as always, scanned the area around them, on the lookout for danger, even in a villa. Seven years ago, Konstantin's father had tasked Miladin with Konstantin's safety, and he'd never completely given up his role as bodyguard. The constant proximity had led to an easiness Konstantin felt with few other men. "I know your situation with Magdalena was far different from mine with Suzana, but have you any advice for a soon-to-be bridegroom?"

Miladin focused his gaze on Konstantin and smiled. "Help her be happy, lord, and then she will help you be happy too. Few people deserve a bit of joy as much as you do."

"And how do I help her be happy?"

"That depends on the woman." Miladin looked as if he might say more, but Aleksander Igorević approached them.

"It's time to prepare for the ceremony," Aleksander said.

Konstantin went to his assigned rooms in the villa. Risto, his manservant, waited there to help him change into a tunic of wool and a dalmatica of silk patterned after one seen in a painting from Constantinople. The rich embroidery made the dalmatica stiffer and heavier than most silk garments, but compared to his armor, it was light and flexible. Risto added an embroidered cape and fastened it with a bronze fibula.

Konstantin's hand went to his side, and Risto chuckled. Risto had once been a warrior, but age and injury had prompted a change from garrison duties. "You won't need your sword at the betrothal ceremony, lord."

"I suppose not." Konstantin ran a hand along the fine fabric of the dalmatica, a gift from his grandfather. Sturdy walls surrounded the villa, and Konstantin's most trusted men would be nearby, some armed outside the church. But he knew little of the villa—nothing of its hiding places, only a cursory glimpse of its strengths. Konstantin had enemies, as did his grandfather. The villa's owner probably did as well, the man who would soon be Konstantin's father-by-marriage.

A pair of shoes had been laid out for Konstantin, thin things that didn't reach to his ankles. He kicked them off and pulled his boots back on, then slipped a knife into the right one. It wouldn't do to go into unknown places unarmed.

Risto stared pointedly.

"No one will see what I have on my feet in a tunic this long." The hemline touched the floor.

The manservant's expression didn't change. "I know you've faced danger before, lord, but Cedozar and his assassins were slain. I don't think your future bride will be a threat."

Konstantin thought of the woman in the garden. "It's not her I'm worried about." That wasn't completely true. He was anxious about whether they would like each other, whether she would be pleased with Rivak, whether she would really ease the burden of his responsibility the way Aunt Zorica had said. "We're surrounded by strangers here."

Risto nodded. It wasn't approval, not exactly. More a commitment to say nothing more on the matter of Konstantin's footwear and hidden blade.

Miladin and Aleksander accompanied Konstantin to the villa's chapel. Upon arrival, Konstantin followed the instructions given by the priest, kneeling in the narthex and holding the candle handed to him. But he had trouble concentrating as the priest droned on about the Apostle Paul's admonitions to husbands and wives and about the wedding feast in Cana, when Christ had performed His first miracle. Because the woman kneeling next to him was the woman from the garden.

Suzana's knees began to ache midway through the betrothal ceremony. Finally, the priest said, "The servant of God Konstantin Miroslavević is betrothed to the servant of God Suzana Baldovinević in the name of the Father, and the Son, and the Holy Spirit. Amen." He repeated it, then added, "Let Thine angel go before them all the days of their life," and in that moment, Suzana was sworn to marry a man she had yet to say a word to. A man who would marry her only because he needed her dowry.

When the service ended, Konstantin stood and reached out to help her to her feet. His hand was firm, the pressure adequate for the purpose but not overly forceful. If he was polite in public, that could work to her benefit. Perhaps he wouldn't beat his wife in front of others, and her survival would simply be a matter of ensuring most of their interactions were not in seclusion.

He led her down the stairs of the church, then left her side for a moment to speak with one of his men. He returned soon after and gave her a respectful bow. "I have a gift." His hands, no longer steady, presented her with an apple and a ring, traditional symbols of betrothal. The rich red skin of the apple was polished and unblemished, and the smooth gold of the ring caught the afternoon sunlight.

Her father and a dozen others watched, though they were not near enough to hear any words spoken. Still, her face heated under the scrutiny. She avoided Konstantin's eyes and reached out to accept the gifts. "I thank you, my lord."

"May I put the ring on your finger?"

"You may." She tried to hold her hand still, but she was nervous and couldn't stop the tremble. His left hand supported hers while his right slipped the simple but flawless band of gold past her knuckle. He tried the fourth finger of her right hand, and when the ring was too loose, he tried the third. There the fit was comfortable and secure.

His touch surprised her. The gentle movements were not what she expected from hands lined with a few small scars, numerous calluses, and several scabs—hands that looked like they would be at home holding sword, ax, or halberd.

He lowered his voice. "I hoped it would be you when I saw you in the garden."

Suzana's gaze had been firmly on their hands rather than on his face, but now she met his eyes. She ought to say something, but all that came out was a simple question. "Why?"

Something in the set of his jaw softened ever so slightly. "It felt right. I could picture you in Rivak. And your face . . . I see beauty there, and thoughtfulness. A man is blessed to have a wife who is pretty and wise."

Pretty and wise? Her mind flashed to the time her father had introduced her to the son of a trading associate. He'd thought her plain and had said so—not in her hearing, but when her father had repeated the claim, she'd sensed he'd barely refrained from striking her. Another glass of wine and he would have. Her insufficient beauty had lost him what would have been a favorable arrangement.

And wisdom? She had little of that. Whenever she made an error in her father's ledgers, he cursed her stupidity and struck her, even without the aid of alcohol.

Thus far, Konstantin was not threatening, but good behavior was expected at a betrothal ceremony. It was later that men revealed cruelty and violence. Her father said a man had the right to hit his daughter or his wife. The villa's priest had concurred but had added that violence should not be without reason. She would try to give her husband no reason to hit her, but what would happen when he realized she was neither beautiful nor intelligent when that was what he expected?

When she said nothing, Konstantin continued, though the hint of warmth no longer touched his lips. "I can't imagine how hard it must be for you to leave your home, but I hope you will be happy in Rivakgrad. I look forward to knowing you better."

What would it be like to be happy? Thus far, she could not read her betrothed's face, but perhaps she could learn to read his moods, learn how she could please him, when she should avoid him, and what he expected of her. Perhaps he would not beat her too much while she adapted.

He released her hand. "What can I do to make the journey more comfortable for you? We can make it in one day, though it would require many hours on the road. Or we can divide the journey into two days. There isn't an inn on the way, but we have tents."

"Whatever you arrange will be fine." That was the best answer. If she picked the wrong choice, the one that didn't match what he wanted, he might hold it against her.

"Would you like to travel in a carriage, or do you prefer to ride? Dama Isidora reported that some stretches were a bit jarring in the carriage. So, you are also welcome to switch off."

All his words were respectful, considerate, kind. If he was always like this, life with him would be a vast improvement over life with her father. But it was probably an act, a display of concern before the new betrothed and her family. Once married, he'd turn out just like all the other men she knew. "Spending a portion of the time in the carriage and a portion on a horse would be most agreeable, thank you."

"And would you prefer an early start and a long day of travel with a comfortable room at the end of it or two days of less rigorous travel but a less comfortable night?"

"I have no preference, my lord." He'd asked her much the same thing before, and she still had no desire to force his hand and suffer his displeasure should her choice disappoint him.

He hesitated. "How long would you like to prepare for the journey? I imagine you have things to pack and goodbyes to say."

Goodbyes? No friendship existed between her and any of those who lived in the villa—her father wouldn't allow familiarity between the family and the servants, and his friends and advisers were all male. Friendship with them would have been improper, even if she'd desired it. Perhaps if her mother had lived, she would be sorry to leave her, but she'd never known her mother, and her father had never forgiven Suzana for killing her in childbirth. "I can be ready to leave as soon as tomorrow, my lord."

One of Konstantin's eyebrows quirked upward. "You wouldn't mind leaving so soon?"

"No, my lord."

"Please, call me Konstantin. We are betrothed, after all, and I hope we will soon become friends." More hesitation. "If you do not mind leaving tomorrow, there are things in Rivak that would benefit from my attention sooner rather than later, and leaving then would let us arrive before the

Sabbath, even if Dama Isidora prefers we divide the trip into two days. If you really have no objections, I'll escort you to your father and see if he balks at our leaving so soon."

"I have no objections, my—" She caught herself before calling him *my lord* again. "Konstantin." She said his name before realizing it would come out as *my Konstantin*, and that sounded far too intimate for the circumstances.

His lips parted, and the mask of hidden emotion cracked for a moment, showing amusement. "I suppose I am yours now." He held out his arm for her. She rested her hand on his forearm while the heat of embarrassment crept up her neck. She kept her eyes downcast as they walked. She had blundered, but he didn't seem to mind—yet. His arm was hard beneath her hand. He wore an embroidered dalmatica rather than his armor, but the firmness of his muscles reminded her of who he was. A noble. To nobles fell the task of waging war, and waging war led men to cruelty.

Suzana did not participate in the discussion that ensued. Konstantin politely asked her father if he would mind if they set out on the morrow. Her father did not mind and sent his steward to see that Suzana's things were readied. Then her father, Konstantin's grandfather, and Konstantin discussed when the marriage would take place. Konstantin suggested after the harvest. Her father suggested it take place sooner. Konstantin's grandfather took her betrothed's view.

Konstantin leaned his head toward her ear. "You haven't said when you wish the marriage to take place. I've much to do before harvest, but if it would please you the way it would please your father, we can manage it before then. We can also put it off a while, but for my part, I greatly desire it to happen before Lent."

The church did not allow marriages during Lent, so Suzana took his request to mean he needed access to the dowry before Easter.

Her father kept pushing for an early marriage. The grandfather insisted that a proper wedding with the right guests would best occur after harvest time. That did not seem so very far off. The betrothal ceremony bound her to Konstantin like rope bound her father's cargo to a ship. The marriage ceremony would change the binding from rope to chain, but regardless, her future was tied to Konstantin's from this point on. She'd spent her whole life trying to please her father and avoid his wrath. Now it was Konstantin who would determine how many bruises would line her arms, Konstantin whom she must learn how to please and not provoke. "Please set the time as is most agreeable to you, my—" She caught herself again before calling him *my lord*. "Konstantin."

What almost looked like a smile pulled at his lips. "My lady, may I call you Suzana?"

He oughtn't call her a lady, not yet at least, but she nodded her agreement. It didn't matter what he called her as long as he didn't hit her.

Chapter Three
Villa of Danger

"You're certain she doesn't mind leaving today?" Dama Isidora asked Konstantin for the second time.

He checked the trunks being loaded into a cart. The stacks were higher now, with Suzana's things added. "I asked her how much time she would like to prepare, and she said she could leave as early as this morning." He glanced at the sun. Too high. They should have left already, but an axle on one of the carts had needed repair, and Miladin's horse had gone lame overnight. Everything seemed to be conspiring to give them a late start. "In truth, I must rely on what she says, because it is difficult for me to guess what she feels."

Dama Isidora laughed.

"I don't find the situation amusing." He was eager to please his betrothed, but he needed a little help from her. She had said almost nothing to him throughout the feast the night before. Perhaps she wasn't pleased that the marriage would take place at harvest's end. Konstantin, too, would prefer more time together before the two of them were officially wed, but he wanted money to hire mercenaries before winter. Not more than he wanted Suzana's happiness, but he couldn't bend to her preferences if she wouldn't reveal them to him.

"I am sorry, Konstantin, but to hear you complain of someone hiding her emotions when you yourself are so adept at turning your face to stone . . ." She'd stopped laughing, but a smile remained. "Dama Suzana and I shall have a good chat on our journey, I think. Keep asking her what she wants. In due course, she will trust you enough to answer."

"I hope you're right. If you will excuse me, Dama Isidora. I must bid my grandfather farewell."

His grandfather stood near Aleksander, both of them surrounded by men-at-arms from Sivi Gora. Grooms from Suzana's villa led out horses, and the men checked the bridles and saddles. So efficient. Why was Konstantin's departure not so smooth?

"I expected you to leave before me," his grandfather said.

"So did I." Konstantin swallowed back frustration. He wanted to get back to Rivakgrad by nightfall, but he'd been willing to take it in two days, had that been Suzana's wish or had Dama Isidora preferred a more leisurely trip. Two days was not so bad—he would still return home earlier than he'd planned.

"I will see you again for the wedding."

Konstantin nodded. The wedding had been set for autumn, after the flurry of harvest was done and before winter hampered travel. "I will pray that the snow does not come early and that you have swift roads now and then."

"I will pray that you and your future bride are ready for a life together by the time I next see you."

"Thank you for arranging it, Grandfather."

"You are pleased with her?"

Konstantin glanced at the hall, where her father's steward had insisted Suzana wait until they were ready to leave. "I am."

"I am glad."

The tug over Ivan's future still hung between them, and Konstantin suspected the matter would come up again at their next meeting, but for now, he felt gratitude. His grandfather had managed to save his lands for him and had brought a woman into his life whom Konstantin wanted to love. "How long did it take for you and Grandmother to love each other?"

Grandfather's lips twisted in thought. He had few wrinkles for a man of his age, and the motion made him seem younger, perhaps because Ivan sometimes made the same expression, and Konstantin was more familiar with it on his brother's face. "Love is hard to measure." He gestured to a nearby pithos of water. "That is water. It is wet, and there is enough there to soak you through. The sea is also water, but it's much larger and much deeper. Yet just because the sea is larger, it does not mean that a raindrop is not also water. Love is like that. For your grandmother and me, it came quickly, and then it grew. Looking back, what we had at the beginning of our marriage seems small compared to what it became. But that does not mean it was not love."

Maybe his grandfather wasn't as cold as he so often seemed. Maybe Sivi Gora and their grandfather wouldn't be so hard on Ivan when the time came for him to leave Rivak. "Thank you for sharing your wisdom, Grandfather. If you have any suggestions on hiring mercenaries, I would be grateful for your advice on that as well."

"I will think on it and bring candidates to the wedding with me."

"Thank you. Godspeed, Grandfather."

His grandfather gazed across the chaos of the courtyard. Konstantin felt his neck heat. The disorder seemed one more sign of Konstantin's inability to do anything right, and no doubt Grandfather could pick out all Konstantin's mistakes, even the ones Konstantin himself couldn't yet pinpoint. But rather than criticize, he simply clasped Konstantin's shoulder. "Godspeed to you as well."

By the time Župan Đurad and his men had left the villa and forded the nearby river, Konstantin's own group had made significant progress. The carts were packed, and half the horses were saddled, including Konstantin's palfrey, so he could escort his future bride to the coach she would share with Dama Isidora. Perhaps today he could draw her into more of a conversation than they'd had yesterday. Regardless, the prospect of seeing her again was pleasant. Perhaps what he felt for her was only a raindrop at the moment, but he could imagine it growing into a sea.

He met Suzana's father on his way to the hall. The man's face was pale and his jaw tense.

Konstantin clasped his hands behind his back. "We're nearly ready. Am I free to collect your daughter?"

"She . . . she's disappeared. I don't know where she is. Neither do any of the servants."

Shock kept Konstantin quiet for several long moments. "Did she run away in the night?"

"No, she was in the hall this morning."

Konstantin tried to breathe through the tension. "Perhaps she returned to her bedchamber. Or went to bid someone farewell."

Baldovin shook his head. "We've searched all the rooms, even the stables and other places she never goes. She's not in the villa."

"Has this ever happened before?" Perhaps his bride-to-be had a habit of disappearing.

"No."

Maybe she didn't want to get married, so she'd run away. It seemed odd to wait until morning when she could have left during the night, but it was blazingly apparent that he knew nothing of how her mind worked. In hindsight, her reticence the day before seemed clear evidence of her reluctance to marry a stranger.

A shout sounded from the top of the wall. "There's a body in the river."

"What?" Baldovin bellowed. "Whose body?"

"A woman. In a red dress."

Baldovin's face grew even paler. "Suzana."

Chapter Four
Among the Rapids

The villa's walls blocked Konstantin's view, but he'd seen the way the river curved around the villa before hitting a straight stretch and flowing to the ford. Trees hemmed in the river upstream, meaning the body would have to be nearly level with the villa before it would be visible by the watchman, so time was short. He raced into the courtyard and mounted Perun.

Miladin turned to him with concern on his face. "Is something wrong, lord?"

"Suzana's in the river." Or maybe just her body. Either way, Konstantin needed to chase her. They were bound together, he and she, no matter what they did or didn't feel for each other. Konstantin urged his horse into a gallop and raced through the villa's gates.

He didn't know how deep the river was, so he rode for the ford. The river had seemed smooth and calm the day before. The surface still appeared placid as he approached, but even if the waves were small, it moved along swiftly enough that Suzana would drift past before he could remove his armor.

In his periphery, an object floated into view, and the flash of pale skin told him it was a person. He rode past a line of trees that blocked his vision, then turned for the ford. Perun's hooves sent up splashes of water, then sheets. Konstantin turned his focus to the person floating toward him and yanked on the reins. Perun threw his head in protest at the rough treatment, but he halted. Konstantin jumped into the water, and the river lapped angrily at his chest as he waded toward the body.

It was a woman—his betrothed. She floated on her back, arms and legs stretched out beneath the surface, with her face and the edge of her skirt above the waterline. Her veil was missing, and her hair stuck to her forehead before spreading into a dark, leafy cloud. Her eyes were closed. The river's current pulled her toward him, and he caught her limp body in his arms. The current didn't release its tug on her and her dress, but Konstantin kept his grip, adjusting his hold so her head was higher.

"Suzana?" he said.

She didn't respond. Her uncovered head had fallen onto his shoulder. He thought he felt her breath on his neck, but it might have been a breeze. He'd once pulled Danilo out of a river, but his cousin had started coughing at once. Suzana remained flaccid, with a white face and lips more blue than red. She was warmer than the river, so perhaps she still lived.

He pushed toward shore and whistled for Perun to follow. The animal seemed to be in a forgiving mood and obeyed.

Miladin, Župan Dragomir, and some of Dragomir's men had ridden after Konstantin, and they waited on the shore, stripping off their armor.

"Konstantin, look out!" Miladin pointed and ran into the water.

Something pummeled Konstantin's side. His lamellar and mail offered him significant protection, but he still hissed as the blow sent pain up and down his ribs. Worse, he almost lost his grip on Suzana. A log floated just downriver of him, bobbing at the waterline. At least it had hit him instead of her. Something else snaked past him. It wasn't painful, but he felt the pressure. What was that?

The log hit the rapids beyond the ford just as a sudden force yanked Suzana from his grip, tugging her downriver. Konstantin dove after her in a panic. He caught a bit of her skirt and tried to reel her in, but something else continued to pull her away.

A rope cut through a wave near the log, and as he pulled Suzana closer, the end wrapped around her waist came into view. Why was she tied to a log?

The riverbed fell away beyond the ford, growing deeper. Konstantin's armor grew heavy, and his head went under. He fumbled with the buckles of his armor but couldn't work the fastenings and keep his hold on Suzana. He surfaced long enough for a single breath. The current was too fast here, the water too deep. He tried to steer them both toward the shore, but the log dragged them along like flotsam.

He broke the surface and gasped, then pulled a knee almost to his chest so he could get at the knife in his boot. He gripped Suzana with one arm and felt for the rope with his hand. His lungs burned as he sawed through the wet rope, desperately trying to sever their connection to the deadweight that would make it impossible for them to escape the river alive.

The rope snapped. The current still carried him downstream, and his armor still pulled him toward the riverbed, but they were free of the log. He pushed Suzana toward the surface as much as he could, but he couldn't tell whether her mouth and nose could draw in air. He could see almost nothing, only a murky glow that showed the border between air and water.

His feet brushed something hard, and he pushed, then gasped for breath when he broke the surface. Suzana responded to nothing, not to his hold, not to the water. She was running out of time. He scraped against another submerged rock and wedged against it, shoving his boot into a crevice and managing to keep himself and Suzana above water while the current flowed around them.

"Župan Konstantin!"

He turned upriver to where Miladin and Perun swam toward them.

"Watch the rocks!" Konstantin meant to shout, but the sound came out weaker than intended.

Miladin kept one arm around Perun as they drifted closer. He'd taken his armor off before coming into the river. Konstantin would have done the same had there been time. "Put her on the horse's back, and we'll hold her on from either side. Is she alive?"

"I don't know." Perun was close enough now. Konstantin pushed Suzana onto the horse's back, and Miladin pulled from the other side. She fell forward, her head between Perun's ears.

Miladin thumped her back, hard. Anger flared in Konstantin's chest that anyone would dare treat his bride-to-be so roughly, but when Miladin repeated the action, water gushed from Suzana's mouth, and she coughed, convulsed, and gasped.

"Back to shore, boy," Konstantin told Perun. It couldn't have been an easy journey for the horse, but he headed downriver toward the shore, swimming with Suzana on his back and a man clinging to either side.

When the horse hit bedrock again, Konstantin urged him more directly from the water. Not long after, Konstantin and Miladin could wade instead of float. Dragomir and his men rushed over to help, taking Suzana from Perun's back and carrying her to shore. One of them, Ilija, moved Suzana's arms, keeping her head low to expel more of the water from her lungs. Additional coughing followed, but her eyes remained closed and her limbs limp. She looked smaller now, wet and bedraggled and unconscious.

"There's swelling on the back of her head," Ilija said when Konstantin reached them.

Despite exhaustion from his struggle in the river, Konstantin felt an urge toward violence. It seemed someone had struck Suzana on the head, tied her to a log, and dumped her in the river. "Why would someone want to kill her?" he asked.

Dragomir frowned. "I don't know. But now that you are betrothed to her, an attack on her is also an attack on Rivak."

Konstantin nodded. He and Suzana were not yet married, but what had happened felt like a strike against his family, one he needed to avenge.

When Konstantin walked into the villa's stables, Perun came to the front of his stall. The horse grunted as Konstantin ran a hand along his forelock, then reached around to pat his withers. Konstantin fed him a carrot, entered the stall and checked his coat, then bent down to examine a scrape on the horse's fetlock. Someone had cleaned it and put oil over it. Konstantin walked a full circle around the horse, then rested his forehead against Perun's forelock.

Konstantin had spent all morning and most of the afternoon pacing the corridor outside Suzana's bedchamber. She hadn't woken, but he had peeked in from time to time, and her coloring had improved. Dama Isidora sat with her, and once Dragomir and Decimir had joined her and promised to remain for a time, Konstantin had felt confident enough in Suzana's safety to check on his horse.

"Thank you for saving us," he whispered to Perun. "I'm sorry about your leg."

As he stood there with his horse, some of the worry eased. Suzana's face must have stayed above water for most of her trip downriver, or she wouldn't have started breathing again. Konstantin had been unconscious before—falls from horses, accidents while training, a narrow escape from an attempted murder. The injuries hadn't addled his brain. Suzana, too, would recover, and then they'd leave for Rivak.

Someone cleared his throat, and Konstantin looked up. Grigorii.

"Are you all right, lord?"

"Yes."

"She hasn't woken?" Grigorii asked.

"No. Unless it's happened since I came to the stables."

Grigorii stood with his hands behind his back. "You asked me to look into the lady's past."

"Yes. What did you find?"

"Twice before, rumors of an upcoming betrothal have circulated through the villa. Last summer, with one of Baldovin's trading partners. Then earlier this summer, with another merchant. It seems the first betrothal was called off because the potential bridegroom was unimpressed. No one would tell me why the second was called off. Since our departure is delayed, I can see if alcohol will loosen a few tongues tonight."

Konstantin shook his head. "Don't bother. I've more important things for you to do tonight. I want to set up a constant watch for my betrothed."

"I'll see to it, lord. We'll make sure she doesn't throw herself into the river again."

Konstantin brought his head around sharply. "She didn't throw herself in the river. Where did you hear such a thing?"

Grigorii looked to the wall, avoiding eye contact. "Several of the men thought she might have tried drowning herself to avoid marriage."

Konstantin felt as though he'd been punched in the gut. Was marriage to him so awful a prospect that Suzana would rather drown? Was that why she had expressed no preferences about when they left or how they traveled, because it was a journey she didn't plan to make? "There was a bruise along her hairline, as though someone knocked her unconscious."

Grigorii hesitated, perhaps because he could sense Konstantin's unease. "There are many ways to be bruised in a river. A log maybe. Or a rock."

Konstantin considered it, but if she had wanted to drown herself in the river, there would have been no need to tie herself to a log. That was the work of someone who had wanted to make her escape—and any potential rescue—more unlikely. Konstantin faced Perun again to give himself a moment to banish any telltale emotion from his face. He couldn't let anyone know how shaken Suzana's near-death had left him. Nor could he show any sign of irritation over speculation and gossip. The truth would win out. God willing, Suzana would wake soon and tell what had happened. In the meantime, Konstantin had work to do.

"Organize a constant guard for her. I'll take the fourth watch. We are to protect her from whomever is trying to kill her." That might include protecting her from herself, but he thought it far more likely that the culprit was someone in the villa.

Chapter Five
An Uncertain Memory

Raw pain gripped Suzana's throat and nose, and a throbbing echoed along her skull. Soft murmurs reached her ears, along with the pops and cracks of a fire. Where was she? She forced her eyes open and recognized her bedchamber. Only it wasn't her bedchamber any longer, was it? She was leaving for Rivak any moment, so why was she lying in her room, and why did the angle of the sun show late afternoon?

"Dama Suzana?" She turned as Dama Isidora knelt beside her. "How do you feel?"

"Not . . . not well." She hadn't woken up ill that morning, but now she felt as if she were recovering from a long sickness. Weakness gripped her, leaving her thoughts jumbled and slow.

Dama Isidora's hand pressed lightly on her forehead. "Are you warm enough?"

Suzana nodded, but that made the ache in her head worse. She was overly warm. The hearth in her bedchamber wasn't normally lit in summer, and a blanket cocooned her. "Why am I back in my bedchamber?" She pulled at the blanket, trying to take it off, only to discover a new pain at her waist.

Dama Isidora helped with the blanket. "What's the last thing you remember?"

"Preparing to leave this morning." She pulled the blanket aside and saw the blue sleeve of her dalmatica. She twisted her arm as if that might somehow change the color. "I thought I was wearing my red dalmatica. What happened?"

Her father strode into view. "That is precisely what you need to tell us. How did you end up in the river this morning?"

In the river? She hadn't played in the river for years, not since her father had told her she was too old for that sort of thing and then had beaten her when she'd gone one last time. "What do you mean?"

"You disappeared this morning. No one could find you until a watchman saw your body floating down the river." Some sort of emotion—anger, most likely—rolled off his stern jaw and tense shoulders.

Fear made Suzana tremble. She didn't remember floating in the river, couldn't even remember what she had eaten to break her fast that morning.

Dama Isidora's voice carried far more gentleness than her father's. "It seems someone knocked you on the back of the head, tied you to a log, and dropped you in the river. We had hoped you would remember who."

"Why would someone put me in the river?" The story seemed far-fetched, but her body had been through something awful, she felt the truth in that. She hadn't felt so sore and abused since that incident in the stables when she was twelve.

"Who did it, Suzana? I'll make sure he's punished." Her father folded his arms.

She pushed herself to a sitting position, but the change did nothing to help her memory. She tried to grab hold of anything from that morning, but she remembered only her dalmatica's red fabric, and she wasn't sure if she remembered putting the clothing on or simply that one of the servants had laid it out the night before. "I can't remember."

Her father scowled. "Now is not the time to be stupid."

Dama Isidora gave her father a glare. "It's not uncommon for someone who has been through an ordeal like hers to have trouble remembering it. Give her time. She barely woke."

"Some of the servants are suggesting you jumped in yourself." Her father's eyes, brown like hers, glared down at her. "Did you do something so shameful?"

Someone thought she'd tried to kill herself? She was wary of her husband-to-be, but he didn't frighten her any more than her father did. If she had wanted to escape misery, she would have tossed herself into the river years ago, not now, not when things were on the brink of changing and might become better. Yet she couldn't remember for sure. "I don't think I did."

"You *don't think* you did?" Her father huffed. "Are you sure you're thinking?"

Dama Isidora cleared her throat as she rose to sit in a nearby chair. "Perhaps it would be best to allow Dama Suzana to rest a while more before you interrogate her further."

Her father's hands tightened and released several times, as if he refrained from striking her only with a surfeit of willpower.

Fear hung round her. Someone had tried to kill her, or she had tried to kill herself. And had Dama Isidora not been in the room, she was certain her father would have tried to improve her memory with a few strikes from his fists. "If I was in the river, how did I get out?"

"Konstantin pulled you out." Dama Isidora picked up a partially embroidered cloth and resumed her work on it. "Almost went under himself, what with his armor still on and that log whipping you out of his grasp."

"There wasn't time to remove my armor," a voice said from the doorway.

Konstantin hadn't been there a few moments ago, the last time her father had spoken. Suzana felt his gaze, intent on her. He wore no armor now, just a simple tunic of wool with a sword belted around his waist. After studying her for a moment, he glanced at her father, then stepped toward her and knelt beside the mattress she lay on. "I am glad to see you somewhat recovered," he said. "How is your head?" He tilted his own head to better stare at a spot below her left ear. His own face was bruised, and there were scratches on his hands that hadn't been there the day before when he placed the ring on her finger.

She felt a flash of embarrassment at his scrutiny; she wasn't even wearing a hair veil. But she needed to answer him. "It is . . ." Her head pounded and ached and made it difficult to concentrate. Should she be brave or honest? "It is tender, lord."

"And your waist?"

She'd felt pain flare around her waist when she'd sat, but how would he know about that? "It is also tender, though I don't know why."

"One end of a rope was tied round your torso. The other end was tied to a log. Do you remember any of it?"

She shook her head. Dama Isidora had mentioned a log, but Suzana had assumed she'd been tied directly to the wood, not strung along like the shackles on the end of a chain. "I don't remember anything of this morning, but I offer you my gratitude for rescuing me."

She watched his face carefully, trying to detect disappointment or anger at her inability to remember. His face revealed nothing, but her forgetfulness was certain to affect his opinion of her.

"What may I do to help your recovery?" he asked.

She wanted everyone to leave so she could rest in silence, but she didn't dare say that aloud. And if everyone left, would her attacker return? Maybe she didn't want everyone to leave. She just wanted them to stop asking her questions.

Konstantin glanced at the fire. "Are you warm enough? I could make the fire larger."

"I am warm enough, thank you."

He surveyed the room. Her father, his steward, and two of Konstantin's men all stood about, along with Dama Isidora. "Then perhaps we should let you rest. I or one of my men will be outside your door. You've only to call if you need anything."

Her father did not look as if he wished to go, but something about the way Konstantin stood and gestured all the men from the room demanded obedience.

Konstantin was the last to leave, and he turned back. "Please send word if you think of anything you need or if you remember something from this morning." He gently pulled the door shut behind him.

"He'll listen, you know, if you tell him what you need or what you want." Dama Isidora kept her eyes on her embroidery as she spoke.

"Why would he listen to a woman?"

"Because he is a different sort of man from your father."

Konstantin had somehow sensed she needed the men to leave, even without her saying anything aloud. She hadn't expected insight like that from a man, so maybe Dama Isidora was right, and he was different.

"His mother was a dear friend," Dama Isidora continued. "She came to Rivak as Miroslav's bride when she was about your age. Konstantin was born a year later. My youngest son was only a little older. They grew up together, trained together as boys, almost went off to war together, but Konstantin was a bit too young for Maritsa. I didn't want Stefan to go either, but he insisted he was ready, so he followed his brothers. None of them came back." Dama Isidora's voice held, but there was sadness in her eyes.

"How many sons did you have?"

"Three, and I lost them all to the Turks at Maritsa."

Suzana had no siblings, and she'd felt no affection from her father for years, but most women loved their children. She'd seen that in the servants, and she sensed Dama Isidora had loved her sons. "I am sorry for their deaths."

Dama Isidora nodded, accepting Suzana's sympathy. "Doubtless Dragomir would have fallen, too, but he was recovering from a hunting accident and did not join the campaign. Or perhaps he would have gone, and the battle would have turned out differently. When he couldn't lead his men, he sent his brother in his place, and Radomir betrayed the army to the Turks."

"Betrayal?" Rumors had flown after the battle of Maritsa, but her father had dismissed them as unfounded.

"Yes. It's a heavy burden our family bears, knowing we trusted someone who caused so much damage. For us. For all of Serbia." Dama Isidora squinted at her embroidery. "Konstantin also lost much at Maritsa. He was too young to go to war, but when his father and his uncle were killed, he became župan. He has listened to his aunt in the years since. He will listen to you, too, if you will speak to him."

"I have seen few men who will really listen to a woman." Konstantin had saved her life, but only because he was desperate for her dowry. If she died before their marriage, he would lose the money he needed to save his župa.

"Konstantin will. Tragedy has hit his family hard, but they've cared for each other. Kindness and concern are natural to him because he's grown up surrounded by them."

Suzana turned Dama Isidora's words over in her head again and again. She wanted Konstantin to be kind, but did she trust Dama Isidora's assertion that he would be? The day before, he had asked her opinion about the timing of the wedding and their departure for Rivak. And he probably wanted to know who had tried to kill her as much as everyone else did, but he'd sent the other men away instead of pestering her, even when she hadn't spoken that need aloud.

She fell asleep with those thoughts on her mind and woke later, when the sun had set and the hearth and a pair of oil lamps offered the only light.

Dama Isidora still sat nearby. Suzana couldn't remember her mother, but she imagined that if her mother had lived, she would have sat beside Suzana on a day like this one. Since she couldn't have her mother, Suzana was grateful to have Dama Isidora.

The kind woman looked up and noticed Suzana was awake. "I'll send someone for your supper. I think it best that you eat."

"I don't feel hungry."

"All the same, you need your strength." Dama Isidora stood and crossed the room, her footsteps full of grace and purpose. Suzana couldn't see whom she spoke with, but she heard her words. "Dama Suzana is awake. Please have someone bring food."

Suzana stood, too, then quickly sat on the nearest trunk when dizziness crawled from her chest to her head.

"Are you all right, dear?" Dama Isidora asked.

"I stood too quickly."

Dama Isidora studied Suzana's countenance. "Food ought to help with that."

"Have you eaten?"

"Yes. I went to the hall for supper, but several of the servants sat with you, and Konstantin left Miladin and Grigorii outside your room when your father insisted he leave your doorway and join the main group for supper."

"He was standing watch?"

"Yes. I daresay he's been worried about you." Dama Isidora offered Suzana the veil that matched her dalmatica, and Suzana arranged it over her hair as a knock sounded at the door.

"Come in." Suzana's throat still ached, but the person who had knocked must have heard, because the door opened.

Konstantin. She'd expected a servant to bring her food, not a župan. What was more, he actually smiled when he saw her perched on the trunk. It wasn't a full smile, the type she'd seen on Dama Isidora's face or the faces of her servants, but it was different from his normal expression. He lifted the cup of wine he held in one hand and the dish piled with fowl, bread, and olives that he held in the other hand. "Where would you like it?"

Suzana slid to one side of the trunk so there would be room for the dish beside her. "Here, please."

He set the dish down and handed her the wine.

"Thank you," she said.

"You're welcome. Are you feeling any better?"

She took a sip of watered wine before answering. "My head does not hurt as much as it did before. Nor do the bruises around my waist."

Dama Isidora busied herself with the fire, leaving the two of them to converse in near private. Konstantin glanced at her and lowered his voice slightly. "Do you remember anything else of what happened?"

She shook her head and nibbled on a bit of seasoned pigeon.

"I, um . . ." He watched her for a moment, then looked away. "If you are unhappy with the betrothal, desperately unhappy about it, I want you to know I wouldn't force you to marry me if you felt that leaving your home and becoming my wife would bring you misery. I am pleased to be betrothed to you, but if your wishes are otherwise, I will respect them."

Canceling a betrothal was difficult. The church would view it as a marriage, and it would affect future prospects for both of them. Suzana could think of only two ways to avoid marriage to a man of her father's choosing: death or holy vows. Perhaps becoming a nun would be agreeable. Her father wouldn't be able to beat her if she went to live in a nunnery. But curiosity about what might happen when she married Konstantin was growing. If Dama Isidora was right, Rivak held the possibility of something better, and she wanted to see if that hope would come to fruition.

"I don't remember what happened this morning, but I am quite certain I did not throw myself into the river." She wouldn't have risked something so widely condemned, especially not when change and potential hope lay on the horizon.

The tension in his face and shoulders eased. "I'd like your opinion on when we should leave. I don't want to take you on a long journey before you've recovered. But someone here tried to kill you, and they could try again. Rivak might be safer for you."

A chill slithered across the back of her neck. Danger had always lurked in the villa in the form of her father's temper. Now threat of murder made it more potent. Dama Isidora had told Suzana that Konstantin would listen to her. She grasped that hope and gave him her opinion. "We should leave tomorrow."

Konstantin's mouth parted in surprise. "That soon?"

"Sitting in a carriage sounds less demanding than fending off another murder attempt."

He clasped his hands behind his back. "Indeed. We can split the journey into two days to make it less taxing."

Suzana picked at a piece of bread. Maybe she and Konstantin really would find happiness together, if she could keep from getting killed long enough to see it through.

Chapter Six
Retribution

Konstantin met Miladin in the hallway outside Suzana's room at the beginning of the night's fourth watch. "Did you see anything?"

Miladin stifled a yawn. "No. It was quiet. I've seen no one from the time I relieved Bojan until you came."

"Good." Konstantin folded his arms and leaned against the wall.

Miladin rested against the bricks beside him. "You like her?"

"Yes."

Miladin waited, giving Konstantin the opportunity to elaborate. Konstantin wasn't obligated to tell him anything, but he was one of the few people Konstantin didn't feel he had to hide his feelings from. Miladin, Aunt Zorica, Father Vlatko, and maybe Lidija. "She's quiet, so I don't know much about her yet. She seems to think carefully before she says anything. I like that she's thoughtful. And she's pleasing to the eye. Grigorii heard she was plain, but he heard wrong." The torch in the hallway flickered. "What I can't understand is why someone would try to kill her."

"There was a malicious edge to it, with the log. Perhaps her father has enemies."

Grandfather had said nothing of Baldovin's enemies, but that didn't mean there were none. Suzana's death would also hurt Rivak, much as the burned crops and destroyed villages had already made it weak and impoverished. The motive would be connected to her father or her husband-to-be, not to anything she herself had done, and that made the attack feel even more wicked. "I want her safe in Rivak. But I also want to find out who's behind it."

"Another mystery." Miladin frowned.

Mysteries. That was something else Konstantin seemed unable to fix.

"You should rest," Konstantin told his friend. "We'll need to be sharp tomorrow."

Miladin didn't argue. Konstantin could have spent the entire watch discussing options and creating plans, and Miladin would have listened and given advice when he had it, but the man was also experienced enough to know the importance of resting when the time came for it.

Konstantin paced to stay alert. Dama Isidora had agreed to pass the night in Suzana's room. His debt to his neighbors was growing. They were like family, even now, even when Decimir and Lidija were not officially betrothed. If only his other neighbors felt like family rather than rivals.

Before dawn came, the noise of servants began to carry through the villa. The sounds were muted, distant. In the kitchens and with the animals. Eventually, a few maids approached the door to Suzana's bedchamber and stilled when they reached Konstantin. He recognized Divna—Dama Isidora's maid. The other, he assumed, was from the villa.

Konstantin stood aside so the women could enter. He listened carefully and relaxed when he heard no cries of alarm. When Divna came out, he stopped her. "Both women are in good health?"

"Yes, lord."

Dragomir came to stand watch just after sunrise, and Konstantin went to wash. He entered the hall to break his fast at the same time Dragomir, Isidora, and Suzana arrived. Suzana seemed less frail now. Her veil covered the bruising, and he was struck again by how beautiful she was. He approached and offered her his arm. She accepted, but after only a few steps toward the table, she halted abruptly. Her nose flared, her skin turned pale, and her breaths turned to gasps.

"Dama Suzana, what's wrong?" he asked.

She shuddered and took mincing steps away from him until her back was against the wall. He followed her gaze, focused on a servant bringing porridge to the main table.

Konstantin found the nearest man from Rivak, Grigorii. "I want that man questioned." As Grigorii moved toward the servant, Konstantin turned back to Suzana. Dama Isidora had joined her, but Suzana gave no indication that she heard Dama Isidora's questions.

"Suzana?" he asked again. He even reached for her hand, but she didn't respond. Her whole body shook with fear, and he felt more than ever a compulsion to protect her.

Baldovin approached with a hard look and a stern tone. “Suzana, this is unacceptable. Pull yourself together.”

She said nothing for a long moment. Then she blinked and looked around and colored in embarrassment.

“It’s all right, Suzana.” Dama Isidora’s calm voice offered reassurance. “What happened? Do you know that man?”

“Of course she knows him.” Baldovin placed his hands on his hips. “He’s worked here for years.”

Suzana inhaled deeply. “Seeing him again . . . I remember . . . yesterday morning . . . he . . .” She paused, swallowed, and looked at the floor. “He told me Dama Isidora wished to see me. I followed him toward the river. When I asked why Dama Isidora was at the river, he held my mouth so I couldn’t scream. He had a rock in his hand.”

Baldovin set his jaw. “Dama Isidora would have been in the courtyard. You should have realized that before you followed someone the opposite direction. Stupid girl.” He muttered the last part.

Dama Isidora glared at Baldovin before turning to Suzana. “I didn’t call for you yesterday morning. I assumed we would talk during our journey.”

Suzana’s gaze fixed on the servant. “He only told me that to draw me out.”

Her fear was almost palpable. Given what had happened, Konstantin understood. He excused himself and went to where Grigorii held the servant, who kept insisting he’d done nothing wrong. Anger at the man burned in Konstantin’s chest, but he inhaled and unclenched his fists. Punishment could come later.

Baldovin followed Konstantin, and he dug his hand into the man’s arm much the way Konstantin wanted to—with a grip that would leave bruises. “Why did you try to kill my daughter?”

“I didn’t—” The man’s response broke off in a cry of pain.

“Yes, you did. Why?”

Splotches of red marred the man’s complexion, and his voice shook. “For the money.”

“And who paid you?”

The man held his tongue. Baldovin elicited another cry from him but no answer.

Even several paces away, Suzana’s face looked gray.

Konstantin caught Grigorii's attention. "The rest of this conversation can take place away from the ladies. Take him away, but don't let him out of your sight."

Grigorii grabbed the man by the arm and led him from the hall.

Konstantin returned to Suzana. "We'll see that he never comes near you again."

She met his eyes and seemed to calm.

He offered her his arm again, and this time, he succeeded in leading her to the table. "I imagine remembering was a shock. Do you still wish to leave today?"

She watched the door where the servant had been taken. "I can think of no reason for him to hurt me."

"He mentioned money."

"Then whoever paid him is the one who wishes me ill, and the threat remains. Leaving today is still the safest option."

"I'll make sure all is prepared." Konstantin excused himself and followed Grigorii and Baldovin outside. He would check his men's progress, but he also wanted to determine who was behind the attack.

The courtyard bustled with activity that, in contrast to the day before, was being made with a speed and smoothness that would have given even his grandfather nothing to complain over. Grigorii and Baldovin weren't there, so Konstantin walked to Miladin, who was preparing his horse. "Did you see where Grigorii and Baldovin took the prisoner?"

Miladin pointed to the stables. "That direction. Who is it?"

"The man who dumped Suzana in the river, but he wouldn't tell us who paid him."

Miladin tested the saddle straps and joined Konstantin, heading toward the stables. "I imagine Grigorii can get the information from him."

"So do I." Grigorii wasn't cruel, but sentiment and softness had both disappeared from his demeanor after his wife and children had been lost to the same sweep of camp fever that had taken Konstantin's mother and sister.

They were halfway across the courtyard when a cry of pain rent the air. The man had tried to kill Suzana, so Konstantin didn't care what methods his men used, as long as they got answers. Still, he quickened his step. Grigorii would know that they needed a name. Baldovin might be more interested in making a gruesome example out of anyone who threatened his daughter.

Beyond the stables was a small side gate that still swung on its hinges. Miladin pushed through first, and Konstantin followed. Baldovin stood with his hands on his hips and a scowl across his face. Grigorii was some distance away, leaning over the man who'd attacked Suzana. Protruding from the man's back was a crossbow bolt.

"He tried to run," Baldovin explained. "Your satnik shot him."

Konstantin walked over and knelt next to the man, who gasped as his injury made it harder and harder for him to breathe. "Who hired you?"

"I already asked him," Grigorii said. "He wouldn't talk."

The man struggled for breath and looked from Konstantin to Grigorii.

"You're dying." Konstantin grasped the man's shoulder. "Confess, and you can meet your Maker knowing you helped protect an innocent woman from whoever is trying to kill her."

The man met Konstantin's eyes and held his gaze, but then his sight seemed to drain away, his breathing ending in a final exhale. And with his death, Konstantin's best chance of finding out who was behind the attack vanished.

Konstantin sat back on his heels. "Did he offer any hints at all?"

Grigorii looked at the ground. "No. I'm sorry, lord. I didn't mean to hit him so squarely in the back. I was afraid he'd get away."

Konstantin could hardly fault Grigorii for taking precise aim. They'd practiced together many times—they always aimed to hit, not to miss. Accuracy had long ago become automatic. "We'll have to hope that whoever wants her dead won't follow us back to Rivak."

Chapter Seven
The Leave-Taking

The busyness in the villa courtyard had died down by the time Konstantin returned.

"We'll be on the road early enough to make it in a day." Miladin gathered the reins for Perun and for his own horse, Grom.

Konstantin glanced at the carriage where Isidora and Suzana would ride. "We could, but Dama Suzana still seemed somewhat frail this morning. I want her away from this villa, but I don't want to overtax her."

Miladin adjusted Grom's bridle. "Your concern for her does you credit. I only regret that it will keep me from my wife an extra night."

"You and Magdalena are both happy in your marriage, aren't you?" Konstantin asked.

"Yes." A look of contentment crossed Miladin's face.

"I may seek your advice, from time to time."

"I am happy to assist you in any way I can, lord." Miladin tightened the girth on his saddle. "Today, my advice is don't give up. Your betrothed may be quiet, but don't take that as rejection. Give her time, a few days to get used to you. Longer, if needed. You saved her life yesterday; that's got to count for something."

Konstantin wasn't so sure. "She doesn't remember me saving her. It might not count for much."

Miladin smirked. "Then I will encourage others to recount your heroics within her hearing."

"I don't want to force it."

Miladin's smile grew. "It won't be forced. The men respect you. My next piece of advice is to help her to the carriage yourself, then see if she needs anything."

Konstantin had already planned to escort Suzana to the carriage. He scanned the horses, pack animals, and carts assembled in the villa's courtyard. They were nearly ready.

Excitement and nervousness accompanied him into the hall when he went to find Suzana. There was no repeat of yesterday's events, with her disappearance and the urgent shouts from the watchman, but Suzana seemed tormented by a different sort of danger this morning: her father. She stood by the hearth, her back to Konstantin as he approached. Her shoulders slumped, and her head hunched forward while her father loomed over her and spoke a steady stream of admonition in a volume soft enough that Konstantin couldn't pick out the words. He could, however, pick out the tightness and displeasure in the man's expression.

Konstantin's father had been demanding, but there had always been love behind the push to learn, the push to improve. Konstantin wished he could have had longer to learn from Župan Miroslav, but that drive to mold Konstantin into the man he needed to be at a pace Konstantin could barely maintain had turned out to be a blessing. Though Maritsa had cut short his time with his father, Konstantin could look back on their time together without regret—they'd done the best they could. Even if it hadn't been enough, they'd tried.

Baldovin's harshness, on the other hand, seemed to lack purpose. Calling Suzana stupid hadn't helped her remember who was behind the attack, nor had it helped her recover from the shock when she had remembered. Konstantin was pleased with Suzana, but marriage involved the joining of two families, and he was not pleased that Baldovin would soon be considered kin. Konstantin hoped the man wouldn't try to exercise the influence a wife's father normally held over a husband, because what he'd seen of Baldovin thus far was repellant.

Baldovin noticed Konstantin and straightened. Suzana must have seen the change in her father's posture, because she turned around. Perhaps the betrothal ceremony had done what was intended, because Konstantin already felt a connection to her. Together they were to lead Rivak. And it was his responsibility to protect her from anyone who might harm her, including her father.

"We're ready to depart." Konstantin placed his feet hip-distance apart and hoped his face hid the lack of respect he felt for his soon-to-be father-by-marriage. "If you will allow me to escort Dama Suzana to her carriage."

"You may," Baldovin said.

"I look forward to returning the hospitality you have so generously shown us when you come for the wedding." Konstantin wished he were a better diplomat. He wanted the words to sound right even if they weren't true. He needed things to work with Baldovin—because he needed things to work with Suzana. "Thank you for hosting us, and thank you for your daughter."

Baldovin's face softened. "I shall be pleased to see you again for the wedding. I'll bring the dowry then."

"Thank you, sir." Konstantin turned to Suzana. "Have you had a chance to say your goodbyes?"

"I have. I am ready to leave."

He offered her his arm. What was it like for her, leaving everything she'd grown up with for a župa she'd never before seen? It took bravery to marry a stranger, especially on the woman's part. He prayed he could make the change a good one for her.

Guilt nibbled at Suzana all day long as she rode in the carriage with Dama Isidora. The older woman wouldn't have any idea that Suzana had lied that morning, putting Dama Isidora at risk by claiming the servant had drawn Suzana to the river with a message from her. Suzana hadn't wanted to lie, not when Dama Isidora had been so kind to her. Lies were dangerous, but the same could be said of the truth. Even as she'd told the lie, Suzana hadn't felt Dama Isidora was in much danger. Suzana's father might beat his daughter or torture a servant named in a murder plot, but he wouldn't dare touch the wife of Župan Dragomir.

"You're still worried, aren't you?" Dama Isidora watched her from the opposite side of the carriage. Divna, Isidora's maid, slept soundly beside her.

"Yes." Suzana didn't feel the need to deny it.

"I've seen a lot of death in my lifetime, but I've never had anyone try to kill me. Perhaps if we figure out who's behind it, you'll be better able to move on."

The attack that had left her unconscious in the river was only one of the things making Suzana uneasy, but it was significant. Maybe more significant than her betrothal to a stranger and her journey to a land that she did not know. "My father's servant said he did it for money. They didn't find out who paid him."

"I know this isn't an easy question, but who would benefit from your death?"

Suzana ran that question over and over again in her mind. "No one. The servants would have less food to cook and fewer tunics to wash, but it doesn't make sense that they'd kill me when on the brink of being rid of me anyway."

"Has anyone else ever wanted to marry you? Jealousy can be a powerful motive."

Suzana shifted in her seat, trying to find a more comfortable position. The jarring of the carriage along the rutted road irritated the bruising around her waist. "I've not spoken more than a few words to any unattached man for some years. Since beauty is not one of my assets, and I have had no conversations of any length with a potential admirer, I cannot imagine anyone developing an interest that would lead to murder to prevent my marriage."

Dama Isidora's mouth pulled tight. "I strongly disagree with anyone who would not consider beauty one of your assets."

"Last year, my father wished to marry me to a trading partner's son. The family found the dowry tempting, but the potential bridegroom was not pleased with my appearance. He married someone else shortly thereafter. I very much doubt he cares enough to notice my betrothal. Besides, he's from Ragusa. That's some distance away. He couldn't be involved."

"One man thought you weren't pretty, and you took it to heart?" Dama Isidora shook her head. "That's only one person's opinion. I don't share it. Nor, I think, does Župan Konstantin."

Suzana glanced at her hands. "He told me, after the ceremony, that he considered himself blessed to have a wife who is pretty and wise. Now I'm afraid I'll disappoint him."

Dama Isidora leaned forward and put a hand on Suzana's knee. "If he already told you he thinks you are pretty, then you obviously have not disappointed him in that regard. And despite what your father has said, you don't strike me as stupid or frail of mind."

Her father had called her stupid time after time, and he had known her since she was born, so his conclusion had to be true. Yet Dama Isidora was right about the first aspect. Konstantin was unlikely to change his opinion on whether or not she was pretty, not overnight. Perhaps in that regard, at least, she met his expectations, so she could stop worrying that Konstantin would decry her as a plain, undesirable bride. She could focus her worry on whether being subject to her betrothed would be easier or harder than being subject to her father. Beyond Konstantin, there was the other worry: the attack that had almost killed her.

"There was nearly another betrothal." Suzana preferred not to discuss the details, but Dama Isidora was right, the mystery needed to be solved. "My father discussed it with the prospective groom's father. They even came to an agreement on the dowry and the bride gift, but the other family changed their mind. My father was displeased."

Dama Isidora waited, perhaps expecting Suzana to explain more about why the betrothal had been called off, but that involved a part of her past Suzana was not willing to share. She glanced toward the window, but the curtains were drawn to keep out the dust. The silence between them stretched, broken only by Divna's steady, gentle breathing.

Finally, Suzana spoke again. "The shame of the broken match fell on my father and me, not on the Kralj family, so I don't think they are behind the attacks. They wanted out of the agreement, so my betrothal to another fits their wishes."

Dama Isidora nodded. "I daresay broken almost-betrothals are usually complicated enough to motivate surprising emotions. Did the Kralj family have any contact with the servant in question?"

"I didn't meet the son. The father came to the villa. He could have spoken with or bribed a servant then, but I don't see why he would have."

"Then, the most likely possibility is that your death was meant to hurt someone else. Your father or your betrothed."

Dama Isidora's words made the world seem a little more dangerous.

"Does your father have any enemies?" the dama asked.

"He trades with many people, and he is skilled at making a profit for himself, regardless of whether that hurts or helps those he trades with. Some owe him money. My death would not cancel out a debt, but perhaps it would give someone satisfaction. I suppose I erred in wishing to leave the villa so soon, because the information we might need remains there in my father's ledgers and lists of associates."

"When you decided to leave, we didn't know one of the servants had been paid to kill you, and you were recovering from quite the ordeal."

Suzana's inability to remember was the reason they hadn't known yesterday. Were her father present in the carriage, he would no doubt hit her for her stupidity. He was unlikely to allow a messenger from Rivak to peruse his ledgers. He guarded them like treasures. He might allow her to see them, but she didn't want to return to the villa when she'd just escaped her father's shadow. But if the answer lay written there . . . perhaps he would send the information she wished for in a letter.

And there was another possibility too. "Does Župan Konstantin have enemies?"

Dama Isidora gave her a sad smile. "A župan always has enemies, I'm afraid. And that means you will always have enemies too."

"Do you suppose they will always want to drown me, or should I remain on guard against poisons and daggers and nooses as well?" The humor fell flat because no matter how flippant the words, she couldn't shake off the fear. Someone had tried to kill her.

Dama Isidora seemed to sense Suzana's unease, because she leaned forward and patted her knee again. "A župan always has enemies, but Konstantin very much wants to be a good husband to you. He is fiercely protective of his family, and that includes you now."

A good husband. She hoped that would prove true. "How often does a good husband beat his wife?"

Dama Isidora looked shocked. "Never."

Suzana wanted so badly to believe her. Husbands had other ways of hurting a wife, with cutting words and domineering control or icy aloofness, but if Konstantin would really never use his fists . . . Suzana could be content with that. Perhaps not happy but content.

The carriage slowed, and the sounds of people and horses grew louder, more concentrated. They were probably stopping to make camp.

"I do not know your father well," Dama Isidora said, "but I have known Konstantin since he was a baby. Based on all I have seen, I can say with confidence that Konstantin will be far kinder to you than your father was. And he most certainly will not strike you."

The carriage rocked wildly as it moved across uneven ground. When it stopped, Župan Dragomir helped his wife, then Suzana from the carriage. Strange, but she felt a bit of disappointment that it was Dragomir, not Konstantin. Still, watching the older couple's regard for one another was illuminating—it was possible for a husband and wife to seem like equals. Was it like that in private, too, or only when others watched?

Around them, men unloaded pack animals and pulled bundles from carts. Dragomir escorted his wife and Suzana toward a pavilion that Konstantin and some of his men were setting up. They finished, and then others brought the pieces of a trestle table and benches so that neither of the ladies would have to sit on the ground or on the logs that some of the soldiers were pulling around the fire. Suzana wasn't ready to sit yet—she'd been sitting in the carriage most of the day—but she appreciated the thought behind the table, and she was grateful for the shade.

"Župan Konstantin, you must dine with us and tell Dama Suzana all about her new home." Dama Isidora waved him closer to the table.

His eyes fixed on Suzana before turning to Dama Isidora. "I would be glad to. I have to see to the watch first and make sure the camp is properly set up. I will join you when the food is ready, and in the meantime"—he turned to Suzana—"is there anything I can do for you?"

They'd left the villa, and he was still being polite. Had she been braver, she might have asked him to walk with her so she could stretch her legs after the long ride in the carriage. But as a župan, he had responsibilities, and she didn't want to interfere with any of them. "Nothing at the moment, thank you."

He kept his gaze on her for several long heartbeats. "If you'll excuse me, then." He strode away.

Suzana stayed under the pavilion as the camp around her took shape. She saw Konstantin with his men, then with the horses. True to his word, he returned to the pavilion just as Župan Dragomir and Dama Isidora's servants set out the meal of fowl, olives, bread, and cheese. He sat beside Dragomir, across from her. The other men, including Dragomir and Isidora's grandson, ate near the fires, leaving their group small.

"Tell your bride about Rivak," Dama Isidora suggested.

Konstantin met Suzana's eyes and seemed to hesitate. "What do you wish to know?"

She wasn't sure how to answer, so as the silence drew out, she settled on a vague question. "What is it like?"

"We have six villages. The grody is part of the largest, Rivakgrad, with perhaps two score hearths. There are several bakers, and they all have different strengths. When we get back, I'll get loaves from all of them, and you can see which you like best."

The servants had put extra bread beside Konstantin, so perhaps it was a food he favored.

He continued, his expression unreadable but his voice kind. "A cloth merchant comes through every summer. We can get whatever you might need for clothing then. And traders come to Rivakgrad often enough, selling everything from Athenian soap to Italian mail. The grody itself is on a hill overlooking the grad, surrounded by a palisade wall. There's a palisade around the town too."

She nodded. Walls hadn't protected her in her father's villa, but hopefully they would protect her in her husband's home.

"We'll live in the grody itself. There are several houses there, the keep, stables, barracks, and chapel. My aunt promised to prepare your room. It was my mother's, years ago."

"Where will your mother sleep?"

Konstantin picked at the chicken that had been placed before him. Her piece had been tough, grizzly, and bland, but she had eaten it anyway. He seemed to be more interested in poking his than in chewing it. "She sleeps with Christ and His angels now."

Suzana felt her face heat. She'd known his father was dead or Konstantin wouldn't have been župan, but she hadn't known about his mother. "I am sorry."

"Camp fever came through the grad three years ago. My mother and my sister Bogdana died. My brother, Ivan, nearly died too. He's had relapses ever since."

"It came to our lands as well," Dama Isidora said. "Took my granddaughter."

Konstantin's face showed sympathy. "It hit the young the hardest." He directed his gaze at Suzana. "I did not see anyone who I thought might be your mother at the betrothal ceremony."

Suzana swallowed. "I killed her in childbirth." She had never known her mother, so it was strange that she still felt grief over her death. Grief and guilt because she'd stolen her mother's life when she'd begun her own.

"I am sorry," Konstantin said. "Did you have an aunt or a grandmother who stepped in?"

"A nurse." A series of them because her father always found something inadequate in those he hired. "And for you? I suppose you were no longer a child when your mother died, but you would have still been young."

"My father survived my mother by a year. And my aunt helped when needed. She is my father's sister, and she married one of his men-at-arms, so she's lived at the grody her entire life."

"Dama Zorica is a dear friend," Dama Isidora said. "I will be happy to have a reason to visit both of you."

"And I suppose you'll bring Decimir?" Konstantin's tone held a hint of playfulness. Suzana had not heard that from him yet, and it piqued her interest. Perhaps her betrothed wasn't always as serious as he'd seemed the last few days.

Dama Isidora smiled. "He is a capable escort, and he also has his reasons to visit Rivakgrad."

Konstantin met Suzana's eyes and explained. "I have three sisters. Two died as children, but Lidija is only a little younger than Dragomir and Isidora's grandson. They are young, but they are fond of each other."

"How many winters has Lidija?" Suzana asked.

"Twelve. My brother, Ivan, has seven, and my cousin, Danilo, has eight. The boys—you'll see them mostly together, often in mischief. They'll all be happy to meet you."

Suzana had never met a cousin and had no siblings. Now she would marry into a husband, aunt, sister, brother, and cousin all in the same day. She hoped they would like her. More than that, she hoped Konstantin would like her, because she was beginning to like him.

Chapter Eight
Danger in the Dark

Konstantin sat on the ground with his back against a felled tree trunk and stared into the fire. Night had fallen long ago, and he ought to sleep, but he was still worried. About Rivak, about whoever had tried to kill Suzana, and about his upcoming marriage.

No flush of excitement or pleasure had colored Suzana's cheeks during their meal. Nor had he noted dread in her eyes or her posture. Neutrality—he could work with that. Neutrality could turn to warmth, and warmth could turn to love.

He hoped she would like Rivakgrad, like him. The villa her father owned was fine enough to grace the main streets of Constantinople or Thessaloniki. Luxuries there had seemed common, and the cook or cooks were certainly more imaginative than the man Dragomir had brought along for their journey. Hunger nibbled at Konstantin's stomach, but none of the food had been enticing enough for him to seek out more. What would Suzana think when she saw palisades of wood in place of walls of stone? Clothing of linen and wool with only rare appearances of silk? Unpaved streets that turned to mud when the rain fell?

But one thing Rivakgrad had in abundance, and he'd seen little of it in Baldovin's villa: love.

Would someone hired as a nurse give a growing child the same type of love a mother could? Probably not. From what he'd seen of her father, he doubted she'd been given much love from him either. Perhaps that was why he'd yet to see a smile cross Suzana's face. Maybe tomorrow he could find a way to spark one.

Grigorii joined him at the fire. He'd been on watch to the north of their camp.

"Anything unusual?" Konstantin asked.

"The merophs aren't even out," Grigorii said. "I expect we'll have a quiet night."

Miladin joined them and handed Grigorii a bowl of stew and Konstantin half a loaf of bread. "I thought you might be hungry again."

Konstantin accepted the bread. "Thank you."

Grigorii raised an eyebrow. "If you do that when you have children, you'll irritate that pretty wife of yours."

"Do what?" Miladin asked.

"Let them get away with not eating what's served by giving them something else later on."

Miladin sat on the log behind Konstantin. "Lord Konstantin is my župan, not my child."

Grigorii chuckled and held up his bowl. "Thanks for this, anyway."

Konstantin bit into the bread. Maybe Grigorii was right. He was spoiled when it came to food because the grody in Rivakgrad had been blessed with a series of talented cooks. He usually ate fowl when served in Rivakgrad's main hall, but today's had been too dry. He had enough things to worry about without forcing himself to eat bland food of unpleasant texture.

Someone shouted in the distance. Konstantin stood, trying to see beyond the fire to the source of alarm. The gallop of hooves pounded through the nearby woods. No one friendly would be riding that hard at them.

Konstantin dropped the bread and reached for his shield. He pulled his spathion from its sheath and called to his men. "Stand together."

He would rather meet other horsemen from the back of his warhorse, but at least part of the garrison was with him. He knew their strengths and weaknesses the same way they knew his. But none of them knew anything about the approaching enemy. He glanced at Suzana's tent—dark and quiet, with Konstantin and the others standing between it and the approaching enemy.

Eight or nine shadows appeared in the darkness. "They're coming through right where I left Čučimir," Grigorii said. "He should have warned us."

The ground beneath Konstantin rumbled, and then the line of horsemen were upon them. Konstantin held his shield high to block their downward strokes. With his sword, he slashed at the horse charging between him and Grigorii. It fell to the ground, and Konstantin stabbed at its rider.

Even with surprise on their side, nine men wouldn't be enough to defeat the seven men-at-arms he'd brought and the ten men-at-arms Dragomir had brought, but it was enough to cause chaos, especially in the dark. One of the enemy cut toward Grigorii, and Konstantin ran at him, forcing him to back away and giving Grigorii a moment to breathe. Konstantin slammed into the man with his shield and hacked high, above the enemy's shield. When the attacker brought his shield up to protect his face, Konstantin hacked low and cut into the man's thigh. It wasn't a fatal blow, but it was enough to slow and weaken him, make him less of a threat. The intruder stumbled back, and Grigorii finished him off.

Konstantin turned to fight another of the bandits who'd been knocked from his horse. He blocked three blows with his shield before seeing an opening and slashing at the attacker's ribs. The man cried out, then fell.

Konstantin looked around. All the attackers were engaged with one of his men or one of Dragomir's men, and unless their skill was significantly greater than the men Konstantin had fought, he wagered the brigands would all be dead soon. The group must have underestimated the strength of the camp, and they'd rushed headlong into a fight they were unlikely to win.

Then a scream rose behind him.

A woman's scream.

Suzana jolted awake when Divna screamed. Three armed men had entered their tent. One held a blazing torch. All held swords. The one nearest the maid grabbed her. "Is this her?"

"Does she look seventeen to you?" one of the others said.

The brawny lout holding Divna threw her to the ground. He held the point of his sword next to her face. "Don't move or you're dead."

Fear seized Suzana's chest. She had seventeen winters. They were looking for her. She slipped from her blankets and tried to find a seam in the tent that she could untie and escape through. The man with the torch waved the light next to Dama Isidora's face and leaned down for a better look. "This one's too old."

Dama Isidora sat up and swung a wooden box at the man's head, but he grabbed her wrist and pummeled the side of her head with the end of the torch. Suzana yelped as Dama Isidora crumpled backward.

One of the men reached for Suzana. She narrowly evaded his grasp as she rushed to Dama Isidora's side. The sound of the torch hitting her head and the woman's sudden stillness was terrifying.

Please don't let her be dead. Suzana hadn't prayed in a long time, but perhaps God would help someone as kind as Dama Isidora.

A trickle of blood dripped across the woman's temple. Before Suzana could see anything more, the soldier caught up to her and yanked her into him, almost crushing her. The torch moved next to her face, and she flinched at the heat. "She's the right age. Are you Suzana Baldovinević?"

Suzana didn't answer. She didn't know what they wanted, but cooperation seemed foolish.

The man holding her changed his grip, and panic seized her more and more tightly as his hands wandered over her torso. "Maybe we can take this one with us and have a little fun first."

Bile burned in her throat, but her body froze in fear as memory and terror tangled around her like ropes. She could hardly breathe.

One of the other men held up his sword. "You heard our orders. Death, and everyone is to see her body so there's no question of her having survived."

Why did someone want her dead? Was this a new enemy or the same foe trying to kill her a second time? The man holding her forced her to her knees. With one hand, he held both her arms behind her back, and with the other, he shoved her shoulders forward, forcing her neck out.

Death by beheading. Her fear flared, and she tried to pull away, but he only held her arms at a more painful angle as a second man approached with a drawn sword.

The flap of the tent flew open, and another armed man ran inside. "No!"

The shout startled the one with the torch for a moment, then he dropped the light and swung his sword at the newcomer. While they fought, the man holding her shoved her to the ground and drew out a dagger.

Suzana's hands and wrists stung from where she'd caught herself. She tried to crawl away, but the man grabbed her hair and tugged her head up and back with an agonizing yank. A blade pressed into her exposed neck. She squeezed her eyes shut, certain death was coming. A bite of pain pinched her skin. Then warm liquid poured over her, and the pressure on her neck disappeared. In its place a heavy weight tumbled onto her back, pinning her to the ground. She'd been trapped like that before, and terror made her whimper.

"Suzana?"

Konstantin's voice. She opened her eyes, swallowed, tried to speak. He'd killed the man who'd been about to kill her, but the corpse now lay on top of her, trapping and constricting her.

Before Konstantin could free her, the third assassin charged for him. Konstantin turned just in time to block a strike with his shield. He yelled and charged at the brigand. His sword sliced into the man's arm, then he slammed the man's face with the upper end of his shield. The assassin stumbled back into the side of the tent. Konstantin's blade followed, stopping next to the man's neck.

The bandit recognized he was defeated and dropped his sword.

"Why were you trying to kill her?" Konstantin yelled.

Blood streamed from the man's nose. He gasped, winced, and spat out a few broken teeth. "Orders. Attack the camp. Kill the woman betrothed to Rivak's župan."

Two more men entered the tent. The one with the hawkish nose, Grigorii, and the one with a scarred face, Miladin.

Grigorii looked from where Suzana lay to Konstantin and the prisoner. "All is under control outside, Župan Konstantin."

"Check on the women," Konstantin ordered. He kept his eyes on the prisoner. "Who sent you?"

"Rivak's worst nightmare." In a movement so quick she couldn't follow, the prisoner struggled. Konstantin flinched to the side, then slid his sword across the man's neck. A cry shot through the tent. The man fell to the ground, and a dagger stained with blood tumbled from his hand.

Suzana should have felt relief, but witnessing another death did nothing to calm the horror that threatened to overwhelm her.

"Did he get you?" Miladin asked his župan.

Konstantin fingered his side. "It's not deep." Then his eyes fell on Suzana and widened. "She's covered in blood. Divna, get the torch!"

Konstantin and Miladin pulled the slain assassin off her. Breathing was easier without his weight crushing her, but her whole body shook.

"Where are you hurt?" Blood splattered Konstantin's face and stained his shoulders. He brushed her hair back, searching for wounds. His touch was soft, not at all like the man who'd pulled her hair so he could better expose her neck to his blade, but Suzana still flinched.

Konstantin's hands pulled back instantly. "I'm sorry. What did I do?"

She needed to answer him. What was wrong with her? He'd just saved her life. But that skill with the sword, that fierceness with his enemies—he'd killed three men in quick succession, and it was terrifying. Dizziness crept up the back of her skull, and queasiness twisted in her stomach. She turned her head to the side and vomited.

Konstantin watched it all, and embarrassment mixed with her nausea and fear.

Miladin put a hand on Konstantin's arm. "I think most of the blood is his, not hers."

Konstantin inhaled. "How is Dama Isidora?"

"Breathing. Unconscious."

Konstantin looked away for a moment. "Grigorii, will you find Župan Dragomir? Then tell Risto that I need him."

"Of course, lord." Grigorii left.

Konstantin turned back to her, but she couldn't meet his eyes. "She's still shaking." He spoke to Miladin, not to her. "Is she cold?" Konstantin seemed to hesitate, then placed his palm against her forehead. This time, she managed to stay calm when his skin met hers, but she still couldn't work up the ability to ask more about Dama Isidora or to explain what had happened. "She feels a little clammy."

"Maybe we should get her to the fire," Miladin said.

Konstantin reached for one of her blankets and pulled it from the bedroll. Then he took one of her trembling hands. "Suzana, I'm going to take you out to the fire. Until the shaking stops."

She managed a nod, nothing more. He helped her sit, then wrapped the blanket around her shoulders and lifted her to her feet. He pulled one of her arms around his neck, then scooped her up into his arms. Miladin opened the tent flap for them. She hated being so helpless, but weakness coated her body as thoroughly as the blood. As Konstantin carried her to the fire, Dragomir rushed into the tent. Even in the dark, worry was evident on his face.

Konstantin sat her on a log before the fire but kept an arm at her back for support. She'd just watched him kill three men. She didn't want to lean against him, but when she tried to ease forward, she felt off balance.

A string of men came to speak with Konstantin. He told one to fetch water and rags. He told another to double the watch and someone else to round up the dead.

She wanted to ask so many questions, but she didn't trust her voice. Tears blurred her vision. Was this what life as a župan's wife would be like, with someone trying to kill her on a daily basis? She couldn't get the image of Konstantin's work out of her mind. What if his anger turned on her? She wouldn't be able to escape. She was completely at his mercy.

She closed her eyes and inhaled, focusing on the rhythm of her breathing and the warmth of the fire, on the fact that Konstantin's sword, as terrifying as it was, had been used to defend her.

When she opened her eyes again, Miladin stood before Konstantin, reporting. "They came past Čučimir's position. He was stabbed in the back. Must have fallen asleep to let someone get that close to him."

"I've never seen him fall asleep on duty before," Konstantin said.

"Nor have I, but there's a first time for everything. There won't be a second, not for him."

Konstantin leaned forward and pinched the bridge of his nose. "Any other casualties?"

"Bojan took a hard blow to the arm, just below his shoulder guard. The cut is wide but shallow. Ought to heal completely. One of Župan Dragomir's men has a few slashes across his legs. He'll need to ride in one of the carts tomorrow. And you."

Konstantin lowered his hand. "Me?"

Miladin motioned to Konstantin's side. "He tried to stab you. You said it's not deep, but I'd feel better if you let me see what your definition of shallow is."

"I doubt it's deep enough to see in the dark."

"Then you can show it to me, and we can both stop worrying about it."

Konstantin shifted positions on the log and held up an arm.

Miladin squinted and pulled at the armor. "He managed to get his blade between two of the lamella. It would be good to have it bandaged, lord."

Konstantin fiddled with his corselet. "When I take my armor off. A while longer."

Another man, one of the few not dressed as a warrior, brought two buckets of water and a pile of small cloths. He put one bucket next to the fire and brought the other to Konstantin. His face had a weathered look, what little hair he had was gray, and he walked with a limp.

"Thank you, Risto."

"Shall I help you out of your armor, lord?"

Konstantin shook his head. "Not yet." Konstantin glanced at Suzana, then back at Risto. "Will you see to it that Dama Suzana is provided with a clean place to sleep? Župan Dragomir might want her in a different tent until Dama Isidora recovers. See what he wishes. Use my bedding or my tent if needed."

"Yes, lord."

Suzana tried to still the tremors in her throat. She still didn't wish to speak, but how could she ever expect to be anything other than scared if she couldn't even work up the courage to ask after her friend? "How is Dama Isidora?"

Konstantin's gaze went to her face the moment she spoke. "Her head will probably feel a lot like yours did after your trip down the river, but we expect her to recover." He took a cloth from the pile Risto had left and dipped it into the bucket. Then he wrung it out and gently took one of her hands. "May I? You're covered in blood."

"As are you, my lord."

He glanced at his hands. "I'll see to it after your needs are met."

She ought to clean herself, but her hands still shook, so she nodded her permission.

He began with her hands and wrists. The water was cool, but that seemed to ease the nausea she couldn't quite shake. Then he washed his own hands in the bucket and switched the used water with the water by the fire. There were servants who could do the work. Divna, though she was probably needed to help Dama Isidora. Or Risto. Someone other than a župan, but there were only three women in the camp, and she wouldn't have been comfortable with any of the other men cleaning the blood from her skin. Not that she was entirely comfortable with Konstantin, but he was gentle as he ran the cloth along the side of her face. The water had heated some, but it still left her skin feeling cooler than it had beneath the layer of dried blood.

She inhaled sharply when he ran the cloth over the back of her jaw. He paused to scrutinize her skin. "He cut you."

"He meant to go deeper. Thank you for stopping him."

He stayed quiet while he cleaned the skin around the cut. "I'm sorry I wasn't there sooner. I intend to keep you safe, but I didn't prove myself very well tonight."

He moved to stand behind her and began cleaning her hair. None of her maids had been so gentle with her hair before, and his actions softened some of the fear and rekindled some of the hope. But then guilt swept over her. "They were looking for me. Dama Isidora tried to fight back. That's why they hurt her." Suzana had killed her mother. And now, after one day, when it almost felt like Dama Isidora might take on some type of maternal role, Suzana had led to her being wounded. She tried to hold back a sob, but she didn't quite manage.

Konstantin came around to kneel in front of her. He took her hand and held it. "She's going to be all right. And so are you, even after these last two days."

She blinked away a tear, wanting to believe him about Dama Isidora and about herself. "Will someone try to kill me again tomorrow? It's like I'm living through a nightmare."

Konstantin shifted, sitting with his back against the log that acted as her bench. "It's frightening, what's happened to you since I came into your life."

The fire cracked. The flames were dying down, and between the reduced light and the angle of his face, it was harder for Suzana to see the blood that still marred him. Most of the other men were sleeping or standing watch, leaving just him and her on their side of the fire.

"I've felt my share of fear," he whispered.

"You have?"

He flung a stick into the fire. "When my father died at Maritsa. There wasn't even a real battle. Župan Dragomir's brother was supposed to set the watch, but he betrayed us, so there was no warning. The Turks attacked at night while the Serb army slept. Like tonight but on a larger scale. So many fell."

Suzana had heard a little of Maritsa. Her father had sold a great deal of armor and weapons in the months leading up to it. Some of the men who perished there had still owed him money for their purchases. Her father had felt the loss but, she sensed, not nearly as much as Konstantin had.

"As time passed, we learned the full toll." Konstantin sighed. "My father. My uncle. Most of our župa's men-at-arms. So many of them gone forever. Only a fortnight before, my father had told me I wasn't old enough to go with him on campaign, that I wasn't ready. And then suddenly, I was to take his place as župan, and at such a time. The Turks had won. I could fight to the death with the handful of men we had left, or I could submit to the enemy who had just taken away the most important men in my life."

He was silent for a moment, surrounded by the firelight. "It was an easy choice in some ways. We hadn't a hope of defeating the Turks, and the people of the župa depended on me to protect them. If I fought, I would fail, and the people would become subjects of the sultan. Maybe they are anyway, but at least this way they have me as a barrier. But easy choice or not, it was a bitter one."

"And you were scared?" Suzana would have been frightened too. She knew all about submission and oppression, but no one had ever depended on her before.

"Yes. All that responsibility. All those people who needed me, and all I wanted to do was cry the way Aunt Zorica and Lidija and Ivan and Danilo were crying. But I couldn't. A župan has to be stronger than that. It was overwhelming. My first order as župan was for someone to saddle my horse, and I rode away all by myself for hours. I cried then. I grieved and thought and prayed as I had never prayed before. And eventually, I came to terms with it all. I was to be a leader to a broken people. That was my task, and God expected me to do my best with it. And I . . . I felt something. Somehow, I knew God would be with me. That it would work out."

He turned to face her. "I felt a little like that again when we rode to your father's villa and I was to marry a stranger. I've tried my best to be a good župan, but I've fallen short. That's why I had to marry, so I could meet the sultan's demands even after all the lands that have burned. But I don't want to fail at being a husband. I want to do it right, and when I saw you in that garden, I felt that same assurance I had the day I became župan. Somehow, it felt like everything would work out." He took her hand gently in his. "And I still feel that, even after yesterday and today."

Suzana watched his blood-smudged face. At times, her betrothed had seemed cold. At times, he had seemed frightening. But at that moment, he seemed like someone she could understand. He'd felt fear—for the future, for the weight of his responsibilities. She felt that same fear, but she didn't feel the assurance he'd spoken of. "I'm still frightened."

Konstantin released her hand and took a cross from around his neck. He placed it in her palm. "As much as I want to, I can't take away your fear. You have to ask God if He can take it from you or help you bear it."

She studied the crucifix in the firelight. Silver, untarnished, on a leather strap, as long as her smallest finger. She didn't know that God would listen to her, even if she prayed, but she'd caught a glimpse of her future husband's soul, there by the firelight, and that glimpse gave her courage.

Divna approached the fire. "Dama Suzana, Dama Isidora is asking for you."

Relief swept over Suzana. She rose too quickly and wobbled as the dizziness came, but a moment later, Konstantin stood at her side with one hand under her arm and the other on her back to steady her. She accepted his help to the women's tent.

Župan Dragomir sat on one side of a bedroll, and Decimir sat on the other. When Suzana and Konstantin walked past Dragomir, Dama Isidora came into view. Her face seemed pale in the lamplight, but she smiled when Suzana entered. "I am glad to see you safe."

Suzana knelt beside her friend. "I'm so sorry." Her throat grew tight at the thought of what the men had done to Dama Isidora—and what they might have done—all because she had tried to help Suzana.

Dama Isidora grasped her hand. "Shush, child. None of this ill is your doing." Her eyes swept over Suzana and focused on Konstantin. "Župan Konstantin, please tell me that is not your blood that covers your face."

"No, my lady."

"Then go and wash it off before you terrify your betrothed. Dragomir, Decimir, you must leave too. Dama Suzana needs a clean tunic, and so I will ask all of you to take your worried faces outside and let Suzana and Divna and me rest in peace. We've had a rough night thus far."

Dragomir asked his wife a few more questions about her head. Suzana met Konstantin's eyes. His battle and the blood had terrified her earlier, but now they did not. She hadn't known warriors could be gentle enough to clean the blood from a frightened girl's hair or that a župan with so much outward strength could rely so completely on God when his responsibilities weighed him down. Konstantin was like no man she had ever before met.

Chapter Nine
Rivakgrad

Konstantin groaned when the sun chased away the darkness of the tent. He might have slept well into the morning, given how taxing the last several days had been, but the wound in his side throbbed with a painful persistence. Miladin had bandaged it the night before, but that hadn't banished the pain.

He opened his eyes and found both Grigorii and Miladin watching him.

"If I may, lord." Miladin placed a hand on Konstantin's forehead.

Konstantin frowned. "I'm not feverish. Just tired and grumpy because my side aches, my stomach is empty, and someone keeps trying to kill my betrothed."

Grigorii cracked a smile. "I'll go see about something for your stomach, lord."

"Did anything important happen after I went to sleep?" Konstantin sat and rubbed his face. He didn't usually have trouble waking in the morning, but he'd stood watch part of last night and much of the night before.

"Everyone is safe," Miladin said. "If that's what you mean. May I check your wound?"

Konstantin nodded.

Miladin tsked when he removed the wrap. "It looks worse this morning."

"Letting you at it a little earlier last night wouldn't have made any difference."

"Maybe. Maybe not." Miladin put another dressing on the wound.

"Suzana needed someone last night. I wanted it to be me." He still wasn't sure if he'd helped her or not, but the trembling had stopped while they'd sat by the fire. And she'd spoken with him. That had to be progress.

"Give it time."

"The way things are going, I'm not sure we'll have much of that."

Miladin sobered. "We'll be home by midday. Things will be better once we're in Rivak."

They had no guarantee that the arson and attempted murder would end, but at least they'd be in a familiar place, where they could notice anything out of the ordinary. They would have walls and a garrison and be surrounded by people just as desperate as they were to keep Rivak peaceful and secure.

Putting his armor on over his injury was uncomfortable, but the injury was also a reminder of how necessary his armor was. Had he not been wearing it last night, he might be dead. Maybe Suzana too. Risto helped him into his mail and corselet, and then Konstantin went to check on the preparations, eat and, with any luck, banish the ache in his head that threatened to turn into a pounding.

Porridge was the only offering, but at least it was warm. He'd overslept, but the others had made a good start of packing the camp and preparing for the day's march. They started taking down his tent almost the moment he left it.

Risto brought Perun over, and Konstantin petted the animal while he checked the saddle and bridle. "Thank you, Risto. For this, and for everything last night." He probably hadn't slept much longer than Konstantin had, not with the need to find clean bedding for Suzana and clean up the blood and vomit.

"Happy to help, lord. Shall I see to anything else?"

"Just prepare for the day's journey. I'm ready to go home."

"As am I, lord."

Konstantin hoped Suzana was ready too. Ready to make a new home. He led Perun to the pavilion to check on the women. Both Dama Isidora and Suzana were up and nearly finished with their meal, despite the attack of the night before. A long scab ran across the corner of Suzana's jaw. He closed his eyes for a moment as the image of the man about to cut her throat flooded his mind. He didn't understand how anyone could do that to an innocent woman. Orders or not, taking a woman from her bed and killing her was evil. Anyone could feel that.

"Good morning, Konstantin." Dama Isidora's voice held only a hint of the exhaustion she no doubt felt. Most of her hair was covered by a veil, but a dark red bruise showed at her forehead.

"A fair morning to both of you. Are you well?"

"Well enough to go home." Dama Isidora waved him to the bench beside Suzana, and Konstantin obeyed. "Things ought to settle down once you and your betrothed are in Rivak."

"That is my hope as well." Konstantin turned to Suzana. Still no sign of eagerness to be with him but no sign of repulsion either. She did, however, wear the crucifix he'd given her. Her hand lay on the table, and he felt drawn to take it with his own, but he wasn't sure how she would react. Maybe with time he'd know what she was comfortable with and which boundaries he needed to respect. "I thought perhaps when we reached the borders of Rivak, you might like to ride with me. You are welcome to stay in the carriage if you prefer, but you'll see the land better from horseback."

The corners of her mouth lifted ever so slightly. Almost a smile. "I would like that. Thank you."

"And until then, what can I do to ease your journey?"

"I am well at present, thank you." She looked down for a moment, then glanced up, almost shyly. "I did wonder if you perhaps would like to keep my cross for me, as you have given me yours." She pulled out a petite cross of gold and offered it to him.

Her hand brushed his as she placed the crucifix in his palm, and her touch sparked a powerful sensation of pleasure. It surprised him to the core, and several long heartbeats passed before he swallowed and found his voice. "Thank you. I will keep it close to my heart." He looped the cord around his neck and slipped the pendant under his tunic.

The rest of the morning progressed normally enough. The roads were dry, the horses obedient, and hope—or maybe it was love—made Konstantin's worries seem lighter whenever he thought of Suzana. Perhaps what he felt for her was only a drop, but that was a start.

When they approached the first of Rivak's villages, Konstantin helped Suzana onto a gentle gelding and rode beside her, pointing out the different crops and explaining the customs of the merophs. He couldn't judge by her expression whether she found the information interesting or dull, but she paid attention to everything he said.

The weather grew more and more contrary to his mood. Dark clouds blew in, and before Rivakgrad came into view, the first raindrops pattered onto his skin. Soon after, the clouds burst. "I should get you back in the carriage before you're soaked." But when he led her back and helped her from the saddle, he realized he was too late. Rain had already soaked her dalmatica, and he didn't have anything dry to give her. That was one more thing he'd failed at.

The rain slowed as they reached the fork in the road that meant it was time to part company with Dragomir.

"Would you like to come to the grody until the weather improves?" Konstantin asked.

"I'd rather return home. I was glad to come, glad to help you, but my wife will need rest after what's happened, even if she's not ready to admit it yet." He pulled his cloak to better block the rain. "Perhaps I need the rest too. I'm not getting any younger."

"Thank you for coming. I'm sorry so many of our plans went awry."

Dragomir grasped Konstantin's wrist. "I will always be Rivak's friend. And your friend. I expect we'll see each other soon. At the wedding, if not before."

The carriage would continue on to Dragomir's župa, so Konstantin had Suzana's horse brought forward once again. Risto even managed to find a dry cloak, but since she was already wet from the earlier ride in the rain, Konstantin didn't know if it would keep her warm.

Her hands felt cold when he helped her from the carriage.

"I'm sorry I let you get all wet," he said.

"The rain came suddenly."

It had, but he'd also been hesitant to part with her. He had the feeling that she wouldn't complain about the wet or the cold, but that didn't mean she wouldn't suffer.

Konstantin motioned Miladin over. "Will you ride ahead and let the grody know we're coming? Tell them to have a warm bath and a large fire ready for Suzana. I don't know if Aunt Zorica will let you leave until after you've filled her in on all that happened, but maybe you can get home to your wife and niece a bit sooner."

"With pleasure, lord." Miladin cut through a field to get around their column, then returned to the road and set his horse to a trot.

Konstantin turned his attention to Suzana. He couldn't see more than her chin because the hood of her cloak was pulled so far forward. "If you look closely, you can see Rivakgrad." He pointed, and her hooded head turned in the proper direction. As they drew closer, he tried to picture how it must look to someone who had never yet seen it. To him, it was home, but as they passed through the lower grad, he couldn't help but notice how dreary it looked in the rain. Few of the craftsmen, merophs, or their families were in view, and the main road had turned into a muddy quagmire. When they rode up the causeway and reached the grody, the courtyard was even worse, coating the horses' legs and building up on the wheels of the carts.

He guided his horse closer to Suzana's. "It looks more cheerful in the sunlight. And it's usually not so muddy." But it never looked as prosperous and clean as the villa she had left.

Danilo ran down the keep's stairs and sprinted through the mud toward him. The boys' dog followed. "Kostya! You're back!"

Konstantin dismounted in time to receive an exuberant embrace from his cousin. He looked over Danilo's head, expecting Ivan to run at him next. Aunt Zorica tried to keep Ivan inside when it rained, but he usually managed to escape despite her efforts.

Perhaps Danilo noticed Konstantin's gaze. "Ivan has a fever again."

Konstantin looked down and read the worry in his cousin's eyes. "How bad?"

Danilo shrugged. "He's been in bed for two days. But this morning, he laughed when I told him a story. I think that means he's on the mend."

It at least meant he wasn't delirious. Ivan had come close to death so many times and then pulled through that it was sometimes easy to assume he'd pull through again and again. But death circled Ivan like a wolf circled a lone lamb. One day, it might strike and carry him off.

Ivan's illness explained why Aunt Zorica stood at the top of the keep steps, sheltered from the rain, but Lidija did not. She was no doubt with their brother.

"Danilo, could you hold Perun for me?" Konstantin asked.

Danilo took the reins with a grin. Konstantin wouldn't have handed his destrier over to a boy of Danilo's age, but his palfrey had not only a gentle stride but also a gentle manner when it came to children. He led Suzana's gelding to the bottom of the steps. His boots were coated in thick, congealing mud, but by helping her dismount at the base of the keep, he could shield her skirts from most of the grime. He felt a tremor in her hand when she accepted his offered arm, so he leaned forward enough to see her face beneath the cloak. She shivered.

Konstantin led her up the stairs at a brisk pace. It wouldn't do for Suzana to survive two attempts on her life only to die of exposure. "Suzana, will you allow me to place you in my aunt's care? She can ensure you're warm enough while I see to the horses and the men."

"Do you not need help with your duties?" she asked.

"I'll have help. For now, I just want you to be warm and comfortable and not shivering in the rain."

Aunt Zorica met them near the top. "You must be Dama Suzana." She reached for Suzana's hand and took it in her own. "Goodness. Konstantin, she is freezing. I hope you haven't neglected her comfort the entire journey."

"I can tell you all about the journey later," Konstantin said. "For now, will you see that she's taken somewhere warm?"

The look in Aunt Zorica's eyes warned him that he'd get an earful later, but he'd deal with his aunt's disappointment then. Maybe he deserved it for failing to keep Suzana out of the rain, but keeping her alive over the last several days had taken nearly all his skill.

"I'm sure I will be well enough if I can sit by the fire for a bit." Suzana's voice still sounded shy, but Aunt Zorica would put her at ease soon enough.

He watched the two women enter the hall, then went back to Danilo and Perun. He lifted Danilo into the saddle and led them to the stables. Others unpacked the carts and cared for the rest of the animals.

"Danilo, have you seen Kuzman recently?" Konstantin reached up to help his cousin dismount, getting a smear of mud across his chest in the process.

"I trained with him this morning, before it started raining. He says I'm improving. Ivan, too, when he's well enough to train. Will you watch us tomorrow?"

"If I can slip away from everything else. Will you find him for me?"

Danilo nodded and ran off.

Konstantin removed Perun's saddle and began brushing him, but he let one of the grooms take over before he finished. Konstantin glanced at Svarog's box, but visiting his warhorse just then would be self-indulgent. He had an ill brother and a threatened betrothed who took precedence.

As soon as Kuzman came into the stables with Danilo, Konstantin walked over to them. "Thank you, Danilo. Now, will you check on Ivan for me? Tell him I'll visit soon, but don't wake him if he's asleep."

"I won't." Danilo's mischievous grin said otherwise, but if Lidija was with Ivan, she'd protect his sleep.

Kuzman watched the boy run off. "I would normally be surprised that you haven't gone to your brother already, but I heard rumors from some of the men."

"The rumors are true if they involve tales of someone trying to murder my betrothed two days in a row. I want the grad's security tightened. Extra watchmen, more strictness at the gates. Will you help me plan it?"

Chapter Ten
WARMTH AND WARNING

After a spell in front of the fire and a warm bath, Suzana dressed in one of the dalmaticas she'd brought from her father's home and listened to the maid's chatter while she arranged Suzana's hair. Servants in her father's home had never held conversations with her. Suzana wasn't sure this counted as a conversation since it was very one-sided, but she liked Jasmina's warmth. The woman, Bojan's daughter of seventeen years, had a cheerful voice and a friendly manner.

"My father said the župan was wounded and you almost killed twice. Absolutely dreadful. But you'll be safe enough now."

Suzana hoped Jasmina was right. She was tired of being afraid.

Jasmina finished Suzana's hair, then placed a clean, dry veil on her head. "I can guess where Župan Konstantin is, if you'd like me to take you to him. Or you can rest."

Suzana might wish to be over her fear, but it quickly crept back. Maybe it wasn't quite fear—more a nervousness. She didn't want to disturb Konstantin, but nor did she want to shirk her duties, and her duties surely included more than sitting around waiting for her betrothed to send for her. "Do you suppose he is in the keep or still tending to the horses?" She had been grateful when Konstantin had sent her inside to warm herself. The combination of rain and ride had sent a chill all the way to her bones, but she suspected a journey into the grody's stables would chill her even more. Duty or not, she didn't feel brave enough for that.

"I'd wager he's in the boys' room, checking on his brother."

The tension that had been building in Suzana's muscles eased. "Then I would be grateful if you could take me to him."

Her new room—formerly Konstantin's mother's room—was warm and comfortable. An icon graced one wall, and a window overlooked the land beyond the grad. One door led, she supposed, to the župan's chamber, but it was currently bolted. The other led back the way she'd come in, and she followed Jasmina through it into the corridor.

Jasmina motioned to a chamber as they passed it and confirmed Suzana's suspicion. "That's the župan's chambers, but he's to sleep elsewhere until the wedding, seeing as how your bedchambers are connected."

Suzana felt her face heat. She'd been ready to leave her father's home, ready to take up her duties in helping her soon-to-be husband rule his župa. But she wasn't ready for all aspects of marriage, no matter how kind Konstantin had shown himself to be. The mere thought of sharing a man's bed made her chest feel tight—and not in a pleasant way. But that, too, would soon become one of her duties.

Jasmina slowed as they approached a nearby chamber.

A child's voice drifted out to her. "What's she like?"

"Well . . ." Konstantin's voice. "I only met her a few days ago, but she's pretty. And she's been very brave. We'll be glad to have her in Rivak."

"She'd have to be brave to marry you." The voice and the giggles that followed were young and feminine.

"Don't laugh, Lidija. Any woman would be lucky to marry Kostya." The boy's voice again.

"But you're always so stern," the girl said. "Have you even smiled in front of her?"

"When was I supposed to smile?" Konstantin's voice was firm but not unkind. "While she was drowning in the river? Or while I was fighting the assassins?"

"Perhaps rescuing her twice will make up for your sour expression." The girl's voice carried teasing again.

Jasmina winked at Suzana and cleared her throat as she turned the corner into the bedchamber. "Is Ivan well enough to meet Dama Suzana?"

"I am!" The boy's voice carried an expectant air that Suzana feared she wouldn't live up to.

Jasmina stepped to the side as Konstantin appeared in the doorway.

His eyes traveled over Suzana's face. "Are you warm enough now?"

"Yes, thank you."

"I am glad for that." He offered her his arm. "May I introduce you to my family?"

She placed her hand on his forearm, wondering if he suspected how much she'd overheard. She hoped not, but she was beginning to sense that he was not an ogre, so regardless, there would be no censure or punishment.

A young woman sat on a trunk at the foot of a bed. Sumptuous embroidery wove across her dalmatica, and her eyes, gray like Konstantin's, held curiosity and welcome. The boy with Turkish looks who had run to Konstantin in the courtyard sat on a bench near the window, adjusting the string of his gusle. And in one of the room's two beds lay another boy, smaller than the other, with a frail, pale face and bright hazel eyes.

Konstantin motioned to the girl first. "This is my sister Lidija. My brother, Ivan. And my cousin, Danilo." He pointed out the boys, then focused on her. "And this is Dama Suzana, who has agreed to marry me at the end of harvest."

All three children seemed to speak at once.

"Does that mean you'll be my sister?" Ivan asked.

Danilo stood and stepped closer. "Can Ivan and I stay up for the wedding feast?"

"Did he do anything romantic when he asked you to marry him?" Lidija seemed intent on her question, as if the manner of betrothal was of upmost importance.

Suzana wasn't sure who to answer first. Konstantin noticed her hesitation and spoke for her. "Ivan, she will be your sister-by-marriage. Danilo, I already told you that your bedtime will depend entirely upon your mother, not on me. And Grandfather arranged the marriage, Lidija. We didn't meet until the betrothal ceremony."

A frown pulled at Lidija's mouth. "You won't let Grandfather marry me off to a stranger, will you?"

Konstantin actually smiled. It changed his whole face, and Suzana couldn't help but stare.

"I know your preference when it comes to a husband, and I don't plan on forgetting it," he said.

Ivan met Suzana's eyes with a solemn look. "Lidija wishes to marry Decimir."

"I met Decimir and his grandparents on our journey," Suzana told Lidija. "His grandmother was kind enough to let me accompany her in her carriage and to help me when I was . . . when I needed help." Suzana wasn't sure if the children had heard details about the attempts on her life, nor did she know how much Konstantin wished them to discuss.

Danilo went back to his instrument. "When someone tied you to a log and threw you in the river?"

Suzana felt her face heat. "Yes."

Konstantin studied his cousin. "How did you hear about the log?"

"The whole garrison is talking about it. How someone tried to kill her twice and you plucked her from the river one day and then stopped a bunch of swordsmen the next." Danilo focused on her. "Were you frightened?"

Konstantin didn't hesitate before speaking. "Danilo, I think it would be wise to focus on the future rather than on the past."

"Did you kill them, Kostya?" Ivan asked. "When the men attacked her?"

Konstantin sighed and seemed to accept that the boys wouldn't let the subject drop without a little more information. "I will always defend my family, fiercely. And Suzana is now bound to our family, so I will always defend her."

Lidija stood and approached her. "Suzana, may I show you around the grody?"

"Can I come too?" Ivan pulled his blanket back and started scrambling from the bed.

Konstantin released Suzana's arm to go to his brother. "Ivan, you need to rest a while longer. We'll all have time to get to know Suzana better, but today you must regain your strength."

Danilo looked from Lidija to Ivan, as if wishing he could be in two places at once. "I'll stay, Ivan. I'll play you a song."

"Thank you, Danilo." Konstantin's words were whispered. He met Suzana's eyes next. "Would you like a tour?"

Suzana had watched Konstantin with his men. He seemed close to some of them but always focused and serious. He was different around his family, more relaxed and playful. Less regal, perhaps, but more approachable. She liked the change. And if she was really to be part of his family, she hoped that he would soon be more relaxed with her too. "I would like that, thank you."

Konstantin slipped into Ivan and Danilo's bedchamber early the next morning. Both slept. He watched, giving Ivan more attention. He seemed settled, his breathing easy. Maybe the illness would last only a few days this time. Or maybe the illness only appeared less all-consuming because the boy slept.

He left and met Aunt Zorica in the hallway, his aunt no doubt about to do the same thing he'd been doing.

"Asleep still?" she asked.

"Yes. I think he seems better, but that might be only because I want him to be better. Aleksander Igorević convinced Grandfather that Ivan is in perfect health, and then this. He asked about Ivan, of course."

"I would expect Župan Đurad Lukarević to ask after his heir and grandson. What did you tell him?"

"That you are a miracle worker, to which he replied that there is a physician in Sivi Gora. But physicians aren't the same as aunts. I won't be able to put him off much longer. And he's right, in some ways. Ivan will be better able to rule Sivi Gora if he spends time there. Maybe he can go in the summers when he's a little older."

"Compromise is often better than outright refusal." She folded her arms. "I keep praying he'll grow out of the sickness."

"As do I." Konstantin had already lost enough family. He didn't want to lose Ivan too.

Aunt Zorica hesitated. "Suzana seems . . . quiet. But more than that, she seems frightened of something."

"Someone tried to kill her two days in a row. It makes me scared, and I assume the effect is stronger on her."

"That's part of it, but I feel like there's something else too."

What would make Suzana scared? Fear of another attempt on her life? Kuzman had organized increased security, but she wouldn't know what it was like before, so it might not make her feel any safer. "I'm doing my best to make her feel welcome and wanted and safe. I'm desperate for this marriage to work."

"We all want the marriage to work." Aunt Zorica put a hand on his arm. "I know you are trying. And you succeeded in saving her life twice."

He shook his head. "She was so scared that second time. Of the men. Of me." She'd flinched at his touch, as if he'd been the one trying to hurt her. He wanted her to trust him, and he wanted to be able to trust her—with his župa and with himself. It wore on him, the constant need to hide his feelings from anyone who might use them against him. He wanted his wife to be his confidant, someone who might learn his weaknesses but never exploit them.

"Give her time," Aunt Zorica said. "Time to get over her fear. Time to grow accustomed to her new home and her future husband. And give her as much of yourself as you can. I know your duties are heavy, but the sooner you can work together without reservations, the better. For both of you and for Rivak."

Konstantin nodded.

"After I've checked on the boys and after we've broken our fasts, I need you in the strongroom. I was going to tell you yesterday, but with Suzana being nearly frozen and Ivan still ill . . ." She trailed off with a frustrated wave of her hands.

"Something serious?"

"We'll worry about it after you've eaten. Nothing will change between now and then."

So, it was serious. Another problem. But sometimes problems were best dealt with over a full stomach.

"It's the taxes. We're missing some of them." Aunt Zorica gestured to the locked chest in the strongroom. Only Konstantin, Aunt Zorica, and the protovastar had keys, and the room was to be locked whenever they stepped away. Čučimir was dead now, leaving only Konstantin and Aunt Zorica with access.

"How much are we missing?"

"Two hyperpyra."

Konstantin unlocked the chest and flipped it open. Roughly a quarter of the space was filled with coins in a variety of metals and origins. Whatever the merophs could scrounge up for their hearth taxes—bronze, silver, and, on rare occasions, gold. Konstantin's household used coinage, too, for the normal purchases that came with maintaining the grody and for trade. "Are you sure it wasn't an accounting error?"

She shook her head. "I saw the taxes when they were gathered and stored. There was no mistake then. And hyperpyra don't go missing over forgotten payments to the butcher. It's too big to be a simple error."

"If someone stole it, why did they take two hyperpyra and leave the rest?" The coins were all stacked neatly. Some were worth relatively little, but three hyperpyra remained as well as a small stack of florins and another of ducats.

"Perhaps they thought no one would notice if they took only a few." Aunt Zorica opened the ledger. "In a way, they were right. I didn't notice until yesterday when I put away the money you didn't spend on your journey, and then only because the piles were wrong. Čučimir and I always keep the coinage separated by type, but the Frankish silvers were mixed with the Venetian grossi. Then I counted and went through the ledger again and noticed the loss."

When collected in full, the hearth tax on townspeople and merophs was barely sufficient to pay the sultan's tribute. Rivak had lands lying fallow season after season because the Great Mortality had left the župa underpopulated. But the sultan would accept no excuses for an incomplete tribute. "We can't afford to lose any more coins to theft. We'll make it this time because of Suzana. But we can't let it happen again."

Aunt Zorica nodded. "It makes me sick, thinking of how hard it was for the merophs to pay their hearth taxes and how careful you are in your spending."

"Can we cut back?"

Aunt Zorica flipped through the ledger. "Can you do with fewer horses?"

That was the last thing he wanted to cut. "I need a destrier, and I need a palfrey. I ought to have a charger as well, in case Perun or Svarog are injured. Anything less will make it harder to protect the župa. And I'm already doing a poor enough job of that."

"It will be the same with expenditures for weapons and armor. Nor can you be stingy with your men. Lords must be generous, or they'll earn no loyalty."

"Clothing?" he asked.

"We've already cut the clothing allowance twice. If we do it again, you'll no longer look like a župan, and that brings its own dangers." She shut the ledger. "If we can get a bit of breathing space—and the dowry will give us that—and if we can prevent any further theft or arson, we'll manage. We'll still need to be careful, but if you have more men to prevent future crops from burning, the taxes will not be so burdensome for the merophs, and they'll have less reason to complain because they'll see the benefit."

"Are they complaining?"

"They don't complain to me, but I don't think anyone has felt safe since Maritsa."

The merophs wouldn't complain to him either, but Konstantin could ask the garrison if they or their wives had heard anything. "Do you always have your keys with you?"

"Yes."

That meant the breach had come from Konstantin or Čučimir. Konstantin normally left his keys in his bedchamber at the bottom of his chest. He retrieved them only when working on administrative tasks. "I need to find a better place for mine."

"Where are Čučimir's?" Aunt Zorica asked.

"They weren't on his body when they brought him into camp." Grigorii had checked. "They must be with his things here."

Footsteps sounded in the corridor, and Miladin appeared. "A group of horsemen have entered the grad's gates. Turks, we think."

Konstantin was not a vassal to the Turks by choice. He had no desire to see any of them in Rivak, and the tribute wasn't due until springtime. Unease turned his blood to ice, but he couldn't show his worry.

"Perhaps just messengers?" Miladin suggested.

"We can hope." Konstantin turned to his aunt. "You'll put everything away and lock up?"

"Yes."

Konstantin followed Miladin from the strongroom to prepare for their unexpected and unwanted visitors.

Chapter Eleven
The Sultan's Emissary

Danilo left the hall as Konstantin approached it. Though normally a cheerful boy, he seemed wary, and Konstantin could guess why. A delegation from the sultan made all of them nervous. But Rivak wasn't strong enough to break their bonds of vassalage, so they would have to remain subservient, no matter how distasteful they found service to the enemy who had slaughtered Konstantin's father and most of Rivak's army on the banks of the Maritsa. The Serbs were trapped, and the longer they did the sultan's will, the stronger he grew, and the less likely they were to ever regain their freedom.

Slavonic words spoken with a Turkish tongue carried to the corridor. "Arslan asks if the boy is Darras's son."

A chill crept along Konstantin's spine. He didn't want the Turks taking an interest in his cousin. He ran a hand over the top of Danilo's head. "Go see how your mother is doing," he whispered.

Grigorii sidestepped the question from the Turk. "You knew Darras?"

Turkish words preceded a Slavonic translation. "They fought together when Lala Şahin Pasha led us to victory at Edirne."

Konstantin had sent Miladin to fetch a few members of the garrison so they would outnumber the Turkish delegation, and when Miladin arrived with Bojan and Kuzman, Konstantin entered his hall.

He was the sultan's vassal, but his father and uncle had given their lives for their people. He wouldn't desecrate their memory with apology or excuse. "It was my uncle's desire to atone for the battle of Adrianople that led him to Maritsa." Konstantin used the city's Christian name rather than its newer Ottoman title. "That, and his loyalty to my father and to the Serbian kral."

When the translation was complete, Konstantin continued. "Welcome. We are prepared to offer hospitality to the sultan's envoy."

The envoy scanned the worn tables and faded tapestries before nodding his acceptance.

Konstantin sent a servant for food. He was new, one of the merophs who had lost his crops in the fire. As he left, Konstantin introduced himself and his men. "I am Župan Konstantin Miroslavević." He gestured to the others. "My satnik, Grigorii, and Miladin, Kuzman, and Bojan."

The Turkish delegation introduced themselves in turn. The envoy's name was Arslan. The one who spoke Slavonic was Esel. The third was Hamdi.

A pair of servants brought bread, wine, and juice, in case the Turks did not wish to partake of alcohol. Arslan chose the juice, and the others followed, either from religious devotion or a show of it.

The translator addressed Konstantin. "We have come from Župan Teodore's grody, and next, we will visit the lands of Župan Dragomir. The duties of your vassalage will require the payment of tribute promptly in the spring, and you will bring it to the sultan along with the army you have been instructed to maintain."

Konstantin did his best to keep a calm face. Military service had been part of his vow of vassalage. He had hoped it wouldn't come, but the summons did not surprise him. "How many men will be required from Rivak?"

"Four score."

Kuzman's lips parted, Grigorii frowned, Miladin put a hand over his mouth, and Bojan shook his head slowly. The number was more than triple their current garrison. Only men hired with Suzana's dowry would allow them to meet the requirement.

"Come spring," Konstantin said, "we will be prepared to meet the sultan's demands."

Arslan raised an eyebrow when the translation was made. He didn't seem convinced, and no doubt, the reaction of Konstantin's men hadn't helped. "We plan to winter in Serbia," he said through the translator. "Given the location of your župa, we hope to spend the majority of our time in Rivakgrad."

Bojan and Miladin showed disdain in their hardened expressions. Konstantin suspected Rivakgrad's central location was only part of the reasoning. The man would also want to verify that Rivak could meet its obligations. If not, whatever military campaign the sultan planned for the spring might be compromised.

"We will ensure you have all you need while you remain," Konstantin said. Rivak's coffers were leaking, but the delegation was blessedly small, and Suzana's dowry was blessedly large.

When Suzana heard rumor of an Ottoman delegation, she felt a stir of curiosity. Rivak was her home now, and if the Ottoman sultan played a role in its existence, she ought to learn all she could. But she also felt fear. She'd heard nothing good about the Turks, not ever. They were dangerous, powerful, and threatening: all attributes she tried to avoid whenever possible.

Danilo walked into the corridor, looking subdued.

"Is everything all right, Danilo?" she asked.

"A delegation of Turks has arrived. They are our enemies . . . and our masters." He continued to a door at the end of the corridor and knocked. His mother answered.

"Grigorii told me I should leave, and Kostya told me I should find you," Danilo said. "The envoy asked about Father."

Dama Zorica cupped the boy's cheek in her hand. "Your father's connection to the Ottomans is complicated. Perhaps it's wise to keep your distance, at least until we know more about the envoys. Will you check on Ivan for me?"

Danilo nodded. He smiled at Suzana as he walked past her again, apparently eased by his mother's explanation, or by his task.

"What do you think the Ottomans want?" Suzana asked.

Dama Zorica folded her arms. "We owe them tribute but not until the spring. We also owe them military service, and perhaps the envoys are making a request now so we have time to prepare. I hope it's something else . . . the last time a župan of Rivak rode off to war, he didn't return."

"Is Danilo in danger?" Suzana didn't know the boy well, but he had a kind smile, and she admired his loyalty to his cousin.

"Probably not, but his father might have been."

"Why?" She assumed Dama Zorica's husband was the uncle Konstantin had lost at Maritsa.

"I suppose it's time you heard that story." Dama Zorica motioned her into the room.

Suzana took in the writing desk, the ledger, the trunks and papers. A counting room, or a strongroom. Her father had one much like it.

"My husband—Darras—was an Ottoman." Dama Zorica sat on the stool in front of the ledger. "He fought for the sultan for a time. Was part of the army that took Adrianople. When Lala Şahin Pasha wished to take full credit for the victory, he poisoned his rival and threatened anyone who didn't bend to his version of events. Darras was faithful to the murdered bey and thus became the pasha's enemy. He was desperate enough to turn to a group of Christian travelers for help, my brother among them. Miroslav saved him, and despite all their differences, they became fast friends."

Dama Zorica closed her eyes for a moment, remembering. "He made a good impression on me. So strong and handsome, wise beyond his years. There had been talk of my marrying Župan Teodore, whose župa borders our lands. But when it came time, I found that I preferred Darras. He converted to Christianity, and then we were married."

"Were you happy?" Something in Dama Zorica's voice suggested a lasting loss, and Suzana wanted to know if marriage to a warrior could really produce the type of union a woman would still grieve over even years later.

Dama Zorica nodded. "Very. I still miss him. Personally, because I loved him. And because times were better then, more secure, more prosperous. Konstantin does his best, but Maritsa left Rivak weak and poor. It's hard to recover from something so devastating." She tapped a leather-bound book lying on the table. "Even our ledger is leaking."

Suzana had spent hours with her father, learning how to manage his payments and receipts, how to track profits and losses, how to spot errors. "Your ledger is leaking?"

One of Dama Zorica's shoulders rose in a gesture of frustration. "Perhaps only the money chest. The protovastar died recently." She forced a wan smile. "Konstantin and I will figure it out well before we add your dowry to the box."

Suzana didn't want to meddle where she wasn't wanted, but Rivak was to be her home now, and she suspected the protovastar had died in the attack meant to kill her. "Do you need help? My father was most precise with his funds, and he taught me."

Dama Zorica's brow knit in confusion. "Your father taught you?"

"Is that so surprising?"

A flush grew on Dama Zorica's face. "From what I heard of your father, I was under the impression that he does not value a woman's mind. But I do not doubt you. Please, come see." She slid her stool to the side and pulled another over for Suzana.

Suzana wasn't sure what to think. Dama Isidora thought it wrong that her father called her stupid. Dama Zorica thought it surprising that her father trusted her with his ledger. Suzana had never known anything other than how her father treated her. She was his child—and he trusted blood. He'd tried to hire others but had quickly grown frustrated with them. She, however, knew his methods and expectations. "My father was not always so sharp with me. He taught me when I was younger. He grew less patient, more critical after—" Suzana stopped herself. Some secrets were best kept hidden. "After I was a little older."

"I see." Dama Zorica looked as if she wanted to ask more, but she turned to the ledger and pointed out its most recent entries. "We're missing at least two hyperpyra. That might not seem like much, but we have many wages to pay and a large tribute to make."

Together they looked through several pages of taxes and expenditures. The man who had written the numbers had possessed a steady hand for his small script. Suzana double-checked all the arithmetic but found no errors in the addition and subtraction. "The numbers look correct, but someone could, in theory, record a different number than what was collected. Skim off part of the taxes, so to speak."

Dama Zorica looked thoughtful. "I hate to doubt the dead, but it's best we know for sure." She stood and took a book from the shelf, one much smaller, and brought it to the table. "This lists the hearth taxes."

Suzana looked at the numbers and searched the ledger for their entry.

Muffled laughter echoed through the hallway, then Danilo and Ivan tried to sneak past.

Dama Zorica stood. "Ivan, what are you doing out of bed?"

The boy gave his aunt an impish grin. "I can stand today without getting dizzy. We're going to spy on the Turks."

Dama Zorica followed the boys out into the hall. "Last time you were ill, you stopped your convalescence too early and had a relapse. You will rest today. In your bedchamber, not about the keep's corridors."

"But I feel fine!" Ivan's lower lip stuck out in a pout. "And the Turks won't suspect us. Plus, I've already missed three days of training. I'm falling behind."

Dama Zorica took her son's wrist in her right hand and her nephew's in the left. "If you still feel fine tomorrow, I will consider letting you go back to your lessons with Father Vlatko. After you've managed that several days in a row, we can discuss a return to your martial training." She met Suzana's eyes. "I'll be back later."

Suzana smiled at the boys, one loyal and sweet, the other stubborn and spirited. She liked them both. When they left, she continued her study of the ledger and the hearth taxes, and soon a pattern emerged. For every ten coins charged by the hearth tax, only eight had been entered into the ledger. Perhaps an incomplete amount was collected from time to time? Homes burned. Merophs died or ran away. But the ratio of taxes charged to funds listed remained constant as she looked through the sheets. That was no coincidence.

"Suzana? What are you doing here?"

She looked up to see Konstantin in the doorway. She swallowed. Was he angry? She couldn't tell, but her father would have been furious to find someone looking through his records without his express permission. "Dama Zorica accepted my help, then she went to see to the boys."

Konstantin glanced at the papers laid before her, then over his shoulder. "We should have a guard nearby."

She glanced at the chest, where she assumed the coins were stored. "I promise I haven't taken anything."

"That was not my concern. My worry is so many of Rivak's most valuable assets being all together in the same room with no one to guard you or the coins."

He stepped closer, and it was just like she was back in her father's home. Suzana had committed some infraction, and now her father would strike her. She pulled back in fear with a single hand raised to block the blow before realizing Konstantin did not intend to cuff her across the head. He'd only been moving toward the window.

He didn't make it that far. His eyes studied her as he backed away, giving her space in the same way he might to calm a wounded animal. "Aunt Zorica said you were afraid of something. I didn't realize it was me."

Suzana's eyes burned, and she avoided his gaze. She could lie, tell him she wasn't frightened of him, but that wasn't true, not completely. He was capable of death; she'd seen that in the tent. He had the power to hurt her—and given enough time, didn't people with power always use it?

He slumped onto the bench. "You thought I was going to hit you?"

She swallowed again, fear still driving her words. "It is what my father would have done had he found someone looking at his papers without his knowledge."

"What have I done to make you think I might hit you?"

"That is what men do, isn't it? When they are displeased with betrothed or wife or daughter."

He rubbed an eyebrow, and his expression seemed pained. "No, Suzana, that is not what most men do. Your father did?"

She nodded.

Konstantin's face tensed. "He shouldn't have hit you, and I'll never let him hit you again." He seemed sincere, perhaps even more when he continued. "And I give you my word that I will never strike you."

"But I am certain to one day disappoint or anger you."

"That doesn't mean I'll hit you. Family is not about control and violence. It's about love and supporting each other. Please believe me, Suzana. Whatever type of family life you had before, this will be different. Better. I want you to believe me. I want to earn your trust, but I'm not sure how."

Her gaze fell on his hands. He hadn't hurt her with them, yet, but could she trust that he would really never turn his power against her? "I have not lived here long enough to recognize what type of control you exercise over your family, but you are very capable with the sword."

"I have worked hard to gain skill with the sword. But I use it only to defend my family and my lands." He looked away. "I will also be forced to use it to serve the sultan's wishes in the coming spring, but in a way that is also for my people. I am less of a župan than I wish to be, but they are better off with me as leader, I think, then as subjects of the Turks."

It all came down to if she could believe what he told her, but words and actions were different things. "Were you not angry when you saw me looking at your ledger?"

"I was unhappy that no one was nearby to protect you. Someone tried to kill you. I don't want another attempt here in the grody, so I arranged extra guards. They should have been nearby, especially now, with three Ottoman strangers in our midst."

She replayed the scene in her mind, trying to look at it from his perspective. Her, alone, where he hadn't expected her. He'd been surprised, but he'd done nothing that should have made her brace for a strike. "I wasn't meant to be alone for long. Your aunt planned to return once the boys are settled. Ivan wanted to return to training, and she wished him to rest another day."

Part of Konstantin's mouth pulled up. "My aunt is capable of many things, but she is not usually armed. I imagine any murderers will be." He leaned forward on the bench, balancing his arms on his legs. "Did you find anything among the papers?"

Suzana had been momentarily distracted by the way the slight smile had changed Konstantin's face, but she pulled her eyes away and brushed her hands along the ledger. "It seems not all the taxes being collected are making their way into your strongroom."

"What?" He stood and came to look over her shoulder.

She found the proper hearth tax and then the corresponding line in the ledger. "See here and here."

He leaned closer, then pulled the extra stool around. "May I sit beside you?"

"You may."

He gave her his undivided attention as she pointed out all the errors, all the times Rivak had been made weaker by theft. At first, she had difficulty relaxing—they were alone, and she had rarely been alone with a man other than her father. Konstantin was close enough that their arms brushed once or twice. But gradually, she felt easier in his presence. He listened to her, and if he held anger for how someone had taken advantage of him, she felt none of it directed at her. When she turned to him, she found that his profile was pleasant. His face had strength, and maybe strength didn't always have to mean danger.

He leaned back when they finished. "What a fool I was not to check. My father trusted Čučimir, so I continued to trust him. If I would have spent even a little time ensuring all was accurate . . ." His jaw hardened, and he shook his head. Then he turned to her, and his face softened. "Thank you, Suzana. I'm very grateful to you."

"You are welcome, my lord."

He raised his eyebrow. "I'll soon be your husband. There's no need to call me *lord*."

"Very well, Konstantin. I am glad I could help."

He kept his eyes on her, and she sensed approval. "You are skilled with numbers."

"Thank you. My father taught me."

"When he wasn't beating you?"

She nodded. Her throat felt dry, just at the mention of her father.

"If I didn't . . ." Konstantin trailed off, then began again. "I don't even want to extend hospitality to him, knowing what he did to you."

"It was within his rights. His priest agreed."

Konstantin huffed. "Any priest who would agree to that cares more about his benefactor's money than he does about God's laws of right and wrong. If I didn't need your dowry so much, I'd banish him from the wedding ceremony. Will it frighten you to see him again?"

Suzana straightened her back. "I can be brave because you do need the dowry very badly, don't you?"

He looked away, and the slight color in his cheeks suggested embarrassment. "Yes. I have merophs who have lost all their crops and need to be fed. And come spring, I am to march with an army of eighty trained men to serve however the sultan wishes. I'm to bring a tribute payment as well. I don't have the money, and I have only twenty-five men-at-arms. No, twenty-four now. And I'll need to leave some behind to protect the grad and the villages." He tapped at the ledger. "Will you help me figure out how many men I can afford to hire?"

"Gladly." Suzana had been in Rivakgrad only a day, and she'd already found her way to the ledgers. In a way, it was familiar. But other aspects of her new home were far different from her last home, especially when it came to the man who ruled. Different—and better.

Chapter Twelve
The Weight of Subjugation

The next fortnight flew by. Konstantin sat with Suzana in the strongroom of the keep, planning how much grain they could purchase to see the merophs through the winter and how many horsemen and foot soldiers they could hire to reach a total of one hundred men—twenty to leave in Rivak and eighty to march for the sultan.

"Catalan mercenaries are highly skilled, but they're also expensive," he told her as they considered their options. "Or we might find Cuman or German men. Albanians."

"Which are most likely to help you safely return?" Suzana asked.

Konstantin grew thoughtful. He was gambling with lives in hiring mercenaries—his and his men's. He wanted dependable soldiers, men who would stand with him and obey his directions, men who wouldn't run at the first—or even at the second—sign of danger. But he also had limited resources. More expensive men would mean fewer options for everything else. "It will depend on their training and on how well we work together more than it will depend on where they were born."

Suzana looked at the numbers again. "Eighty men. So many, and yet I would almost see you take more. It would be safer for you, wouldn't it, with more men?"

"Probably. But also harder to find food and sufficient water. Most of the men will take along a page or a groom. We'll be well more than eighty when we march. But I won't have to pay the servants—each man will take care of his own."

She frowned, and he admired the curve of her lips. Maybe she would miss him if he didn't come back. Or maybe she was simply worried about plans for her dowry. He would miss her—every day he was more and more sure of it. It surprised him sometimes, how God had arranged for him to marry a woman who was so perfectly suited to Rivak and to him.

Yet being perfectly suited for Rivak's needs didn't mean Suzana would be happy. He couldn't tell if she felt any affection for him, but he no longer saw signs of fear, and they cooperated well on the župa's finances. That was something.

The patter of small feet sounded near the door. "Kostya!" Ivan appeared, then Danilo. "Danilo's arrow hit the center of the target from all the way across the bailey. You have to come see!"

Danilo grinned. "It wasn't all the way across the bailey, just most of the way."

Konstantin glanced at the books. He enjoyed working with Suzana, but they were nearly finished for now. Later, there would be more decisions to make, when specific mercenaries were contacted and wages negotiated. He would have long ago been ready to leave the strongroom had the company been any less pleasant. "I will come in a moment." He turned to Suzana. "If you do not mind."

She gave the boys a small smile. It made her lips even more lovely than when they had frowned. "I do not mind."

"Will you come, too, Dama Suzana?" Ivan's exuberance had yet to dim.

Konstantin blessed his little brother for his question—something he'd wanted to ask himself but had been unsure if he ought to. She might feel obligated to accompany Konstantin, but he doubted she would feel any compulsion from Ivan.

"I would like to see Danilo's fine shot. And I would like to see your progress as well, Ivan." Suzana looked at each of the boys in turn.

Ivan straightened his shoulders. "I can mount a horse without a block now, as long as the horse has stirrups and the saddle is firmly fastened."

Konstantin turned a laugh into a cough. "The stirrup would be up to your navel, wouldn't it?"

Ivan squared his feet. "That is why the saddle must be firm, because I have to climb a bit. And I'd not try it on Svarog. He's too big, and he would never hold still for so long."

"Nor would we dare touch him without your permission," Danilo added. "He can be mean."

Konstantin nodded. A horse like Svarog could trample a full-grown warrior and do far worse to boys of seven and eight.

They left the strongroom, Konstantin locked it, and then he offered Suzana his arm. She took it, and her light touch sent warmth all the way from his arm to his chest, like the glow and comfort of a campfire in winter.

When they reached the bailey, several targets stood in line on the side of the grody nearest the barracks. Kuzman sparred with one of the younger members of the garrison, but they pulled apart as Konstantin's group approached.

Kuzman gave Konstantin a respectful bow. "Lord."

"Ivan has been boasting about Danilo's aim." Konstantin already knew Danilo was rapidly developing skill with the bow, but he wanted to see it too.

"His aim rivals that of most members of the garrison." Kuzman took a small unstrung bow from where it rested against the palisade and handed it to Konstantin. "This bow from there, and the arrow is still in the target." Kuzman pointed to the respective locations.

"Well done, Danilo." Konstantin handed the bow to his cousin. "Will you show me?"

Danilo took the bow and looked steadily at the target, then marched back to where he had made his earlier shot.

"Go back farther this time," Kuzman suggested.

The rest of the group drew away, giving Danilo—and his arrow's projected flight path—plenty of space. Danilo carefully strung his composite bow, then tested the hold before nocking his arrow. He lifted, drew, and loosed. The arrow flew into the target—not as close to the center as the previous one but nearly so.

Danilo beamed as he shot a second, then a third, fourth, and fifth, making a cluster of strikes in the target's center. He unstrung his bow and jogged back to Konstantin and Kuzman. "May I join the garrison now? That's the requirement, isn't it—five shots from the end of the bailey that hit the target?"

"That is one of the requirements, yes." Konstantin brushed his hand along Danilo's hair. "But I believe there are also height requirements. Then there's your mother. I doubt you'll get her permission for another seven years, at least."

"But you're the župan," Danilo said. "You can countermand her."

"Perhaps I can, but I daren't." Konstantin took the bow. "Before you join the garrison, you must also build up your strength. This is a good bow, and you use it well. But it doesn't have the draw weight to pierce armor."

Danilo lifted his chin slightly. "Then I shall practice with a larger bow."

Kuzman picked one out for the boy. "This one ought to work. Enjoy it today. Tomorrow, your arms will be too sore to hit much of anything. After that, it will get better."

Ivan stiffened, and Konstantin glanced round to learn the cause of the change: the Turks.

Konstantin nodded politely, giving Arslan and Esel permission to approach. Danilo moved to stand beside Suzana, and Ivan stepped closer to Konstantin.

Arslan said something in Turkish, and Esel translated. "His father was also good with the bow. Archery is in his blood. Are your other men as skilled? If so, the sultan will be pleased with your army when it is time to campaign."

Konstantin glanced at Suzana. She, too, seemed nervous around the Ottomans. Everyone did, though Kuzman covered it by busying himself with the weapons. He'd given Konstantin that piece of advice years ago—frayed nerves were best hidden under a flurry of activity. Yet Konstantin couldn't always throw himself into secondary tasks. He had to stand and face his duties as a župan, and that included showing politeness but not weakness to the Ottoman envoy. "We are even now debating the benefits of hiring archers."

The smallest movement around Arslan's left eye showed understanding even before Esel made his translation. He knew more Slavonic than he let on. Konstantin would have to be careful to say nothing in the presence of the Turks that he didn't want the sultan to learn.

Konstantin turned to Esel, not wanting to reveal his newfound knowledge. "Perhaps you could tell me what sort of troops we are most likely to face on campaign, and I could plan my army accordingly." Konstantin hoped the sultan wouldn't order him to subdue other Christians. Being vassal to a sultan was humiliating enough without adding the sting of fighting against his coreligionists.

Arslan waited for the translation, spoke, and then Esel gave his response. "Perhaps that information will be available when the time draws nearer."

The knowledge would do him far more good now, before he decided which mercenaries to hire. Perhaps the sultan feared Konstantin would warn his intended target, or perhaps the emissaries didn't themselves know the sultan's plans. Regardless, Konstantin would have to march to war in the spring, and it seemed the man who summoned him was keeping all details about the campaign a secret.

Suzana had felt something change when the Ottoman emissaries had joined them, a gloom like the chill of a sudden storm. The Turks eyed her betrothed much the way her father eyed those who owed him money. Power. The Ottomans had it. And they would use it.

Konstantin had said he would always defend his family, and she was beginning to understand why. His family would soon be her family, too, and she was coming to care about each of them. She couldn't stop the Ottoman levy or erase the sense of oppression that came whenever the Turks were near, but she would try to ease the current discomfort.

She swallowed, reminded herself to have courage, and spoke. "Ivan, I believe you had something you wished to show us with your horse."

Wariness over the Turks had made Ivan seem younger, but now he straightened. "Yes. I'll go fetch him."

"I'll go with you." Danilo followed his cousin—either to escape the Turkish envoys or to protect Ivan.

The Ottomans made a bow and excused themselves. Good. She didn't like the way they seemed to be sizing Danilo up, as if anticipating when they could use him, too, for whatever purpose the sultan deemed important.

Konstantin watched the Turks go and put a hand over hers, where it rested on him arm. "Shall we follow the boys to the stables?"

The stables? Suzana hadn't set foot in a stable for close to five years. Perhaps Rivakgrad's stables would feel different from her father's, but her heart thumped along at thrice its normal speed, and the slick sweat of worry heated the back of her neck beneath her veil. She managed a nod and let Konstantin lead her after the boys.

"Arslan understands Slavonic."

Suzana clung to Konstantin's statement, trying to focus on Ottoman intrigue instead of her irrational fears. "He does?"

"I'm almost certain. I'm not sure why he pretends he doesn't—maybe he hopes we'll be careless around him and say something we prefer he not know."

Suzana glanced after the Turks. It must be lonely for them in Serbia, among a people who didn't want to be bound to them, but she could summon no sympathy for them. They were either tyrants or spies or a combination. "Do they know about the dowry?"

"I assume so. Arslan need only count our garrison to recognize how short we are of the required troops. He's clever enough to figure out that your dowry is the likely solution to all our shortcomings, but I'd rather not give him any information we don't have to. I am vassal to the Turks by circumstance, not by choice."

They were closer to the stables now, and she had to squeeze her hand tight to keep it from trembling. She didn't want to go inside, but nor did she want to make a scene. One of the garrison men rode his horse across the bailey and dismounted on the other side of the stables.

"That's a beautiful horse." She'd seen almost nothing of it, other than its color, but she was desperate to avoid the stables and hoped Konstantin would lead her over to look at the animal.

He complied with her unspoken wish. "Bojan, will you hold up?"

Bojan held the horse in place, and Suzana stroked the horse's nose, then neck. Gray flecks spotted the otherwise white coat, and three of the horse's feet had gray socks. Konstantin asked after Bojan's recovery and how the mare had ridden; Suzana gathered it was a young horse, only recently of age to be saddled.

Ivan and Danilo led a gelding from the stables. Though it was not the tallest of mounts, it was a full-grown horse, not a pony, and the stirrups were level with Ivan's stomach. She gave the white mare a final pat and turned her attention to the boys. Danilo held the lead rope. Ivan lifted his left foot to a ridiculously high position, then grabbed the strap as high as he could reach. It took obvious effort, but he managed to pull himself onto the back of the horse. His legs weren't long enough to reach the stirrups, but he took up the reins and walked the horse around the bailey.

Konstantin smiled softly as he watched. It would have been easy for him to lift the boy back to the ground when he returned, but Konstantin let Ivan dismount himself. Suzana winced at the drop, but Ivan grinned.

"Well done," Konstantin said. "But most horses wouldn't let you get away with something like that. You may do it occasionally on Radegast but not on any of the larger or less patient mounts."

Ivan nodded. "Yes, Kostya."

Konstantin lowered himself to the boys' height. "You are both turning into fine warriors. One day, you will make the family proud."

Only when the boys had gone into the stable did Konstantin straighten. He turned to Suzana and let out a sigh. "I wish they didn't have to grow up so quickly, but in lands like these, we need warriors the moment they are of age. The sooner they master horse and weapon, the better chance they'll have of living longer than their fathers did."

Suzana's father had been so eager for her to marry into a noble family, but he had thought only of the prestige, not of the responsibilities that came with the honor. She wouldn't be expected to fight, but ultimately, she would have to watch her new family ride off to war, knowing there was no guarantee they'd ever return.

CHAPTER THIRTEEN
SHADOWS OF FEAR

ALEKSANDER IGOREVIĆ ARRIVED A FORTNIGHT before the wedding with news from Konstantin's grandfather. "There's a German captain who can provide the mercenaries you need. Ulrich once served with your grandfather. He wasn't the captain then, but he's gathered a group of men now. He says they're disciplined and well-armed, and your grandfather trusts him."

"How many in the company?" Konstantin asked.

"Three score and ten."

It wasn't quite as many as he wanted, but if he could find a few others—merophs or craftsmen or their sons—to fill out the garrison he would leave behind, it might be enough. He glanced around the hall. His bride-to-be, his sister, his brother, his aunt, his cousin . . . they needed to be safe. So did the merophs. "How much?"

"Five dinar a month. Double for the captain. Plus a bonus for each enemy killed. You would be responsible for medical care and provisioning, and they're to keep four-fifths of any plunder they take." The wages Aleksander named were not cheap, but if they were well-trained, it would be fair. Could Konstantin afford fair? He'd have to discuss the numbers with Suzana, but he thought they could make it work without letting any of the merophs starve.

That decision could wait. At present, Suzana, Lidija, and the boys were practicing the steps to the traditional wedding dance, so Konstantin wouldn't interrupt.

"Your grandfather will bring Ulrich to the wedding. You can meet him then and discuss whether you wish to come to an arrangement. But now, if you will excuse me, I'd like to check on my horse. He caught a stone in his hoof. Bojan offered to look at him."

"Bojan is good with horses, but I understand your desire to tend your mount. I'll have someone prepare your rooms in the meantime." Konstantin saw Aleksander to the bailey, then caught Risto's attention and asked him to prepare a room for his grandfather's envoy.

Later, Konstantin expected Aleksander to ask after Ivan again. A few more years, that was all Konstantin wanted. As he returned to the hall, Konstantin hoped he and his grandfather could agree to a compromise.

Sometimes life was like that. Compromise. Balancing different wants and needs into something that would work, even if it wasn't perfect for anyone. And occasionally life surprised him with the perfection of select elements. Suzana, for instance. He'd agreed to marry her because her dowry could save his župa. That would have been enough. But she was so much more than a bride with a dowry. He liked working with her. He liked looking at her. He liked the way she was fitting in so well with his family.

Across the room, Suzana and the other kolo dancers changed positions. The height disparity between her and Ivan made her dip to the left, and both of them laughed. Konstantin could spend hours watching the way each element of her face changed when she smiled or laughed.

"Konstantin?"

He pulled his eyes away, surprised that Miladin hadn't addressed him as župan or lord. Humor lined Miladin's face, as if he were about to laugh.

"Have you something amusing to report?"

"No, but I had to call you thrice before you heard me." Miladin shifted his glance to Suzana. "I suppose you were distracted."

Konstantin felt heat creep up his face. "Did you look into the taxes?"

"Yes. They were all gathered according to the list you gave me."

That meant the money had disappeared *after* the merophs had paid their taxes. Čučimir had probably been involved, but Konstantin couldn't question a dead man. Were any of his other men secretly stealing from him, hurting the župa he was trying so hard to save?

"I take it the news is not what you hoped for," Miladin said.

"No." It would have been easier to think someone had given the merophs a lighter burden even if it hurt him. But now the merophs had done their portion and the theft would make Konstantin less able to fulfill his part of the trust between lord and subject, less able to defend them and their lands.

"I am sorry to deliver it, then." Miladin smirked. "Especially when you seemed to be enjoying your view."

Konstantin glanced back at Suzana. She said something to Danilo, and he laughed. So much of Konstantin's hope rested on her. It didn't seem fair, and yet she seemed to smile more each week. They were friends now. The small drops of love Konstantin's grandfather had spoken of were growing larger, more powerful, more pleasant.

Miladin folded his arms. "I take it you look forward to the wedding."

"For my part, yes. As to her part . . . I cannot tell." He wanted to marry her, now for personal reasons as well as the practical ones. But if she didn't feel the same, the pain of rejection would pierce him like a blade. He could be patient, could wait if she needed more time than he did to feel comfortable as man and wife, but his hope wasn't strong enough to survive if she spurned him completely.

"Some women like gifts. Flowers or jewelry. It might give you a better idea of her feelings."

Konstantin nodded, and in the next moment, something suitable came to his mind.

The next morning, Konstantin made all the arrangements, and in the afternoon, he asked Suzana to accompany him outside. "I've a surprise for you."

"A surprise?" She wore a blue dalmatica, setting off her fair skin and brown eyes to perfection.

"Yes." He watched the emotions play out on her face. Confusion, then pleasure, but he would give her no clues. She had seemed to like Dola when they'd last been near the stables. Bojan had promised Konstantin that the young mare would be the right combination of gentle and energetic, and her white coat was striking. Konstantin could think of nothing he'd like more than a horse were he the one receiving the gift. Dola was a beautiful, well-behaved horse for a beautiful, talented woman.

He took Suzana's hand and led her. She slowed as they approached the stables. Lidija did that too—women's shoes were more delicate, and ladies, in particular, had to be cautious about where they stepped in an open bailey, especially near animals. Konstantin scanned the ground. Several boys from the burned village had been tasked with keeping the area clean in exchange for earning their food. They seemed to be doing the job well enough.

She slowed even further when they passed through the door.

"This way. You're going to love it." But even as he spoke, his confidence started to fade. Konstantin loved horses, but Suzana's face showed none of the excitement he would have expected. Stiff lips and jaw, a hand no longer so flexible, eyes like those days when he'd first met her and danger had lurked.

Uncertainty swirled around him. She did like horses, didn't she? She'd ridden well, with no sign of distress, when they'd traveled to Rivakgrad from her father's villa. And she had approached Dola of her own accord that day when Danilo had shown them his skill with the bow and Ivan had shown them how he could mount from the ground. Perhaps the cost worried her. He had, after all, been quite clear in explaining Rivak's limited funds. Did she fear he was spending her dowry before they were even married?

"Dola was born to one of my father's old palfreys," he said as they reached her stall. Perhaps that would make it clear that he hadn't spent money on the horse. Or did that dilute the value of the gift? "She's named after the old Slavic goddess of Fate. We are Christians here, of course, but we like the old names, and I thought it fitting since fate seems to have brought you to me just when I needed you." That sounded wrong too. He didn't want to give credit to fate when he was certain God was behind the blessing. Maybe they should name the horses after saints instead. "We can change the name if you prefer something else."

She had let go of his hand completely. He didn't dare take it again. She swallowed and squeezed her eyes shut. Her breaths came in quick gasps.

"Suzana, are you all right?" Konstantin waited for an answer. She swallowed again, opened her mouth, then closed it.

Uncertain of what else to do, he unlatched the stall door and led the horse into the aisle. This was not how he had foreseen the gift-giving playing out. Suzana looked frozen. Konstantin had seen that look before, on the faces of new men in skirmishes with brigands. But Suzana couldn't be frightened of Dola—she'd petted her not that long ago. And surely she wasn't scared of Konstantin anymore—they'd gone over numbers for the German mercenaries together that morning, and she'd seemed warm toward him then.

"Suzana?"

No response, but her breathing, if anything, was more rapid.

"Would you like some fresh air?" Maybe that would help. He reached for her arm to help guide her out.

She flinched, almost as hard as she had that night in the dark camp when they'd both been covered in blood.

Then she ran.

Shocked, he followed her path to the door, slowly, not wanting to alarm her or make her think he was chasing her. By the time he reached the open bailey, she was already halfway across it. He leaned against the stable's outer wooden wall, wondering where he had gone wrong.

She slowed as she reached the grody's chapel and ducked inside. He didn't follow her. He'd asked the grooms to give him privacy in the stables, so he would need to put Dola back into her stall.

He returned to the horse. The mare nickered at him and playfully butted his shoulder. Konstantin rubbed behind her ears. "I suppose that wasn't how you expected it to go either, was it?" He moved to Dola's side and rested his forehead on her neck, trying to absorb some of her calm.

She nickered again.

"No, I don't think it was you. She liked you well enough that day Bojan saddled you. So, I suppose that means there is something wrong with me." Konstantin leaned into the horse as the sting of rejection set in. "I've made a mess of everything else, but I wanted to get this right, because I think I'm falling in love with her."

A sound like someone clearing his throat sounded nearby. For a moment, Konstantin hoped it was one of the animals, but the sound had been more human. He turned around to see Arslan several stalls away. Either he'd been behind his horse, out of view but listening to the entire encounter between Konstantin, Suzana, and Dola, or he'd come in the back entrance when Suzana had run out the front.

Of all the people who might have overheard him confiding in a horse, why did it have to be a Turk?

"I suppose you heard all that. And understood every word." No doubt Arslan would recount it to the sultan along with his report on all Rivak's weaknesses and all its assets that could be exploited to help the Ottomans expand their empire.

Arslan raised an eyebrow rather than answering.

Konstantin grunted and led Dola toward her stall. "Fine, keep pretending you don't understand Slavonic."

"How long have you known I understand Slavonic?" The words were heavy with accent.

Konstantin considered lying, but there seemed little point in that. Any advantage he'd had by knowing Arslan understood Slavonic even though he pretended not to had been lost with his last statement. "Since the day Danilo's arrows hit the target from across the bailey."

"For someone who claims to be failing at everything, you managed to uncover my ruse quickly enough."

Konstantin said nothing as he opened Dola's stall and led her inside. Yes, he'd discovered Arslan's ruse, but in a moment of frustration, he'd squandered the secret without any thought.

"What exactly do you think you are failing at?"

Konstantin fastened the stall door. "The only reason I'll be able to make the payment to the sultan, hire the required number of troops, and keep my merophs from starving is because I'm marrying a woman with a significant dowry. If not for her, Rivak would crumble."

"But since you do have her and her dowry, there will be no reason for the sultan to do anything other than allow you to continue your governance."

Konstantin tried to mask his emotions, but they all seemed closer to the surface than usual. "Finding Suzana was not my triumph. I've others to thank for arranging it."

"Just as you have others to blame for impoverishing your župa and leaving you barely able to meet your obligations to sultan and merophs."

Why was Arslan trying to make him feel better? Perhaps it was another trick, one so clever that Konstantin could pinpoint neither the reasoning nor the motivation behind it.

"You are pleased with her?"

Lying about this would do no good either, so Konstantin answered truthfully. "As I told the horse."

"Yes, as you told the horse. When I see you and your betrothed together in the keep or in the bailey, I suspect that her feelings are not so different from yours. Caution, hope, affection. You say the problem is not the horse. I wager the problem is not you either."

Konstantin didn't want to like Arslan, but he felt some of the hostility burning off. "Then what happened? She flinched and ran away."

"If it is not you and not the horse, then it must be something else. A smell. A sound. A place. Something that combined with the past. I have seen it before, when powerful memories of painful events are sparked and become waking nightmares."

Suzana's past held many unpleasant memories. Maybe her father had beaten her in the stables. Konstantin walked to Perun, stabled nearer Arslan's horse. As he nuzzled his favorite palfrey, he felt some of the worry leave him. "Thank you, Arslan. I don't know why a sultan's envoy would bother assisting a vassal with matters of the heart, but your words are like a salve."

Arslan bowed gravely. "My loyalty will always be first to my sultan. That doesn't mean I can't help his vassals find happiness. I had a wife once. She was the greatest joy of my life."

"*Had* a wife? What happened to her?"

Arslan looked across the stable as if he were looking back in time. "Illness after childbirth. The infant was also lost. Love your woman while you can, young župan. Love is worth your best efforts."

CHAPTER FOURTEEN
THE WEIGHT OF THE PAST

SUZANA SAT ON THE FLOOR of the church, trembling with the raw strength of her worst memory. She wanted to banish it from her head forever, end its absolute control over her. Men wielded such power—a single act could strike her with a force that left her hurt and cowering at the mere memory.

Sweat dampened her clothing and nausea swirled in her stomach, but at least she could breathe now. And she saw her real surroundings, not the visceral setting of the past. Painted murals decorated the stone walls of the grody's chapel, and the smell of incense hung in the air. The nave remained empty and would for some hours while Father Vlatko tutored Ivan and Danilo.

Poor Konstantin. He'd done nothing wrong. But in her mind, it hadn't been Konstantin who had reached for her arm, and the grip hadn't been soft. It had been just like her father's steward all those years ago.

A blackbird chirped and warbled nearby, drawing her attention to the picture of Christ in all His glory. The colors of the paint had faded, and the angle of the afternoon sun left that side of the chapel in shade. The painting drew the eye regardless. Yet the face, divine or not, depicted a man, and she'd never been able to completely trust a man.

The church door squeaked as someone pushed it open. Suzana tensed until she recognized Dama Zorica. She motioned to someone out of sight, then shut the door behind her. "Konstantin thought you might be in here. He wanted to know if you were well but wasn't sure you would welcome his company."

Tears stung Suzana's eyes. "I . . . I didn't intend to make it so difficult. I know he is trying."

Dama Zorica sat on the hard stone ground beside her. "Are you not also trying? Leaving your home to join an entirely new family? Spending hours poring over the ledger? Trying to trust a man you've only just met, maybe even trying to love him? It's not an easy thing to bring two strangers together, even when both of you are trying. The responsibilities of a župan, or of a župan's wife, are no small matter. Nor, I think, is the weight of your past."

A weight. That was what it felt like. Something heavy, lugging her backward, holding her captive, sabotaging all progress. She liked Konstantin, wanted to like him even more because they were bound together, and she wanted their connection to bring both of them joy, not pain. "I want to let it go before it pulls both of us under."

"I would like to help you. And Konstantin is desperate to help you."

Suzana squeezed her eyes shut. She would have to tell Konstantin. He was to be her husband, and he deserved to know. But telling him about her past . . . it would hurt. And it might change the way he felt about her.

Dama Zorica patted Suzana's arm. "You don't have to confide in me. And you don't have to confide in Konstantin, though secrets between husbands and wives should not be treated lightly. But even if you don't wish to tell either of us, you don't have to carry it alone."

Suzana met Dama Zorica's eyes. If she weren't to tell her husband-to-be or her husband-to-be's aunt, whom did Dama Zorica mean? The dama shifted her gaze to a fresco depicting the Christ. "You can tell Him. He'll help you carry your burdens. And He's easy to confide in because He already knows."

Suzana had attended church from a young age because being accused of heresy would have been bad for her father's business, but she'd never felt close to God. It was hard to feel close to anyone when everyone she'd known her whole life had been either a servant, paid well for anything they did for her, or a harsh father, himself a little broken. God was distant, and He was too busy to help a frightened girl like her.

Dama Zorica spoke again, and emotion weighted each of her words. "I've needed His help before. So often. When Konstantin's mother died, I lost my best friend, only a day after losing a beloved niece. Then a year later, I lost my husband and my brother. I loved them all. I missed their wisdom, their friendship, their strength. I was suddenly the matriarch of the family. Konstantin was župan, but he and all the others looked to me, and I wasn't sure I could be strong enough. Strong enough to give Konstantin the advice he needed when he was so young and so burdened and so heartbroken.

Strong enough to raise my son without my husband to help me. Strong enough to keep Ivan alive through all his illness. Strong enough to step in for Lidija's mother as she grew from girl to woman."

So much sorrow. And so many responsibilities. Suzana had yet to love someone enough to feel true sorrow at their loss, but she was beginning to understand how it might hurt, and she had tasted a little of how burdensome responsibilities could prove. "How did you do it?" Suzana asked.

"I prayed. I pleaded for help over and over again. It didn't become easy, but I did the best I could, and somehow, God made it enough. When I was up all night trying to keep Ivan's fever down and I somehow managed to get through the day, even without any sleep. When I remembered the right memory of Yaroslava and was able to tell Lidija and make her smile. When I would sit here, in this church, wondering how to teach Danilo something and have an idea come to my mind. The tragedy didn't disappear, but God helped me bear it, helped me be enough, despite how inadequate I felt."

Suzana wanted help. She needed help, because she's been trying for five years to do it herself, and she still felt just as helpless, just as broken. "How?"

"Faith and trust and time. Courage too."

That was what Suzana needed. Faith to trust a God she barely knew. Courage to tell Konstantin so there would be no secrets between them. "Do you know where Konstantin is?"

"I believe he is training with the garrison. That seems to help him when he is worried."

Guilt settled on her. She'd added to his burden, and it was already heavy enough.

Dama Zorica stood and extended a hand to her. "Let me show you my favorite fresco."

Suzana accepted Dama Zorica's help and followed her to the other end of the church. Much of the church's artwork depicted Saints, most of whom she couldn't name, or a grisly Day of Judgment. Some portrayed Christ in all His power and majesty. There were angels, too, and the Virgin Mary with a gold nimbus to show her holiness. But in the corner where Dama Zorica had led her, Christ reached out to lift the woman who'd been plagued with an issue of blood. A healing Christ rather than a distant Christ or a judging Christ. The image caught Suzana's attention in a way none of the other artwork had, and the warmth of comfort grew in her chest.

"Take as much time as you need." Dama Zorica laid a hand on Suzana's arm, and then she excused herself.

Suzana spent a long time staring at the painting, thinking, and then pleading on her knees. For healing. For faith. For the courage to give Konstantin the truth as to why she had run from him in the stables. The light on the walls shifted, illuminating some of the artwork and covering some in shadows. She looked at every single painting but always turned back to the one Dama Zorica had shown her.

When the scent of supper wafted from the kitchens and the sun coming from the windows shifted to an even lower angle, Suzana knew it was time to leave. Time to face her past before it poisoned her future. She felt a spark of courage and hoped—prayed—it would be enough.

Konstantin stood waiting for her when she approached the hall. His hair was damp from bathing. He met her eyes, but he stayed where he was rather than approach her, as if uncertain about whether she wanted him to escort her to supper.

Dread crept into her chest—not fear of Konstantin but worry about the conversations they needed to have. For now, she needed only to apologize. She gave him a small bow. "My lord."

He returned the gesture. "My lady."

She swallowed hard. "I am sorry. I . . . wasn't myself this afternoon. Perhaps after we sup, we can speak more?" She didn't want to discuss anything in the hall, where they might be overheard.

He offered her his arm, and she took it. "I would be pleased to speak with you, at whatever time you feel is best."

Supper seemed to stretch out. Fresh bread and goat cheese, olives and lentils, wine and new greens. She ate but barely tasted the food. She caught Konstantin looking at her from time to time with one eyebrow slanted in worry. He picked at his food almost as much as she did, though that wasn't abnormal for him.

At last, the meal ended. Konstantin discussed the night's schedule for the guards and watchmen with Miladin, listened to Ivan and Danilo tell him about their learning with Father Vlatko, and then he turned to her. "May I escort you around the bailey?"

She nodded. The trepidation returned, and she prayed for courage as they left the hall and went out into the night. She wanted her relationship with Konstantin to be a good one, for both their sakes.

Neither of them spoke as they walked past the kitchen, where servants who had waited on those in the keep were now enjoying their meal, then past the barracks. The sun had set, but a blush of lavender still showed along the horizon. The rest of the sky was a deep sapphire running to black.

They slowed along the palisade, midway between the armory and the gate of the causeway that led down to the grad.

She prayed again, inhaled, and spoke. "I owe you an explanation for what happened at the stables."

"I would be glad to hear one." Konstantin's voice was gentle. He leaned against the wall and waited, quiet and expectant.

Suzana's throat felt dry. Telling him was hard, but they stood on the brink of marriage. Time after time, he had shown her that it could be a good marriage, if she didn't ruin it with untruths and secrets. "I don't want our marriage to start with any lies between us."

"Nor do I." His eyes searched her face.

"I spoke falsely in the villa when I remembered the servant who took me to the river. It really was him—I wouldn't have accused anyone if his face weren't clear in my memory. But he didn't tell me that Dama Isidora wanted to speak with me. He said it was the cook. My father insisted on distance between the servants and the family. Most obeyed, but the cook was friendlier than the others. I thought she might really want to say goodbye."

"Do you think she was involved?"

Suzana shook her head. "She wouldn't hurt me. He only said her name because he knew he could draw me out with her request. But if my father heard, he would have asked questions."

"Would that have been so awful? She could have confirmed that she knew nothing about the request, that your attacker used her kindness as a lure."

The evening breeze blew a chill between the back of Suzana's neck and her veil. She shivered. "My father doesn't ask questions with only his mouth. He also uses his fists."

"So you lied to protect the cook from a beating like the ones you experienced so often?"

"Yes." She kept her gaze on the ground. Emotion was so rare in Konstantin's face—if any appeared now, it would be disappointment. Or perhaps anger that she'd lied when he was trying so hard to discover the threat behind the attacks. The wind blew again, and then a warm layer was placed on her shoulders. She looked up to see Konstantin smoothing the folds of his cloak now wrapped around her. He pulled the wool cloth closed in the front, ensuring it gave her the most warmth possible.

"Father Vlatko might advise against lies, but I think God will overlook your telling one to save an innocent woman a beating." The wind tugged at his hair. The more time she spent with him, the more she was coming to admire the sweep of his eyebrows and the depth of his eyes, the symmetry of his nose and the strength of his jaw.

She wasn't used to such gentleness, such care. She wanted to fall into it, let it wrap her up the same way his cloak had wrapped her up, but she still had another confession, and it would be even harder to make.

"You're trying so hard to be good to me." She paused. She could leave it at that, tell another lie about what had happened in the stables. Say it was about something else—anything else. But he would find out. She could hide it from everyone else, but not from her husband. It was better to tell him beforehand so he wouldn't feel betrayed. "I don't want to disappoint you."

"I don't think it's possible for you to disappoint me." He took her hand and held it softly. She cherished that warmth, the regard the simple gesture seemed to convey, but he was bound to yank his hand away soon, of that she was sure.

"When we're married . . ." She bit at her lip, trying to form the right words, but there were no right words for something so wrong. "I'm not the pure, unblemished maiden men expect their bride to be."

As she'd predicted, his grip on her hand slackened. "I won't be the first man you've been with?"

"No."

He folded his arms and looked into the distance. "The rumor my grandfather heard—that's why your earlier betrothal was broken off—because they found out?"

"Yes."

He inhaled deeply. Her father would have struck her by now, but she'd come to know Konstantin wouldn't do that, no matter what she told him. Still, she could detect his resentment. "Who was he, this lover of yours?"

"He was not my lover."

"But didn't you just say—"

She shook her head to interrupt him, then pressed forward, even though the process of explaining pulled up memories that were hard to relive. "I did not lie with him by choice. I was twelve, and he forced me."

Konstantin's head snapped toward her. "When you were twelve?"

Suzana nodded. "He was one of my father's men. He gave me a pony, and one day when we happened to be alone in the stables, he—" Her voice broke. The details didn't matter anyway, just that she had been shamed, defiled, and tainted. He had pushed boundaries before, done things she hadn't liked, things he had threatened to reveal as a way to push past more boundaries. But that day, in the stables, he'd smashed through all laws of decency, and he'd left her damaged beyond repair.

Konstantin's arms fell slack at his side. "That's what you remembered when I gave you a horse in the stables."

"Yes."

"I'm sorry, Suzana. I'm so very sorry."

He was apologizing? After learning his bride was spoiled?

Konstantin took her hand again, and his voice was earnest. "Tell me who did this. I will find him, and I will kill him."

She shook her head. She ought to be relieved that his anger was for the man who had hurt her rather than for her, but anger could easily shift.

"Please, Suzana. He wronged you horribly and must be punished. Justice demands it. So does honor."

"You can't kill him, Konstantin, because my father killed him five years ago. And then he regretted it—every time he saw me, he remembered that he'd tried to avenge me, and it had cost him his best friend. Vengeance didn't stop my nightmares or make me pure again or bring either of us peace. It pushed my father to drink, and with it came more violence toward everyone, including me. That day broke me, and it changed him, and justice didn't make it better. Justice and honor and shame soured an already frail bond between father and daughter, and it never recovered."

Konstantin looked at the ground. Weariness and defeat bowed his shoulders.

"My father said it would have been better to die than allow myself to be shamed like that. But I was too small, and he was too big." The man had threatened her afterward, told her he'd kill her pony if she told anyone. But she'd barely been able to walk. A groom had seen something was wrong, and her father's shouts had been enough to make her confess. Her pony had survived despite the broken secret, but she had never ridden him again. Tears stung her eyes, but she kept her voice steady. "So many times, I thought he was right. Death would have been better. For me. For him."

Konstantin laid a gentle hand on her shoulder. "Death is not better than hardship. If I could take this hurt from you, I would, but I would never wish you away just because someone in your past wronged you."

"It might not stay in the past. People will find out." Serbian tradition included a showing of the blood stains on the bedclothes the morning after the wedding. For them, there would be no blood stains—her virginal blood had been spilled long ago, left on the straw of a horse's stall. "When they learn the truth, they will despise me and think less of you."

Konstantin's hand moved to her back, and she let him guide her into an embrace. She couldn't recall the last time someone had given her a hug, and she wanted to cling to him. His arms enfolded her, and she hesitantly raised her hands and entwined them about his waist. His body was firm against her, welcoming, comforting. When he spoke, she felt the vibrations in her chest as well as heard the words with her ears. "I'm not worried about what everyone else might think. I'm worried about you."

He held her for a long time. She'd expected their conversation to end with anger or hurt feelings, not with the compassion and comfort she'd been aching for all her life. He ran a hand along her back, and she relaxed even more into his strength and kindness. "Does it make you nervous . . . about when we're married and together?"

Her mouth felt dry. She was beginning to trust Konstantin—she was even beginning to recognize an attraction for him. But what if memories of the past haunted her in the bridal chamber?

"Of course it makes you nervous." He relaxed his embrace and moved his hands to her arms, then stood back so he could look into her face. "I never want to hurt you or push you into something you aren't ready for. I will be gentle, and I will be patient."

"But you need an heir."

He glanced away for a moment, then met her eyes again. "Yes, I need an heir. And you're so beautiful, Suzana. Every time I talk with you, I find something new to admire. I want trust, and I want friendship and love and passion. But we have time enough to take it slow."

She wanted all those things, too, but without the pressure of a timeline imposed by others. They already had trust and the start of friendship. Maybe even the beginnings of love, because no one else had ever shown her so much concern.

His fingers ran softly across her cheek. The tender touch spoke of affection and promise, seemed to soften all the sharp edges of hurt that had haunted her for years.

"Thank you for trusting me with your past," he whispered. "I will do all I can to ensure that your time as my wife is full of happiness instead of pain."

Chapter Fifteen
Uneasy Allies

Konstantin hungered after vengeance for days. He'd been unable to save his father and his uncle, he couldn't drive away the illnesses that plagued his brother, and he had no choice but to honor the Ottoman envoys while they stayed in Rivakgrad. Now he was powerless to ease the pain of Suzana's past.

But maybe that wasn't entirely true. They spoke more and more freely with each other now, whether on walks around the bailey, sessions in the strongroom, or on rides around the countryside—after either a groom or Konstantin brought Suzana's horse from the stables so she didn't have to enter the building herself. He recognized a calm in her manner that hadn't been there before. Maybe sharing her burden had made it lighter. More and more, he felt that their marriage could bring them both joy, and as the harvest was brought in and stored, he grew more and more eager to be Suzana's husband.

The wedding approached, and guests began to arrive. First some of his neighbors, Župan Nikola and Župan Teodore. Then Suzana's father, Baldovin. Soon the keep teamed with guests and their servants.

Baldovin waylaid Konstantin shortly after he broke his fast the day before the wedding. "Suzana has disappeared. Do you know where she's gone?"

Suzana had been in the hall for their morning meal, so Konstantin doubted she was in danger. More likely, she was avoiding her father. Konstantin had enlisted his aunt and sister to help her in that pursuit, but they also had to maintain the pretense of respect and cordiality, even if Konstantin really wanted to break each of the man's fingers for all the times he'd struck his daughter.

Konstantin inhaled and slowly exhaled. At least the man had punished the brute who had assaulted Suzana in the stables, but Konstantin wasn't sure he could ever forgive him for being unloving and abusive when what she had needed was a safe haven. But Konstantin was desperate for the dowry Baldovin had brought, so his contempt had to be masked. "She may have appointments with the seamstress."

Baldovin's nostril's flared. "That's what she was busy with all of yesterday."

"Perhaps the garments are complicated."

"It's important that I see her."

A father had the right to see his daughter before her wedding, but not in private. Konstantin would be by her side for support and, if needed, for protection. "I'll speak with her and arrange something. Before the wedding."

Miladin approached, and Konstantin excused himself, motioning Miladin to follow him outside.

He searched for a place where they wouldn't be overheard. In normal times, finding relative privacy in the bailey was a simple matter. That wasn't the case today, with wedding guests spilling into the courtyard to enjoy the mild weather. "Aunt Zorica told me that a large wedding is necessary to show the proper prestige as a župan. I don't doubt her, but I wish she were wrong."

Miladin smiled. "It will be over soon enough. Then the extra people will leave, and you'll have your bride to yourself all winter."

All winter with Suzana. That would be his reward for putting up with guests he would rather avoid. "Miladin, do you know much about women?"

"Lord?"

Konstantin felt heat creeping up the back of his neck. "I've spent a lot of time learning to read and learning to ride a horse and learning how to use each of my weapons. But some aspects of marriage are still a mystery to me." Konstantin had never even kissed a woman before. He wanted advice, and he wasn't brave enough to ask his aunt or most of the men in the garrison. He didn't want to ask Miladin either, but it was better than the alternative: ignorance. Konstantin had seen part of the love Miladin and his wife held for each other. And he knew Miladin wouldn't spread gossip to the rest of the garrison.

"I will give you advice, lord, but . . ." Something caught Miladin's eye. "Grigorii's coming."

The satnik rushed toward them, not fast enough to cause alarm, but Konstantin sensed an urgency.

"Is something wrong?" Konstantin asked when Grigorii drew closer.

Grigorii nodded. "A group of brigands raided the village by the river, took everything worth carrying off. Kuzman and Bojan are there, sent one of the villagers for reinforcements. Sounds like the bandits have holed up in the church. They can't escape without risking Kuzman or Bojan getting a few of them, but even with the villagers' help, our men don't have the strength to storm the church without reinforcements."

It was an hour's walk to the village, but they'd make it quicker by horse. "How many bandits?"

"The messenger from the village seemed uncertain. About ten."

Tomorrow, Konstantin would be a bridegroom, but today, his duties as župan came first. "Danilo! Ivan!" They were at the range with their bows, but to Konstantin's relief, they came quickly. "Ivan, run to the stables and tell the grooms to have Svarog saddled and barded. Then find Risto and ask him to meet me in the armory."

"Have Grom saddled too," Miladin added as the boy headed to the horses.

"Danilo, ask your mother to meet me in the armory. I don't want the guests to think anything is wrong. Can you ask without alarming anyone?"

"Yes, Kostya." Danilo ran off. The running didn't bode well for keeping the guests unaware of events, but Danilo ran more often than he walked, so perhaps that would allay any suspicion.

"Grigorii, round up as many men from the garrison as you can. Those who aren't on watch. Have them ride out in ones or twos through different gates. We'll assemble outside the palisade rather than in the bailey. By the western gate." Most of the garrison would be on watch, on patrol, or off duty in the lower grad, but perhaps a dozen would be in the barracks or in the keep.

Grigorii glanced at the barracks, then back at Konstantin. "Lord, Župan Teodore brought a contingent of men, as did Župan Nikola. We could ask for their aid."

Asking them for help would be admitting weakness. The župans had been invited to the wedding so they could be impressed with Rivak's hospitality, not so they could be begged for help with internal matters. And while Konstantin could use the extra men, he didn't trust them. "They aren't to be told."

Grigorii frowned. "We'll barely match the bandits in strength, lord."

"Then we'll have to hope they're less skilled than we are." In normal circumstances, Konstantin would order the gates to the grody closed while he was gone. Then it would take but a few men to defend it, and more could ride with him. But he couldn't do that today, not while hosting a score of wedding guests with questionable allegiance. He needed to leave enough men to ensure the gates would open for him when he returned.

Grigorii nodded and strode to the garrison.

Konstantin headed for the armory. Miladin kept pace with him. "You're to stay, Miladin."

"Lord?"

"If I take all the men who aren't on watch with me, the men Župan Teodore and Župan Nikola brought will outnumber those I leave behind. I need someone I trust here—a man who can lead. The garrison might respect my aunt, but battle strategy is not among her talents."

"I would rather be by your side, lord."

Konstantin gripped Miladin's arm in gratitude. "I know. And I would be glad to have you, but more than I need you in the village, I need you here. If Dragomir or my grandfather had come early, it might be different. Them I trust enough to ask aid of."

"What of Aleksander Igorević? Would you let him ride with you?"

Aleksander's hair had long ago turned gray, but he was among Sivi Gora's best warriors. "If he wishes to ride with us, I will accept his help. Will you ask him?"

"I will, lord. Would you trust him to stay behind so I can accompany you?"

"And admit that I need his help to hold my own grody? That would get back to my grandfather by nightfall, maybe before, and I don't wish that."

Miladin nodded in resignation and went in search of Aleksander.

Zoran had arrived at the armory before Konstantin, as had Father Vlatko, who was helping Zoran into his mail hauberk.

"Ten bandits holed up in a church?" Zoran asked. "Is that what you heard, lord?"

"Yes, but the number is a guess." Konstantin stripped off his outer dalmatica, something designed for entertaining guests on the eve of a wedding, not for battle. He usually armored himself in his own quarters, but today, discretion was required.

Zoran reached for a padded tunic and helped Konstantin into it. "We can hope for fewer and plan for more."

Konstantin glanced at Father Vlatko. "Pray it's less than ten."

More men from the garrison came as Father Vlatko guided Konstantin's mail hauberk over his head. Risto arrived and helped with Konstantin's lamellar corselet and splinted greaves.

Aunt Zorica entered and stood near enough to hear but distant enough to be out of the way. "A feast is planned for the evening meal."

"I hope to be back in time to host." Konstantin pulled on his gauntlets. "But if not, downplay my absence and carry on without me. Most župans are called away to deal with brigands from time to time, so perhaps it won't seem unusual. And make sure Baldovin stays away from Suzana. I want to be with her when she has to face him again. I'm leaving Miladin. Anything the two of you can do to prevent Župan Teodore or Župan Nikola from realizing their forces together are stronger than those I've left behind would be appreciated."

"I'll call the entertainment early, if needed," Aunt Zorica said.

"I'm sorry that it falls on you. I hope it won't be too awkward." Konstantin tugged on his helmet.

"I'm the one who insisted we invite our neighbors, including Župan Teodore." Aunt Zorica and Župan Teodore had almost been betrothed once. Almost, but it had come to naught when Aunt Zorica and Darras had fallen in love. "I'll think of something."

"And Suzana . . ." Konstantin wanted to say goodbye to her, but he would be back soon. Sending for her would only arouse suspicion. "Keep her safe."

His aunt nodded.

Grigorii and Zoran rode out the grody's gate as Konstantin entered the bailey. A few horses were assembled but not so many as to indicate heavier action than a routine patrol. Evidence of their real intent would still be hidden. Two members of the garrison milled about, and he waved them on, then approached two other mail-clad figures.

Two rather short mail-clad figures. He pulled the coif off one of the heads to reveal Ivan and the coif off the other head to reveal Danilo. "You two are not to follow."

Danilo's lips pursed in earnest angst. "But I can hit the bandits with arrows if they try to leave the church. If they're normal brigands, then they probably aren't wearing mail, and then I can use my light bow—and I never miss with it."

Konstantin put a hand on the boy's shoulder. "Someday. But not now. Besides, I need you both here. The men on watch won't be relieved until later. You'll have to tell them their watch will last longer than planned. Only the members of the garrison must know, none of the guests. The men in the tower or at the gates might require your eagle eyes for a time if they need a moment to eat."

Next, he grasped Ivan on the shoulder. "You must help Danilo. When the garrison is all warned, you are to protect Dama Suzana and Lidija."

"Are they in danger?"

Konstantin knelt. "Yes. And I'm depending on you to keep them safe."

"Yes, Kostya."

Konstantin straightened and checked Svarog's saddle. "You're brave boys. Thank you for your help." He led Svarog past Father Vlatko and lowered his voice to a whisper. "See that the boys don't follow me."

The priest nodded.

Konstantin mounted his warhorse and went down the causeway. The big stallion offered a rougher ride than Perun, but in battle, Svarog became a weapon. His teeth, hooves, and utter disregard for noises that would unnerve most other animals made it worth the sore haunches Konstantin would have the next day after a ride so long. He could have taken both animals, but that would have drawn too much attention.

When he reached the grad, rather than riding through town to the main gate, Konstantin turned off to the western gate, which passed fewer homes. Even so, his open-faced helmet revealed his identity, so people recognized him and waved. He waved back but didn't slow, didn't give anyone the chance to offer their congratulations for the upcoming nuptials or to ask his judgment on whatever matters were troubling them.

He stopped at the gate and told the guards where he was going and why. "I'm sorry you won't be relieved as planned. But celebrations are coming soon. They'll make up for it, I hope."

"They will, lord," one of them said. "Be careful. Those brigands have always run off before. Who knows what they'll do when cornered."

Konstantin nodded. He rode through the gate, then turned back. "See that my cousin and my brother stay inside the gates."

"Yes, lord."

Grigorii and five members of the garrison waited along the moat outside the palisade. A little farther along were Arslan, Esel, and Hamdi. They wore leather lamellar and carried weapons.

Konstantin glance at Grigorii, who gave him the smallest hint of a shrug. It seemed he hadn't expected the Turks to be there either. Konstantin urged Svarog toward Arslan's horse.

Esel spoke first. "I have been asked to inform you that the three of us will ride with you. Rivak is nominally the sultan's. By assisting you, we are serving him."

Three men. Konstantin could use three more men, but he knew nothing about their abilities and had little reason to trust them. "You would risk injury or death for Rivak?"

Esel went through the motions of translating for Arslan, and Arslan kept up the pretense for his reply. "We grow restless in the full grody, and you need to defeat the brigands quickly. Župan Teodore looks upon your lands as a thirsty man looks upon a cup of pomegranate juice."

Unease trickled across Konstantin's neck. Even after the betrothal was canceled, the family had never been sure if Teodore coveted Rivak or Aunt Zorica. The Turks, at least, seemed to think it was the land rather than the lady.

Grigorii rode his horse over to Konstantin's and lowered his voice. "They might stab us in the back."

That was possible, but Konstantin didn't see how that served the sultan. Konstantin was leaving guests he didn't trust in his grody, and now he would also have envoys he didn't trust at the village church.

Aleksander Igorević and four of Rivak's men-at-arms rode through the gates.

"That's all that's coming, isn't it?" Konstantin asked Grigorii.

"We're just waiting for Miladin."

Konstantin shook his head. "I asked him to stay."

"You did?" Surprise sounded in Grigorii's voice.

"Someone has to keep an eye on our guests." Even the Turks had noticed the risk. Konstantin raised his voice so each of the assembled men could hear. "For too long, these bandits have plagued us. They've burned Rivak's crops, disturbed the garrison's sleep, and sown fear in every home. It is time they answered for their crimes, and we thank our friends who have agreed to assist us." He gestured first to Arslan, then to Aleksander. "Speed is our ally—Kuzman and Bojan need more than merophs to help them against the bandits." Konstantin clicked at Svarog and urged him into a canter toward the village.

Chapter Sixteen
Whispers in the Chapel

Suzana suspected something was not as it should be when a group of men rode from the grad. The shapes she watched from her bedchamber window were far too small for her to identify by name, but the number indicated more than a mere patrol.

Rivakgrad had begun to feel more and more like home to her, but the guests who filled the keep and spilled into the grody's other buildings made her uneasy. With so many strangers about—plus her father—she hesitated to leave her bedchamber. It would be easier to stay away, but she shared a duty to entertain the guests, especially the other župans' wives.

Not that they seemed to want her about. When she'd greeted Dama Emilija upon her arrival the day before, the woman had lifted her chin, looked down her nose, and given her a smile that oozed contempt. No one else—not Konstantin or his family, not Dama Isidora or Župan Dragomir, had so much as mentioned the fact that Suzana was not noble born. In contrast, blood seemed to matter a great deal to Dama Emilija. Suzana had found the courage to tell Konstantin about her past, but facing Dama Emilija again would require a level of bravery Suzana might not possess.

But duty called. Konstantin let it guide him. She must do the same. And she wanted to know why so many from the garrison had ridden out and if Konstantin was among them.

She went down the stairs from the family's rooms to the main level of the keep. Dama Zorica stood on the opposite side of the hall and quickly excused herself from a conversation with Župan Nikola's wife, Dama Violeta. Dama Zorica threaded her arm through Suzana's, leading her away from the others.

"Was Konstantin among those who rode out?" Suzana asked.

Dama Zorica nodded. "There was an attack on one of the villages. He hopes to deal with it without the other župans realizing he's left. Or barring that, without them realizing how frequent attacks like this have become."

"Show no weakness?"

"Advice he has taken to heart perhaps too well." Dama Zorica frowned. "He asked me to make sure you are safe, especially from encounters with your father. And we're to entertain the guests ourselves if he doesn't return in time."

He'd thought of her before he'd ridden off. But rather than seeking her out, he'd given instructions to his aunt. Habit perhaps. Someday, maybe, he would trust her the same way he trusted Dama Zorica. She wanted him to trust her like that, wanted him to think of her first when he needed aid. "What should I do?"

"You may have to assist me as hostess if it takes him longer than he thinks it will to deal with the brigands."

"Dama Emilija does not like me."

"She does not like me either." Dama Zorica lowered her voice. "I wish they wouldn't have come. A marriage was considered between Župan Teodore and me. When it did not happen, his disappointment was greater than mine. But their župa borders ours, and he and Konstantin will campaign for the sultan together. Cultivating friendship, or at least cooperation, will help them both."

"Did he love you?"

"I believe he loved the idea of being Miroslav's heir should anything happen to Konstantin. That was before Ivan's birth."

"And Dama Violeta? She seems glad of your company."

"Our mothers were cousins. She is a friend, but I am uncertain of her husband's intentions."

Around the hall, servants kept light fare available for anyone who wished it. A man played a gusle and sang about an enchanted vila from the mountains. The lyrics were familiar to Suzana, even though her father had scoffed at the notion of the fair, swift creatures who were part angel, part nymph. In her father's villa, he would have shown off his icons or tapestries, but the grody's artwork was faded. "Perhaps we could escort our guests to the church in the lower grad to see the frescos there."

Dama Zorica smiled. "We can show them Father Vlatko's illuminated Bible as well. The artwork is lovely, and if we allow it, Father Vlatko will give them an in-depth lecture about each illustration."

The artwork in Rivakgrad's church lacked the power Suzana had seen in more richly patronized churches, but the combination of color and light pleased the eyes, and the scent of incense pleased the nose.

When she paused beneath a fresco of the Judgment Day, her father approached. A familiar fear, the tension of worry and anticipation of ill, came with his presence. She'd greeted him when he'd first arrived, but she hadn't been alone then, and having Konstantin beside her had given her courage. She still had his protection now, because she was in his grad. Perhaps God's protection, too, because she was in His church.

"You have been safe since you left?" he asked.

"There was another attempt on my life during our journey, but I have been safe since then."

"I heard of the attempt. I am glad nothing more has come."

She nodded her thanks for his well-wishes. Had she died, it would have saved him the significant cost of the dowry, but it also would have ended his chance of being united with a noble family.

"Things are well with your husband-to-be?"

"I think we will be happy together." Perhaps happy was too mild a term. She was beginning to hope for more than happiness—for the trust, friendship, love, and passion Konstantin had spoken of.

Her father looked at the ground. "When you are married, the župan is likely to find out about your past. There are ways to make things seem as though they were never broken . . ."

"He already knows."

Her father's eyes widened. "He's taken you before the wedding, has he?"

"No." Konstantin had been completely proper in his affections. "I told him."

Her father clasped his hands behind his back. "And his reaction?"

"For the man who wronged me, anger. For me, compassion."

The silence stretched out, broken only by distant murmurs from the other visitors.

"I am pleased you have found someone who can offer you compassion. I gave you justice when I punished the man who wronged you, but that did not seem to help."

Was that an apology? He had never apologized before, not to anyone, not within her hearing. "Thank you for the justice, Father. I think . . . I think it helped a little, though I know it gave you a heavy burden."

He looked at the ground again.

As the silence stretched on, she noticed Dama Zorica nearby, ready to intervene if needed. Lidija and Father Vlatko also watched. "Have you been well, Father? The attacks on my life may have been intended to harm you."

"The villa has been calm in your absence. Quiet. Maybe a little too quiet."

She stared at him again. Was he saying he missed her?

"I am pleased that your new life seems likely to offer you happiness. I hope it does." He gave her the barest of smiles and then walked away.

It didn't erase all the times he had called her stupid, all the times he had hit her, all the times he had told her she was unattractive or ruined. She wasn't sure she could trust one conversation after so many years of abuse, but how she had longed for a bit of affection from him, some show of regret for all his wrongs.

She'd fought emotion so often in the wake of abuse, but now she fought it in the wake of kindness. It wouldn't do for anyone to see her with tears—she didn't want to explain and doubted anyone would understand anyway. Konstantin's family had experienced tragedy and loss but rarely deliberate pain. Without the pain, would anyone comprehend the whirlwind of sensations a scrap of kindness could create?

Suzana went to the narthex and waited behind a pillar where no one would see her tears. She wanted to tell Konstantin about her conversation. She sent a prayer heavenward for his safety, then prayed with gratitude. No one had given her a choice as to whom she would marry, but God had given her someone she could confide in, someone she could trust when she wasn't sure whether her father's change was real or an illusion.

Soft footsteps crossed the stone behind her.

"Your men, combined with my men, outnumber the men Konstantin left."

"What of it?"

"Rivak is vulnerable. And poorly led—you've seen the burned fields and how everything is slipping into poverty. Konstantin was too young when his father died, and his people are suffering. But with the right leadership . . ."

A grunt. "And I suppose you think *you* are the right leadership?"

"I'd do better than Konstantin."

Suzana held absolutely still, not daring to move lest the men notice her. She wanted to defend her betrothed, but these men seemed to value strength, so she doubted they would listen to a female only barely a woman.

"I'll not betray Miroslav's son when he's done nothing wrong."

"Incompetence can hurt the merophs as much as wickedness can."

"Since when have you cared about merophs?"

A sigh. "He rode off this afternoon with part of his men to deal with brigands. If he doesn't return, I trust you will join me or, at the very least, allow me to do what is best for Rivak, for Serbia."

"Taking his lands for yourself?"

"If he doesn't return, Rivak will be leaderless. Someone will have to step in to prevent chaos. I don't want the mess he's created spilling into my lands."

"*If* he doesn't return, we can look at our options."

"By then, it might be too late to act."

"To act before would be dishonorable."

The voices moved off. Suzana didn't recognize either, though she assumed they belonged to Župan Nikola and Župan Teodore. She peeked from behind the pillar. Župan Nikola disappeared into the nave.

Župan Teodore held back, just for a moment. He glanced her way, locking eyes with her.

Fear made her freeze as he glared and strode toward her.

"Perhaps no one taught you that it's rude to listen to the conversations of your betters," he growled.

Suzana's throat went dry. Župan Teodore's voice was the one that had been most menacing toward Konstantin. He stepped closer, and she stepped farther away. After a few paces, she realized he was backing her into a corner. She took a step to the side, but he matched her movements, making escape impossible. Her eyes sought anything she could use as a weapon but found nothing useful. Would he try to silence her? Here, in a church?

A small figure darted from behind another of the pillars, and suddenly, Ivan stood between her and the župan, his diminutive hand grasping the hilt of a narrow-bladed knife.

Župan Teodore glanced at Ivan's blade. "Bringing weapons into a church, are we?"

"I'll use it in a church, too, if I have to." Ivan's young voice matched Župan Teodore's in volume and in coldness. Suzana couldn't see the boy's face, but his posture was unyielding.

An ominous sneer played across Župan Teodore's lips. "I believe we've had a misunderstanding. You are both too young and inexperienced to realize how quickly everything can change. A župan must plan ahead for every possibility. I'm sure Župan Konstantin does the same."

Ivan widened his stance. "He planned for the need to protect his betrothed."

"And you are her protection?" Župan Teodore chuckled. "It seems rumors of Rivak's desperation are not far off. I'd thought them exaggerated, but it seems the weakness is understated." With a final look of contempt, Župan Teodore turned and stalked away.

Suzana inhaled completely for the first time since Župan Teodore had entered the narthex. She put a hand on Ivan's shoulder. "Are you old enough to have a knife so long?"

He relaxed his stance and presented the knife for her view. "I'm old enough to have something much longer, but my aunt might be upset if I brought a sword into a church."

Suzana had assumed she would find safety in the narthex of the church, but now she regretted sneaking away from the nave. Ivan had noticed, but no one else had. Would that be a constant battle for her—the pull for privacy always pitted against the need for protection?

Ivan put his knife away and seemed more his age again. "Do you think he was going to hurt you?"

Suzana had felt the threat, heavy and imminent. But surely the župan wouldn't have really harmed her—not in a church, not when so many others were nearby. "I don't know." She squeezed his shoulder. "Maybe we should join the others."

Ivan escorted her inside. Had Konstantin been like that twelve years ago, when he would have been Ivan's age? So eager to be a warrior, so willing to stand up to danger, even if that danger were three times larger than he was? What would happen to her—and to their family—if Konstantin didn't return?

Chapter Seventeen
A Besieged Church

Konstantin glanced at his odd mix of men—eleven Serbs from Rivak, a Serb from Sivi Gora, and a trio of Turks. He hoped Grigorii's suspicions were unfounded and that Arslan and his men would be a help rather than a hindrance. They had little reason to assist brigands but did have a clear incentive to keep Rivak orderly and at peace. And Arslan's words in the stables had rung true in Konstantin's heart. Love was worth Konstantin's best efforts. Other duties, too, demanded his best efforts, but simply listening to Suzana had made a difference.

Kuzman rushed over to him when a meroph led them to the church. "Thank you for coming, lord."

Konstantin dismounted and pushed thoughts of his bride aside. He couldn't allow any distractions. "Tell me what happened."

"We met a girl on horseback. Said her village was under attack, so we came back with her. The brigands didn't kill anyone, but they tied up the merophs who resisted. We released the prisoners and sent off a messenger. The villagers aren't warriors, but the brigands aren't so impressive either."

"How many?"

"Started out as fourteen. We've killed three and wounded several others. They're no stronger than eleven now."

"Are they all in the church?"

"Yes. They tried breaking out but gave up. They've been fools to wait so long. They could have assumed we would only grow stronger."

Konstantin studied the structure. Simple but built to last, with stone walls and a tile roof. The men inside had the advantage of shelter, but Konstantin's group numbered seventeen, plus the villagers. Storming the church carried risk, but the size of that risk depended on their opponents.

"No arrows or crossbows?"

"None that we've seen."

"Armor?"

"A few had brigandines. I saw no mail, though half had helmets of some sort."

Konstantin weighed the risks and possibilities. He would attack—of that there was no question. The men had threatened a village that depended on him for protection. Even if he could afford a show of weakness in front of the merophs, he couldn't afford a show of weakness in front of the sultan's emissaries. Nor did he want Aleksander telling his grandfather that he'd been cowardly. Yet report of foolishness would have equally bad consequences, so caution and planning were needed. "How many entrances does the church have?" He directed his question to both Kuzman and the meroph.

"Three," the meroph said. "The narthex and two side entrances, plus the windows."

The windows were large enough that a man could escape through them, if he could reach them, but that seemed unlikely given the height of the church and the position of the windows. The village might be poor, but generations ago, someone had built a chapel to instill awe in those who worshipped there. The church would be the pride of all who lived nearby. Konstantin had best drive the bandits out with as little damage to the building as possible.

"Arslan?" Konstantin turned to the Turks first.

Arslan glanced at Esel, who answered. "Yes?"

"Will you and your men guard the far door to make sure the brigands don't escape out the west side?"

Esel performed the charade of translating, and the Turks agreed.

Konstantin assigned a meroph to show them the way.

"Grigorii, take two men and guard the narthex. Bojan, you'll have four men to hold in reserve. Go where you're needed. The rest of you, with me." Konstantin led his remaining men along the stone bricks to the eastern entrance, stepping where they would be less visible should the men in the church try to peek out. The door there was small—it would be easier to break down and easier to repair when the bandits were defeated.

He didn't expect the door to open for him, and that proved right. Konstantin set Kuzman and Zoran to work with their axes. After a few strikes, the planks around the lock splintered. Then Zoran gave it a sharp kick, and the door swung inward. Splintered bits of wood flew through the air and fell to the ground. Three men charged from inside the church. A large one in a helmet and leather lamellar ran right for Konstantin with an ax.

Konstantin raised his shield and stepped to the side, blocking the blow and moving away from it at the same time. He thrust his spathion at the attacker's unarmored thigh, and the man fell with a cry.

Another man was on him a moment later. Konstantin twisted away from the javelin and knocked it aside with his shield. He sliced his sword into the man's flesh. The brigand collapsed in a writhing mass of blood and agony.

Zoran took care of the third man, and Kuzman finished off the one Konstantin had wounded. Konstantin kept his shield close as he approached the door of the church. Light from the windows dimly illuminated the interior, showing faded frescos and a worn altar.

Aleksander touched Konstantin's arm. "Careful. Those three targeted you."

Had they attacked him because they'd recognized him as župan or because he was part of the group blocking their escape? Either way, Konstantin would move forward.

Kuzman joined Konstantin in the doorway so anyone leaving the church would face both of them, not just one or the other. With the burly sword master at his side, Konstantin stepped inside.

Most churches had few obstructions, but the inside of this one was piled with debris. The bandits must have stolen furniture from every home in the village. Most of the trunks, chairs, and tables were in pieces. The church didn't smell like incense. Instead, the scent of wine and plum brandy caught Konstantin's nose. Maybe they'd stolen that, too, and broken some of the containers.

A handful of men slipped from behind a pile and ran for the opposite door. They ripped back the latch and yanked the door open, revealing Arslan holding a scimitar and ready to wage war. As more of the bandits gathered to escape, Konstantin and the men he'd brought with him hurried to catch them in the rear. The bandits outnumbered the Turks, but if caught between Arslan's group of three and Konstantin's group of six, the bandits would be hard-pressed to outfight them.

More of the brigands converged on Arslan. A crash sounded behind Konstantin, and a pile of broken furniture and shredded tapestries fell in front of the door. From somewhere in the narthex, a torch flew through the air and landed on the pile. Flames spread with the speed of a destrier in full gallop, completely encircling Konstantin and his men.

That was why the church smelled of alcohol. All the broken bits of the merophs' possessions had been soaked in it so they would burn with fury.

Thick smoke quickly overpowered any lingering hint of drink, and the heat built quickly. The stone walls of the church wouldn't burn, nor would the fire reach Konstantin or his men in the center of the paved floor, but the smoke might choke them.

"Can we break through?" Konstantin shouted to be heard above the snapping flames. All around him, piles of furniture held towering columns of fire. He pulled his cloak over his mouth, but already, his eyes watered and a tight irritation gripped his throat. The church had become an oven.

"It's too thick," Kuzman shouted. "The smoke's rising, so get on the ground."

The center of the church held nothing other than the six trapped men. No benches to push aside the blazing piles that surrounded them. No jugs of water or earth with which to smother the flames. Zoran wetted his cloak with the contents of his waterskin and passed it around to the others huddled on the floor. Sweat trickled down Konstantin's face and coated his torso. Breathing took more effort now and brought less and less relief from the increasing heat and the thickening smoke.

The village had a well. Grigorii, Bojan, and Arslan might have to deal with the bandits first, but then they'd battle the flames, as would any merophs who hadn't fled when the brigands arrived.

Konstantin coughed, aggravating the pain in his scorched throat. Beside him, Aleksander collapsed. Konstantin grabbed the man's shoulder and shook, but his grandfather's satnik gave no response.

No sign of rescue could be seen through the swirling smoke. His eyes stung, and his vision blurred, but he couldn't tell if it was the smoke or a sign of impending death. Konstantin had failed again, and this time, it might cost him his life and the lives of some of his best soldiers.

Chapter Eighteen
PROVOCATION

Death had haunted Konstantin's kin as long as he could remember. It had stalked his grandfather's family in Sivi Gora, taking his grandmother, two aunts, and four uncles before his birth. Death had prowled the grody and battle camps of Rivak, too, snatching away baby Militsa, then his mother and Bogdana, then his father and his uncle. Now it shadowed Konstantin, lurking close, preparing to pounce.

Kuzman shook his arm. "The fire near the narthex isn't so high now. We might be able to break through." The voice was part wheeze, part croak.

Konstantin tried to focus. Every thought was heavy, as if it were sheathed in layers of mail. His throat and eyes burned, but he blinked and coughed and looked toward the narthex. All was a blur of bright flame and dark smoke. But he trusted Kuzman, and he wanted to live. Standing seemed too difficult and too dangerous, so he crawled, following Kuzman's lead and drawing ever closer to the source of the heat.

"What of the others?" Konstantin asked. Four men lay on the church floor, unmoving.

"We'll come back for them once we find a way out."

Konstantin nodded against the pounding fog that clouded his head. He wasn't sure he could break past the flaming barrier at all, let alone do so while carrying someone else.

Kuzman kicked a bit of burning wood from the flaming debris, and it tumbled toward them. As Kuzman scooted it out of the way with another shove, the blazing pile before them collapsed further, leaving flames that climbed only to hip height.

Kuzman hauled Konstantin to his feet. He twisted his cloak and pulled it around his shoulders so it wouldn't drag. "We run through."

Kuzman half pulled, half dragged Konstantin through the flames. The heat scorched but lasted only moments. Then it was over, and they were beyond the flaming barrier. Kuzman's trousers had caught fire. Konstantin ripped his cloak off and smothered it. The air beyond the flames was marginally better. His motions still felt sluggish, but maybe he could make it through again to grab some of the others. He turned, but Kuzman took his arm and led him to the door.

"First we find a complete route through. We have to get you to safety before we worry about anyone else, lord."

Konstantin shook his head. "Those men have families. Children."

Kuzman coughed again and pulled free the lockbar holding the door of the narthex. "If you die without children, Rivak falls into ruin."

That may have been true, but Konstantin couldn't leave the others. He used the lockbar to make more of a path for the others to escape, and as he finished, merophs ran into the church, carrying buckets of water. Now that the way was clear, Konstantin inhaled and rushed back through the path. He came across Zoran first and tried to lift him, but weakness still gripped Konstantin's body. A few breaths of fresh air hadn't been enough. He needed more time to recover, but his men couldn't wait. They needed to be rescued now.

Kuzman caught up to him and took one of Zoran's arms. Together they hauled him from the church into the fresh air. When they were clear of the smoke, they lowered him to the ground. In the next moment, Konstantin's legs gave way, and he crashed down next to Zoran's unconscious form.

More merophs ran to the church with buckets in their hands. Any battle that had taken place outside must have ended. A few bodies Konstantin didn't recognize littered the ground—the enemy, not his men nor the villagers.

"Stay with him, lord," Kuzman said.

Konstantin would have liked that—to sit beside Zoran and do nothing but breathe clean air and feel the cool breeze on his face, but he struggled to his feet and took an unsteady step toward the church. "There are still three inside."

"And none of them are as important as you."

That voice. Konstantin's head jerked around to stare at a man on horseback. His grandfather. He gave Konstantin a knowing look, then ordered his men-at-arms into the church to rescue those trapped inside.

"Why are you here?" Konstantin asked.

"I thought I was traveling to see my grandson married. It seems I nearly saw him burned alive instead, but at least both events had a church for the setting."

Konstantin tried to follow his grandfather's words, but his brain was still too muddled.

His grandfather raised one eyebrow at Konstantin's confusion. "We were on our way to your grad when we saw your men chasing after a group of brigands. Then we saw the smoke."

As Grandfather spoke, Grigorii, Bojan, and some of the others rode back to the church. They brought with them no prisoners. Bojan dismounted near Konstantin. His mouth hung open as the men from Sivi Gora brought out Aleksander and the other two who had been trapped in the church. Soot coated their skin, and their heads hung forward limply. Billows of smoke still escaped from the narthex.

"What happened?" his grandfather asked.

"They set a trap, and I walked right into it." Konstantin moved toward the men who'd been rescued from the church. "Are they alive?"

Someone Konstantin didn't recognize laid the man he carried on the ground and put an ear to his chest. His blue eyes looked up and met Konstantin's. "Yes, he still breathes." The man's Slavonic words were strongly accented. He wasn't from Sivi Gora or anywhere else in Serbia.

Zoran, who'd had more time to recover, coughed and blinked his eyes open. Aleksander wheezed as another of the rescuers sat him down and gave him several solid thumps across the back. Konstantin went to the third, Akinin. His breathing was shallow but steady.

Horror showed on Bojan's face. "We didn't know you were trapped. We just saw them force their way past the Turks. They killed Hamdi."

"How many escaped?" Konstantin strode to the side of the church, and as he turned the corner, he extended his count of the enemy to three dead and two dying.

"Four."

The pounding in Konstantin's head made it hard to decide whether Bojan and Grigorii had done right in chasing the brigands or if they should have stayed to support their župan. He slowed as he approached Arslan, Esel, and the body of Hamdi. Clothing concealed the wound but blood stained the fallen man's chest, revealing the fatal strike's location. Arslan looked up and met Konstantin's gaze. He was dry-eyed but somber.

"I am sorry this happened." Konstantin's words felt inadequate. There was risk in battle—the Ottomans knew that, and they'd volunteered. Still, Konstantin felt responsible. "You will wish to bury him soon?" Konstantin's uncle had once told him of Muslim burial traditions.

Arslan nodded, not waiting for Esel's translation.

"What do you need?"

"White cloth for a shroud. A spot of land."

"We have cloth at the grody. You may have your pick of land."

"Thank you."

Konstantin almost apologized again, but he hadn't asked them to come, he hadn't been the one to strike down Hamdi, and a župan did not apologize to his men when their friends were slain in battle.

He returned to those still recovering from the smoke. "Bojan, see if you can find a cart for the body." Konstantin fished a coin from Svarog's saddlebags. "Either pay one of the merophs to drive it to Rivakgrad and back, or pay him for its use."

"Yes, lord."

Konstantin walked through the church. The merophs had fully extinguished the fire, and now smoke stained the walls, and scorch marks blackened the floor. Konstantin didn't linger inside. The air stung his irritated eyes and his aching throat.

His grandfather joined him in the narthex. "Thanks be to God that you escaped." Grandfather motioned Konstantin toward cleaner air and placed a hand on his shoulder. "Your heart is noble to wish to save your men when they were trapped in the church. But you can't wage battle with your heart alone. You must also use your mind. The death of any of your men is a tragedy. Your death would be a disaster. You must remember that—your family and your župa depend on you. That means you must do all within your power to stay alive, even if it costs you. And it will cost you—each of the men who die at your command or who die to defend you—that cost is part of your burden as their leader."

Konstantin nodded, accepting the older župan's wisdom even as he struggled to agree.

Grandfather didn't continue the lecture about the myriad other mistakes Konstantin had made that afternoon, but he did motion for two men to approach, including the blue-eyed man whose native tongue was not Slavonic. Grandfather gestured to the older of them. "Ulrich, captain of a

German band of warriors for hire." He shifted his hand to the one who had helped rescue Konstantin's men. "Otto, his second."

"Welcome to both of you. And I offer my thanks. Your timing was most fortuitous," Konstantin said.

Otto smiled, the gesture brightening his face.

Grandfather motioned for one of his men to bring his horse. "You can discuss things when your head clears, but I think we'd best be on our way, or we'll be late for the banquet."

By the time he reached the grody, exhaustion coated Konstantin as thoroughly as the smoke and dust did. Miladin met him at the grody's gate and filled him in as he led Svarog across the bailey. "The banquet is long over. Your aunt told the guests it was a minor matter that drew you away, but the appearance of the party suggests otherwise."

Konstantin glanced at Kuzman and Zoran, both covered in soot. "Were there any problems?"

"None that I'm aware of," Miladin said. "We have men keeping an eye on our guests' men-at-arms."

"Suzana is safe?"

"I saw her at supper. She looked in good health and was gracious to Dama Violeta. Lidija did an admirable job trying to charm Dama Emilija, though that is no easy task."

Konstantin nodded. "Am I as filthy as Kuzman and Zoran?"

Miladin smiled rather than answer the question directly. "Several fresh baths are ready in the barracks, if you would like to bathe there, lord. Or I can have someone prepare one in your room."

"The barracks will do." Konstantin called a few servants to fetch white cloth for the Turks and to warn his aunt to expect a hungry crowd, then he rushed through the bathing process. Usually, he preferred relaxing at length in the warm water, but he meant to attend Hamdi's burial that night, and there would be preparations for the wedding.

While Konstantin bathed, Risto brought fresh clothing and cleaned his armor. The mail shouldn't have still smelled so strongly of smoke, but as Konstantin slipped it on, the scent transported him back to the burning church. Maybe he only imagined the smell, but that time in the church, trapped between flames, scarcely able to breathe, it would not soon fade from his mind.

When he was presentable, Konstantin fastened his spathion and headed for the keep. When he was halfway across the bailey, Suzana's slight form appeared on the stairs to the keep. She rushed down and embraced him tightly. He didn't mind—liked it even—but it surprised him. He'd held her once before, that night when she'd told him about her past, but that closeness had been more gradual.

"I was so worried about you," she said.

He held her, content to have her near. In contrast to the thick smoke of the church, she smelled of something floral, fresh and light and enticing. When he'd left, he hadn't thought there'd be much reason for anyone to worry on his account. Brigands were rarely warriors of distinction—just men with better weapons than the merophs. "I'm sorry I didn't come to you sooner." He hadn't wanted her to see him covered in soot and blood. "I underestimated my enemy. A mistake I'll try not to make again."

One of her hands brushed against his cheek. "You have enemies here in the grody too."

"I do?"

"Yes." Suzana told him what she'd overheard at the grad's church.

As she finished, shock made him tense, and then anger made him agitated. "Župan Teodore was bold to threaten you in your own church."

Worry pulled at her lips. "I should have screamed, but it was hard to do anything, hard to even think. He left us alone when Ivan came, and though Ivan was brave and determined, he's hardly old enough to threaten someone like Župan Teodore—he didn't have to leave, but he did. That makes me think he would have backed down before hurting me."

Konstantin ran his hands along Suzana's arms. "He might have thought two victims were twice as likely to call for help. Regardless, he is no longer welcome in my grody. Conspiring to take my family's lands should I die might be forgivable. Threatening my bride is not. Will you be all right if I go take care of a few things?"

Her body immediately tensed. "You plan to confront him?"

"Yes."

"What of the rules of hospitality? He is an invited guest. Sending him away could damage your reputation."

Konstantin weighed the likely consequences of his intended action. "Reputation be hanged. Župan Teodore is already my enemy. Sending him away before the marriage ceremony won't change that; it will just bring it into the open. I already have to suffer your father attending the feast. One man in attendance who frightens you is more than I wish. I'll not tolerate two."

She took his hand. "My father seemed different today. Almost kind. I'm not sure what it means, but while I am in Rivakgrad, I do not think I have anything more to fear from him."

He studied Suzana's clear face and bright eyes. She had changed since Konstantin had first met her. Confidence, inner strength, and peace seemed to be replacing fear, pain, and indecision. Love for this woman may have been a rainfall before, but now it felt like a flood. "I will be the most blessed man in the world when I take you as my bride tomorrow. Men like Župan Teodore haven't earned the right to witness it. I'll send him on his way."

Her hold on his hand tightened. "You'll make sure you outnumber him when you speak to him?"

"I'll have the men on alert, where I can call them if needed." He doubted Župan Teodore would be so foolish as to attack him in his own grody, but he'd wear armor and take several men. He lifted Suzana's hand and gently kissed her knuckles. "I'm sorry today didn't unfold the way we planned. But I look forward to becoming your husband."

A smile warmed her face. "I shall be glad to be your wife."

He led her back into the keep and toward the safety of the family's private rooms. Only propriety and a long list of things to see to managed to pull him away from her. Soon the time would come when he wouldn't have to bid her farewell at the end of each day. For now, it was better for him to focus, not on her but on what Župan Teodore would do when Konstantin asked him to leave.

First, he found Grigorii in the corridor near the hall. "Where are Župan Teodore's men?"

"Most are in the garrison. A few are in his quarters with him. Why?"

"Because I'm going to ask him to leave."

Grigorii's eyes widened. "Lord, is that wise?"

"While we were absent, he tried to pull Župan Nikola into an alliance to divide Rivak between themselves—or perhaps Župan Teodore was planning to take it all. Then he threatened Suzana because she overheard."

"And you trust her account?"

"Without question. I'd like you to accompany me, in case there's trouble."

Konstantin motioned Bojan over next. "Will you gather a few of our men? Ten. Armed. I'd like you all to wait near the guest house, out of sight, but where you can come at once if I call for you."

"Yes, lord. May I ask who we ought to be on guard against?"

That was a fair question. The guest house—formerly an administration building—currently hosted his grandfather, Župan Nikola, and Župan Teodore, plus their entourages. The garrison was packed like a quiver full of men from four župas, and that number would be five when Dragomir arrived. "Župan Teodore and his men."

Bojan headed for the garrison, while Konstantin and Grigorii went to the hall. There Aunt Zorica presided over a late meal for Župan Đurad, his men, and the members of the garrison who had been with Konstantin in the village.

"Did Suzana tell you what happened in the grad today?" Aunt Zorica asked.

"Yes. I assume you've heard what happened at the village?"

"I did."

"I'm going to tell Župan Teodore that he is no longer welcome here."

Grandfather looked up from his meal. "You'll make an enemy of him if you humiliate him with a dismissal."

"My betrothed told me much the same thing," Konstantin said. "But Župan Teodore has already proved himself an enemy. Anyone who threatens my betrothed is not welcome at my wedding."

"You'll have to serve with him when the sultan calls you in the spring." Grandfather's tone suggested he wasn't trying to change Konstantin's mind. He was simply reminding him of all the consequences.

"I know. And that will make the sultan's service more difficult, but I would rather Župan Teodore openly menace me on campaign than secretly menace me and my bride at our wedding and beyond." Konstantin glanced at Miladin. "Will you come with me?"

"Of course, lord."

"Would you like some of my men?" Grandfather and his men-at-arms still wore the armor they had traveled in.

"I believe my garrison can manage it," Konstantin said. "But if we run into trouble, I'll gladly accept your help again." He glanced around the hall. "The boys?"

"You wish them to help send Župan Teodore on his way?" Grandfather raised an eyebrow.

"No. I wish to see that they aren't getting into mischief."

Aunt Zorica gestured toward their room. "I told them they must retire early tonight if they wish to stay up for the entire feast tomorrow. Lidija promised them a story and took them to their bedchamber."

Konstantin would give his thanks to Ivan later for trying to defend Suzana. Someone else should have been there—someone with more skill than a boy of seven—but Ivan had done his part. Konstantin was proud of him. And relieved that neither Ivan nor Suzana had been injured during the incident.

Accompanied by Grigorii and Miladin, Konstantin left the keep and went to the guesthouse.

Bojan met them on the way. "All is prepared, lord."

"Good." Konstantin slowed his stride. "Does anyone know which chambers Župan Teodore is staying in?" Konstantin knew the building well enough, but Aunt Zorica had been the one to assign quarters to the various guests.

"I do, lord." Grigorii had a grim look on his face as he took the lead. He stopped outside the chambers along the building's northwest corner.

Konstantin paused for a moment. With Miladin, Grigorii, and Bojan at his side, he didn't think Župan Teodore would attack him. If he did grow violent, the four of them could manage a fighting retreat, and enough of his men waited nearby to reinforce them. His grandfather's men could be called too. Konstantin wasn't declaring war, exactly, but he was stirring up conflict, or at least bringing it into the open. Regardless, it was his best option. He rapped on the door.

Župan Teodore's steward answered the knock and bowed politely. "Župan Konstantin."

"I wish to speak with Župan Teodore."

The steward motioned them in. "Please enter."

Konstantin didn't need to be invited inside a room in his own building. "We'll wait here."

The steward's eyes widened slightly in confusion. "If that is your wish."

"It is."

The steward excused himself, leaving the door open. Miladin and Grigorii both kept their hands on their swords. Konstantin, too, itched to touch his hilt, but that might be too intense a provocation.

Župan Teodore seemed annoyed by Konstantin's presence but not surprised. "I would have thought the bridegroom too busy to honor his guests with individual visits the day before his wedding, but perhaps this is meant to make up for your absence at the evening banquet?"

Konstantin straightened his back. “I’ve come to bid you farewell. I expect you, your family, and all your retainers to be gone by tomorrow’s third hour.”

Župan Teodore lifted his chin. “You would dare tell me to leave?”

“Your invitation to visit Rivak and my hospitality will end tomorrow morning. You can leave before then with whatever excuse you like. After that, you are no longer welcome.”

Dama Emilija appeared from behind a curtain being used to divide the room. Her brows were drawn in, and her hands fisted. “Župans do not treat other župans with such discourtesy.”

Konstantin forced calm into his voice. “Which is the greater discourtesy? Asking someone to leave before planned? Or conspiring against one’s host, then threatening his host’s bride when she discovers the plan?”

Dama Emilija tilted her chin in a defiant slant. “That lowly merchant’s daughter is a bad influence on you, young župan. She’s inventing lies and causing you to disregard the most basic codes of honor.”

Irritation flashed through Konstantin’s chest, and he hoped it didn’t show on his face. “Honor suggests I reserve my hospitality first and foremost for my family and my friends, not for neighbors who threaten my lands and my bride.”

Dama Emilija glanced at her husband. His stern face showed nothing but contempt as he spoke. “I said nothing to threaten her.”

“Not all threats are spoken. But this one is: be gone tomorrow by the third hour.” Konstantin preferred not to mar his wedding festivities with battle. He might have every confidence of defeating Župan Teodore, but he was unlikely to do so without incurring casualties, and he couldn’t afford to lose any men. He prayed the enemy župan would leave without a fight.

Župan Teodore’s hand crawled toward the hilt of his sword, but he glanced at Grigorii and held off. Grigorii must have noticed the movement, too, and the determination in his face and warning shake of his head must have been enough of a deterrent.

Konstantin took a step back. “I’ll leave you to your preparations.” He didn’t want the standoff to escalate into something he’d be unable to control. Proximity might provoke greater anger, and that might lead Župan Teodore to a rash vow, something he wouldn’t be able to back away from without loss of pride.

Župan Teodore said nothing, so Konstantin took another step back, then turned on his heel and marched away. He had a burial to attend, a group of unwanted guests to monitor, and a marriage to plan.

Chapter Nineteen
Bound with Silk

Suzana stood atop the keep while Župan Teodore's entourage saddled horses and packed carts below in the bailey.

"He's late." Dama Zorica stood beside Suzana along with Lidija and the two boys. "I suppose that's a way for him to concede while maintaining a bit of control."

"This will cause trouble, won't it?" Guilt nipped at Suzana. Konstantin had many reasons to send Župan Teodore away, but the only one he'd shown emotion over had been the man's threats to her. She was grateful Konstantin wished to protect her, but what if she'd driven him to make an enemy?

Dama Zorica put a comforting hand on Suzana's arm. "There was trouble before. Konstantin was right to bring it into the open. Župan Teodore won't forget this slight, but nor would he have forgotten had Konstantin let him get away with intimidation and schemes of takeovers in his own grody. It would have been worse to show himself too weak to defend his rights to his land and the safety of his bride."

Suzana hoped Dama Zorica was right.

Danilo peered to the west. "I think that's Dragomir."

Suzana turned to follow his gaze but saw only a cloud of dust along the road in the distance.

"How can you tell?" Lidija squinted.

Danilo shrugged. "That's the road they'd take, and they're expected soon."

"Do you suppose Decimir is with them?" Lidija watched the group's approach, but Suzana kept her focus on the bailey below. Konstantin was down there, as were all his men, fully armed, waiting for Župan Teodore's departure.

Konstantin appeared to wait with patience, and she wouldn't have expected anything else from him. Sometimes his calm was so extreme that it made it hard for her to understand what he wanted and what he thought, but today, that calm meant it was unlikely Župan Teodore would provoke him into anything rash. The other men seemed less patient. Some fidgeted, and others cast glares. As long as Konstantin was present, she didn't think his men would deliberately stir up trouble, but if Župan Teodore's men said or did anything foolish, it would be like throwing a spark into a pile of hay.

Konstantin glanced at the top of the keep, where he'd sent his family. He met Suzana's eyes but scanned past her soon after. At the moment, she was a beautiful distraction he couldn't afford.

"Should we tell them to hurry?" Grigorii whispered. The third hour had come and gone. Župan Teodore and his men were purposely stalling.

"I don't wish to provoke them. We outnumber their group, but they could still hurt us, and we cannot sustain any losses." Konstantin would need all his men in the spring and all of Ulrich's mercenaries, though that arrangement remained unsettled. Yesterday's events had left no time for a serious discussion, and by the time Župan Teodore left, all attention would turn to the marriage.

"I do not wish for a battle either." Grigorii studied the men-at-arms in Župan Teodore's entourage. "But you gave him a clear ultimatum. He will think you weak if you don't hold him to it."

Rivak was frail. Konstantin couldn't change that overnight. Standing by might weaken his prestige, but confrontation would weaken his garrison, and that was the more serious risk. Grigorii grimaced as some of Župan Teodore's men unloaded something from a cart so they could shuffle the bundles into better position.

"Yesterday, you questioned me when I planned to dismiss him," Konstantin said. "Now you think I should insist he leave at once."

Grigorii's face colored. "I didn't mean to question you, lord, but circumstances changed when you made your demands."

That was true enough. And though the danger had existed before, it felt more real now, which was why he had sent his family to the tower and asked Kuzman to organize their protection.

Grandfather emerged from the guesthouse and walked to stand near Konstantin. A show of support. Župan Nikola remained out of sight. He'd given no word that he would leave before the marriage, shown no outward sign of solidarity with Župan Teodore. Konstantin hoped Nikola would stay neutral or end up on Konstantin's side, but the risk of offending Župan Nikola by failing to show Župan Teodore hospitality was real.

Finally, at the fourth hour, Župan Teodore and his group left the grody and traveled down the causeway to the lower grad. Konstantin crossed the bailey and climbed the watchtower beside the gate, where Miladin waited.

"I feel as though I can finally breathe again," Miladin said.

"You arranged for a few of our men to follow them to the borders?" They'd discussed it last night, after Hamdi's burial.

"Yes, and I posted men along the route. In other circumstances, I would suggest shutting the gates behind them, but I think I see Dragomir's group approaching, and merophs are streaming in for the wedding."

"I shouldn't have invited him in the first place."

"A župan must do many things out of duty and expectation."

That was true enough. He'd accepted his betrothal to Suzana out of duty and desperation. But marriage would be different. That, he would enter into wholeheartedly. He glanced at the sun. Wholeheartedly and soon.

Suzana entered the keep's hall with Dama Isidora and Dama Zorica. Konstantin waited there, dressed in a long robe of embroidered silk. He looked up from a conversation with Ivan and Danilo to stare at her. She wore a veil over her face, so he wouldn't be able to see her expression, but she smiled anyway. His beard was newly trimmed, and his hair was clean. The wedding robes gave the impression they were designed to: he looked like an emperor. Regal and mighty, everything her father had hoped for in this marriage. Suzana saw the majesty and the power, but more than that, she saw a friend and a partner.

Her own bridal clothing was an opportunity for her father to show his wealth, and the quality of the fabric was the finest she'd ever felt or seen. The jewels placed on her wrists, ears, throat, and veil would likely pay a sizable band of mercenaries for a season. She felt the weight of the fabric and the jewels, but mostly, she felt the promise of the new life she would soon begin.

Her father, Konstantin's family, the visiting župans, and their kin and advisers lined the hall. Both bride and bridegroom signed the contract, and then Konstantin took her hand, and escorted by the wedding party, they began the walk to the large church in the lower grad.

At the bottom of the causeway, Konstantin leaned his head toward hers. "I cannot see your face through the veil, but even so, you look beautiful."

They entered the grad, and a swell of people, all of them cheering with excitement, made it impossible for Suzana to reply verbally. She gripped his hand, and he gripped hers in exchange.

The ceremony itself began when she and Konstantin stood before the altar, with the guests filling the church behind them. After Suzana folded the veil back from her face, Father Vlatko handed bride and bridegroom white candles with small, bright flames that swayed with each shift in the air. They held the tapers in their left hands while prayers were read, and their right hands were wrapped together with a silk sash. At the betrothal, Suzana had thought of marriage as a binding of two people by rope or chain. She'd been wrong. She and Konstantin were now bound to each other, not with something harsh but with embroidered silk. Something soft. Something beautiful. Something that could bring them joy.

The symbolism, the scriptures, the prayers—they all reminded her that she could trust Konstantin, and she could trust God. Tears crept from her eyes as emotion overwhelmed her. They were supposed to face the altar—marriage was a promise with God, after all, even more than it was a promise with each other—but she met Konstantin's eyes often. His expression remained calm, but she saw the happiness in his eyes.

When it was time for the crowning, Father Vlatko placed a golden and crimson crown on her head, identical to the one he placed on Konstantin's head. The crowns were switched between bride and bridegroom three times before one settled atop her head. She felt its heft. Symbolically, the crowning gave them honor as they started their marriage under God's watchful eyes. It was also one step closer to being a župan's wife. Her father would be pleased at her rise to nobility. She was also pleased, but for a different reason. She had felt love from very few people, but she felt it from the man she was marrying.

Konstantin watched Suzana throughout the ceremony. She seemed happy, despite the tears, and he felt the same. He tried focusing on Father

Vlatko's words as the priest read the story of Jesus turning the water to wine at the marriage in Cana, but Suzana distracted him. She did nothing to consciously pull his mind from the ceremony, but her beauty and dreams of their life together chased away all other thoughts.

Father Vlatko handed him the cup of wine he and Suzana were to share. The ceremony was almost over. They shared the cup, just as they would share their lives. Then they followed Father Vlatko as he led them around the altar three times, and after another blessing, the ceremony wound to a close. The crowns were removed, and their hands were unbound. He passed his candle to Father Vlatko and reached for Suzana so that he was holding both her hands in his. The expression on her face took his breath away when she smiled up at him. She was stunning, and she was his to cherish, his to love, his to care for.

"Suzana, I will do everything I can to be a good husband to you."

"And I will do all I can to be a good wife to you."

Their whispered promises would linger forever in his memory, but the two of them could not linger near the altar. Duty required much of a župan on his wedding day, even when all he wanted was time alone with his bride. Family already crowded round to share their well-wishes, and merophs and townspeople who hadn't been able to fit inside the church waited in the streets for a glimpse of their lord and his new bride.

"I liked your crowns." Ivan took Suzana's hand and grinned at Konstantin.

Dama Isidora laid a hand on Suzana's arm. "I couldn't be happier to have you as our neighbor."

Župan Dragomir nodded his agreement, and the smiles and wishes for good health and a large family continued as they left the church and walked the crowded streets. Miladin and a few of the others stayed nearby for security, but there were no assassins, just well-wishers. Even Arslan and Esel waited outside the church to show their approval—or perhaps to gather information for their sultan.

Konstantin felt lighter as they walked along the causeway to the grody and the keep. He still had worries: animosity with Župan Teodore, brigands who might again attack crops or villages, and a sultan who held the fate of Rivak in his hands. But today was a new start. Suzana was by his side, and everything about the future now seemed illuminated by promise and hope.

CHAPTER TWENTY
THE BEDDING CEREMONY

GUESTS FILLED THE GREAT HALL for the wedding feast. Suzana wasn't used to having so many eyes on her. She sat with Konstantin at the head table, eating slowly because apprehension and anticipation kept her appetite at bay. The guests were not so moderate, eagerly partaking in the plentiful food and wine while the musicians played. Whenever the scrutiny of the guests left Suzana feeling vulnerable, Konstantin brushed his hand over hers, and gratitude that God had given her a husband who was so good eased her worry.

The feast lasted long into the evening, and then most of the guests danced the kolo, linking arms to form a chain as their feet moved in rhythm to the flutes and pipes. She was grateful that Lidija had practiced so often with her and even more grateful for Konstantin's look of approval as he danced by her side.

When the kolo finished, Dama Zorica and Dama Isidora whisked Suzana to her bedchamber. They helped her remove the elaborate wedding garments and replaced them with a simple robe. Something that was easy to put on and easy to take off. The silk was soft against her skin, but she was too nervous to enjoy its smooth texture.

"Are you familiar with bedding ceremonies?" Dama Zorica asked.

"Only a little." She'd never been to a wedding feast before her own. She'd heard servants tell of the bawdy songs sung as the wedding party escorted the married couple to their bedchamber but didn't know at what point the guests left. "How long do people stay?"

Dama Isidora unfastened Suzana's hair and combed it out with long, soft strokes. "I imagine Konstantin will send them all away as soon as the bed is blessed."

Dama Zorica smoothed Suzana's embroidered dalmatica. "He will try, but Konstantin spends a great deal of time training with the garrison, and they will all have had more wine than is wise. I expect teasing and mischief, like at Miladin's wedding last year."

"What am I to do?" Suzana was nervous to be alone with Konstantin but far more nervous *not* to be alone with him.

"Ignore them." Dama Zorica gave her a gracious smile. "At my bedding ceremony, Darras had to escort several of his friends to the door, some a little forcefully. Father Vlatko dislikes the tradition as much as I do, so we shall do our best to make it as short as possible." She turned to Jasmina, who stood on the edge of the room. "Tell them we're ready."

Dama Isidora seemed to sense the question Suzana had but was too scared to voice. "And after everyone has gone, enjoy your time with your new husband. Tell him when you enjoy something or when you don't enjoy something. He's a good lad, but he can't read your mind."

Dama Zorica chuckled. "He's a man now, not a lad, but I still remember him as a baby. You both are so young." She took Suzana's hand. "You look enchanting. Come, we'll lead you through the back way. We can't avoid the crowd that's bound to follow the bridegroom up from the feast, but that doesn't mean we have to parade you through the corridor."

Suzana's bedchamber contained a door that led to the main corridor and a second exit that she had never before used. Dama Zorica lifted the lockbar that had been in place since Suzana's first night in Rivakgrad and cracked open the door. It squeaked loudly.

Dama Zorica pulled the door fully open. "I'll have someone grease the hinges tomorrow. It's been a long time since Rivak's župan had a wife. It will be good to have a couple in the home again."

They went through a narrow hallway, then through another doorway that led to a larger room. She hadn't seen it before but knew it must be Konstantin's. A fire burned in the hearth, and someone had carefully folded the covers back from the bed and arranged flower petals on the floor. She scarcely had time to note the other furniture and the heavy wool curtains that, no doubt, hid shuttered windows when the sound of the bridegroom's escort echoed through the corridor.

What an awful tradition. Her attraction to Konstantin had grown over the summer, but she was nervous to be a bride. She didn't need a flock of gawkers and well-wishers to make things even more awkward.

Some of the voices broke out in song, and then the door swung open, and Konstantin and a score of others entered the bedchamber. She stiffened when she saw that her father was among them, and that made everything worse. Konstantin would forgive her for not knowing what to do, for not knowing how to hide her embarrassment. Her father wouldn't.

Dama Isidora patted her on the shoulder and leaned next to her ear to whisper. "You don't have to worry about your father anymore. Your husband now has custody of you."

Konstantin met her eyes. His face seemed impassive, as if he didn't care about any of the commotion going on about him. But perhaps he sensed that she did, because he held up a hand and called for peace. "I thank you for your well-wishes, and now I bid you a fond farewell."

Several soldiers ignored him and continued with their song. Konstantin walked over to them and put a firm hand on each of their shoulders. "Not that song, not in front of the boys."

Suzana scanned the room and caught sight of Danilo and Ivan next to Lidija. Ivan yawned, and Danilo's eyes looked drowsy. She doubted they would remember any of the songs, but she didn't think Konstantin stopped the songs for their benefit; he did it for hers.

Župan Nikola stood near the back of the crowd, his face almost as phlegmatic as Konstantin's but redder than normal, like he'd had too much wine. Most of the men and women seemed that way—a little too merry.

Father Vlatko was an exception. He motioned for Suzana to sit on the bed, then had Konstantin sit beside her. She barely heard the words he said as he blessed the marriage bed and the union. She'd enjoyed the crowning at the church, but now she felt as if a storm raged around her—but there was a calm in that storm, sitting right beside her.

The moment Father Vlatko finished, Konstantin stood and thanked the priest, then began escorting others to the door, beginning with her father, then making his way through the loudest of the guests. He thanked them for coming, and if they didn't make their own way to the door, he guided them that direction until they understood what was wanted.

Ivan rubbed a fist to his eye and walked toward her. "I don't understand. I don't need anyone to tuck me into bed at night unless I'm sick. You and Konstantin are both older than I am. So why did we all come see you to bed?"

His innocence made her smile. "It's an old tradition, I suppose. Do you know that you are my brother now?" She turned to Danilo, who, as usual, was right beside the other boy. "And you are my cousin."

"Lidija said that when you have children, I'll be an uncle." Ivan grinned. "Will you have a baby soon? I'd like to be an uncle."

Konstantin appeared beside the boys. "Lidija will see you both to your own beds." The room had mostly emptied. Only Konstantin's siblings and cousin, his aunt, and his manservant remained.

Lidija reached for Ivan's hand.

"But I'm not—" Ivan's words broke for a yawn. "I'm not sleepy."

"Of course not." Konstantin gave his brother a gentle smile. "But I think perhaps I am ready to retire, and I can't very well go to bed until you've gone to your own room."

Dama Zorica ushered Danilo from the bedchamber, followed by Lidija and Ivan. Konstantin shut the door behind them and turned to Risto. "Perhaps help with the top layer." Konstantin's dalmatica was as ornate—and probably just as heavy and restrictive—as hers had been. She was married to the župan now, but she still stood and averted her eyes as Risto helped remove the ceremonial clothing, leaving Konstantin in a simple linen tunic. "Thank you, Risto. That should be all until morning."

Suzana turned to see Risto lay the dalmatica across a trunk and leave the room.

Konstantin bolted the door behind him and leaned his back against it. A smile pulled at his mouth, and he chuckled. "I understand that marriage is something that involves the whole community, but I wish the seeing of the bride and bridegroom to the marriage chamber ended in the hall, not in my room."

He walked toward her and reached for her hand. "Will you sit by the fire with me?"

She nodded and let him lead her to a cushioned bench. He sat beside her, so close that their knees touched. They had shared a few embraces, but they hadn't been alone for those, not really. Watchmen and others in the bailey had been able to see them. Now the doors were barred, and no one would interrupt them until morning. A nervous tension gripped her, and she did her best to force it away.

"You're so beautiful." His fingers tangled with hers. "May I call you *my Suzana* now?"

She felt herself smiling at his words and at his touch. "You may, my Konstantin. Or should I call you *my Kostya*?"

"You may call me either." His eyes ran all over her face, and his lips softened, as if pleased with what he saw. "Thank you for marrying me, my Suzana."

She glanced at their entwined hands. "I wasn't given a choice, but if I had been, I would have chosen you."

"Now that we are married, I promise I will give you as many choices as I can. I want us to work together because we want to, not because we are forced to. And tonight, you can decide what we do or don't do." He raised her hand to his lips and kissed it. The gentle motion was a confirmation of his promise. He offered her freedom, and she would forever be grateful to him for that.

He raised his other hand to her hair and ran his fingers along the strands that trailed down her back. "There's still so much I don't know about you. What type of flowers you like and what type of foods you hate."

She smiled at his question and at the pleasant sensation of his hand running along her back. "Most people would ask what type of foods a person enjoys. That would be the shorter list for you, wouldn't it? What you like versus what you don't like?"

"I'm not that picky, am I?"

She hadn't ever teased him before, but she enjoyed the way his face changed when he laughed. She would make it a goal to tease him again, soon. "You seem to have clear preferences on which cuts of meat you prefer, and I've seen you eat few vegetables." As a župan, he could afford to be picky because meals in the hall were meant to serve a great many people. None of the food he rejected went to waste.

"Why eat vegetables when I can eat plum pastries?" His mouth pulled mischievously, and she found the expression so appealing that she almost brought her hand up to touch it.

"People have given me reasons for eating vegetables," she said. "But none of them seem important right now." No one had ever asked her what foods she liked or disliked before. Sometimes she'd been given a choice of items from a banquet or feast, but Father, nurses, and companions had always expected her to eat what was placed before her. "I don't care for boukellaton because it is bland and dry nor for walnuts because they leave my mouth sore."

"Then it's a good thing you aren't a soldier. We eat hardtack often. I don't think it's so bad if you can soak it in olive oil or wine first." He studied her face. "It's also good that you aren't a soldier because I don't think I could pay attention to anyone else on the battlefield if you were there. Memory of those first days after the betrothal . . ." He shook his head. "I shouldn't bring those up tonight."

This time, she didn't resist the urge to touch his face. Her fingers felt along his temple and into his closely cropped beard. "Thank you for rescuing me."

"I will always do all I can to keep you safe. And to make you happy, so tell me more about what you like, what you enjoy."

Suzana relaxed with her shoulder next to his. It was comforting, leaning into the muscles of his arms, and then he wrapped an arm around her, and she leaned into the muscles of his torso. She had known many men who wielded power, but she no longer feared that Konstantin would wield his against her. "I like autumn, when the leaves turn colors and the air turns crisp. Sunrises and sunsets. Sitting by the fire and staying warm on a wet day. And the feel of silk against my skin."

Konstantin's eyes ran along the lines of the silk robe she currently wore. "I like horses. The way new snow makes everything look clean. Well-made swords and bows. And the shape of your mouth." He stared at her lips and lowered his voice. "May I touch your mouth, Suzana?"

"You may."

He brought his hand to her face. Softly, he traced the edge of her lips, and his touch was among the most pleasant sensations she'd ever felt.

"Like a recurve bow." He ran his fingers around her mouth again. "The perfect shape."

Next, he asked about her childhood and told her about his. Her father had been strict and cold. His had been demanding but supportive.

"Your family has had hardships," she said, "but there has always been love too."

His fingers traveled from her chin to her shoulder. "You're part of it now. Part of that family. Part of that love."

She'd felt that love since coming to Rivakgrad, especially in the moments she'd found with Konstantin. "You really love me, don't you?"

"Yes."

Something in her chest seemed to transform, shifting aside hurt and worry and replacing it with joy. "I love you too."

The firelight was dim now, but it still showed his expression: calm and pleased. "Suzana? May I kiss your mouth?"

She swallowed. She knew she could say no, but she didn't want to turn him down, didn't want to pass up the chance for her first real kiss. Her hesitation sprang from inexperience, not from lack of desire. "You may."

She closed her eyes as he leaned toward her. His breath whispered across her skin, and in the next moment, his lips met hers. The moment was flawless. Him and her and the soft sensation of two people coming together in hope and affection. He kissed her once, twice, and then again. This was what it felt like to trust and to love. Potent emotion and a new overpowering happiness tangled up inside her.

He ended the kiss and smiled. "Your lips are every bit as perfect as they look."

"I think that's the largest smile I've ever seen from you." She lifted a hand to touch his cheek, his mouth. "My Kostya. We really belong to each other now, don't we?"

He caught her hand and placed a kiss on her palm. "Yes."

"You may kiss me again. If you wish to."

His hand smoothed her hair and moved along her neck. "I very much wish to kiss you again."

The kiss began much as the other had, soft and sweet and poignant. Then it grew. His lips caressed her mouth, and their arms entwined, and they pulled each other closer, discovering passion in all its beauty and all its power. Konstantin's lips found the scar on the corner of her jaw, and the kisses he placed there left her feeling giddy. Then his lips brushed across her ear. "Do you wish me to stop?" he whispered.

"No." She kissed him again in the dying firelight. He nuzzled into her neck, making a burning path along her skin with imploring lips and warm breath.

Four knocks that were so loud and so sudden that they made her flinch shook the door of the bedchamber. "Župan Konstantin!" Grigorii's voice.

Konstantin searched her face before turning to the door. "What is it?"

"A village is burning. We think we can catch the brigands if we hurry."

He turned back to her for a long moment, still breathing hard from their kisses. He looked down, then at the door, then at her again. "I have to go."

She nodded as disappointment and dread replaced the elation she'd experienced only moments before.

Konstantin rushed to the trunk and threw open the lid. "Have my horses saddled and send Risto with my armor," he called toward the door.

Suzana stood. Perhaps this was what it would be like to be married to a župan. He would always have responsibilities that outweighed her. And she was coming to realize how difficult it would be to watch him ride off and not know if or when he would return. She put another log on the fire. He'd need better lighting when he put on his armor.

She turned to watch him. His back was toward her as he stripped off the long tunic he'd worn beneath his wedding garments and replaced it with a shorter tunic, one that wouldn't impede him so much in battle, but not before she saw the grace and strength of his well-muscled body, from his neck all the way to his ankles. She'd never suspected that a human body could be so pleasing to the eye. When the bedchamber had swarmed with people, she'd been nervous about the process of man and wife coming together in the flesh. Now she ached inside that those sweet moments had been snatched away.

"Can I help?" She didn't know how to assist with his armor, wouldn't want to make an error that would make him less safe, but she wanted to support him in any way she could. That was her duty because she was his wife and because she loved him.

He pulled on a pair of trousers and turned to her, then clasped her arms and kissed her softly on the mouth. "Just promise you'll let me kiss you again when I get back."

She put her hand briefly to his cheek. "I promise." Now she had something new to add to her list of favorite things: not just autumn leaves and sunsets and silk but also her husband's kisses.

Another knock on the door.

"Just a moment," Konstantin called. He went back to his chest of clothing and grabbed a small knife. He went to the bed and pulled the blankets completely back. Then he pulled his clothing aside and made a small slice into his own thigh.

Suzana gasped as she stepped toward the bed. "What are you doing?" She kept her voice quiet, not wanting the men on the other side of the door to hear. Why on earth had he cut himself?

He gathered a bit of blood on the knife, then wiped it onto the bedsheets. "Someone will check. And if they don't find blood, they'll think something is wrong with you or something is wrong with me. I think it's better this way."

"But . . ." She couldn't think of what else to say. He was on his way to battle. Surely a cut large enough to bleed would make him more vulnerable, yet he'd done it to keep her secret and protect her reputation.

"I wish I didn't have to go." He went to the door and slid the bolt free, letting in Risto and Miladin.

Chapter Twenty-One
In Search of Justice

When Konstantin found the men who had burned his village and interrupted his wedding night, he was going to do something truly awful to them. Impalement, perhaps.

"What do you know about the fire and the men who started it?" he asked Miladin, who walked beside him.

"Almost nothing. Grigorii spoke to the messenger. Neither of us wanted to disturb you, but we assumed you'd want to know."

"You were right to tell me."

"You could stay, lord. It's your wedding night."

The pull to stay with his bride and bask in all their shared expressions of love was strong, almost overwhelming, but what type of župan sent his men off to do his duty for him? Especially tonight. Battle against the elusive brigands and tension with Župan Teodore had strained the garrison. Most of them had probably drunk too much wine while relaxing at the wedding banquet. Konstantin wasn't the most experienced of the men, nor the most skilled, but he was their leader, and the sting of disappointment and the underlying rage at being ripped from Suzana's side had cleared his mind. "It is my duty to lead my garrison and defend my people and their homes. That doesn't change, not even on my wedding day."

They crossed the bailey swiftly. Most of the men were already armored and mounted on their horses.

"Dragomir and my grandfather's men will remain here, yes?" he asked Miladin.

"Yes, lord. Unless you'd like us to ask for their aid. The messenger reported less than ten brigands."

"I don't think we'll need their help." But Konstantin could trust Dragomir and his grandfather to protect his interests should Župan Nikola turn on Rivak.

Miladin gave Konstantin a leg up onto Perun. "It should be a simple enough matter to track them down and capture or kill them. But the ones yesterday set a trap. I recommend caution, lord. I assume this is revenge."

"Agreed." Konstantin counted his men-at-arms. Twenty in all would ride. "How long did the drinking last after I left the banquet?"

"Those who overindulged are remaining behind. Enough time has passed that the men who ride are mostly sober."

Mostly rather than completely sober was not ideal, but danger and the crisp night air ought to keep them alert. If there was any chance of stopping the brigands preying on his lands tonight, he had to take it.

He glanced back. A figure wrapped in a cloak stood near a torch on the top of the keep. Suzana, watching him go. When they rode from the grody, he kept his eyes forward. But his thoughts darted more than once back to the woman he left behind.

The scent of smoke grew stronger as they approached the village. Konstantin dismounted from Perun and switched to Svarog, then maneuvered his new mount next to Grigorii's stallion, Yarilo.

"You don't suppose Župan Teodore is involved, do you?" Konstantin had shown his neighbor dishonor. He expected dishonor in return rather than pillage, but slighted men were sometimes unpredictable.

Grigorii scanned ahead and to the side. "I can't be certain, lord, but I think the brigands are the same ones we dealt with yesterday. Their last attack was before you asked Župan Teodore to leave Rivakgrad. That attack can't have been revenge for withdrawing hospitality, so I don't suppose this one is either."

Konstantin slowed Svarog as they reached the village outskirts. Something wasn't right. The flames had taken hold of the buildings, but none of the buildings had fallen in on themselves. Given the distance between the grad and the village, he would have expected the fires to be more advanced. "It would have taken some time for the messenger to come to Rivakgrad. And we rode swiftly, but the distance still eats up time. Why do the fires look as though they were set only recently?"

Grigorii shook his head. Even in the poor lighting, bewilderment touched his expression. "The messenger said brigands set the village on fire. Maybe they started at one end and the fire spread after he left?"

Konstantin urged Svarog along the road through the village center. Heat from the flames on either side turned the road into an oven. Svarog whinnied and grunted and seemed reluctant to continue. Konstantin urged him on. None of the homes they passed seemed to have been burning any longer than the ones at the edge of the village.

Grigorii followed, though his horse was even more reluctant than Svarog to walk between the burning cottages. Merophs ran about with buckets of water, and others used cloths to fight the flames. Grigorii stopped one of them. "Is everyone accounted for?"

"Yes. Most left to attend the wedding and stayed with friends or kin in the grad. Those of us who returned tonight are all accounted for."

"Which way did the brigands go?" Konstantin asked. Catching them was his highest priority. He had to prevent this same thing from happening to any of his other villages.

The man pointed north. "They left not long ago, lord. They took a trail that leads through the woods."

Konstantin peered into the dark distance. From those woods, the bandits would have been close enough to attack this village and the one where he'd been trapped the day before.

"I can lead you to where the path leaves the road, lord," the meroph said.

Konstantin nodded and pushed his horse past the worst of the flames to where several of his men had gathered. "Bojan—keep four men with you and help the villagers put the fires out. We'll come back once we've defeated the brigands." His words expressed confidence he didn't feel—the bandits had outsmarted him more than once. But perhaps tonight Konstantin would end their threat once and for all.

"Yes, lord." Bojan wasn't normally the type who liked to be left behind, but Konstantin didn't wish to leave any of the younger, less experienced men in charge of organizing the fire fight. He wanted Miladin and Grigorii with him, and he didn't think Kuzman or Zoran were ready to deal with fire again, not after nearly dying in the church the day before.

Konstantin turned to his men. "These brigands have menaced our lands long enough. Accept their surrender only if they give it quickly; otherwise, show them no mercy." He turned to their guide. "Can you ride?"

"Yes, lord."

"Grigorii, get a horse for him."

Grigorii borrowed Bojan's mount for the meroph, and then the group rode until they reached the woods. Their guide slowed on the edge of the trees, as did the rest of the party.

"Are you familiar with the woods?" Konstantin asked the meroph. Most of the village's inhabitants would gather firewood, mushrooms, and berries from the forest.

"Yes, lord. I can show you." He led them along the main path, one wide enough for the horses, though branches brushed against Konstantin's leg, and he had to duck often to avoid low-hanging boughs. The soft tap of a drizzling rain sounded on the nearby leaves. Maybe that would help those fighting the fire.

The meroph stopped, dismounted, and walked back to Konstantin. "I think I saw a campfire through the trees."

Konstantin dismounted, as did Miladin and Grigorii. The four of them walked forward, leading their horses. Miladin pointed out the soft orange glow first. The flames themselves weren't visible, but the warm light they cast on the surrounding trees was.

Konstantin didn't want the brigands to escape again. They might have sentries, but this time, they had no church to hide inside. The wind through the trees was strong enough to drown out the sound of normal footsteps, and the rain was picking up. It, too, would mask their sounds, especially if they left their horses behind.

"Miladin, I want you to lead half the men around to the south. I'll take the others around to the north. If they see you, attack then. If not, wait for me, and we'll attack from both sides at once."

"Yes, lord." Miladin headed back to the others.

"Shall I come with you, lord?" Grigorii asked.

"Yes." Konstantin grabbed his horse's lead rope so he could tie it to a tree.

Grigorii glanced at Svarog. "We'll do more damage if we attack from the saddle. They might flee, and having at least part of our group mounted gives us flexibility."

A destrier was a mighty weapon, and the prospect of fighting with a horse that could be positively savage toward the enemy was appealing, maybe more so after the night's earlier disappointments. Konstantin mounted Svarog again, and Grigorii mounted Yarilo. The meroph, now on foot, led the way, finding paths large enough for the horses. The branches were low, and Konstantin and the other men on horseback leaned over till they were nearly flat against their mounts' backs. An owl hooted in the distance, and the wind and rain whistled through the branches.

The small path widened, then reached a tree that split the path in two, though the division was not even. The meroph took the narrower path, but Svarog wouldn't be able to make the pass between tree trunks, so Konstantin went the other way. The glow of the enemy's fire growing nearer directed them onward.

Svarog snorted, and his weight shifted. Momentum pulled horse and rider downward. The crack of splintering wood sounded, and Konstantin tumbled through a shower of straw and leaves. He smashed into dirt and stone, and the weight of his horse rolled over his left leg. Svarog screamed in the shrill way that only a horse in horrible pain could.

Dizziness and nausea pummeled Konstantin like a massive wave. A combination of clouds and thick trees meant little moonlight made it beyond the edge of the pit he'd fallen into. He reached for Svarog's thrashing head and tried to calm him in the dark, but the horse's cries and the flaying of his legs became even more intense. Konstantin heard his name being called, but he kept his focus on Svarog.

Sharp pains in his own side and leg sent firm protests as Konstantin tried to move. He patted Svarog's head, then followed the horse's outline down his neck to his back, wincing as he moved. He expected Svarog to find his feet, but the horse remained on his side. Konstantin's knee bumped into something, and he explored it with his fingers. A thick stick, protruding from the ground. He followed it upward to the sharpened tip.

He heard his name again, but the sound echoed strangely in his ears, and when he tried to answer, his mouth was too dry. He patted Svarog again, running his hand along the mighty destrier's side until he brushed against a stave much like the one his knee had bumped into, only this one was slick with warm liquid because it had pierced his favorite horse.

"Oh, Svarog." Konstantin's voice cracked. He didn't need better lighting to know his horse was doomed. "I should have gone on foot."

Svarog's thrashing grew less vigorous, and Konstantin's ears finally recognized Kuzman's voice. "Župan Konstantin, can you hear me?"

"Yes. Don't come down. He's dying, but his legs could still break bones."

"And you?"

Konstantin's head swam, and points all along his side burned. He was injured, but he could make it home. If by some miracle the brigands hadn't heard his crash and Svarog's cries, he could even direct the attack against them.

Another voice shouted. "Watch out!"

A shower of dirt and pebbles trickled across Konstantin's shoulders and quickly grew to a deluge. He threw his hands up to protect his head as the landslide's contents grew larger and more dangerous. A boulder smacked into his shoulder, then one bashed into his side. The dust choked his throat and made him cough. Svarog screamed again. A burst of pain radiated from the back of Konstantin's head, and then he remembered nothing more.

Chapter Twenty-Two
Casualty and Crisis

Suzana had tried falling asleep after Konstantin and his men departed, but sleep had proven elusive, so she'd gone to the grody's small chapel. Hours later, she still knelt there, holding a candle and praying for her husband's safe return.

Most of the day had felt like a dream. A beautiful dream that she'd been pulled from the moment that knock on the door had come. And if Konstantin didn't come back . . . it would turn into a nightmare.

She couldn't tell how quickly the night passed; she only knew the party hadn't returned, because the stables were across the bailey from the chapel. She'd hear the fall of hooves when they returned. For now, silence gripped the grody. The inhabitants and guests slept on, ignorant of the župan's call to leave his bride on his wedding night.

If her husband did not return, Rivak would be vulnerable. No one would follow her leadership, not when she'd been Konstantin's wife less than a day and had no child. They were unlikely to support Ivan either, not while he was young and frail and promised to Sivi Gora. Would Župan Teodore try to take the župa? And would Župan Nikola help him? The uncertainty swirled round, for her, for the family, and for the župa.

The clomp and thud of hoof beats sounded from the courtyard, strong and steady, moving faster than expected across the bailey. As she rushed from the chapel, a rider flashed past her, then dismounted before the keep and ran up the stairs.

A messenger bringing good news wouldn't be in such a desperate hurry, especially when most of the grody's occupants still slept. Konstantin had ridden with the men, so they couldn't be rushing back to consult with their župan. A messenger now would be searching for Konstantin's grandfather or his aunt . . . or his wife.

Risto waited outside the chapel, no doubt part of Konstantin's increased security. "What does it mean?" Suzana asked as she darted across the bailey, terrified of what the messenger had to say but in desperate need of his information.

Risto kept pace with her. "I know not, my lady. Perhaps they need reinforcements."

"If reinforcements were needed, wouldn't the messenger have gone to the garrison? Or one of the other župans?"

Risto's face fell. "Perhaps he brings ill tidings."

That was what Suzana feared, and that fear was growing. If death had visited one of the men-at-arms, there would be little urgency to reach the grody before the main party. If something had happened to the župan, speed might mean everything.

A torch and two shadows appeared not far ahead of them as Suzana and Risto went to the corridor with the family's rooms. They stopped outside Konstantin's bedchamber and knocked gently. When there was no answer, they pushed inside.

Moments later, Suzana and Risto caught up to them: Dama Zorica and Bojan.

"What's happened?" Suzana asked.

Bojan turned to her and bowed quickly. "Župan Konstantin has been injured. I rode ahead to prepare his treatment and warn you, my lady."

"How bad are his wounds?"

Bojan's chin quivered for a moment before stilling. "I pray he still lives."

Horror and dizziness washed over her. Her legs felt weak, like they could no longer fully support her. Konstantin might be alive, and if he was, he would need all the help she could give him. And if he was not alive . . . then as his widow, she would need to look to the concerns of his family and his župa. "Is there a physician?"

"The last physician did not return from Maritsa. I stopped to wake Magdalena, Miladin's wife. She's stitched up several members of the garrison over the last few years." Bojan glanced at his own arm. "She's coming here."

Dama Zorica excused herself to wake the servants. Risto set to work arranging the bed linens.

"How did it happen?" Suzana asked.

"The brigands set a trap. A pit like hunters might use to capture large game. Konstantin fell into it. The staves didn't pierce him, but part of the side collapsed and buried him. We had to dig him out. He . . . he wasn't conscious when I left, but he still breathed."

Suzana put a hand on the hearth to steady herself. "Were they targeting him when they trapped him in the church and when they drew him into a pit?"

Bojan moved his shoulders in frustration. "I'm not sure, my lady. I wasn't there either time. That's twice I haven't been there when he's needed me."

"He needs you now. We have to assume he's still in danger. As is his family." If Konstantin were killed, the role of župan might fall to Ivan, and despite the boy's courage, he remained an easy target.

"The brigands were all killed. Miladin's group finished them off while the others dug out Konstantin and I oversaw the battle against the fires." His tone spoke of disapproval for his role.

"Someone hired the man who threw me in the river. He could have hired the brigands too. He remains a danger."

Bojan stared into the fire chamber's dying embers. He added a few logs and used the fire iron to coax them into a steady burn. "The attempts on your life seem a long time ago. I hadn't thought to connect them, but you're right. It's best we assume a threat remains."

"We need extra guards. For Konstantin. And for Ivan." Suzana couldn't let anything more happen to either of them. Rivak's garrison had been working so hard for so long. The German mercenaries were still unknown, untrusted, but Konstantin and Ivan's grandfather might step in. Blood was involved, and his heir. "If we need more men, we can ask help of Sivi Gora."

Bojan nodded. "I'll ask Župan Đurad to lend us a few guards."

As Bojan left, Jasmina and Dama Zorica entered carrying water. Bojan and Jasmina drew away for a moment, long enough to say a few words to each other and for Jasmina to place a hand on her father's shoulder. A woman Suzana recognized as Miladin's wife came not long after and requested more light and hotter water.

Between tasks, Dama Zorica put her arm around Suzana's shoulders for a quick embrace. "If this will be too hard for you, you don't have to stay."

It would be hard; she could sense it. But not knowing, not being there—that might be harder.

The scuffle of boots sounded in the hallway and grew louder. Miladin and Grigorii carried Konstantin between them. Suzana resisted the urge to run to them and stayed out of the way while they placed her husband on his bed. He was barely recognizable. Dirt and mud coated him, and in some places, the layers were thicker and soaked with blood.

The bedchamber swarmed with activity, but Suzana caught the worried looks that passed between Miladin and Magdalena.

"You had best remove the armor and everything else so I can see the damage," Magdalena said to Miladin, Grigorii, and Risto. Dama Zorica and Jasmina prepared the water, and Suzana remained frozen in the center of the room.

Her husband's face showed little emotion when awake and none now, but that might have been because dirt and mud cloaked it so completely. Grigorii tugged off one of Konstantin's boots, then removed the other. His displeasure at the current situation was easy to pick out, as was Miladin's concern.

"What happened to the brigands?" Dama Zorica asked.

"We caught them by surprise." Miladin pulled Konstantin's tunic free. "One or two may have escaped, but none we caught survived long enough to question."

Magdalena examined the swollen, discolored skin that lined Konstantin's side. Suzana felt herself sway. His skin had been perfection when he'd pulled the same tunic on not so long ago. Grigorii took her elbow. "You look like you ought to sit down, my lady."

She let the satnik guide her to the trunk. "Has he ever had an injury like this before?"

Grigorii glanced at his župan. "A rival for rule of Rivak once tried to kill him, but . . . I think this is worse. He's never before been buried alive."

Buried alive. Suzana felt as if she could barely breathe. "Will he recover?"

"Magdalena will have a better idea than I do."

Miladin's wife was currently stitching closed a gash on Konstantin's shoulder. Suzana thought it unwise to interrupt. She glanced at Konstantin. She'd once been frightened by his power, but now it was his vulnerability that had her terrified.

Suzana woke when a crack of sunlight shone on her face. She lay near the hearth, on the same cushioned bench where Konstantin had kissed her only the evening before. She couldn't remember falling asleep, but someone had covered her with a blanket. Last she remembered, Magdalena, Miladin, Grigorii, and Dama Zorica had been sitting with her husband. Now Lidija perched on the bed beside her brother, and Jasmina and Bojan sat on a trunk across the room. All eyes fixed on her as she sat upright.

"How is he?" she asked.

"He hasn't woken." Lidija's voice wobbled, and she quickly clenched her jaw shut.

Konstantin lay in the bed's center. Suzana stood and approached him. He'd been washed the night before, and then the bed linens had been changed so he could rest without the grime from the pit. The bruises along his face seemed darker now, as did the ones on his shoulders. The rest of his body was covered by a blanket.

Suzana sat on the side of the bed opposite from Lidija and studied her husband's face. The scab on his lip had darkened. She brought a finger gently to his mouth, felt the air move with each of his breaths, and remembered her promise to let him kiss her again. Slowly, she lowered her head and kissed him gently on the forehead.

"What does he need?" she asked.

Lidija blinked away a tear and shook her head. "I don't know."

Suzana wasn't sure what her husband needed, but she could sense what her new sister-by-marriage needed. Suzana stood and walked around the bed, then drew Lidija into an embrace. One sob escaped, and then a slew of them racked the girl's body, as if she'd been holding it all in and was now free to grieve. She was scared for her brother. Suzana was scared for him too.

She told Lidija what she most wanted someone to tell her. "He loves you too much to leave you so soon. Time and prayers. That's what he needs."

Perhaps that was what Konstantin needed, but Rivak needed leadership, so as the day passed, Suzana discussed security with Bojan and hosting responsibilities with Dama Zorica. The boys remained away, distracted by the new bodyguards arranged by Župan Đurad. Konstantin remained unconscious through several changing of the guards and three visits from Magdalena and Dama Zorica checking his bandages.

Suzana's feet felt heavy as she stepped toward the hall for the evening meal. She would have rather stayed by Konstantin's side instead of dressing in formal clothing and going to supper, but failure to appear at the meal would signal to all that the župan and his župa were in grave danger. Giving Rivak the appearance of strength would do her husband more good that evening than sitting beside his unresponsive body.

Miladin stepped to her side when she entered. "May I escort you to your seat, Dama Suzana?"

She nodded. As they crossed the hall in full sight of the guests from the wedding, she felt all eyes on her. "Have you heard anything I should be aware of?"

"Župan Nikola will leave tomorrow morning, as planned. Župan Dragomir had intended to leave after this meal but has offered to stay longer, if that would be suitable. Župan Đurad says he cannot stay indefinitely but can extend his visit for some time, if that is your desire."

"And the mercenaries?" Suzana and Konstantin had planned to discuss their hiring today. Suzana hoped she wouldn't have to make that decision without Konstantin's input. Ulrich and Otto looked like competent warriors, but she hadn't seen them in action, and even if they were proficient with their weapons, it didn't mean their entire company would be as skilled. And loyalty, too, was vital. Assuming Konstantin recovered, could she trust them with her husband's life when he went to fight for the sultan in the spring?

"They will want a decision by the time Župan Đurad leaves. Has Župan Konstantin woken?"

"Not yet, but that does not need to become common knowledge."

"No one will hear it from me, my lady." Miladin seated her at the head of the women's table.

Župan Nikola approached her and gave a bow of respect. "My condolences, Dama Suzana, and my hopes for your husband's speedy recovery. Please know that I am at your service should you need anything."

"Thank you." His sentiment was right, but she didn't fully trust him. When tempted by Župan Teodore, he hadn't said he would refrain from trying to seize Rivak if Konstantin were killed, only that it would be dishonorable to do anything against Miroslav's son before a crisis emerged. Now that crisis was here. With Župan Teodore some distance from Rivak and Župan Nikola near its heart, would he take the opportunity to turn events to his benefit?

Župan Dragomir and Dama Isidora came to greet her when Župan Nikola went to the men's table.

Župan Dragomir helped his wife into the seat beside Suzana's, then said, "We will pray for Župan Konstantin's quick recovery. I would have ridden out with him had he asked. We stand with Rivak, and with your family, regardless of what happens."

"Thank you."

"What do you need?" Dama Isidora asked.

Suzana felt herself smiling. She needed the meal over quickly so she could return to Konstantin's side, but that might show weakness, and that would be dangerous. "I would be grateful if you and your contingent could stay until tomorrow afternoon."

Dama Isidora ran her fingers across the table linen. "Župan Nikola is leaving tomorrow morning, correct?"

"Yes."

Župan Dragomir nodded. "We will stay until he has left and all his contingent has faded from view. Longer if needed."

Next Župan Đurad visited her. She supposed he was family now, but she'd always been intimidated by the combination of his stern face, powerful status, and fierce reputation. Overhearing his opinion of her—a girl who was too young to know her own mind—had done little to lessen the uneasiness. Yet he was their surest ally, and he was responsible for her marriage to Konstantin. Even if Konstantin never recovered, his influence had changed her for the better, and she would be forever grateful to the severe župan for his role as matchmaker.

As she turned to the župan, she tried to maintain a face as devoid of emotion as her husband's normally was, but she wasn't sure she'd succeeded. "Miladin said you might be able to extend your stay in Rivakgrad. I would be most appreciative of your presence for a while longer."

"When the snow covers the top third of the mountains." Župan Đurad gestured to the north, and though she could not see the peaks through the grody walls, she knew the landscape. "I can stay that long, but no longer. I am also willing to leave a few of my men behind until spring as bodyguards for my grandsons."

Suzana locked eyes with the župan, waiting for the catch.

"I can do the same thing next winter, and in the spring, they'll bring Ivan to Sivi Gora for the summer."

Ivan and Danilo sat with men who were not part of Rivak's garrison. They seemed happy. But this wasn't her decision to make. "I will pass your offer on to my husband when he is recovered."

One of the župan's eyebrows moved ever so slightly, as if surprised she hadn't immediately agreed to his offer. He glanced at Ivan. "Very well."

Dama Isidora leaned next to Suzana's ear as Župan Đurad walked to the head of the men's table. "I don't think he is used to people who do not immediately acquiesce to his plans."

Suzana felt heat rising along her neck. "I won't hand Ivan over unless Konstantin believes it is a good decision."

Dama Isidora smiled. "You did no wrong in putting the decision off. I only wish to point out that the župan is used to getting his way. Except from Konstantin. And now, from Konstantin's wife."

Suzana prayed she would remain Konstantin's wife and not his widow.

Chapter Twenty-Three
Scraps of Time

Svarog's cries filled Konstantin's head. Clouds cloaked the moon, and tree branches veiled the stars, yet Konstantin could see every stake that had impaled his warhorse. He tried to reach for Svarog's muzzle, to give the poor animal a bit of comfort. Svarog snapped at Konstantin's hand. Konstantin tried to pull away, but something held him in place. He glanced down to see a stake protruding from his lamellar corselet. Then the rocks began falling on him. He couldn't breathe, couldn't move, couldn't avoid the pain and destruction gaping after him like a wolf on the hunt.

Konstantin gasped. The image disappeared.

Just a memory distorted by dream, but waking didn't bring an end to the pain, and the terror he'd felt lingered, strong enough to taste.

"Konstantin?"

The voice was soft, hesitant. Feminine. He turned toward it, or at least, he tried. His limbs were in mutiny, refusing to obey the orders he gave them. He could force neither his eyes nor his mouth to open. Pain pulsed all around his head. Most headaches he felt in the temples or along the back of his head, but this one hurt everywhere.

Something moist and cool touched his forehead. Not warm enough to be blood and more damp than wet. The pain eased ever so slightly. Low voices murmured in the distance. He couldn't understand them, so he concentrated on the square of his forehead that didn't hurt quite as much as the rest of him.

He slept. He didn't remember falling asleep, but he must have because things felt different when he awoke again. Pain still laid siege to his head. To his side, too, and his left leg.

His eyes finally opened to a blurry image of his bedchamber. Either the shutters and curtains were pulled, or it was night outside, because only firelight from the hearth lit the chamber. He turned his head toward the window, looking for telltale cracks of light around the curtain. None showed, so the sun was down.

More came into focus as he stared. A shadow by the door became a figure. A guard? He'd never had a guard in his bedchamber before. There was no need. A causeway, wall, and watchtower protected the grody, and only those considered trustworthy were free to walk about the bailey and the keep. But that wasn't entirely true. Some of the wedding guests had proven menacing.

The wedding. Another shadow near the bed, in a chair, with slow, barely audible breaths.

Konstantin squinted. "Suzana?" His voice left his parched throat as a croak.

The woman in the chair didn't stir, but the man across the room did. In only a few heartbeats, he was at the side of the bed.

"My župan?" Miladin, but with dark shadows under his eyes.

Konstantin swallowed, trying to work some moisture into his mouth. "Why are you here?" The question came out slowly, each word an effort.

"Your wife requested a guard for you, lord." Miladin grimaced. "Something you both have in common, I suppose. A desire to protect each other when danger is stalking."

Konstantin hadn't insisted on guards standing watch inside Suzana's bedchamber. He turned his eyes to his bride. He'd expected to wake up the morning after the wedding with her sleeping nearby, but not in this manner. "I'm thirsty."

Miladin strode to the door and pulled it open with a creak. Another man—Konstantin couldn't tell who in the dim light—carried on a short, hushed conversation with Miladin. In the meantime, Konstantin studied his wife. Her head tilted back against the wall. As much as Konstantin admired the elegance of her neck, the position didn't look comfortable.

"Shouldn't she be sleeping in a proper bed?" he asked when Miladin returned.

"She wished to stay by your side, lord."

Konstantin glanced at the bed. He lay in its center, but Suzana was small, and the bed was large. "There's room here."

"Shall I move her?"

Konstantin managed a nod. "And tell me what happened. I remember the pit."

Miladin took a deep breath. "Kuzman and Grigorii dug you out. The brigands we went for are no more."

"Any members of the garrison harmed?"

"No."

That was a weight off Konstantin's shoulders. "The village?"

"Bojan and the others couldn't save the buildings already burning, but they kept the damage from spreading. Half the homes there were uninhabited anyway."

"And Svarog?" Konstantin already knew the answer, but he asked anyway.

"I'm sorry, lord. He couldn't be saved. We barely saved you."

Konstantin squeezed his eyes closed. Poor Svarog. He shouldn't mourn so much for a horse, not when far heavier losses plagued Rivak.

Miladin waited, and when Konstantin had no further questions, he turned to Suzana. The instant Miladin's hand touched her shoulder, she jerked awake. She inhaled sharply and stared at Miladin with wide eyes.

"My lady, he's awake."

Her eyes found Konstantin's a moment later, and she simultaneously smiled and began to cry. She moved to sit on the bed and ran her hand over his forehead, pushing back his hair. "We've all been so worried." Her eyes searched his face. "How do you feel?"

Miladin had disappeared into the hallway, leaving them alone. Konstantin considered telling her he was fine, but he wasn't. Weariness gripped him, pain nipped at him, and he mourned the loss of his warhorse. "I might ask to bow out of the post-wedding festivities."

Her fingers, still running through his hair, paused. "What do you mean?"

"There's a banquet planned, isn't there?"

"Our wedding was almost three days ago. All the guests have left, save my father with his men and your grandfather with his."

That should have been his first question, but he'd assumed he'd slept for a few watches of the night rather than a few days. His body had never taken that long to sleep before.

He was saved from coming up with a reply when Miladin let Risto in with a cup of something. Watered wine, he discovered when Suzana helped him sip it.

The liquid helped calm the burning in his throat. It did little to ease the panic eating away at him. Three days. All manner of disasters could have happened in three days. "What happened while I was recovering?"

"Everything is well. Your family is all in good health, save you. No members of the garrison are injured. We've received no reports of bandits or arsonists preying on Rivak. And your guests wished you a speedy recovery. Župan Dragomir and Dama Isidora left behind a single man to act as messenger when you recovered or . . ." Suzana's voice drifted off. "Well, you've woken, so that will be the news he brings them."

Konstantin closed his eyes. "I'm glad Župan Teodore was not here to take advantage of my weakness." What a nightmare that would have been, to wake up to a struggle between his garrison and Župan Teodore's. Or to Rivak already conquered by its neighbor. Had that happened, he likely wouldn't have lived to wake at all.

"You have loyal allies. Your grandfather and Župan Dragomir would have stood for your interests."

Konstantin had enemies, but he also had friends. Suzana seemed to understand that as well as he did. He studied her face. The room was only dimly lit, but it showed enough. He found beauty when he saw her, but he also recognized the signs of worry and weariness. He glanced at the chair she'd been sitting in. "I hope you haven't been spending all your nights in a chair."

"Not all, my lo—my husband."

My husband. She'd never called him that before. Until recently, it hadn't been accurate. "There is room beside me."

She glanced down. "So there is, but I did not wish to disturb your recovery, nor be in the way when Magdalena or your aunt came to check on you."

Magdalena came in then to see to him, and Suzana moved to the hearth. Konstantin answered Magdalena's questions and did his best to hide his grimaces when she changed his bandages and checked his cuts and contusions. The skin had broken in only a few places, but bruises covered his body.

"The skin around the sutures doesn't look infected." Magdalena rubbed a salve over a cut on his shoulder. "Other than a few of your ribs, your bones seem whole, which is nothing short of a miracle, given what I heard of the trap."

The trap. Had it been a trap rather than an abandoned hunting pit? He'd not had time to think it through before, but bandits had set a trap in the church. Surely this had been planned too. And he'd ridden right into it.

"I can't give you orders, lord, but I would discourage any training with the garrison until the ribs are healed. You need to rest as much as you can until your health is restored."

Rest? He'd been in bed for three days. He had a župa to take care of, one fragile enough to feel a few days' neglect.

Risto stepped forward as Magdalena left and helped him change into a clean tunic, then pulled the linens from the bed so they could be washed. Miladin had to hold Konstantin up while the fresh linens were laid. The whole process was excruciatingly painful. Mortifying as well. How had he become so weak and helpless?

"Magdalena is right, lord," Miladin said softly while Risto straightened the bedding. "And I'd say that even if she weren't my wife. You must rest. Everything in Rivak is well now that we know you're on the mend. Dama Suzana managed the guests and their departures with acumen."

"She's a fast learner." A blessing, because he'd planned for an entire winter together and part of a spring before she had to take over temporary custody of their župa. The bandits had altered the timeline.

Miladin lowered him back to the bed. "Yes, and she's hardly left your side."

Suzana approached again and pulled the blankets over him.

The shock of how weak he was left him flustered. And tired. So he followed the advice of those around him and went to sleep without learning any more of what had happened while he'd been unconscious.

When he woke again, slits of sunlight broke through the edges of the curtains, and the fire in the hearth had died. Kuzman sat near the door, whittling on a stick with a small knife. And Suzana lay by his side. Her head rested on a pillow, turned slightly toward him. Not a single flaw marred her skin other than the scar along her jaw. Her eyes remained closed, her perfect lips relaxed in sleep. He reached over to smooth her hair, but the moment he lifted his arms, angry bruises woke all along his torso. He inhaled sharply enough for Kuzman to look up.

The loyal soldier approached the bed with hardly a sound and spoke in a whisper. "Lord, I am grateful to see you on the mend."

"Thank you for digging me out of that pit."

Kuzman's eyes stayed on the floor. "I should have scouted ahead. Or gone down into that pit at once to get you out, before the landslide."

Konstantin shook his head slightly. He had a vague memory of Kuzman calling to him from the surface, but Konstantin had been too focused on his stallion. "Svarog would have broken your bones. Or we would have both been trapped in the landslide."

Kuzman still wouldn't meet his eyes. Guilt? Embarrassment that he served a župan who was currently as helpless as a baby? "What would you have me do, lord?" Kuzman's face finally softened. "The boys are eager to see you. Your aunt and sister as well."

Konstantin glanced at Suzana. She still slept. Kuzman had whispered. He doubted Ivan and Danilo would do the same, and Miladin's report that Suzana had remained at Konstantin's side meant she needed her sleep, especially if she'd fallen into the habit of sleeping in a chair. "I will see them when Dama Suzana awakes."

A smile creased Kuzman's bearded face. "Every bridegroom should have the chance to watch his bride wake in private. Shall I wait in the hall, lord?"

"Yes. Thank you."

Kuzman shut the door quietly behind him. A soft murmur met Konstantin's ears—probably another man in the hall acting as guard or runner.

Suzana's breaths formed a soft, slow rhythm, something he could hear only when he concentrated. She looked at peace, and he tried to memorize every little detail. The sweep of her eyelashes, the curves of her ear, the straight line of her nose, and her mouth—still the shape of a recurve bow.

The light grew brighter, but Konstantin wasn't in any hurry to get on with the day. Getting out of bed was going to hurt, and he was perfectly content watching his wife. No. Not perfectly content. Only pain and an acknowledgment that she needed sleep kept him from waking Suzana and kissing her the way he had on their wedding night.

She woke with a deep inhalation, a slight turn of her head, then the fluttering of eyelashes. A shy smile graced her mouth as she focused on him.

"Good morning," he said.

"And to you." She raised herself on an elbow. "How do you feel? Are you in pain?"

"Only when I move."

Her smile disappeared into a look of concern. She traced her finger across his forehead and along his cheek. Probably along a cut or a bruise, but her touch was gentle enough not to aggravate it. "I've been so afraid I would lose you when I had barely had a chance to know you. I've never had a friend before, not until I met you."

Never had a friend? It wasn't fair that she'd been given such a lonely and harsh childhood. But he was here now, and he'd survived the brigands' trap, and he would do what he could to be a good friend, husband, and lover to her. "We'll have time now." He prayed it would be a long time, but the summons of the sultan awaited him come spring.

She gave him a sad sort of smile. "You are the župan of Rivak. That is who you are, and with that title comes responsibility and danger. I understand that. It scares me, how little control I have over what your enemies do. And I know your duty to your župa will always come first, but I will be grateful for every scrap of time I can have with you."

She leaned in and planted a soft kiss on the corner of his mouth. He felt the smoothness of her lips, the warmth of her breath, and the tickle of a hair that fell onto his cheek. He turned to follow her mouth as she pulled away, wanting to turn that gentle kiss into something more.

She snuggled next to his shoulder. "Does this hurt any of your bruises?"

"No." The warmth of her body nestled along his side. Silence marked the passing of time, but it wasn't awkward. The quiet between them was comfortable.

"Do you remember what happened that night?" she asked. "I heard some from Grigorii and Miladin, but not all."

He told her what he remembered. His voice cracked when he recounted the injuries to Svarog, and she found his hand and laced her fingers through his. "It's different in my dreams. Twisted." He closed his eyes. "What a nightmare." He glanced at the top of her head, still touching his shoulder. "What happened after I was injured?"

She told him how she'd handled all the guests and each of their reactions. Her memory painted the picture completely for him. He wasn't surprised. He'd come to expect that from her—an eye for detail and a precise recounting of events.

"Do you think I should accept my grandfather's offer?" he asked when she finished.

She shifted, turning so she could see his face. "That is not my decision to make."

"Ivan is your brother now too. And I've come to value your insight."

She shifted onto her elbow again. "Your grandfather is a rock of a man . . . but I've seen how quickly things can change. When you came back and we weren't sure if you would live . . ." Her voice cracked, and she swallowed. "Kostya, I wasn't ready to lose you. I wasn't ready to be the župan's widow. I may understand Rivak's finances, but I don't know enough to command the garrison or run the household. Ivan will need to know all those things if he is to become župan. And since he is to become župan in Sivi Gora, he will best learn there."

Konstantin had heard much the same argument from his grandfather, but Suzana had experienced it. She knew what it was like to be overwhelmed with a sudden weight of responsibility. Heaven willing, Ivan would not be forced to shoulder Sivi Gora's leadership for many years. But men aged. They died in battle or from illness. "Ivan is still so young."

"He is. But your grandfather has not requested him for two more winters. And your grandfather does not show love in the same way your aunt does, but he has affection for Ivan. And for you." Mirth invaded her voice. "And you have given Ivan much practice in detecting small hints of affection from stern men."

He almost laughed but caught himself. Laughing would hurt.

Suzana's mouth parted in surprise. "You have a dimple. I don't think you've ever smiled enough for me to see it before. That, or it's been too dark." One of her fingers found a spot just above the growth of his beard.

He turned his head into her finger and gave it a kiss. "Mighty župans aren't supposed to have anything so childish as dimples. Keep it a secret."

"But I like your dimple." She studied his face. "What else don't I know about you?"

He gave her another smile. "You have the rest of autumn, all of winter, and part of spring to find out."

The clatter of feet sounded in the hallway. Voices of varying volumes, and the louder ones were easy to recognize. "I do believe my brother and cousin are waiting to see me."

"They have been most anxious for you. Shall I let them in?"

"Yes, but tell them not to jump on the bedding."

Suzana climbed from the bed. She wore a long tunic, and she fastened a belt around her waist. Her slim, very appealing waist. She opened the curtains but paused at the shutters. "Would you prefer them open or closed?"

"Open, but slowly."

She complied, watching for his reaction to the light after so many days with his eyes closed. She stopped with one shutter open and one still mostly shut. "I'll open them the rest of the way later." She smoothed her hair as she walked to the door, running her fingers through it and pushing it over her shoulders. Those were the types of motions Konstantin could be quite content watching for an entire morning.

Danilo and Ivan were in the room approximately two heartbeats after Suzana opened the door.

"I knew you'd get better!" Ivan shouted as he ran toward the bed.

"Be gentle," Suzana said. "His body is still bruised."

Ivan stopped abruptly at the side of the bed. Danilo slowed barely in time to avoid a collision. A grin had lit Ivan's face only a moment before, but now a different expression showed in his wide eyes and blanched skin. "But they said you were better!"

Danilo peered over Ivan's shoulder, his expression nearly identical to his cousin's.

Suzana took Ivan's hand. "The scrapes and bruises will take time to heal."

Ivan nodded gravely.

"Do I look so hideous?" Konstantin asked.

Ivan's mouth opened, then shut again. "I'll find the plate Lidija uses to see her reflection. I'm sure she'll let you borrow it long enough to see." Ivan crept closer.

Konstantin glanced at the doorway. No one besides the boys had come in yet, so he made the silliest face he could, and that drew a smile from his brother and a chuckle from Danilo.

"Grandfather's men taught me how to play Nine Men's Morris. And yesterday, I won. Danilo won too. We played it a lot. And Danilo is learning to use the bigger bow." Ivan's face grew less animated. "I'm still on the smaller one."

The boys sat gently on the bed, telling Konstantin all about what had happened since the wedding, and then Konstantin yawned, and Suzana led the boys away so he could rest. He watched her talk with them, fitting into his family so seamlessly. He'd known he needed a wife who could manage Rivak in his absence, but he hadn't expected to need her help so soon. Regardless, she was showing herself to be completely capable of her new role.

CHAPTER TWENTY-FOUR
BARGAINS

SOME THINGS COULDN'T BE PUT off until bruises were healed and headaches were gone. Konstantin waited one day further to see his grandfather and used the time to ponder his younger brother's future, trying to find a balance between what Ivan needed now and what Ivan would need when he became a župan.

When Grandfather arrived, he took his time visually examining Konstantin. "Are your injuries as painful as they look?"

Konstantin nodded slightly. He'd seen his reflection, knew his face was covered in dark bruises and small cuts. He still didn't feel strong enough to get out of bed, but he was at least propped into a sitting position. "I expect a complete recovery. Until then, I expect a good deal of pain."

His grandfather grunted, then gave his thanks when Miladin brought a chair for him. Suzana sat on a bench along the wall, giving the men a chance to discuss what was needed but staying nearby. Grandfather explained his plan, much as Suzana had already told him. He would leave a few of his men to ensure Ivan's safety and assist with his education and training. The men could stay until Konstantin returned from his military service to the sultan, giving the boy extra protection when his brother and most of Rivak's garrison were away.

"Until my betrothal, I would not have anticipated the need for a boy like Ivan to have a bodyguard. A personal physician, perhaps, but not his own dedicated protectors. Now . . ." Konstantin didn't finish. Someone had tried to kill Suzana, and the bandits had tried to kill him. His family was alive only by God's mercy. "Not this next summer but the summer after."

"That is my request, yes. From Easter until the harvest begins."

Ivan would be gone through all the best weather for training, but Sivi Gora had sword masters and horse masters nearly as good at Kuzman and Bojan, and perhaps having twice as many teachers would benefit the boy. Ivan's health was normally better in the warmer months, so he'd be less likely to fall ill while away from Aunt Zorica, who had always nursed him back to health, and from Danilo, who had always cheered him during his convalescence.

Konstantin would miss Ivan. But Ivan's fate had been determined with the betrothal of their parents—the second male born to the union was to become heir of Sivi Gora. "I will discuss it with Ivan and recommend he accept the agreement."

Grandfather raised an eyebrow. "He's young to be given a decision such as that."

"He is young, but he is also brave, and he will go with less reluctance if he feels he has been given a choice."

Grandfather tilted his head to the side. "That trait will serve him well when he is župan because a župan must be brave. I hope you will do all you can to show him that he is needed in the land he is destined to lead."

"I will."

"There is also the matter of the mercenaries. Do you wish to hire them?" his grandfather asked.

"I would prefer more time before I decide." If Konstantin hired Ulrich and Otto, he would either be depending on them to keep his lands safe in his absence or relying on them to supplement his own men while they waged battle. Trusting them with his family and župa or trusting them with himself.

"I would prefer you have more time, too, but the weather is changing. I will need to leave before you have completely recovered, and they will want an answer by then."

"Tell me what you know of them." Konstantin would rather have first-hand knowledge, but he trusted his grandfather.

"Ulrich once saved me from a Hungarian assassin. He was younger then, part of a company rather than leader of one. They served with me for five years. Ulrich is good at sensing danger, and you seem to be surrounded by it."

"And Otto?"

"I know he hates Hungarians."

"Rivak shares no borders with the Hungarians." They menaced Sivi Gora, but they had yet to threaten Konstantin's lands. "Instead, I am vassal to my greatest enemy. Can he serve with Turks? Or against them, should circumstances change?"

"I believe so. You can ask him, should you feel up to it in the next few days."

Konstantin would have to ration his energy, as there were pursuits more enticing than the hiring of mercenaries competing for his time and attention. But he was a župan before he was a husband. "I will meet with them as soon as I am able to do so in the hall rather than in my bedchamber."

His grandfather gave a nod of satisfaction.

Konstantin turned to Suzana. "Suzana, do you feel the finances are in order for us to hire Ulrich's company, should we wish to do so?"

"They are."

Grandfather raised an eyebrow as if to question Suzana's involvement. Konstantin had never met his grandmother, so he didn't know how that relationship had worked, but he saw no reason not to use his wife's mind when it was clearly sharper than his own on matters of money. Better to depend on a wife one trusted than to depend on a protovastar who had, by all evidence, cheated him.

Grandfather was right when he said Ivan needed more time in Sivi Gora. But he was wrong if he thought Suzana should not be involved in discussions about the župa. She, too, might be thrust into a role that would make the župa dependent on her leadership. She almost had been, with the trap that had killed Svarog and wounded Konstantin. Or perhaps not since a widow was generally of only moderate power unless she was regent for an heir, and the two of them had not as yet had time to create an heir.

"She is a merchant's daughter," Konstantin said. "Counting and allocation of coins is second nature to her, and her dowry will pay the men in question, should we hire them."

Grandfather glanced at Suzana, who met Konstantin's eyes and seemed pleased with his words of confidence.

"Your face has grown more and more pinched the longer I sit with you." Grandfather stood. "I will leave you to your recovery. And to your conversation with your brother."

The discussion with Ivan took place in Konstantin's bedchamber the next day, but this time, Konstantin sat on a chair rather than in his bed. The upright wooden back brushed against no fewer than five large bruises, but if he held very still, the pain remained steady and low.

"Ivan, someday you will be the župan of Sivi Gora," Konstantin said.

The boy had been told that often enough; it was no surprise, but Ivan's lips twisted with uncertainty. "I would rather stay here with you."

Konstantin looked at the ground, wishing for the same thing. Someday, Lidija would marry and live with her husband somewhere other than Rivak. If she married Decimir, she would be only a few hours' ride away. Sivi Gora was a much farther journey.

"We can't always make the choice that is most comfortable, Ivan. A župa needs a good leader. One who is brave and can lead them in battle. One who is caring and can see to the needs of the people. One who is close to God so he can bring down divine blessings."

Ivan looked at him with wide eyes. "But I can't lead anyone in battle. I can't even launch an arrow from a full-sized bow."

"Not yet, perhaps, but you are brave, and you are determined. The skill will come with time."

"What if it doesn't?"

"It will. And Grandfather wishes to be more involved in its development. He also wishes you to learn more about the župa you will one day lead."

"But I want to stay in Rivak."

"I wish you could stay. But more than that, I want you to be better prepared than I was when the time comes for you to be a župan. I knew Rivak, but I was expecting more time with Father. You must begin learning from Grandfather so that you can better serve the people of Sivi Gora when you lead them."

A frown was etched on the boy's face, but determination was present, too, in the set of his jaw and the steadiness of his eyes. "When will I have to go?"

"Not for another year and a half. You'll spend next summer here, then travel to Sivi Gora the summer after, but only for the summer. You'll be able to spend most of the year in Rivak until you're grown."

Ivan relaxed. A year and a half was a long time away for a boy who had seen only seven winters.

"Are you willing to go?"

Ivan nodded. "Yes, Kostya. I want to be a good župan, like you and like grandfather. And I still have much to learn."

The days that followed passed slowly for Konstantin. Poultices and soaks in a tub of hot water eased the pain of his injuries, and time reduced his weariness and the ache in his head. Suzana brought the ledger into his room to show him how they could fund the hiring of the mercenaries, and Konstantin met with the men in the hall. Walking there the first time left him winded, but as he met with the Germans more and more, he came to like Otto's easy laughter and feel a growing confidence in Ulrich's efficient manner.

When they reached an agreement with the Germans, Konstantin felt as if an enormous burden had been lifted. Suzana's dowry had once again kept him from complete failure as a župan. Though he, like Ivan, still had much to learn, it looked as if now he would have the time he needed.

Suzana felt a familiar dread when she saw her father in the hall, but she needed to speak with him. Ivan, Danilo, and their bodyguards sat across the room near the hearth, playing a game, and she had fewer reasons to fear her father when he was sober and others were nearby.

"You look tired." He said it without contempt, so perhaps it was not meant as an insult. It was undoubtedly true.

"My husband is recovering from serious wounds. Sleep has been a luxury."

Her father glanced round the hall. "It is not so rich a župa as I had imagined, but surely they have healers and servants to see to his needs."

She led the way to a table where they were unlikely to be overheard. "His friends and his servants do attend him. As do I because I wish to be with him as much as I can."

Konstantin's face relaxed when he slept, losing the sternness that had initially made her so wary. She could watch him for hours, remembering the way he'd kissed her, the way his mouth and his hands had made her yearn for something more.

Her father brushed a hand across his tunic of imported velvet. "It seems you have flown from one cage to another."

Life in Rivak was not a cage, but she didn't owe her father an explanation. He'd never shown concern over her happiness before, so she saw no need to confide in him now. "Father, we still don't know who tried to kill me. Or why. I ask for access to your ledger to see if anyone might have sought to hurt me in an attempt to hurt you."

"I do not carry all my ledgers with me. Most are at the villa, locked away."

Suzana pushed ahead. "But you usually take the most recent one with you wherever you go. Do you have it here?"

"I do."

"May I look?"

He nodded reluctantly. "You and your husband, if he wishes. No one else."

She understood the conditions. Secrecy had always been important to his success. "Thank you, Father. I also have another favor to ask of you."

"You may ask."

"My husband will need a good horse to carry him into battle come spring."

"So buy one. Your dowry was generous."

The dowry was generous, but hiring mercenaries and refilling the granaries had reduced it significantly, and they might need to hire mercenaries again should the sultan wish Rivak's service more than once. "Mercenaries are expensive."

"Yes, I know. I've been hiring men to protect my shipments and my person for several decades. I certainly hope Rivak will prosper, but I do not believe in pouring more money into expensive investments before they have given me any return."

"I see." She had hoped generosity would suit his pride, but she wouldn't beg her father for a warhorse. Still, Konstantin would need a good one, and she could hardly go searching about Serbia herself for the right animal. "I am not an expert on destriers. Perhaps you would be willing to act as my agent in a search for an appropriate animal at a fair price."

"An appropriate animal at a fair price will be costly."

"I know." She had brought the dowry to the marriage, but she now had few assets she could control without her husband's consent, even when she wished to surprise him. They would have to discuss whether a new destrier or a reserve of coin for future mercenaries would be of greater benefit. Unless . . . "Was the jewelry you purchased for my wedding costly?"

"Anything less would reflect poorly on our family's rising status."

She hesitated, fearful of offending. She might be tied to her husband rather than to her father now, but old habits, like a violent temper, did not disappear in an instant. "Of similar value to a destrier?"

"Yes."

"Now that the wedding is past, few people will see my jewelry and think well of my father's wealth. A fine horse, on the other hand, could prove key in securing battlefield victories for my husband, and those successes would be widely known."

The muscles along her father's jaw tightened. "You would trade your jewelry for a destrier that you are unlikely to ever ride?"

He made it sound like a large sacrifice—and she was giving up something beautiful—but Konstantin had given her friendship and love, and she wanted him to return to her after the sultan's battles. "I would . . . if it will not greatly displease you."

He studied her for a moment. Perhaps she should have asked Konstantin's grandfather to be her agent. Župan Đurad would know how to pick a good warhorse, but the distance between Rivak and Sivi Gora was great, and winter weather might prevent delivery of the horse until spring. She wanted her husband to have time with his horse before he depended on it in battle. The consequence of incompatibility or unfamiliarity could be deadly.

Her father smoothed his tunic. "If that is your wish, I will find a magnificent animal for you. Damascene or Thessalian, I think. Soon, so the young župan has ample training time."

"Thank you, Father. And the ledger?"

"I'll have it brought to you."

A week after his injury, Konstantin sat next to Suzana in the strongroom, studying the names in the ledger.

"This man, Giacomo Toderino, might have reason to feel he was taken advantage of." Suzana's finger pointed out the entry. "My father came off far better from their dealings. Do you know him?"

She'd asked him about ten others, all of them strangers to him, strangers to Rivak, and in each case, he'd answered the same. "No, I have not met him." He could ask his aunt—perhaps she would recognize a name, someone who might be a common enemy, or a contact from before Konstantin was made župan.

Suzana glanced at him. "Do you need to rest now? I don't want to overtax you while you recover."

Konstantin looked at the book. It wasn't difficult to sit at the table and peruse the names; there were just other things he was more interested in at present, like the way her lips pursed and parted as she spoke. "Your father leaves in a few days, does he not?"

"Yes."

"Then we had best keep working." The thick ledger would take them several sessions to analyze.

Suzana continued her perusal of the records. "What of Markos Vojnović? He deals in furs."

"Maybe . . . a long time ago. But he was selling furs to us and received adequate compensation. My mother thought he received too high a price."

She asked him about three more names but looked up when he put a gentle hand on her shoulder. He let himself smile. She didn't seem to have any idea how lovely she was, how intoxicating it was to watch her. "Your skills at deciphering a ledger are admirable, but today, it is your beauty that holds me in awe."

She blushed but didn't pull away.

"May I kiss you?" he whispered.

She nodded and leaned toward him. He reciprocated, meeting her lips in a moment that burst with pleasure and warmth. Her kiss was exhilarating. When he was young, Konstantin had wanted to fly, and this was how he'd imagined it—a soaring, heady feeling that overwhelmed him in the best possible way. It was hard to breathe, but breathing didn't seem to matter, just the overwhelming sensation that came from her mouth against his. He pulled away for a moment, saw the contentment on her face, and followed his initial kiss with a few more, gentle and pleading, sweet and satisfying.

He shifted so he could pull her closer and bumped his rib on the table with the ledger. Pain shot through his side so hot and so sudden that he gasped.

Suzana's eyes fluttered open, then watched with alarm. She held a hand toward his injured side but didn't touch it. "Are you all right?"

Slowly, he released the breath he was holding. He'd been in heaven, then been thrust into hell. But her concern convinced him he wouldn't be stuck there, not for long. He wanted to wish away the need for rest, but clearly, some parts of his body were not yet ready for loving Suzana the way he craved. He took a shallow breath. The pain hadn't gone away, but the shrillness had softened. "Perhaps we should go back to the ledger."

Suzana hesitated, studying his face as if she, too, wished they could avoid the ledger for a while longer. She brushed her fingers along his cheek, her touch soft as silk, her affection a promise of something more to come. Then she cleared her throat and began again. "A wine merchant named Vlastimir Cvetković? He owes my father a great deal of money."

CHAPTER TWENTY-FIVE
FAREWELLS AND FONDNESS

THE FIRST SNOWFALL DUSTED THE peaks of the mountains, warning all travelers that any journeys not completed soon would involve muddy roads and frozen nights. Suzana stood with her husband and his family to bid the last of their guests farewell. Konstantin didn't show it, but she suspected the effort of standing to bid his father-by-marriage and his grandfather farewell wore at him and his wounds. He'd need to rest after this, but for the moment, he stood tall, as the two groups supervised the loading of their mules, horses, and carts. They would travel together for the first days of their journey, the larger numbers offering better protection to them both.

Her father said his goodbyes first. "You will be well?" he asked her.

"I will. Thank you, Father." She would not miss him, but she was grateful that his wealth and pride had led to her marriage.

Župan Đurad Lukarević approached her next. "You are different from what I expected you would be. You may take that as a compliment."

Suzana was too surprised to reply. The older župan moved beyond her to embrace his grandsons and granddaughter. "I wish you a speedy recovery," he told Konstantin. "And much happiness."

When the groups left the bailey, Suzana turned to her husband, searching for signs of exhaustion. Magdalena had wrapped his ribs to help support whatever injury still needed time to heal there, but she noticed the lines of pain that formed around his eyes when he moved too quickly. His bruises had changed from black and blue to green and yellow, but they hadn't disappeared. She put a hand on his arm. "Should you rest now?"

Konstantin glanced at the keep. "I think a bath first. The warmth helps with the pain."

Ivan, standing nearby, gave his brother a look of perplexity. "You just took a bath yesterday. And you haven't trained since before the wedding."

"It's part of my healing."

Ivan's eyebrows scrunched together, and his face turned in clear disapproval of daily baths.

The boys went to practice their archery, and Konstantin went to arrange a bath. Suzana felt tension melting away as she strolled around the bailey, the sunlight warming her face and hope lighting her steps. They still didn't know who had hired men to kill her, but the local bandits were defeated, Konstantin was recovering, the mercenaries were arranged, and the last of their guests had departed. Though she was grateful to each guest in some way, most had also made her nervous, and their absence offered relief.

After a climb to the tower to watch the guests ride away, she returned to the keep. In her bedchamber, she removed her formal dalmatica and replaced it with something simpler. With only the Turkish emissaries and the two guards from Sivi Gora augmenting those who lived in the grody, less formal clothing would suffice.

She had changed her tunic but not replaced her veil when footsteps beat a slow pace in the passage between her chamber and Konstantin's, then a soft knock sounded in the open doorway, where Konstantin now stood. Damp hair dripped onto the collar of his clean tunic. He smiled—an expression so rare on his face that her breath caught. "I hoped I might find you here."

"Did the bath help with the pain?"

"It did." He held up a long strip of cloth. "Would you help with the wrap? I took it off for the bath and don't want to send for Magdalena."

"Of course I'll help." She hadn't done it before, but she'd observed the process, so she followed Konstantin to his room. His door into the corridor was closed and bolted already.

"Do you want me on the edge of the bed?" He gestured toward the blanket, where Magdalena had asked him to sit when she'd wrapped it the day before.

Suzana nodded. Konstantin pulled off his tunic, and she was immediately struck by two things: the high number of fading bruises, and the muscular build. His body drew her eye and threatened to draw her fingers. She confined her touch to the smooth linen as Konstantin situated himself on the bed, bare-chested save for the gold cross she'd given him.

"Here?" She placed a gentle hand over the largest of his contusions.

"Yes."

She placed one end of the cloth on his chest. Experience with the procedure meant Konstantin knew he should hold it there, out of the way, until the binding was ready to be tied off. His hand brushed hers, pausing for a moment. The warmth of affection sent heat from the end of her fingers up along her arms and into her lungs. She met his eyes. He smiled enough for his dimple to show, and it took several long moments for her to remember the task before her.

She wound the wrap around his back and chest, trying to focus on the linen instead of the scent of fine Greek soap. Konstantin watched her, and his scrutiny made her face heat. Attraction pulled and grew into longing. She bit her lip, trying to bring her mind back to her role as temporary nurse. "Is it too loose? Too snug?"

"Perhaps a little tighter."

She arranged the cloths a little differently, running a hand over his chest. His breathing changed, but she didn't think that was a result of pain.

"There. That's the right pressure," he said.

She wound the cloth round him six times. She had to adjust the tightness once more, then she tied it off and let her fingers linger on his skin.

When she spoke, she kept her voice a whisper. "Perhaps you should stand to make sure it is still the proper pressure even in a different position." Reluctantly, she pulled her hand away and stepped back. "How does it feel?"

He stood and raised his arms and moved them gently around. "It's perfect. Thank you."

"And the pain?"

He shrugged. "Today, it is not so strong. When Grandfather left, his embrace didn't hurt. But I told everyone else that the bath would wear me out and I wasn't to be disturbed until supper."

"Shall I leave so you can rest?" She didn't really want to leave, but nor did she want to interrupt his recovery.

He glanced at the floor, almost bashful. "You are free to leave whenever you wish, Suzana. But I was hoping you would stay."

She swallowed. Looked at his mouth, his bare skin, his piercing gray eyes. "I would like to stay."

He took her hand and gave it a gentle kiss. "You have proven more wonderful than I ever imagined. Thank you."

The combination of his touch and his gratitude confirmed her decision to stay. "You have surprised me in the best possible way. I didn't expect to find friendship and love in marriage. I had merely hoped to avoid misery."

"I'm glad your rather low expectations have been exceeded." He chuckled. "I love you, my Suzana."

"And I you," she whispered back.

"You don't have any idea, do you?"

She searched his eyes, wondering what he meant. "Any idea of what?"

"Of how beautiful you are."

She shook her head. "Many people have assured me I am quite plain."

He reached for her cheek, and his soft caress made her sigh. Something about the way he looked at her made her feel beautiful, regardless of what others had said. And his touch—it made her feel as if she could do anything.

"Whoever said you are plain was a blind fool." One of his fingers brushed across her lips, and his expression, already warm, turned to adoration.

"There's that secret dimple again. Your smile changes your whole face, like a spark turning into a flame."

"Then I will smile more often when I am alone with you." His right hand continued to her jaw, and his left arm twined around her waist. "That should be easy because you make me so very happy."

She closed her eyes against emotion strong enough to threaten tears. Her love for her husband was so beautiful and so powerful, she could barely breathe.

His finger brushed back a few strands of hair. "May I kiss you, my Suzana?"

Some questions were best answered with words. This one was best answered with action. She stood on her toes and pressed her mouth to his. He smiled beneath her lips and kissed her back.

CHAPTER TWENTY-SIX
SUZANA'S GIFTS

BEFORE KONSTANTIN HAD MET SUZANA, everything had been falling apart. His treasury and granaries had been nearly empty, part of his župa burned, and there seemed no hope for improvement. It had been an unending downward spiral.

Now, as the late crops were brought in and the leaves changed colors, everything was different. Suzana's dowry had replenished the treasury and the food stores. She'd brought hope to Rivak and hope to him. He hadn't done everything perfectly, but when it came to his role as a husband, he was succeeding, and their marriage was thriving.

One morning, amid the lightest of snowfalls, Ivan barreled across the bailey. "Kostya! You must come see!"

"Where is your hat, Ivan?" Catching a chill might lead to illness, especially with the change in weather.

"Don't worry about a hat." Ivan's joy bordered on laughter. "Come and see!"

Konstantin caught his brother's arm and placed his own fur cap on his small head. He could indulge in his brother's excitement *and* ward off the illnesses that seemed to strike the boy with regularity.

Danilo met them partway to the stables. "It's extraordinary!" His mouth formed a perfect circle of awe.

A crowd had formed, with Suzana and most of the garrison gathered around the most beautiful horse Konstantin had ever seen. Black coat with a white star and white socks, much taller and more powerfully built than any of Rivak's other horses. Konstantin slowed his approach. He had no idea where the horse had come from, but at the moment, he didn't care. One didn't question splendor of such magnitude. One simply stood in awe of it.

Bojan held the lead rope. He grinned at Konstantin. "Do you like him, lord?"

The crowd parted for Konstantin as he approached the horse. The animal turned a wary head toward him, then snorted and stamped a hoof. His muscles were huge. Konstantin held a hand near the horse's nose, letting the animal get used to him, then ran his hand along the muzzle. "I've never seen a finer animal. Where did he come from?"

Bojan looked past Konstantin to Suzana.

Konstantin turned. "Did you have something to do with this?"

Suzana beamed as she joined him beside the massive horse. "I asked an agent to find a destrier for you. Something to carry you safely back to me when you're called away."

The warhorse was his. He ran his hands along the horse's withers, along its back. The stallion was in perfect health. He'd never seen its equal. A horse like this was worth . . . His hand paused on the animal's back. He met Suzana's eyes and lowered his voice. "We can't afford a horse like this."

"It was a trade. The dowry remains untouched until Ulrich arrives with his mercenaries, save for what we spent on the grain."

"But how?"

"I'll tell you later." Suzana glanced at the horse. "For now, I think you ought to try him out."

Anticipation pulled at Bojan's face. "Shall I fetch your saddle, lord?"

"Yes. Thank you."

"Will you take me on a ride?" Ivan asked.

"And me?" Danilo stood right beside his cousin.

"Both of you in turn, but not until I've got a feel for how well he obeys."

Bojan and Konstantin saddled the horse, which snorted a few times but stayed mostly still. Konstantin checked the girths and mounted the stallion. He didn't normally have so large an audience when he tried out a new horse, but he was used to being scrutinized.

A clicking sound from his mouth and a slight increase in pressure from his legs set the horse moving. A few more clicks and the horse was trotting—the bailey was too small for anything faster. The horse had power, more even than Svarog. Konstantin still missed his old destrier, and he recognized the strong possibility that he would have to return this horse to meet his other financial obligations, but he would enjoy the splendid beast while he could.

The stallion followed each command, so Konstantin rode back to the stables and dismounted. He ran his hand along the animal's neck. "I think it's time to take him outside the grad. But first, he needs a name."

"Father had a horse like this." Ivan's comment surprised Konstantin. The boy had been only five when their father had died, and Ivan rarely spoke of him.

"So he did." Konstantin studied the horse. Miroslav's destrier hadn't had a star, nor been quite so large, but the dark coat and the white socks were similar.

"Veles," Danilo said. That was less of a surprise because Danilo had been a year older, and he'd always been fond of horses.

"Perhaps it is time we had another Veles in the stables," Konstantin said.

Veles. The old god of earth, water, and the underworld.

Suzana had watched Konstantin ride out earlier and had seen him try the horse at a gallop along the road from the grad, then use a more sedate speed for trips with Ivan and Danilo riding in front of him. Much later in the day, Konstantin found her in one of the corridors. He glanced along the hallway, and after confirming they were alone, he flashed a smile, wrapped her in an embrace, and swung her in a circle. If the exuberance gave him any pain, he hid it completely.

"Veles is perfect and magnificent and beautiful, and I don't know how we can afford him, but I will never forget that you found him for me." He rested his forehead against hers.

"I didn't find him myself. My father did."

"Don't tell me I need to whirl him around to show my gratitude." His fingers ran lightly along her neck.

She laughed. "No. He was my agent, but he did not pay."

His expression turned serious, and he pulled away to better see her face. "The horse is magnificent, Suzana, but we went through the accounts. There wasn't enough left for a destrier like that, was there?"

"The money did not come from the treasury. I told you I made a trade."

"What did you trade?"

"Some jewelry."

He studied her face. Lifted the hand with the finger that wore the gold ring he'd given her. Placed a kiss on that finger, then on the inside of her wrist. "What jewelry?"

"The set from our wedding."

His eyebrows drew inward. "But . . . didn't you want it?"

The jewelry had been beautiful. She could almost imagine that her father had given it to her in part to show affection, but he'd told her himself that the gift had been a display of wealth, not sentiment. "I want you to be safe more than I want jewelry, and it is my prayer that a proper warhorse will help you come back home to me."

"You have given me so much." His voice grew soft with emotion. "You didn't have to give up your jewelry for me too."

"But I wanted to. Kostya, you've given me safety and friendship, and those have been far rarer than gemstones in my life."

He gave her a sober look. "I would be angry at your father for giving you such a lonely childhood, but it's hard to be angry at him when he picked out such a wonderful animal. And it is hard to feel anger when I'm surrounded by so much love."

He bent toward her and brushed his lips against hers, then waited, seeking her permission for a more thorough kiss. She wound her fingers into the hair at the back of his neck and returned his kiss, at least until footsteps sounded along the end of the corridor and a male throat made a polite cough to warn of his approach.

Grigorii stood some distance away, doing his best to give them privacy by looking at the wall.

"What is it?" Konstantin's face was stern, but his voice was not.

"Several merophs from one of the far villages seek your wisdom in settling a dispute."

"Tell them I will come. Soon."

"Yes, lord." Grigorii bowed slightly, then retreated.

Konstantin turned back to her. "Will you come with me?" He kissed her before she had a chance to answer. "It's one of those duties you might have to deal with when I leave in the spring." Another kiss. If he kept it up, she'd never catch her breath long enough to answer. "Sometimes it's awfully dull, but it's important to them." As his lips explored hers, his hands ran along the sides of her torso and around her back.

She finally broke off the latest kiss with a laugh. "You should not have told Grigorii you would preside over disputes soon if you intended to kiss me like that."

His smile revealed his dimple as well as a rare hint of mischief. "Will you come? I'd rather take you to our bedchamber, but if duty requires my attention elsewhere, I would still like you by my side."

"I will come. And I will sit close enough to learn from my župan's wisdom but far enough away that I shan't distract him."

"Sit beside me. Your župan manages to remember most of Dušan's code, thanks to Father Vlatko's tutoring, but his wife is his greatest asset. He would be glad of her insight." He reached for her hand and led her toward their duty.

Konstantin kissed his wife gently on the forehead before getting out of bed. She sighed and shifted slightly in her sleep before settling back into a beautiful stillness. Winter had brought a slower pace to life in the grad, broken only by the arrival of Ulrich's mercenaries a fortnight before. Konstantin spent much of his time training with the garrison and incorporating the mercenaries into the župa's plans for defense and military service. Today was the Sabbath, so Konstantin had no training to rush off to. He slipped back into bed, waiting, pondering. They slept in the same bed each night, but he hadn't actually seen Suzana first thing in the morning for almost a fortnight. For most of their marriage, Suzana had been up as early as he, but things had been different the last moon or so. She was acting like him at mealtimes—picky, drawn to safe, bland items of food. And more than once when she'd apologized for sleeping in so late, she'd mentioned a feeling of queasiness. It couldn't be a normal illness that caused fatigue and an overly discerning stomach, because if she were ill, surely the symptoms would have spread to Konstantin by now. Ivan, too, because it seemed that when anyone sneezed within five paces of him, he came down with a fever.

Konstantin had been old enough to remember his mother being ill before Bogdana's birth and before Ivan's birth. He also recalled Aunt Zorica's near constant nausea while carrying Danilo. He and Suzana had certainly been married long enough for her to be with child, but he hesitated to ask—he didn't want to pressure her to produce an heir. That timing was up to God.

If she was carrying his child . . . maybe an heir . . . a baby that was part of him and part of her . . .

No, he'd best not get his hopes up.

Did Suzana know, and was she keeping it a secret from him? Maybe she wasn't sure yet. Or maybe she hadn't noticed the signs. Her mother hadn't been around to tell her about things like childbearing, and that might not have been a subject her tutors addressed.

The light coming through the windows grew brighter. Suzana stirred and twisted toward him. "Good morning." Her soft, sleepy voice met his ears like sweet music.

He ran a hand along her cheek and kissed her softly on the mouth. Then again, not quite so softly. Her skin was warm from the blankets, her smile calm and content.

"It's nice to have you still here when I wake up." She snuggled closer. "I've been so sleepy lately."

"Just tired?" he asked.

Her hand shifted under the blanket. "Sometimes I also feel unwell in my stomach."

That could be caused by pregnancy, but it could also be some internal ailment. He would be a poor husband if he let dreams of a baby distract him when she needed some other type of care. "Anything else?"

"Sometimes a little tenderness—" She broke off and stumbled from the bed and over to a corner where a chamber pot was hidden behind a screen. She retched.

He followed, picking up a clean cloth to hand to her.

She wiped her mouth with a shaking hand.

"Has this been happening often?" he asked.

"Yes. I hoped you wouldn't have to see it. I can think of few things less attractive than vomit."

He chuckled. He bent down and pulled her into him, then put a hand on her forehead. No fever. "Do you need to rest more?"

She nodded, and he lifted her from the ground and carried her back to the bed.

She laughed softly. "I'm capable of walking."

"I know, but I'm trying to make up for all the mornings when I haven't been here to help you." He placed her on the bed, then sat on the edge of it, debating how much he should or shouldn't ask.

"You look as if you wish to say something," she mumbled.

She was getting good at reading him, or he was doing a poor job hiding his emotions. That was one of the beauties of his bedchamber—he could share everything with her, even his thoughts. But this openness was new to him, each aspect tentative. "Given your symptoms, do you think perhaps you should see someone?"

"Like who?"

"Maybe a midwife?"

"A . . . a midwife?" Her face grew thoughtful. "I had my last menses after the hunt Župan Nikola hosted." Her eyes widened, and she put a hand to her mouth. "It's been nearly two moons. That has to mean . . . doesn't it?" She moved her hand to her abdomen. "I don't feel any different."

"Other than the sleepiness and the queasiness?"

She sat up, and he pulled her onto his lap, then kissed the side of her neck just behind her delicate ear. "I think, my beautiful, wonderful wife, that you are with child."

"A baby." Her whisper held a hint of awe as she leaned into him. "I hoped it would happen soon."

The emotion hit him then, so hard that he had to blink back tears. "You have given me everything, Suzana." Her dowry, with its ability to rescue Rivak. Herself, as an advisor, a friend, and a lover. A warhorse of unmatched magnificence, bartered for at personal sacrifice. And now a child.

Her hand reached for his cheek. "I hope those are tears of joy and not tears of fear."

He cleared his throat. "Župans don't cry."

"No. And they don't have dimples either." Her lips brushed his jawline. "But my župan is going to be a father . . . at the end of the summer, I think. Will you be back by then?"

He looked away. "That depends on the sultan." The sultan's power always hung over them, but he resented even more than usual its intrusion into this happy, private moment with his wife.

A child.

His child. Her child.

Not even the sultan could ruin the magic of that marvelous fact.

Chapter Twenty-Seven
PARTINGS

Suzana pulled her wool cloak more tightly around her shoulders as she stood in the wind-swept bailey. Though it was spring, it felt more like winter. Perhaps she ought to have worn fur. Before her, the men of the garrison and Ulrich's mercenaries waited beside their horses, as did Arslan and Esel. The baggage wagons had already taken the path down the causeway and through the grody, then turned east, toward the sultan and his demands.

Lidija stood beside her, sniffling. Suzana tried not to follow her example. She had sobbed the night before into Konstantin's chest when their passion was spent and the coming separation had loomed large. She would not cry today—at least not when her husband could see. He didn't want to go, and her anguish would only make his burden heavier.

Konstantin spoke with Kuzman and Bojan. Most of the garrison would depart with Konstantin, but he had insisted on leaving men he trusted to take care of his family, including the two he currently spoke with. Ten of the garrison in total would remain, along with the bodyguards Konstantin's grandfather had left. Merophs would serve as watchmen. Most of them had fields to plant as well, but the sultan's burden fell on them too.

Veles snorted as the young groom led him away from the worst of the press. Suzana approached the huge beast and placed a hand on the animal's face. "Bring him back to me." Konstantin would travel most of the distance on Perun, but she expected Veles to carry him into battle.

The horse pulled away, but his head seemed to nod, and Suzana took comfort in that.

Konstantin had moved on to say his goodbyes to his aunt.

Lidija was next, and she flung her arms around her older brother. "You'll be gone for so long."

"You're just jealous that I'll see more of Decimir than you will."

Lidija wiped a hand across her cheeks. "I could come with you."

"Absolutely not. But I will pray for you. And I'll keep an eye out for Decimir, though I imagine Župan Dragomir has already appointed his best men to protect him."

Lidija clung to her brother a little longer, then took a gulping breath and released him. Suzana pulled the young woman into her arms while Konstantin said goodbye to Danilo and Ivan.

"Someday, we will ride with you," Danilo said.

Konstantin grasped his cousin's shoulder. "Someday, I will be glad to have you by my side. And today, I am glad to leave two brave young warriors-in-training behind to protect Rivak and my family while I am gone."

Danilo looked near tears, but he managed to hold his emotion back while Konstantin embraced him.

"Will you bring something back for me?" Ivan asked during his farewell hug. "Something from far away, something that's hard to find in Rivak or in Sivi Gora?"

Konstantin nodded. "We'll pass the seashore, and many great cities. I'll find something for you there. And while I'm gone, you'll obey Aunt Zorica? And Suzana?"

"Yes, Kostya." Ivan pulled a small enameled icon of the Virgin Mary from a pouch on his belt and handed it to his brother. "This is for you. It's supposed to be Mary, the mother of God, but I think it looks like Suzana."

Konstantin studied the icon, then showed it to Suzana. The hair color was right, what wasn't hidden beneath a veil. The facial features were too small for a good comparison, but the icon showed a Mary heavy with child. Suzana could not see the new curve in her abdomen through her clothing, but they'd told the family that she was with child, and it seemed Ivan was already anticipating what changes that might bring to his sister-by-marriage's shape.

"Thank you, Ivan." Konstantin smoothed the boy's hair, then turned to Suzana.

Lidija drew back, giving the two of them a moment alone.

He held out his arms, and Suzana stepped into his embrace. They'd already said everything they needed to say. How much they would miss each other, how she was to act and plan should brigands make an appearance again, what to do if the worst should happen and he did not return. But he had more words for her. "That icon reminds me that I'm going to miss so much." His voice was a whisper, but she heard it easily as she rested her head in the curve between his neck and shoulder. She could feel his pulse from there, feel the pain and sorrow that he hid behind a mask that only those who knew him best could see around.

"Come back to me, my Kostya."

"I'll do my best." He held her tightly, then planted a soft kiss on her cheek and turned for his horse.

A single tear fell in a warm path down the side of her cheek, then grew cold as the wind blew and Konstantin mounted Perun. Grigorii and most of the men were already on their horses. Miladin gently pried his niece's arms from around his neck and handed the weeping child to his wife so he, too, could mount. Suzana understood the little girl's desire to hold on a little longer.

Konstantin led the men from the bailey, and as they disappeared into the causeway, Ivan tugged on Suzana's arm. "We'll see them longer from the tower."

Suzana followed Ivan and Danilo to the top of the keep. The view from there extended in every direction. To the south, a line of dust showed that Župan Dragomir's group, too, was heading east. They planned to travel near one another—close enough to offer support if attacked but far enough apart that they could more easily find water. She'd sat in on all the planning, all the coordination, and had heard and sensed the unspoken worries. They would travel through Greek country first—feral lands with nominal allegiance to the emperor in Constantinople, himself a vassal to the sultan. In reality, local strongmen controlled the lands. The Serbs hoped they would pass unmolested if they did nothing to provoke the local kephales to anger and showed nothing to tempt them to greed. After that, their journey would take them to Ottoman lands. They would cross the Bosporus and fight under the sultan's command. It was a far-off place, a far-off battle, with an unknown outcome. That risk existed was certain. The sultan would not have called upon his Serbian vassals if his enemies in Anatolia weren't strong.

Dama Zorica and Lidija joined them on the tower as the bailey emptied.

Lidija picked out the line of Župan Dragomir's troops almost immediately. "I wish they would have stopped here before they went east."

Dama Zorica put her arm around her niece's shoulder. "We can hope for a visit when they return."

Lidija cried again. "I still remember saying goodbye to Papa and Uncle Darras before Maritsa. I never saw them again."

Maritsa was nearly three years in the past, but it still haunted all of Rivak. Suzana wondered how Konstantin felt now, with his home and family behind him and unwanted service to the sultan ahead.

Dama Zorica wiped Lidija's eyes. "This is not Maritsa. But I know it is hard, so I had Nevena make honeycakes for the men . . . and for those of us left behind. She gave some to Sveta and Magdalena and ought to be serving the rest of them in the hall now."

Danilo and Ivan pulled their eyes away from the disappearing line of men marching to war. "Honeycakes?" Danilo repeated.

Dama Zorica nodded.

Ivan took his sister's hand. "Come on, Lidija. I want two."

Dama Zorica turned to Suzana as the three children went back inside. "Are you all right?"

Suzana gazed into the distance. Rivak's banner flapped in the breeze, and the line of horses stirred up dust. "I miss him already. And if he doesn't come back . . ."

"His father did not come back, nor did his grandfather. While the Ottomans hold power, it is the lot of župans to die in battle. Either in service to the sultan or in rebellion against him."

Suzana blinked sharply to clear her vision. Though they were alone, she lowered her voice. "Rebellion? How could Konstantin hope to break the Ottoman yoke?" Suzana was intimately familiar with the numbers in the ledger. She knew what it cost to run a župa, what it took to maintain an army. Rivak wasn't strong enough or rich enough to rebel.

Dama Zorica's face grew sober but determined. "If God did not wish us to be free, I do not think He would have given us such a hunger for liberty. Hope doesn't have to be practical in order to be real, in order to be just. The timing is not right, not now. Maybe not for years. But that doesn't mean we stop dreaming of it." She placed a hand on Suzana's arm. "I hope Kostya will always come back to you. And I am so pleased that you are proving adequate to the burdens placed upon you. Rivak will be in good hands should it fall to you, whether we are vassals or free Serbs. But we should get you inside. You look chilled."

Suzana followed Dama Zorica into the keep. The coming months would be focused on replanting the fields that had been destroyed the previous year by brigands. And on waiting. Waiting for a baby. Waiting for the župan's return. Waiting for the strength they would need to gain their freedom.

The boys' excited calls greeted them as they entered the hall, and Ivan ran toward them. "Would you like a honeycake, Suzana?"

She forced a smile. "Can I trust you to save one for me? I wish to go to the chapel and say a few prayers for your brother's safe journey."

Ivan placed the cake he had offered her on the table and eyed it. A few crumbs from his own cake clung to his small mouth. He stepped away. "Danilo and I can pray too."

She cupped the boy's face in her hands. The resemblance to his brother was there, if she searched for it. "Thank you. An abundance of prayers will do him good."

CHAPTER TWENTY-EIGHT
ANATOLIA

KONSTANTIN WOKE WHEN THE SUN neared the horizon, turning the sky to the east pink and orange. The weather had been pleasant the night before, so they'd slept under the stars or under the baggage wagons rather than setting up tents. Their journey thus far had taken them through Thessaloniki and Constantinople, where they had restocked their supplies. Then they had crossed into Asia. None of the Serbs, Konstantin included, had ever been so far from home.

He fingered the small cross Suzana had given him. The strap was just long enough for him to hold before his face. She would be busy preparing for the birth of an infant and overseeing Rivak as crops were planted and grown. One of the reasons for taking a wife was to have someone to look after things while the husband was away. That partnership was essential, especially for a župan, but gratitude at her abilities didn't soften the ache he felt in her absence.

He rose and went to check on his horses. Perun came to greet him at once.

"What a good horse you are." Konstantin ran his hands along the animal's coat, then checked each leg. Perun had carried him many miles over the last moon, and he remained fit and dependable.

Next, Konstantin turned his attention to Veles. The warhorse was equal parts feisty and mighty. He was untested in battle but had shown he had a vast store of endurance to go along with his impressive speed. And nothing seemed to scare the horse—though irritations certainly came frequently enough. Konstantin was no longer one of those irritants, so he gave Veles plenty of attention: checking his legs, rubbing the length of his back, and adding oats to his hay.

The camp had begun stirring before Konstantin had left his bedroll, but the activity grew as the sun rose. Their campsite lay on a rise, offering a sweeping view of the land around them. Father Vlatko's voice rang out in a hymn, as it did every day at dawn and at dusk.

"Riders approaching," one of the sentries called.

Konstantin glanced around the camp's perimeter to make sure all the sentries were in place. They sometimes skipped setting up tents, but they always dug ditches around the camp at night for protection and to keep the animals in place. "How many?"

"Five."

Konstantin joined Miladin at the camp's main entrance to watch for the incoming riders. They were barely visible.

"They aren't from Dragomir's camp," Miladin said. "He's a mile to the west of us."

As the men came closer, their headdresses became more and more distinct. Turks. But he doubted they were hostile. Five men, no matter how impressive their abilities, were unlikely to attack a camp of eighty warriors, plus camp followers.

Konstantin motioned one of the grooms over. "Jakov, ask the Ottoman emissaries if they will join me. We may need their language skills."

The boy ran off. He slowed his pace as he approached the Ottomans, wary of the foreigners but obedient to his župan's request. Jakov headed back to Konstantin, and Arslan and Esel followed.

"Peace be unto you," Konstantin said as the emissaries joined him.

"And unto you." Arslan studied the incoming riders.

The men let their horses slow to a gentler pace as they approached the steeper ground leading up to Rivak's camp. They dismounted at the camp's edge. A wise decision, given the armed crowd that awaited them.

With friendly voices, they called a greeting in Turkish.

Konstantin looked to Arslan, who answered the newcomers before translating. "They're from the sultan. Sent to lead us to his army."

They followed the Turkish guides for three days before joining the sultan's army. Dragomir's group arrived the same day. Župan Teodore's men had arrived a fortnight before them, and over the next eight days, all the other vassals joined the camp. They paid the sultan their tribute and, as was expected, gave him gifts befitting his high station. On the day the last Christian contingent arrived, the sultan invited the župans to dine with him in a large silk-lined tent with a long leather mat spread down the center to hold the food. The Serbs were placed at the end of the mat, far from the sultan, his sons, and his pashas.

Župan Dragomir inserted himself between Konstantin and Župan Teodore, for which Konstantin was grateful. He had no desire to see Župan Teodore again, let alone converse with him. But Župan Teodore conveniently ignored Konstantin, saving him the trouble of determining what, if anything, he should say to the man who had threatened his wife and wanted to steal his lands.

Communal bowls were set before those present, filled with pungent stews. In Rivak, they ate with knives, forks, and spoons, but Konstantin followed the examples of the Turks and used his right hand to dip his bread into the spicy mixture, scooping up part of it. His first bite was edible, but the texture of something in his second bite made him shudder. He would have to eat it with a calm face. Vassals did not turn up their noses at food served to them by the sultan. The next time he dipped, he let only a bit of the broth soak in.

Some of those present held conversations, but they were not boisterous, and most were spoken in Turkish.

Konstantin leaned next to Župan Dragomir's ear. "Do you understand anything they're saying to each other?"

"No. Decimir has picked up a little of their language, but he was not invited to sup with the sultan." Župan Dragomir scanned the other guests. "His lack of invitation does not grieve me."

Decimir wasn't a lamb, not exactly, but the hosts felt like wolves. In time, when Konstantin had children of his own—sons who would join him in battle—he, too, would want distance between them and the Ottomans.

When the meal ended, Konstantin took his turn in front of the sultan, kneeling, pledging his loyalty, and kissing Sultan Murad's foot. Other Ottomans watched—some clearly warriors, there to protect the sultan and ensure his vassals did proper obeisance, others in fine clothing that showed wealth, though undoubtedly, they were fighters as well. Three young men, older than Decimir but younger that Konstantin, also watched. They were the sultan's sons.

Konstantin buried his feelings deep during the ceremony. The Turks were present to witness his humiliation, but none of his men were, and that was a blessing. Could warriors like Miladin and Grigorii follow a man into battle when they'd seen him kneeling before a foreign sultan and kissing his foot? And what of Ulrich and the mercenaries? They worked for pay, but he would depend on them during the upcoming campaigns. He needed their respect.

He left the sultan's tent and found Župan Dragomir waiting for him. "And that is another reason I am glad Decimir was not invited to dine with the sultan," he said in a low voice. "Come, I'll walk you back to your men. The Karamanids are not your only enemies here, and I know many who will be devastated if you don't come back to them. I doubt Župan Teodore will try anything in the open, but it's probably best that you not wander alone when he is near. All manner of accidents can happen while on campaign."

Konstantin followed, still weighed down by the humiliation of kissing the foot of the man responsible for his father's death. Worse than the act was the subservience and impotence attached. "I am glad my men and my family were not witnesses to that ceremony."

Župan Dragomir sighed. "It stings, doesn't it? Perhaps it will not sting forever."

Did Župan Dragomir mean the bitterness of subservience would pass into acceptance or that the vassalage would not be permanent? Konstantin longed for freedom, but the possibility seemed faint and distant, at least for now. Footsteps sounding behind them kept Konstantin from asking for clarification.

Arslan hurried to catch up to them. "Peace be unto you, Župans Dragomir and Konstantin."

Konstantin and Dragomir returned the well-wishes.

"The sultan requests that you be ready to march tomorrow morning, by what you would term the second hour."

"We will be ready," Konstantin said. "Do you have any advice for us?"

"Be prepared to fight. The Karamanids will not wait for a declaration of war before fighting back."

Chapter Twenty-Nine
Speed, Blood, and Fury

The sultan's army marched the next morning. With him were his Serbian, Bulgarian, and Greek vassals, the mounted Turkish akincis that moved with a swiftness unmatched by any others, the heavily armored sipahis who formed the disciplined core of the sultan's troops, and a plethora of ghazis, raiders who offered the sultan their allegiance in exchange for the opportunity to plunder. They marched for nine days, and then they found the enemy and prepared for combat.

As the enemy army arrayed themselves in the distance, Sultan Murad's forces formed a wide battleline. Konstantin and his men waited at the center right. The Serbs from Rivak formed a mounted group, ready to charge and break into the enemy line should they be called to do so. The mercenaries had joined with Župan Dragomir's foot soldiers. Most of Ulrich's men had horses, but they used them only to speed their movements. The mercenaries were not trained for battle on horseback, and few had mounts that wouldn't bolt in fright when the sights and sounds of war surrounded them.

"What did you think of them during their raids?" Konstantin asked Miladin. The Karamanids had sent fleet-footed horsemen out to observe the advancing army. Most days, they shadowed the bulk of the sultan's forces, staying far enough away that they were seen but not pursued. Twice, they'd probed closer and clashed with some of the akincis.

"Skilled. I can ride a horse, and I can shoot a bow well enough. But both at the same time?" Miladin shook his head. "Fast and dangerous, but if they shoot from a distance, I think our armor will stop most of their arrows."

"Our men have armor, but many of our horses will be vulnerable." Veles wore armor, as did Grom and several others, but the majority of the animals did not.

The Karamanids drew closer, and dust rose into the air, hiding the troops beyond the first few rows of warriors. The same was true of the Ottoman side. Konstantin couldn't see through the haze to the far end.

Arslan rode along the front ranks, stopping at each group to give them instructions. When he pulled up near Konstantin, he relayed the orders quickly. "You are to be part of the main advance. Stay level with the groups on either side of you."

Konstantin nodded his understanding. Župan Nikola was to his right, beside the sultan's own sipahis that formed the line's center. Župan Dragomir was to his left, with most of the other Serb vassals beyond that, each group gathered beneath their banners.

The advance began. Though Konstantin was not eager to fight for the sultan, he was eager to demonstrate courage in battle. Perhaps if he earned renown as a warrior, brigands and greedy neighbors would be more reluctant to threaten his lands.

The sound of hooves and the clatter of weapons and armor filled the air. Konstantin, like most of the Serbs he rode with, carried a shield and long spear. He wore a spathion at his belt for close combat and for backup should his spear break or stick in the enemy, and he'd strapped an ax, bow, and quiver behind Veles's saddle. He also had a dagger at his waist and a knife in his boot. Sweat trickled along his back under his mail and armor as the sun beat down on them. His open-faced helmet shaded the sides of his face and his neck, but it did nothing to cool his skin.

As the opposing forces grew closer, they picked up speed. Konstantin urged Veles into his fastest canter—he didn't want him to gallop because then he'd outpace the other horses and separate himself from his men. They were stronger together, fighting side by side.

He lowered his spear and homed in on a Karamanid with a wide, pale turban. The lines converged, but the spears Konstantin and his men carried had longer shafts. They sliced into the enemy before the enemy's weapons threatened them. Men cried, and horses swerved as the two lines crashed together in a combination of speed, blood, and fury.

Veles plowed over a fallen enemy, and Konstantin aimed at a new target. Arrows fell toward him and his men, launched from a distance, but Konstantin used his heavy almond-shaped shield to protect his face, and the arrows lacked the drive to penetrate his mail or Veles's barding.

One of the Karamanids unhorsed Grigorii. Amid the dust of the battle and the swirl of activity, Konstantin couldn't see if he moved, just that he'd been knocked from his saddle. Konstantin skewered an enemy warrior standing between him and his fallen satnik, then guided Veles closer and thrust his spear at the man trying to hack at Grigorii with a curved scimitar.

"Are you injured?" Konstantin asked.

Grigorii struggled to his feet. "Not badly."

Konstantin struck at another enemy riding toward them with speed. Zoran and Miladin appeared on his left. More enemies attacked from his right. Konstantin's spear stuck in one of them, and as the man tumbled to the ground, the shaft of the spear pulled from Konstantin's hand.

Miladin caught the reins of the Turkish horse. "Grigorii, take this one."

When Grigorii settled into the saddle, the four rode forward, forcing a path through the enemy. Konstantin used his spathion now. Its blade did not reach as far as the tip of a spear, but both edges were sharp, and Kuzman had taught Konstantin well. Many of the Karamanids wore leather cuirasses and helmets of metal, but most of their arms and necks were covered only by a layer or two of fabric, and Konstantin's blade sliced easily into their vulnerable limbs. Not every stroke was a killing blow, but it was enough to take the men out of the battle, and the rush of the wounded trying to find safety added to the chaos of the enemy host.

Konstantin's small group of horsemen mixed with Župan Nikola's men and slaughtered the Karamanids with a calm efficiency. The enemy advanced, but none made it past the Serbs.

The same couldn't be said of the line's center, where a much larger Karamanid force had thrust itself. Perhaps their scouts had noted the diverse makeup of the sultan's army and thought the juncture between Slav and Turk would be the best place to break their foe. The plan held wisdom: the different tongues made coordination more difficult, and though they all fought under the sultan's command, they were reluctant allies.

A score of Karamanid horsemen in heavy armor formed a wedge and drove at the juncture between the Ottomans and the Serbs. Another group did the same thing against the sipahis. Konstantin continued to fight off the enemy facing him and his men, but that assault was slowing and losing momentum. The action to the right of him, on the other hand, threatened to pierce the line in two places. The men between the Karamanid thrusts would be cut off, surrounded, and probably annihilated.

The men under threat were not his comrades or his brother Serbs. They followed a sultan who had sent an army to kill his father and make

Konstantin a vassal. But they needed help, and Konstantin's group, though not large, was powerful enough to stop the Karamanid encirclement.

"Miladin." Konstantin pointed. "We can stop that pincer movement."

Miladin studied the battle lines. "We can. Is that your command?"

"It is." If the Karamanids succeeded, the rest of the line would fall into disorder, leaving everyone on the Ottoman side—including his men—at risk.

Konstantin called to the others by name, then waited while they lined up on either side of him, knee to knee for a charge. Miladin plucked a spear from a nearby body and handed it to Konstantin. He pointed to the wedge of Karamanid warriors trying to separate the Turk and Serb elements of the Ottoman army. "Our task is to break their advance and prevent a breach. Show everyone how powerful the warriors from Rivak can be. Onward!"

The men followed his lead, keeping pace with him as the horses increased speed and galloped toward the enemy. As before, the long Serbian spears hit their enemy moments before the Karamanid scimitars and javelins could threaten them in return. Veles's force seemed not at all diminished, but Konstantin's arms were battling fatigue. The same would be true for his men, hopefully for their enemies.

Konstantin ripped the spear from its most recent target and rammed it into the next man. The group of Karamanids were being forced to turn away from the sipahis and focus the brunt of their fury on Konstantin and his men. It felt a little like kicking a wasp nest and bracing for the retribution. Konstantin had led his men into the most dangerous part of battle—but danger would have found them regardless, and his men had trained with a fierceness that came from seeing their garrison nearly wiped out along the banks of the Maritsa, then seeing the villages of their župa burned to the ground by brigands.

Three more thrusts with his spear, and three more enemies were knocked from their horses. But with the fourth, the spear pulled from Konstantin's grasp. He switched to his spathion again and commenced the work of slashing and thrusting at those within reach of his blade.

As he hewed toward one of the Karamanids, another rode toward him. The man leaped from his horse and seemed to fly at Konstantin, grasping his shoulders and propelling both of them off Veles's back and onto the churned-up earth below.

The air rushed from Konstantin's lungs, and his helmet fell from his head. He still gripped his spathion, so despite the burning need to inhale, he focused on thrusting his weapon into the man who had dragged him from his horse. The man fell atop Konstantin's shield, and the warmth of his blood spilled across Konstantin's arm.

Another Karamanid horseman noticed Konstantin's plight and rode toward him with murderous intention. Konstantin shook off the man he'd just slain and stood, bracing for the attack. The enemy raised his scimitar over his head, then brought it quickly down. Konstantin thrust his shield up to block it and slashed his spathion along the side of the man's horse. The animal shied away from the pain, sending the rider on a crooked path.

More men charged at him through the dust of battle. They came on foot, but they came in force. Konstantin hefted his shield into position and waited for a few heartbeats, then moved toward them—he wanted momentum to work for him when he met the enemy. Spathion met scimitar in a peal that promised death for one side or the other. An unexpected calm settled over Konstantin. The man he fought held only average skill. Thrice their blades crossed, and then Konstantin jabbed the man through the stomach. As he fell back, a pair of Karamanids attacked him. They, too, were far easier to duel with than the men he spent hours practicing with from his own garrison.

But battle could drain a man of strength with dangerous swiftness. Konstantin's arms were weary, and each stroke of the sword reminded him that his muscles would not last forever. Another enemy, then a pair of them, then three more in quick succession. The sun grew oppressively hot, and scarcely a breeze ran through his uncovered hair. Two more and then the steady stream of enemy seemed to slow. Konstantin lowered his shield ever so slightly and looked around. Nearby, the rest of his men stood over fallen enemy soldiers. The Ottoman line had held, and the right wing of the Karamanid attack had disintegrated. Farther along the line, the Karamanids' left wing seemed to be withdrawing.

Miladin came over to him. Weariness showed in each of his steps, but he held his head upright, and his eyes remained alert. "I kept trying to reach you, but they cut me off again and again."

Grigorii followed, eyes wide as he took in the bodies of the fallen Karamanids, dead and dying, that surrounded Konstantin. "Are you well, lord?"

Konstantin nodded. "I am not injured. But I've lost Veles. And my helmet."

Miladin walked a few paces away and plucked an iron helmet from the ground. He dusted off the leather aventail and handed it to Konstantin. "I believe this is yours, lord, and I believe your destrier is among the footmen."

Konstantin placed his helmet on his head. The sun had warmed it to an uncomfortable temperature, but he was grateful for the extra protection, especially if the sultan ordered them to pursue the enemy while the Karamanids were retreating and vulnerable. "We'd better find our mounts."

Chapter Thirty

WARY ALLIES

The Karamanids retreated, and the army serving the sultan pursued all that day. The ghazis and the akincis bit at the retreating forces at every opportunity, but the Karamanids maintained discipline. No panic left them open to widespread decimation, other than what they had suffered when the battle lines had clashed.

As the sun dipped below the horizon, the sultan sent word that his army would stop and rest. Konstantin and his men were exhausted, and some had minor wounds. The same was true for the mercenaries. When the grooms and camp followers caught up to the men, everyone worked to set up tents and care for the animals.

Konstantin spoke with each man from the garrison, checking their health and fitness for battle in the coming days and thanking them for their gallant fighting. He also spoke with the mercenaries, including two with serious wounds.

"If they avoid infection, they ought to make full recoveries, but they might not fight again on this campaign." Ulrich filled Konstantin in on how the battle had proceeded for the men on foot, finishing with approval at the arrangement that placed his men near the footmen that Župan Dragomir's satnik led. "Our crossbows pair nicely with their javelins."

Konstantin nodded. "Good. We'll likely do the same thing next time the battle lines are drawn up. If the Karamanids are up for another battle."

"We'll see them again, I think. They were hurt today but not defeated, and more will rally to their cause as we push farther into their lands."

Sobered, Konstantin went to check on Veles. The battle had left Konstantin weary, but all his men had come through, and though it was possible the Karamanid ranks would grow, the added men would likely be merchants, farmers, or herdsmen rather than warriors.

"You fought valiantly today, lord." Miladin had come to tend Grom. He smiled despite a bruise forming along the right side of his face. "Your father would have been proud of you."

"Given the banner we follow, I'm not so sure." Konstantin kept his voice low. By preventing a breakthrough, he'd saved his men. But he'd also saved some of the sultan's men, and his father had ever considered the Turks his enemy. What would he think of his son following the horse-tail tug of Sultan Murad?

Arslan approached, making Konstantin glad he'd not spoken louder.

With Arslan was another Turk, one dressed in the clothing of a sipahi, with a powerful build and a face that showed experience. His piercing eyes studied Konstantin.

"Peace be unto you, Arslan. I am glad to see you uninjured." And that was true—Konstantin disliked serving the sultan, but he liked Arslan.

"Peace be unto you. Are you and your men well?"

"Yes. A few wounded, but we expect them to recover. Quickly, if they are given rest."

"The sultan has not yet decided if he wishes to pursue the enemy while they are still reeling from today's battle or give the men a chance to regroup and recover."

That meant Konstantin would have to prepare for both possibilities until the sultan made his decision and shared it with his vassals.

Arslan gestured to the other man. "This is Kasim bin Yazid. He led the sipahis who fought near Župan Nikola's men. He wishes to meet the man who broke the Karamanid pincer."

The man spoke in Turkish.

Arslan translated. "He did not expect you to be so young. But he credits you with saving his life. He is grateful for your timely aid to his sipahis and your role in keeping the Ottoman line from breaking."

For a moment, Konstantin wondered what would have happened if he hadn't come to the aid of the sipahis. The flower of the Ottoman army might have been destroyed. But that destruction could have grown to include Konstantin and his men. Or would they have been able to successfully extricate themselves from the fray while the Karamanids waged destruction on Konstantin's Turkish overlords? He didn't think the Karamanids were strong enough to completely break the Ottoman army. And unless the Ottoman army was well and truly broken, vengeance would fall quickly on any vassals who performed poorly in battle. With at least partial sincerity, Konstantin said, "I am glad my men and I were in the right place at the right time."

"And with the right skills and the bravery to use them," Kasim said through Arslan. The envoy continued. "Kasim wishes you to join him as his guest at the sultan's table."

"When?"

"Tonight," Arslan replied.

Konstantin was not eager to attend another meal with the sultan. He preferred the food he was accustomed to—even the bland campaign fare. And he did not relish the reminder that his people had been subjugated by the Turks. But he wasn't sure this was the type of invitation he could refuse without causing trouble. "I have a watch to set with my own camp. And I have enemies that I am loath to meet when unaccompanied."

"Many have told me of your skill on the battlefield," Arslan said. "I do not think those who might wish you harm could outmatch you. Take my advice. Accept the offer. Set the watch quickly, or have someone else arrange it. Put on clean clothing, and bring a bodyguard. Do not turn down the chance to dine with the sultan when he is pleased with your valor."

Konstantin nodded. "Please tell Kasim that I am honored by the invitation." Attending the sultan's meal was less repulsive than most of his other duties as a vassal. "If he wishes to wait in my tent while I change and see to my men, I would be pleased to extend my hospitality. If he wishes to go on ahead, I will do my best to catch up to him."

Kasim said something to Arslan, who translated the reply. "He would be happy to accept your hospitality."

Konstantin had been hoping he wouldn't. Kasim bin Yazid was a stranger who did not seem to speak Slavonic, and everyone in Rivak's camp sought rest, not unwanted guests. But politeness was required. Konstantin wasn't eager to ingratiate himself with the sultan, but it could prove useful. Perhaps a friendly sultan would be less inclined to suspicion should Konstantin's yearning for freedom ever be revealed.

As they led Arslan and Kasim toward the camp's center, Konstantin lowered his voice and spoke to Miladin. "I would be grateful if you would accompany me."

"Of course, lord."

"Has anyone arranged the watch?"

"Grigorii assigned one of our men for each watch of the night, and Ulrich assigned two of his."

Three men per watch. Given the size of their encampment, it ought to be enough. "See that the men are ready to act quickly should the need arise."

"Yes, lord. I'll remind them now, if you like, then meet you at your tent."

While Miladin went to the men, Konstantin led the Turks the remaining distance to his tent and ushered them inside. Arslan did not drink wine. If Kasim followed Muslim tradition, nor would he. It seemed pointless to serve hardtack on the way to a meal with the sultan, but a host needed to offer the men something. Risto was setting up Konstantin's bedroll, but he stopped what he was doing and pulled several cushions from a trunk to offer the visitors. When the Turks were seated, Konstantin motioned Risto closer and lowered his voice. Arslan might hear, but Konstantin fully expected him to pretend he didn't. "Do we have anything other than wine and hardtack to offer our guests?"

"Vinegar, lord. Or dried dates."

"Offer them dates, please."

Konstantin excused himself and went to find water for washing. The day before, they had set up camp near a stream, but the battle had changed their position, making the drawing of water an extensive chore. Regardless, Konstantin couldn't visit the sultan covered in the dust of battle. He allocated a pail of water from one of the barrels they pulled in carts and used it to wash hands, hair, and face. With any luck, they'd camp close enough to water in the coming days that he could bathe more thoroughly in a stream.

When he returned, he found Kasim bin Yazid snacking on dried dates and holding Konstantin's icon of the Virgin Mary, the one Ivan had given him.

"He wished me to ask if it is yours," Arslan said.

"It is."

Kasim asked another question, and Arslan translated. "Do you worship the woman?"

Konstantin tried to pick his next words carefully. From what he knew of the Ottoman's religion, they didn't approve of icons or of most other images. That wasn't so odd—the emperors in Constantinople had at times eschewed images and at times embraced them, and the difference in opinion had been sharp enough to cause civil war. "I worship God the Father,

His Son, and the Holy Ghost. The woman is venerated for her role as the mortal mother of God's Son. I keep the image because it reminds me of my Redeemer, my brother, and my wife."

Kasim studied the image a little longer before placing it on the trunk he'd no doubt dug it out of. He said something to Arslan.

Arslan had the decency to look embarrassed by Kasim's blatant disregard for his host's privacy and property. "He asks if you are happy in your marriage. Shall I tell him yes?"

"You may."

"Kasim says his wife displeases him, so he will search for a new wife."

Konstantin had no wish to become involved in the sipahi's marital troubles but didn't wish to offend by not engaging in conversation. "How is it done among your people if a wife is not pleasing?"

Arslan exchanged words with Kasim. Konstantin pulled off his surcoat and replaced it with a fresh one. He kept his mail. Walking around without any protection would be foolish. Even armies that had suffered setbacks could send out raiders, and Konstantin didn't wish to be trapped in a distant part of the camp without everything he might need to combat a Karamanid ambush.

"He will not divorce his wife, as her family is too powerful. But he is allowed four wives if he can support them, and he expects this campaign will give him the wealth for at least one more."

Two wives? Konstantin was glad he could focus on his clothing for the moment. It made it easier to hide his distaste. Perhaps Kasim had been unlucky in marriage. If he'd been blessed with someone as perfect for him as Suzana, there would be no need to look for another wife. "I see." He didn't really but wasn't sure what else to say. Konstantin straightened his clean surcoat. "I am at your disposal."

Kasim placed a final date in his mouth and stood. Arslan followed suit, and the three left the tent. Miladin waited for them outside, the ends of his hair, like Konstantin's, damp from his efforts at hygiene.

The walk to the sultan's pavilion was pleasant, with the cool evening air offering a welcome change from the dry heat of the day. Despite the battle, the men they passed had set up orderly camps. Men cooked over small fires, bedrolls and tents formed tidy rows, and grooms fed and cared for horses, mules, and donkeys. Contented laughs floated through the air, a sign of high morale.

Konstantin had visited the sultan's tent before, but the size and luxury struck him anew. Sultan Murad wielded a power no Serb had held for a generation.

Miladin was directed to the end of the leather mat, some distance from the sultan and his leading pashas. Kasim motioned Konstantin to follow him. He bowed to the sultan, and Konstantin did the same. If the sultan insisted on another prostration that involved Konstantin kissing his toe, Konstantin would regret bringing Miladin.

But instead of asking obeisance, the sultan stood and clasped one of Konstantin's shoulders. He spoke briefly but earnestly, Turkish words that sounded harsh and incomprehensible in Konstantin's ears.

Arslan translated. "He thanks you for your timely maneuver that saved his army from breaking. He will not forget this service."

Konstantin didn't want to lie, but nor did he wish to take a misstep with the sultan, and standing there, in that tent, with the mighty Murad right before him meant diplomacy ought to outweigh candor. "Please tell him I am pleased to be found adequate to my duty."

That ended the interview, much to Konstantin's relief. Kasim led him to a spot before the mat, much closer to the sultan than Konstantin's previous position, and before long, the first course was served. The food was still strange, as was the language, but the men around him no longer looked at him as they might an insect. He had proven himself to the Ottoman leaders. For better or for worse, he needed to use his new status as best he could to help his people.

Chapter Thirty-One
Pushing Boundaries

Suzana shifted her market basket into one hand and knocked on the door of the two-level home in the lower grad.

Miladin's wife, Magdalena, pulled the door open and gave Suzana a cautious smile. "Dama Suzana, your visit is an honor to our home. Will you come in? I have bread still warm from the oven."

Suzana hesitated to accept the invitation because Magdalena's welcome seemed subdued. It would also mean boredom for the man acting as her guard. Yet Suzana's feet were sore after wandering the market, and fresh bread sounded appealing. "Thank you."

Magdalena led her inside, past a loom with a growing length of wool cloth, then beyond a stone hearth, and offered her a chair at the trestle table positioned beneath a window.

"Do you bring news of the men?" Magdalena asked as she placed a slice of bread with skorup on it in front of Suzana.

That explained why Magdalena seemed so tense. Like everyone with a loved one away at war, she feared ill tidings.

Suzana shook her head. "I've heard nothing of the campaign."

Magdalena relaxed. "I shouldn't have assumed, but this is the longest Miladin and I have been apart since our marriage. It's hard not to worry. I dreamed about a memory a few nights ago, when Miladin was almost killed." Magdalena touched her forehead in the same spot where her husband's face was scarred. "It . . . I've felt unsettled ever since."

"I worry too." Suzana said a silent prayer that Magdalena's dream was only a memory, not a premonition. Suzana tasted the warm bread with the creamy topping. "This is delicious."

"Miladin's mother makes the best skorup in Rivakgrad. I'll pass on your compliments when she and Sveta return from the market."

"I saw them there." Suzana had spent most of the morning negotiating with traveling merchants over the family's upcoming needs for cloth. She had left Dama Zorica and Lidija debating between two colors of silk, and she had seen Miladin's mother and niece not far from there. She bent and pulled a soft fur cap from her basket. "A furrier from the north was there, and he had two of these." She handed the cap to Magdalena.

"It's so soft." Magdalena studied the cap. "And so tiny. Is it meant for an infant?"

Suzana nodded. "The last time the midwife visited me, she mentioned your condition, so I thought I would take both caps. One for your baby. One for mine."

"But this . . . is it sable? I hate to think of the price."

"I have been watching my father negotiate prices since I was your niece's age. Trust me, it was a bargain. Besides, I've heard stories of both you and your husband saving Konstantin's life. I think you've earned a few luxuries."

Magdalena looked up from the cap, though her fingers continued to move across the soft surface. "Thank you."

"Whenever I start to worry too much about Konstantin, I remember that Miladin went with him, and that makes it easier." Suzana looked at the last few bites of her bread. "I know they would both rather stay in Rivak, but I am glad they can look out for each other."

"It's a generous gift. You have my gratitude."

Suzana smiled and finished her bread. "I'm afraid I can't stay long. I left my guard with most of the purchases. Konstantin insists I not wander about the lower grad without an escort." The guard was a member of the garrison too young to march with the army.

Magdalena looked thoughtful. "A distant relative with a weak claim to the župa tried to kill him in the lower grad shortly after his father died. And someone has tried to kill you before. Rivakgrad is usually safe, but Župan Konstantin is wise to give you protection."

The attacks against her the previous summer seemed so long ago. Suzana no longer worried about her own safety; she worried about her husband's. Regardless, she would continue honoring his arrangements for her protection.

Suzana left the cozy home and returned to the grody with her escort. Ivan and Adamu, one of the men from Sivi Gora, sparred with wooden swords in the bailey. When Suzana, Dama Zorica, and Lidija had left to visit the market, both boys had been working with Kuzman. She'd watched them then, noting that though Ivan and Danilo lacked power, they had speed. Their footwork was well-coordinated and natural, as if they'd practiced so often that the motions were second nature to them.

But that training had begun some time ago, and now Ivan's face was flushed and his hair wet from exertion. He blocked blow after blow coming from his opponent, and though Adamu used only moderate force, his blows came with a speed that made them hard to follow.

Adamu stopped and held back for a moment.

"Again," Ivan said.

Suzana watched the session repeat once, then twice, and then Ivan staggered and would have collapsed had his trainer not reached out to steady him.

"Did you train the entire time I was gone?" Suzana asked.

Ivan sucked in a deep breath. "I did."

"But you were ill only a few days ago. Oughtn't you take your training more slowly? A body has limits, Ivan."

His limbs may have drooped with fatigue, but the eyes that stared back at her held fiery resolve. "If I never push those limits, then they will never change."

The contrast of his weary body and determined face surprised her. She glanced around for Danilo, surprised that he hadn't told Ivan to stop long ago. But it was not a boy's job to keep his cousin from overexerting himself. She turned her anger on Ivan's trainer. "You ought not push him so. He is still a boy."

Adamu did not answer immediately. "He is only a boy, my lady, that is true. But he is destined to be a župan. My župan, in fact, and the determination he has shown today has given me a glimpse into how great he can become. Forgive me for wanting to see how hard he could push himself."

"I can do another round, Adamu." Ivan's breaths still came in gasps.

"No." Suzana reached for Ivan's wooden sword. "The rest of your day will involve tasks of a less physical nature."

Ivan held her gaze for a while, as if determining whether he had to obey. He finally nodded and relinquished his sword, but that may have been only because his aunt and sister had returned from the market. Dama Zorica pressed a hand to his forehead before insisting on rest and leading him toward the keep. Lidija followed.

When they were out of earshot, Suzana turned to Adamu. "That boy may be destined to be your župan, and he may be destined for greatness, but he is still fragile, and his brother has placed him in my care. Do not push him until he collapses again, not in Rivak."

Adamu bowed his head. "As you wish, my lady."

"Where is Danilo?"

Adamu glanced at the range. "I believe he is practicing his archery."

"Until his arm will no longer move?"

"No. Kuzman has taught the boys to stop when fatigue affects their aim."

"And when were you planning to stop Ivan? When he fell to the ground?"

Adamu looked after the small figure walking to the keep. "I planned to see how far he would go before he stopped himself. I wish we lived in lands that did not require boys to study with the sword from such a young age, but he and his cousin will someday need to defend themselves. They must learn the proper techniques and the proper discipline, or they will not survive their first battle. He impressed me today, lady. And his grandfather, too, would have been impressed."

"He may have impressed you, but he will never lead you into battle if he does not live to reach manhood."

"I will be more cautious with his limited stamina in the future, my lady," Adamu promised. "But sometimes the sons and grandsons of župans do not have the privilege of reaching manhood before their duties require them to shoulder a man's burden."

Konstantin had not been given the privilege of time. Suzana didn't know if Ivan would either, but rather than following the boy into the keep, she went to the church to pray. She owed God gratitude for the promising crops now growing in last year's burned fields, and she wanted to plead with Him on behalf of her husband and her husband's small brother.

Chapter Thirty-Two
In the Shadows

Konstantin tucked the cross from Suzana back under his tunic. A hot, dry wind blew along the line of horsemen as they followed the Ottoman sultan farther and farther into Karamanid territory.

"He'll have to release us in time to journey home before the snow falls, won't he?" Zoran, riding ahead of Konstantin, spoke to Grigorii. "Snow comes early in some of the passes."

"I don't know if the sultan understands our weather." Grigorii's voice held gloom—something becoming all too normal for him. "Or cares, for that matter."

"I just wish I knew how my family was. We've been gone for nearly two moons, and the Karamanids don't seem to be losing yet."

Maybe Konstantin would plead the need to be with his men more often the next time an invitation came to dine with the sultan. He was growing more easy in the presence of the sultan, the sultan's sons, and the sultan's top advisers. But if the morale of his men was faltering, it was Konstantin's job to improve it. Like them, he longed for his family. Suzana would likely be showing her condition by now, and he was missing all of it. Lidija, Ivan, and Danilo, too, might all change in the course of a summer. He wanted to be with them, but that would happen only with the sultan's permission.

Melancholy and worry gave him something to feel, but they wouldn't change his circumstances. He urged Perun to catch up with Zoran's horse. "What do you think of the scimitar, Zoran?" Perhaps a distraction would do the man good, and he was passionate about weapons.

Zoran and Konstantin launched into a vigorous discussion about the merits and weaknesses of scimitars, spathions, and the long two-handed swords men from the west tended to favor. In the end, they both decided they would prefer a spathion and a shield.

"You look thoughtful, Grigorii. A different weapon for you?"

Grigorii shook his head slowly. "My thoughts are elsewhere."

"On what?" Zoran asked. "A girl back in Rivak?"

Grigorii huffed. "No. On enemies. Is it possible to admire an enemy?"

Konstantin hated Sultan Murad for what he had done to his family and his župa, but he could recognize the man's wisdom when it came to organizing his troops and the admirable way he balanced listening to his advisors and maintaining decisive authority. Konstantin would learn all he could from the sultan even while wishing he could rebel against him. He gave Grigorii his answer. "Yes, it's possible."

The deep rhythm of a drum signaled the alarm. The sound came from the portion of the sultan's army marching ahead of them—Kasim's sipahis.

"It must be another Karamanid ambush." Zoran had been riding without his helmet, but he shoved it onto his head now.

Everyone in Rivak's contingent put armor on when they dressed each morning, so they were ready to defend against just such an attack, but the size of the army and lay of the land meant they saw the enemy only when they were nearly upon them. Jakov brought Veles forward and switched horses with Konstantin.

"Can you see what's happening?" Konstantin asked as Miladin guided Grom next to Veles.

"No. Too much dust, and the Karamanids do not dress so differently from the Ottomans."

"They're coming around the sipahis' left flank," Grigorii called out.

Konstantin saw it then, the group of raiders, scimitars drawn, charging with speed past Kasim's men.

"Form a line!" Konstantin called. He turned to Jakov. "Tell Ulrich to form up behind us."

As the men from his garrison arranged themselves for a charge, Konstantin peered at the skirmish swirling before him. The Karamanids were attacking hard and in force. Over the past fortnight, they'd fallen into a pattern: attack, hurt the Ottomans as much as they could, and then withdraw before an effective counterattack could be organized. They never stayed long, and when they met strong enough resistance, they withdrew. They were unlikely to win battles that way, but the constant harassing made it hard to sleep at night and left all those who rode with the sultan on edge.

Konstantin motioned his men forward. Galloping in near unison, they lowered their spears and plowed into the Karamanids trying to flank the sipahis. The Karamanids quickly retreated.

"Should we pursue, lord?" Grigorii asked.

Konstantin's gut said no, and he decided to follow it. If Sultan Murad defeated all his enemies in Anatolia, he could more fully subdue his vassals in Serbia. The men of Rivak had to fight with competence, but there was no need for recklessness. And something about the retreat gave Konstantin pause. They were coordinated in their movements, more so than most men in the midst of a retreat. "We wait."

Kasim's sipahis had no such hesitations. They followed the retreating Karamanids like a pack of wolves striking down prey—all instinct and hunger. The Karamanid warriors, in contrast, formed a perfect crescent, one that grew deeper and deeper, forming a pocket around the sipahis.

"They're riding into a trap." Konstantin saw the danger, but it was too late to give Kasim's men any warning. At that moment, the retreating Karamanids turned around and charged at the now-encircled sipahis.

"Do we rescue them?" Grigorii asked.

Now that he knew the Karamanid plans, intervention lost some of the risk. "Yes, but first, we let the mercenaries thin their ranks. Ride to Ulrich. Have his men loose several salvos, then we'll break open the line for the sipahis to escape through."

"Yes, lord."

As Grigorii rode off, Konstantin explained the plan to the others. All the while, in the center of a ring of Karamanids, Kasim's sipahis fought for survival.

Ulrich acted quickly. The men rode forward and dismounted, leaving their horses with grooms stationed outside the range of Turkish arrows. Then they ran closer, aimed, and brought down a score of enemy horsemen. The second salvo had roughly the same results, but as the bolts flew, the Karamanids turned to the new foe. They would organize a charge against Ulrich's men soon, and Konstantin didn't want that. The mercenaries wore armor, but not enough to stop a scimitar swung with the full force of a warrior and a horse behind it.

"Caution as we move around the crossbowmen." Konstantin led his horsemen through the mercenaries. "Break open the Karamanid encirclement, but do not push into the center of the fray. We fight on the edges, where we can retreat if they attempt to spring another trap."

Konstantin and his men charged forward. He skewered one of the Karamanids, then another, and then Veles thrashed his hooves into the wounded men on the ground. Konstantin held back, not allowing himself to be drawn too far into the skirmish.

In the distance, the Karamanids remained virile and coordinated. Closer to Konstantin, they disintegrated as sipahis and Serbs battled them from opposite sides. Konstantin pushed closer. His spear broke, so he took out his spathion. He slashed at a man on a horse, and the Turk's back arched as he tumbled to the ground and his horse ran wild, frightened and desperate. Konstantin slashed at another enemy on foot, driving the end of his blade into his opponent's neck. Then another man on horse. And another.

Several sipahis tried to break free of the Karamanid encirclement, but the enemy surrounding them fought hard. Konstantin hacked and hewed his way closer to the men fighting so desperately. Miladin and Zoran followed. Konstantin struck down another pair of Karamanids, and then he shoved his spathion into one who had wounded a sipahi and was about to finish him off.

The enemy warrior fell, and the wounded sipahi turned. It was Kasim, and he quickly accepted Konstantin's hand so he could pull him up behind him on Veles. More and more of the Karamanids were retreating now—really leaving, not setting a new trap. Konstantin did not pursue, but Ulrich's men shot more of them as they left. When they were gone, the dust settled on at least a hundred bodies. Roughly half were Karamanid. But the other half were Ottoman. Kasim's sipahis had been ravaged.

Commotion swirled around Konstantin as men set up tents, prepared perimeter defenses, and tended their horses after another day of war. Konstantin could have delegated care of Veles and Perun to his groom, but he wanted time with his animals. The calm they brought was welcome after seeing so many broken bodies that day.

Miladin found him as he was finishing. "Lord, Župans Dragomir and Nikola have arrived."

Their visits were unexpected. Only something important would bring them from their own camps after a battle like the one they'd just fought.

Konstantin met the župans and Decimir near his tent. "Welcome," he said. "I am honored by your visit." Small entourages from both županas joined men from Rivak at their fires.

Župan Nikola studied Rivak's encampment. Konstantin would no doubt have done likewise had their positions been reversed. While on campaign, a man needed to always be aware of his surroundings, and Župan Nikola had learned that the hard way. Unlike Konstantin's father and uncle, Župan Nikola had survived the disaster at Maritsa, living long enough to put the hard-earned caution into practice. "I wish to discuss a matter of importance, and Župan Dragomir assures me you are the right sort of man."

"I hope I am." Konstantin pushed aside the flap of his leather tent and allowed the others inside, uncertain why Župan Nikola wished to see him, Dragomir, and Dragomir's heir but not the other Serbian vassals who were setting up camps for the night.

Risto opened a trunk to pull out cushions for the guests to sit on, then lit another oil lamp and slipped from the tent.

"What do you know of the Karamanids?" Župan Nikola asked when the four of them were left alone.

"They are fierce fighters," Konstantin said. "And clever. They only fully engage when they have an advantage. They trapped the sipahis well today."

"And beyond their skill on the battlefield? What do you know of them?"

Župan Dragomir studied the flame of the lamp. "They are Turks, like the Ottomans. Both wish to control the same trade routes and collect the corresponding custom duties. The Karamanids are positioned along many of the land routes from the south and the east. Some of the shipping routes too. I doubt we'll take their capital in Konya, nor gain control of the Black Mountain in a single campaign. But we are helping the Ottomans take some of the lands that lie between their respective strongholds."

Župan Nikola absently twisted the ring on his left hand. "And as we gain more power and glory for the sultan, will that make him so rich that he no longer needs our tribute? Or so powerful that he will control us even more completely?"

Konstantin looked around the tent. They were alone, and Župan Nikola's voice was barely above a whisper. No one outside would hear, and secrecy was vital when discussing anything other than complete loyalty to the sultan. "I do not imagine a sultan would give up tribute unless he were compelled to do so."

Župan Nikola leaned forward, seeming pleased that Konstantin had come to the same conclusion he had. "So, we all agree that helping the sultan will not bring us more freedom."

"Careful, Župan Nikola." Župan Dragomir kept his voice quiet and calm. "None of us enjoy our vassalage, but we have much to lose if the sultan feels he cannot trust us."

"We also have much to lose if we help the sultan gain more power than he already has." Župan Nikola planted his hands to either side of his cushion.

"What do you propose?" Konstantin wasn't ready to reveal his own rebellious aspirations, but curiosity pushed him to learn all he could of Župan Nikola's plans.

"If the Karamanids attacked from the south, and if we attacked from the west, would the sultan be able to defeat us both?"

Konstantin did everything he could to make his breathing appear normal, but inside, thoughts and emotions churned. An alliance against the sultan? It carried tremendous risk. It also carried tremendous potential. "Are you in contact with the Karamanids?"

"No." Župan Nikola looked away. "But I wish to know how many Serbs would stand with me should I find the right messenger and make contact with the right beylik."

"Have you spoken with others?" Župan Dragomir asked.

Župan Nikola twisted his ring again. "If I make my inquiries in small groups, the conspiracy remains limited should the sultan hear of it. He may find out I seek an alliance with his enemies, but he would not know who else might risk rebellion. Until the time is right, I prefer to work in the shadows."

"Then you do not believe that time has come?" Konstantin could picture his life without vassalage to the sultan, and it was significantly better for him and for his people.

Župan Nikola shook his head. "It will not come during this campaign."

Hopes that had been rising fell but didn't completely disappear. Konstantin did not wish to remain Murad's vassal, but by himself, he had no other options. Together, perhaps, the Serbs could gain their freedom. "*Only unity can save the Serbs.*"

Župan Nikola smiled. "Saint Sava. We will need unity indeed. And patience."

Konstantin wished he could discuss potential rebellion with others—Suzana, Aunt Zorica, Miladin, or Grigorii. Even more, he wished his father, and not he, would be the one to make the choice. Fealty to an enemy or rebellion that might lead to destruction? For better or for worse, the choice was Konstantin's, and in his heart, he already knew the answer. "When the time is right, I will stand with my brother Serbs."

"As will I," Župan Dragomir said. His grandson nodded his agreement. "But we must use caution and be certain the time is right. We will increase our strength and keep the sultan from gaining power too swiftly. Until then, we will work, as you put it, in the shadows."

Chapter Thirty-Three
A Burden of Grief

Suzana closed the ledger and locked the strongroom. She allowed herself a smile of satisfaction at how much Rivak's finances had improved in a single year. Moving forward, the rents would be sufficient to cover all the grody's needs as well as hire mercenaries, should they be needed again.

Her hand rose to the bulge in her abdomen. It seemed like so long ago that Konstantin had ridden off to war, and his return wasn't expected for some time yet, but she ached to see him again, yearned to share all her hopes for the baby. The future—for their family and for Rivak—seemed bright.

"Suzana!" Danilo barreled around the corner and stopped in front of her. Excitement lit his swarthy face. "Come and see!"

Ivan skidded to a halt beside his cousin. Their faces were different from each other—their skin, hair, and eyes did not match—but today, they shared an expression of wonder and delight. "There's a new foal! Will you come?"

"I would be happy to." She strolled with them from the keep and across the bailey to a gated enclosure by the stables, flattered that they wanted to share their wonder with her. Lidija already watched from behind the fence along with Bojan, Jasmina, Magdalena, and Svetlana. The foal was a pale tan in contrast to the mare's rich chestnut, but both had a similar blaze across the face. The newborn stood on wobbly legs as the mare licked it from face to hindquarters.

"Is it a filly or a colt?" Danilo asked.

Bojan squinted. "I'll check later. For now, it's best not to interrupt."

"Miraculous, isn't it?" Magdalena asked with a smile.

"It is," Suzana said.

Magdalena leaned closer and lowered her voice. "And the process is even more miraculous when it's your baby. How are you feeling?"

"I've more of an appetite lately. I still want to sleep far longer than is normal, and sometimes, my body aches with the growth, but if I could only know my husband will return to me before the baby comes, that would make everything perfect." Suzana noted Magdalena's figure: her condition was more obvious now than it had been when Suzana had last seen her. "How are you feeling?"

"Better than with any of the previous times. When I was married to my first husband, we did not always have enough food, and he was not as careful of my health as Miladin and his mother are. This time, I am far more hopeful."

"You've lost babies before?"

Magdalena's face grew wistful. "Many times."

Magdalena's toll, though not unusual, felt incredibly heavy. As Magdalena and her niece returned to the lower grad, Suzana said a silent prayer that this time, the woman would be blessed with a healthy infant.

Gasps of delight pulled Suzana's attention back first to the boys, then to the foal they watched as it took its first tentative steps with a few gentle nudges from its mother. Horses always reminded her of Konstantin now because he loved them so much, though Danilo's passion for them might be even deeper.

She missed her husband. She tried to stay busy with preparation for the baby and organizing the grody's stores and sometimes even by sitting in on Ivan's and Danilo's tutoring. She had picked up a little Greek from them, but yesterday, in place of language work, they had examined the organs of a recently slaughtered pig, and the sight had turned her stomach.

She stayed for a while longer, watching the new foal—a colt, Bojan had discovered when the time was right—and enjoying how the boys and Lidija reveled in the gentle newness of life. Then she went to the chapel to say prayers for her husband's safe return.

A year ago, she had found little peace in churches. Little peace anywhere. But now the chapel was among her favorite places in the grody. Worry for her husband and his small army was constant, but most days, Suzana managed to bury that worry in prayers. Men in Konstantin's family might be destined to die in battle, but she felt it would not happen yet for her husband. He would come home to her, at least a few more times.

An achy sort of pain hit her as she left the church. She inhaled sharply, wondering at its cause, then she rested against the wall of the church and took deep breaths until the ache seemed to ease. But something about the pain in her loins made her nervous. It wasn't a familiar type of hurt.

Another step and it was back, sharper than before, making her hunch over. Her neck and torso felt clammy and nausea turned in her stomach.

"My lady?"

She held her breath and glanced up. Kuzman stood before her, a wooden practice sword in his hand. Danilo and Ivan, similarly armed, stood just behind him.

"Are you well?"

"I . . . I'm not sure." The midwife who visited her from time to time had told her birth pains were unlike other pains, but it was too early for the baby to come. "I think I need to rest."

"Danilo, go fetch your mother." Kuzman gently touched her arm. "Let me see you back to the keep."

Suzana accepted Kuzman's assistance and took a few steps, then had to pause as the pain flared and her eyesight grew fuzzy. Something warm trickled down her legs. She gasped for breath as the pain increased again, sharper and more powerful than before.

Kuzman scooped her up as her footsteps faltered, with one arm under her knees and the other across her back. He wasn't running, exactly, but he was moving far more quickly than she had been.

She faced backward, so she saw Ivan bend to the ground, touch something, then pull back in alarm. He ran after her. "Suzana?"

Kuzman shifted his hold on her. "Whatever it is, Ivan, it will have to wait."

Ivan held out a finger smeared in red. "But why is Suzana bleeding?"

Dama Zorica's hand pressed gently against Suzana's forehead, wiping it with a cool cloth. They were alone in Suzana's bedchamber. Jasmina and the midwife had changed the bed linens and cleaned the room so that it looked as if nothing had happened.

Looks could be incredibly deceiving.

"How do you feel?" Dama Zorica asked.

Suzana closed her eyes. The pain lingered, though not as strong as the waves that had knocked her off her feet. But grief—that pain loomed large. "I feel as if my heart's been torn out."

The baby had been a boy. So small. Limbs like twigs. A few wisps of dark-brown hair. She'd wanted him so much, but he'd been dead before he was born. All the plans she'd had for him now felt false. They would never be fulfilled, and the sadness of all that potential cut off before he could take even one breath felt suffocating.

Dama Zorica grasped her hand. "I know it hurts and that right now, it feels as if your heart will never heal. But does it feel as though your body will recover?"

"The physical hurt is . . . My body has recovered from worse, I think." Suzana squeezed her eyes shut, letting tears leak out. "Konstantin doesn't even know." He had cried tears of joy when he'd found out she was with child. What would he do when he learned of their child's premature death?

Tears streamed down Dama Zorica's face, but her voice held. "I know it is hard. For now, focus on resting and recovering. I'm sure that is what Konstantin would tell you if he were here."

She had longed for Konstantin before, but now, she *needed* him. She wanted his arms around her, wanted him to grieve with her, needed him to tell her it wasn't her fault and he still loved her and that somehow everything would work out. He'd fixed her heart before. She needed him to fix it again because it felt as if all hope, like a candle, had just been snuffed out, leaving her in the dark with her grief and pain.

The next morning, Suzana woke to whispered voices.

"Don't wake her, or your mother will scold us." Ivan's voice.

"Here, or on the bed?" Danilo's voice.

Suzana's body throbbed. She loved Ivan and Danilo, but that morning, she agreed with whatever Dama Zorica had told the boys. She would rather be left undisturbed. She had rested on and off the night before, but lingering pain and heartache had made it difficult to sleep.

She kept her eyes closed. If the boys didn't know she'd woken, they wouldn't expect her to say anything brave. That was beyond her this morning, after the whole world had fallen apart the day before.

One of them sneezed, and they bumped into the bed no fewer than five times. Eventually, the voices and shuffles faded, and she was alone again, and that was suddenly worse.

Was it too late to call the boys back? Danilo played the gusle for Ivan when he was ill, and a distraction—any distraction—suddenly sounded like the best of ideas. She didn't want to think about the baby boy who would never feel his mother's arms around him. Never feel the warmth of sunshine on his face. Never see a horse or a bird. Never taste a plum or an almond. Never grow up to take his father's place as župan.

When she opened her eyes, only a small amount of light made it through the pulled curtains. No wonder the boys had bumped into the bed so often. The darkness seemed overwhelming, but the task of opening the window to let in light felt inordinately difficult.

The curtain was but two steps away. She could manage that much. She slowly sat. That made the pain worse but only by a little. Standing did the same. Using the bed and then the wall to balance herself, she took small steps to the curtain and tugged on one end.

Light streamed in. If only sunshine could banish heartache the way it cut through darkness. She turned toward the bed and inhaled sharply. Spread across the floor were wildflowers. Pink and red and yellow and orange. So many of them—more than she would have thought two small boys could carry.

She sat on the bed and cried again—with sorrow because she had lost her son but also with gratitude because of the love behind the scattered wildflowers.

CHAPTER THIRTY-FOUR
THE DANGER OF AN UNDEFEATED FOE

BOTH ARMIES GREW MORE CAUTIOUS after the raid that had nearly killed Kasim. The Karamanids were less bold when they probed the sultan's army. The Ottomans were less reckless in their pursuit, and Konstantin, like his men, merely hoped that the campaign would soon be over so they could return to Serbia. Thus far, none of his men had been killed. He wanted to keep it that way.

Then a group of Ottoman akincis led a nighttime raid through the main Karamanid camp, and much like the Ottomans had at Maritsa, they surprised and broke their enemy. Sultan Murad pressed the pursuit. The remnants of the Karamanid army lacked the strength to mount raiding parties, so they retreated, and the Ottomans, with their Christian vassals, followed them south.

The sultan assigned Konstantin to search one of the caravansaries they passed to make certain no warriors lingered among the stone walls and courtyards. Refugees, mostly women and children, had flocked to the roadside inn. None of them tried to stop Konstantin and his men when they rode through the main entrance.

He glanced around at the wide courtyard before them, probably used as a market in times of peace, and at the numerous arches and portals made of local stone. He divided his men into groups of ten. "Have the people wait in the market while we make sure no one is hiding. Confiscate any weapons but leave everything else." The refugees were on the losing side of a war. Konstantin knew what that felt like, what it would be like for the people as they struggled to find sufficient food to survive the coming winter.

A few of the caravansary's inhabitants protested, but a glimpse of a mercenary's crossbow or a man-at-arm's sword quickly silenced them. Despite

Konstantin's orders, he soon saw one man leave an alcove with a chicken tucked under his arm. Not far away, one of his men argued with a woman over a goat. Konstantin dismounted and dug through his saddlebag for a coin purse. He and Suzana had carefully planned the expenditures needed to feed the army while they campaigned. A splurge on chickens and goats in Anatolia was not part of the plan, but better food would lift morale. Hardtack, dried meat, and wine were growing tiresome for him too. The women here were not his enemy, so Konstantin gave them appropriate coins for the animals they lost. He dealt only with women. They were Karamanids, so their men were all on campaign.

Miladin approached with a quiver of arrows. "We've found a few bows and a stock of arrows. No scimitars thus far."

Konstantin took one of the arrows and examined the workmanship. "I think war swept away all the men and most of the weapons. Have you seen anyone who might be a danger?"

Miladin scanned the Turks crowed in the courtyard. "Even a child can be dangerous if they drop a rock from the right height, but I don't see anyone who concerns me. Still, I wouldn't want to sleep here. The design is admirable and the walls strong, but they see us as the enemy."

Sleeping in the caravansary had never been part of Konstantin's plan. "Let's catch up with the rest of the army." He felt no love for the Ottomans, but in these distant lands he needed them. Caught out on their own, he and his men could easily be ambushed, even by the weakened Karamanid force.

They rode from the caravansary with the confiscated weapons and purchased livestock, confident that the women and children they left behind would not be a danger to the Ottoman army. Grigorii rode next to Konstantin. "The Ottomans have been destroying the settlements they pass so the Karamanids can't go back for shelter or food."

"The villages, yes, but not structures of stone." Konstantin doubted the Karamanid army would make its return in force this summer. And he had seen how devastating fire could be. It would take Rivak years to recover from war, famine, and a series of brigand raids. He had no desire to cause that type of hardship. He fought against the Karamanids out of compulsion; he did not wish them harm.

Grigorii stayed quiet for a long time. Konstantin wondered at the silence and gave his satnik a long look. Grigorii's mouth pulled into a smile that didn't touch the rest of his face. "At least we'll eat well tonight. Do you care for goat?"

"That depends on how it is prepared."

A rider in a turban galloped toward them. Esel. He slowed only when he was close enough to be heard. "The Karamanids have attacked again."

"How large a force?" Konstantin asked.

"Large enough. I'll lead you there." Esel turned his horse around and seemed ready to ride off again.

"Wait—let me tell my men what to expect." Konstantin rode near the front of the group. He urged Perun along the line of men all the way to the rear, telling them to prepare for battle and watching them check their armor. He traded Perun for Veles and returned to the head of his column.

"So many battles." Grigorii tugged on his gauntlets.

"Maybe this one will be decisive." If the Karamanids were gathered for a last stand, a victory today might end the campaign.

They traveled swiftly but did not gallop. Their horses had to be ready to fight when they arrived. And no one was willing to part with the two goats and eight chickens they'd secured, so some of the horses carried extra weight.

A cloud of dust appeared in the distance, along the horizon, low and spreading.

"What did you see before you came for us?" Konstantin asked Esel. The battle lines would have shifted since Esel rode for reinforcements, but Konstantin didn't want to be blindsided when a bit of information could mean the difference between success and failure.

"They formed a line—a crescent really. Their right flank was hidden in the forest. We engaged with their center and left, and then their right emerged and struck. The akincis are all dispersed, so only the sipahis and the Christians hold the line."

"Where did Župan Dragomir's men fight?" Duty and brotherhood made defending his fellow Serbs a priority.

"Near the left."

That meant they would be among those hit hardest by the hidden Karamanid attack. "That is where we ride." Konstantin waited a moment to make sure Esel had no counterorders from the sultan, but he said nothing. Konstantin motioned Ulrich forward. "Aim for the enemy as best you can. We're rescuing Župan Dragomir, so you'll be able to distinguish his men from the Karamanids easily enough. Come as close as possible, but keep your horses nearby in case you need to retreat."

"I will see to it, Župan Konstantin."

Konstantin turned to give his men-at-arms their instructions. "Župan Dragomir's men are in danger. They are your friends and your brothers. You know what to do."

They rode again, faster than before. They moved behind the lines where Ottomans and Karamanids clashed in combat that seemed to favor neither side. Then, as they approached the left end of the sprawling battle, Konstantin recognized Župan Dragomir's banner.

Konstantin pushed Veles forward. The Serbs and Karamanids had no doubt begun their clash in lines, but that order had disintegrated into a melee of individual duels and skirmishes. Konstantin used his spathion to slice into the exposed flesh of every Karamanid he saw who battled one of Dragomir's men. Miladin, Grigorii, and the others did the same.

Twenty paces away, Decimir dueled with a large Karamanid warrior. The enemy towered over the young man, and of Decimir's two bodyguards, one lay unmoving on the ground and the other fought against two men at once. Decimir blocked each strike that came toward him from the scimitar, but his opponent pushed him back. Decimir stepped around an impaled horse with enough strength to thrash its legs about, and then the Karamanid lunged again and hit Decimir's shield with enough force to rock him backward. Decimir stepped on a corpse, slipped, and fell to the ground. He threw his shield up to block his foe's next blow, but it was only a matter of time before he was defeated.

Konstantin plucked a javelin from a dead horse and galloped closer. He hurled the shaft and struck the man before he could finish off Župan Dragomir's heir. Konstantin said a silent prayer of thanks for his success. Lidija would be heartbroken should Decimir fall in battle and so would Župan Dragomir and Dama Isidora. They'd already lost enough.

Decimir looked up at Konstantin. At about the same time, his remaining bodyguard slew the man he'd been fighting and rushed back to Decimir's side.

"Stay close," Konstantin said.

Decimir was brave enough, but he hadn't yet gained the strength of a full-grown man. If separated from the others, he was vulnerable.

Konstantin split his mounted men, ordering Grigorii to lead half to circle round and attack the Karamanids hemming in Dragomir's men from the east. He led the rest to push back the enemy fighting his ally from the west. He saw little of Ulrich's men as the battle continued, but he noted their handiwork when crossbow bolts slammed into the enemy, often in the moment Serbian warriors most needed a reprieve. The Karamanids slowly began falling back. One turned and ran. Then another and another. Most fought on a while longer, but panic and certainty of defeat spread and became a rout as more and more of the Karamanids fled.

Župan Dragomir limped toward Konstantin. He was missing both horse and helmet, but relief lit his face when he saw that his grandson still lived.

"Do you think we should follow?" Konstantin gestured at the retreating enemy.

"That is a real defeat, not a feigned one." Dragomir accepted a horse—not his normal mount—that one of his men brought. "So, yes, I think we should follow, with caution." He gazed around, and his eyes fixed on the body of one of his men. "With caution and vengeance."

Chapter Thirty-Five
In War's Aftermath

Konstantin and the others rode forward until the dust of battle cleared, and then the screen of trees opened to reveal a large clearing. The Karamanid camp. The enemy continued their retreat, and few slowed as they passed among the rows of tents. Seeing the panic, others fled as well, including the camp followers. Boys too young to be soldiers but old enough to care for horses ran, and so did women. Ottoman sipahis cut them off and slaughtered them.

It wasn't war. It was butchery. Some threw up their hands in surrender, but the Ottomans showed no mercy.

Grigorii and most of the men he'd led in an attempt to save Dragomir had rejoined Konstantin's group, minus one man who had been killed and several who had been wounded. The losses had sobered them all, but now Grigorii's face tensed.

"Are you all right?" Miladin asked him.

Grigorii inhaled audibly. "It reminds me of Maritsa, only that slaughter took place in the dark."

Konstantin dismounted. The need for swift action had passed. "Grigorii, go back to the battlefield. See to the wounded. Take a few men with you in case you run into stragglers."

Grigorii nodded. "Thank you, lord."

Konstantin wanted to join his satnik, but he needed to be sure the Karamanids were well and truly defeated. The enemy had surprised them countless times over the course of the summer. He didn't want to walk into another ambush.

"They took us by surprise?" Konstantin asked Župan Dragomir.

"Yes. We would have been overwhelmed had you not come. Thank you."

"You'd do the same for us."

"I would, but I lost many men today. I am but a weak ally now." Župan Dragomir swallowed and cleared his throat, probably to stave off emotion.

One of Dragomir's men asked him about orders, and Konstantin walked on, leading Veles. He, too, had lost a man, and several of the wounded had injuries severe enough that the number threatened to rise. Maybe he shouldn't have divided his forces. Dragomir's men might have held. The Karamanids attacking them would have retreated when the rest of their army broke. Now Konstantin would have to tell at least one family that their loved one was not coming home. That was a weight he did not want to bear.

The Karamanid camp was chaos, but the way the tents had been erected showed order. Strange that he and his men had traveled so far to fight against these people. In reality, they had a common enemy: the Ottomans. Would the Karamanids, too, become vassals? And someday would Sultan Murad or one of his sons use Karamanid warriors to fight against the Serbs should they dare wage a war for freedom?

Straggling men still fled through the camp. Some were wounded, some were whole, and most were cut down. Konstantin ordered his men to stand as a group, ready to defend themselves if needed, but the battle was over. What remained was pillage, and he didn't want his men involved in that. The sipahis had no such qualms and ran in and out of tents, taking whatever caught their eye.

A woman screamed. No, not a woman—she was but a girl, probably Lidija's age. Kasim dragged her toward a nearby tent.

Suzana had told Konstantin of the pain—immediate and lasting—that came from rape. Konstantin's ire spiked instantly. "Let her go!"

Kasim did not speak Slavonic, but some things didn't need translation. He held the scrawny girl to his side, his arm pinned around her shoulders as she tried fruitlessly to escape. He laughed and said something in Turkish that Konstantin didn't understand.

His spathion pulled free with a slight tug as Konstantin marched closer, repeating his command. "Release her!"

Kasim raised an eyebrow in challenge.

Konstantin lifted his weapon.

The sipahi leader cuffed the girl on the head and threw her to the ground, where she lay whimpering. Then he drew out his scimitar, and several of his men joined him before the tent.

As Konstantin took another step forward, Miladin grabbed his shoulder. "Lord, your motive is noble, but this will get you killed."

Death was not certain. One on one, Konstantin didn't think Kasim could beat him. The sipahis who stood with Kasim were all well-trained, but some of them might sympathize with an innocent girl.

Konstantin made to move closer, but Miladin tightened his grip.

"Let me go." Konstantin tried to tug away from Miladin, but Miladin was stronger. He'd never before disobeyed, and Konstantin's rage, already built, quickly grew large enough to include his rebellious man-at-arms.

"Please, lord." Miladin's face, like most of the men, was coated in a layer of dust, blood, and sweat, but the intensity of his request was plain to see. "Your father charged me with your protection."

That didn't justify disobedience. "My father is no longer your župan." Konstantin pulled again, but Miladin's hold remained in place. Konstantin changed his grip on his spathion but couldn't quite bring himself to strike down Miladin, regardless of his insubordination.

"Lord, if you attack Kasim, his men will kill you. I can't defend you from so many sipahis, and the rest of our men can't see what's happening through the tents, so they won't know you need help until it's too late. You might delay her pain for the length of a brawl, but after Kasim's men kill you and kill me, someone else will take and use her. You can't save her. If you try, you'll die, and so will I. And, Konstantin, you are not the only man who left behind a wife who carries his first child."

The plea gave him pause. Miladin had used his name, not his title. And he was right. Konstantin could kill Kasim and free the girl for a moment. But that would earn him and his men a death sentence. The Turks outnumbered them, and they were far from home. Yet the girl was so young, and no one deserved to be made a sipahi's plaything. "She's scarcely more than a child herself."

"And I grieve for her." Miladin tried to pull Konstantin back, away from Kasim, but Konstantin wasn't ready for that, not yet. "But you cannot save her. Is she worth your life and the life of all the men who have followed you? Because that's what it will cost—your life and mine, then all our men who come to our aid. Probably Dragomir's men too. If you don't walk away, scores will die. Maybe hundreds."

"I have to do what is right." And Miladin was exaggerating the casualty count.

"Not when you are powerless to succeed."

"So, you would have your župan become a coward by turning his back on the innocent?"

"It's not cowardice, Župan Konstantin." Župan Dragomir put a heavy hand on his shoulder. "It's our reality."

Konstantin hadn't seen Župan Dragomir join them, but he listened as the older man continued. "Your duty is to your people, your family. You cannot keep them safe if you do not return to them. And you will not return to them if you cross one of the sultan's men, because the sultan will show you no mercy. You'll die and your family will be destroyed. Your widow and your sister will be married off to one of the sultan's favorites. Ivan might escape, if he makes it to Sivi Gora before messengers from the sultan arrive to issue new demands. Otherwise, he'll be put in your place, wholly unequal to the task, or he'll be executed so Rivak does not rally behind him. Danilo will be taken for the sultan's service, and your people will be under the direct yoke of the Ottomans. Is that what you want?"

Konstantin shook his head and clenched his jaw.

Dragomir adjusted his stance as one of the sipahi sneered. "I have long admired your desire to help the helpless, but this fight was lost when your father fell at Maritsa."

Anger still pulsed through Konstantin at the injustice, and now at his impotence. How could he turn his back on an innocent victim? But how could he condemn himself and all his men to death and his family to grief and misery? Would Lidija, married off to a Turk, be treated any better than the girl Kasim was even now dragging into a tent? And what would a Turkish husband do to Suzana?

"Come. Leave the devils to their pillage." Dragomir put a firm hand around Konstantin's upper arm, and Konstantin allowed himself to be led away. Away from the Karamanid camp falling to the plunder of the sipahis, past the dead corpses falling to the plunder of crows and vultures. Miladin followed behind with the horses.

Župan Dragomir's men had already begun setting up camp. He led Konstantin to his own tent and put a cup of wine in his hand.

Battle had left his throat dry, so Konstantin drained the liquid. It was strong, but not strong enough to deaden his memories. "I never wanted to be vassal to the sultan."

Dragomir sat across from him on a cushion that showed some of Dama Isidora's embroidery. "Nor did I. We were forced to make a choice between submission or death. And that submission must be maintained because the consequence for rebellion is still death."

"If all of us unite . . . if we find allies. Like Župan Nikola said."

Dragomir looked at the ground. "I have been looking for allies since word of Maritsa reached me. But now I've seen how vast the sultan's army and lands are, and I worry. You remember the camp fever?"

"Yes." It had struck down members of both their families, done the same to their garrisons.

"That was mild compared to the Great Mortality. We still haven't recovered. Then came famine. Our lands are weak, Konstantin. Our people are too few."

"So, we're doomed to bow to the sultan's will?"

Župan Dragomir sighed. "Not forever, but we must grow stronger if we ever wish things to change. We need more merophs to till the ground, better harvests, more wealth to buy arms and the men to wield them. It can happen, but not in a season. Not even in a year. I do not want to die a vassal of the Turks. Sometimes I fear it will be my grandsons, not me, who live to see a day of freedom, but preparing for that day is my life's mission."

"I also do not wish to die a vassal of the sultan. But I don't want to live as a vassal of the sultan either." Especially not after what he'd seen today.

"If you wish to live, you will have to endure it and keep a hope that it will not last."

Hope. Konstantin couldn't feel hope at all. He accepted a refill for his wine cup and drank it slowly. "Kasim might not understand Slavonic, but I imagine he understood most of what I yelled at him. He might seek vengeance." He'd never known Kasim well enough to like him, but having him as an ally had been useful. Changing him from supporter to opponent could carry heavy consequences.

Župan Dragomir frowned. "Words are not the same as actions. You saved his life. Perhaps that will soften his anger. That, and the woman you wanted to save."

Konstantin felt bile rising in his throat. He wished he hadn't saved Kasim's life in battle. Raw, deep hatred pulsed through his veins. For Kasim, for the sultan, for his own weakness. He still wasn't sure if Župan Dragomir and Miladin had been right to stop him, but their motivations were in the right place. His own motivations felt muddled. What was he doing in Anatolia? He was no better than a slave.

Konstantin finished his wine and stood. "I should see to my men."

Župan Dragomir stood to walk him to the tent's exit. He put a hand on Konstantin's shoulder. "We can't provoke the sultan. We must obey him when he tells us to hold a line or make a charge. But there is no need to risk our lives or the lives of our men for the Ottoman cause. Remember that. Save your bravery and Rivak's strength for when we can make a stand as free men rather than as vassals."

Konstantin had always tried to do everything to the best of his ability, and that included waging war. But Župan Dragomir was right. If freedom was his goal, then daring maneuvers to protect his overlords would not help him reach it. The sun hit his face as he left the tent. He knew what he needed to do as a vassal: only what the sultan required, nothing more. But what of God's requirements, especially when it came to protecting the innocent?

Miladin waited outside. He seemed hesitant to approach too closely. Understandable since Konstantin had nearly threatened him with a sword. "Lord? Are you well?"

"No. I am not well, but I am ready to be practical rather than emotional." The battle had stoked his feeling to a feverish pitch, but now, weariness and a growing sense of gloom dulled the rage and indignation. "What are our losses?"

"Akinin is dead, and Predislav is unlikely to survive the day. Two of the Germans are dead. Another mercenary took an arrow in the shoulder. They've removed it. Father Vlatko thinks he'll live if they keep it clean, but the damage may be permanent. The other wounds are smaller."

If Konstantin wanted to garner Rivak's strength—and he did—then no deaths and no injuries would be his goal, and that wish would temper all his movements from now on. "Which of the mercenaries were killed?"

"Erasmus and Ludolf."

Konstantin knew their faces. Erasmus had been tall and quick to smile. Ludolf had been too young to grow a beard. The losses from his own garrison hit even deeper. He'd been training with Akinin and Predislav since he was a boy, knew Akinin's young daughter and Predislav's aged mother. "Any word from the sultan?" Konstantin asked.

"No."

They mounted, and Konstantin followed Miladin back to where the other men from Rivak were setting up camp. He remembered the words the two of them had spoken and felt a stab of guilt. Miladin had told him news, and he'd said nothing. "Magdalena is with child?"

"Yes, lord."

"I am happy for you."

The edge of the battlefield seemed the wrong place to discuss the miracles of new life and the joys of a wife and a family, but it was an apology, of sorts. What Konstantin wouldn't give to have Suzana waiting for him in his tent, where he could pour out all his grief and frustration and sorrow over his inability to rein in Kasim's cruelty.

Then he inhaled sharply. What would Suzana think of him and what he'd failed to stop? He was a župan. He was supposed to lead his people in strength and righteousness, not in weakness and subservience. *Compromise.* It wasn't always a word tainted with weakness, but today, it was. Helplessness, cowardice, and disgrace—they all coated the situation, and they coated him.

Arslan arrived at Rivak's camp late that night, after the sun had gone down and all light had disappeared, save the sparkle of distant stars and the glow of small campfires. Konstantin felt more trepidation with every step the envoy took toward him. Word of the threats Konstantin had made against Kasim would have reached the sultan's ears by now, and Sultan Murad was unlikely to overlook defiance from a vassal.

Arslan greeted Konstantin with the traditional phrase. "Peace be unto you."

"And unto you." Konstantin said the words and felt the irony. Peace. They were on campaign, at war, helping the sultan subdue the Karamanids the way he had already subdued the Serbs. There was no peace for the army. And no peace for Konstantin.

"I have news for you."

"Please, come." Konstantin led the way into the tent. He still wore his armor and his sword, so if Arslan had been sent by the sultan to execute him, Konstantin could put up a fight. He might even be able to defeat Arslan and ride away, but if Sultan Murad wanted Konstantin dead, he could send a pack of akinci raiders after him, and it was a long way home to

Rivak. Konstantin thought a public execution was more likely, as it would send a message to all the other vassals.

Konstantin sat on a cushion, motioned for Arslan to do the same, and waited for his sentence.

"Rumors are circulating that you nearly fought Kasim over a woman."

"She was more girl than woman. I did not wish her for myself. I only wished to stop Kasim from hurting her."

Arslan looked away.

"Kasim is married," Konstantin said. "His actions will hurt two women. The captive girl and his wife."

Arslan crossed his arms. "I do not approve of what Kasim did. But defying him was unwise. We are at war. Some of the sultan's troops are paid only from the pillage they are allowed to take."

"Some, yes, but that is not true for the sipahis, and even if it were, it hardly eases the girl's pain."

"Most men care little about the pain of women."

Konstantin had already stirred up animosity with Kasim and the sultan, perhaps with Arslan too. They were wrong to disregard female suffering, but saying so aloud would not improve matters. "Does the sultan wish to punish me?"

"No. Had a different man threatened Kasim, the result may have been different, but Sultan Murad remembers your valor. For now, he will allow the incident to pass. And the campaign is drawing to an end, so you and your men may return home."

Relief ran over him. Konstantin would live to return home, and they could begin their journey soon. "Please tell Sultan Murad that I am grateful for his mercy."

"I will," Arslan said. "When will you leave?"

"I will consult with Župan Dragomir before deciding. I have a handful of wounded. He has many, and that may slow us, but I think we are both eager to return home."

"I recommend that you complete your journey before Župan Teodore does. And be cautious. Kasim was once your defender, but he will not forget your slight."

CHAPTER THIRTY-SIX
IN SEARCH OF HEALING

A WEEK HAD PASSED SINCE Suzana lost her baby. Her body still felt weak and damaged, but the physical aches had diminished. The pain in her heart, however, did not go away, and she yearned for her husband's return, but she managed to cry less often. She had wanted her baby desperately, but she was still young. There might be another chance to bear a child.

She visited the chapel more frequently than before, praying for strength to carry her burden of grief. Church law called the loss of an unborn infant a sin, so she would have penance of a year. It didn't seem fair, but abstaining from richer foods three times a week was a small slight compared to her overwhelming sorrow.

In addition to praying for herself, she prayed for Konstantin. Lidija joined her most days, but she was not present the day Suzana's father came to visit.

"I was told you might be here." She hadn't heard his footsteps, so the sound of his voice startled her.

"Welcome to Rivak, Father." Unease worked its way across her arms and neck. If she were to number all the days when she had been in the company of her father, the majority of those days would have involved no violence, but many had, so fear in his presence was ingrained. "Will you be visiting us long?"

"A day or two. I have things to see to, but I was passing this way and thought . . . well, I wanted to speak with you."

The church held no benches. Worship was performed on one's knees or on one's feet. Suzana held her breath and stood, hoping she could suppress a wince because movement still brought pain.

He glanced at her abdomen. "So, the rumors were correct. The child was stillborn?"

"Yes. He came too early." Was that why her father had come? He had never been one to offer comfort or sympathy, but he always protected his assets. And a grandson who would inherit a župa was an asset.

Her father adjusted the cuffs of his tunic. Suzana was tempted to step back in case disappointment made his temper flare, but her father was sober, and she was a noblewoman now, so perhaps he would not hit. Beyond that, he didn't seem so imposing or threatening in the calm of the church. She doubted he grieved over the lost child, but he did seem subdued. "Hopefully your husband will return and another child can be produced. But you must think of the future. If the župan does not come home . . . a childless widow has no power, no future. We can find another baby and claim it as your own. I worked too hard to get you here to let it slip away. You must have an heir, Suzana."

She shook her head. "Word has already spread that the baby died."

"No, we can say the child *nearly* died, that it was not expected to live but pulled through with the grace of God. The information I received came through curated channels, not from meroph gossip."

"I will not pass off another child as my own."

He stepped closer, and she stepped back. "If you have another child, you can discard the spare. But going childless is not a viable option when your husband's return is uncertain."

Suzana would not lie about an infant. She had been powerless as her father's daughter, and by law, she would have few rights should she become Konstantin's widow without becoming regent to an heir. Yet regardless of what happened, she was part of Konstantin's family. Love would sustain her in that role, not lies.

He stepped closer again, probably to press his point, but this time, she did not step back. She lifted her chin and stood her ground. "Konstantin and I have made a commitment to lead our people with honesty. And I will not take a child from another woman and give her the heartache I have felt."

"You could find an orphaned child. Women die in childbirth often enough."

She walked past him toward the door. "I will not play with the future of an infant, promising an inheritance that I intend to snatch away if another child comes. I am pleased to extend hospitality to you, Father, but this is no longer a topic for discussion."

Even as she said the words, she braced for him to come after her and strike her for her defiant words. But the only footsteps to echo across the paved chapel floor were her own.

"Wait, Suzana."

She paused and turned slightly, facing him again.

"There are other things I wish to discuss with you."

"Perhaps in the keep? You are no doubt weary from your journey. And Dama Zorica has suggested I refrain from going too long without sustenance. I am still rebuilding my strength." Suzana also wanted a chair and a location that was not so isolated. Her father had held his temper thus far, but she didn't know how long that would last.

He nodded, and she waited for him so they could walk to the keep together.

"How are things at the villa?" she asked.

"The villa is quiet. Prosperous. Hot in the afternoons and pleasant in the mornings." He broke off to hold a cloth over his mouth while he coughed.

"Do you enjoy the quiet?" she asked when his coughing stopped.

"Only at times."

Suzana had been a quiet child and a quiet youth, so she doubted her move to Rivak had much altered the level of noise, but maybe her father felt her absence. If she still felt the loss of her stillborn son, surely he felt the change when a child known for seventeen years left home. Maybe she had even been missed.

Inside the keep, Suzana helped herself to an early plum. "Would you like one?" she asked her father.

"No."

He'd always been fond of fruit. "Are you well?"

He strode to a table on the side of the hall, near the hearth and away from where Lidija and Jasmina brushed wool in preparation for spinning. Suzana joined her father.

"I . . ." He coughed again, over and over. And when he pulled the cloth away, it was spotted with blood.

"Father?" Alarm wove through her voice. "Shall I send for a healer?"

He shook his head. "There is no need for your healer. I have a physician, and he has advised me to put my affairs in order."

Shock hit Suzana the same way the slam of her father's fists had so often before. He'd always been so large, so strong. "The physician does not expect you to recover?"

"No." He leaned his arms on the table. "I had hoped to live longer. One of the things I found so appealing in the match with Župan Đurad's grandson was the precedent already set. The oldest heir to the groom's family. The next boy to the bride's family. I thought with time, I might train a successor."

Suzana remembered what it was like growing up with Baldovin as guardian and father. Under no circumstances would she agree to send a beloved child to live with Baldovin as a guardian and grandfather. It seemed now that the request would never come.

"Putting my affairs in order . . . I believe that includes where I stand with you."

She waited, hoping for a kind word but not expecting it.

"After that incident in the stables . . ."

An incident. Was that what it had been to him? It had changed her life, broken her, left her so frightened of men that she'd almost pushed Konstantin away before even giving him a chance.

Her father coughed again. Jasmina brought him a cup of wine, but he didn't drink from it. When the coughing subsided, he continued in a subdued voice. "After that, every time I looked at you, I was reminded that I had failed. And I have failed at very few things in my life. Failure to protect my only child was a bitter memory. Everything changed that day. You were different. I was different. The villa was different."

Suzana looked at her hands rather than at her father's face. She had been different. Frightened and fragile, and the one person in her life who could have helped her heal had been emotionally distant. Physically distant, too, other than when he'd been violent.

"All that guilt and all that hurt," he continued. "I shouldn't have let it come out so often. I would grow so frustrated when you made an error in the ledger. If you weren't pure enough to be married off because of what my steward did to you, and if you weren't smart enough to help with my business—our future—then what type of legacy would I leave? Nothing but failure."

Silence stretched between them, heavy and tense. She inhaled, unsure she really wanted to make a confession, but she spoke anyway. "The errors in the ledger were not because I did not know how to balance the figures. There were times when I thought you had taken advantage of someone, times when I learned of a person's situation and saw a need that might be met if I changed a few numbers."

Her father grunted. "You should have consulted me."

"I did not think you would listen. What was best for your business was always your upmost priority, not the hurts and needs of those you traded with. I stopped years ago. You always caught the error, and then it did not help anyone else, and I ended up with bruises."

"If your errors were intentional, that makes it betrayal. Or theft."

Adamu and the boys entered the room and snatched up a few plums.

"You should have known theft was wrong." Her father's voice was rough with anger. "Against God's law."

Adamu met her eyes and lifted an eyebrow in silent question. His task was to be a bodyguard for Ivan, but without using words, he offered to come to her aid. She shook her head. The current conversation with her father was difficult but not dangerous.

"I did not know God back then," she said.

"You were taught."

"After *the incident*, I learned that I was worthless to you and no doubt worthless to God. I had no hope for myself, not then. If I was ruined anyway, why not help someone else?" She inhaled a shuddering breath. "Now I recognize how important trust is to a family. I couldn't trust you not to hurt me, but I am sorry I made it harder for you to trust me with your ledgers."

Her father stared at the hearth for a long time. A small fire burned there, not needed for heat but meant to be a source of flame for other fires. A flame—light—was like that. It could spread from place to place, but it had to start somewhere.

"My relationship with my daughter was the affair I most needed to put in order. That is why I came. I wish to say that I'm sorry I could not stop what happened to you in the stables. And I'm sorry I couldn't control my temper. I would ask for your forgiveness."

Suzana's eyes stung with emotion. He had beaten her so many times. He had let her down again and again when, as an innocent child, she'd needed comfort and reassurance. She didn't want to keep hold of the hurt and disappointment, but it still felt vivid and raw whenever she remembered her past.

Forgiveness was part of family. She'd felt a taste of it before her wedding, when her father had stood with her in the church and wished her happiness in her new life. With time, she had accepted his tentative step in repairing their relationship, and the emotional scars she carried had hurt a little less. Would they heal even more if she forgave him now?

Forgiveness did not mean she approved of his violence. It didn't mean she would trust him with her own child should her father live long enough to see her give birth to a second son. It simply meant she could move on, let go of the pain, and leave matters of penance and punishment to God.

She reached across the table and put a hand on his. "I forgive you, Father."

His expression softened, easing as if a weight had been removed, and a single tear rolled down his cheek.

Chapter Thirty-Seven
The Journey Home

The army was three days past Thessaloniki when Konstantin walked by a tent and overheard Miladin and Grigorii. It didn't take long to deduce that he was the subject of their conversation.

"He's not himself lately," Miladin said. "You've heard him at night."

Grigorii's voice came next. "I have, and I believe he would rather we pretend we haven't." Grigorii was right. Konstantin preferred that those who slept nearby pretend not to notice the nightmares that pulled him from his sleep, sometimes with screams, more often with gasps and jerks. They were worse than the nightmares he'd had after his injury and Svarog's death. Much worse because they were mostly memory, and waking didn't prove the dreams to be false.

Miladin huffed. "That may be his preference, but ignoring it isn't fixing it. He should be happy. We're going home. The losses we suffered are regrettable, but those killed are few in number, and the sultan himself commended him for his valor."

"Our župan has always been good at hiding what he feels."

"This is more than hiding his feelings." Miladin sounded frustrated. "Surely you've noticed the difference. This is something heavy, and it doesn't seem to be easing. He drinks too much wine at night. He no longer looks at the necklace from his wife or the icon from his brother. He avoids Father Vlatko. And he's unhappy. He may mask his reactions, but I can still tell when he's happy and when he's miserable."

Konstantin moved on. The sun had slipped over the horizon, and it was time for the tent to be packed and the men to be on their way. Konstantin suspected that Miladin had initiated a campaign to cheer him up. No doubt Grigorii was the latest recruit, after Miladin, Father Vlatko, Ulrich, and a dozen others had tried to help. But they were all wasting their time. The guilt that haunted Konstantin couldn't be swept away because nothing any of his men said could change the past.

Whenever the wind blew through the trees, it sounded like a woman's cry. One of pain and devastation, of someone irreparably harmed because something had been irrevocably taken. Was that the sound Suzana's heart had made when she'd been attacked in the stables, and was the girl Kasim had taken suffering the way Suzana had? More likely, her pain was worse because she would have neither sympathy nor justice, for no one would punish a sultan's favorite like Kasim.

Konstantin knew the wreckage such violence could cause, and he owed it to Suzana to stand against it. More than that, he owed it to God. As long as he could remember, Konstantin had felt God's hand in his life, but now that peace and assurance were gone, and he felt empty inside. God had given him everything, and Konstantin had faltered.

Once or twice, he had thought of approaching Father Vlatko, but the priest was in deep mourning because his brother was among the fallen. Predislav had held on to life for a full two days after the battle, two days of anguish and suffering that had left a sadness on the priest's face long after, two days of anguish and suffering that Konstantin might have prevented had he given his men different orders.

Not long into the day's ride, Grigorii maneuvered his horse next to Perun. "We'll be back within the fortnight."

"Yes."

"The merophs will be preparing for harvest. Assuming there weren't any brigands burning crops again while we were gone."

Konstantin closed his eyes briefly. He hadn't any right to ask God for anything, not when he'd walked away from that girl's pain, but he wished he could pray for the safety of his people and have confidence that God might hear him. "I thought all the brigands were defeated that night I fell into the pit."

"Not more than one or two made it away, but you know how it is. A few men are enough to stir up trouble. There are always people willing to steal and destroy."

They rode in silence for a time. If brigands had returned, Suzana would organize patrols and drive them away. Her wit, combined with Aunt Zorica's experience, would see any enemy defeated as long as the group wasn't too large. That was another blessing God had given Konstantin: two dependable women who cared for him.

"It will be good to be home," Grigorii said.

Konstantin wanted to be home. All the people he loved most waited in Rivak. People who thought the best of him, people he didn't want to disappoint. He wanted to see them again, but would they forgive him when they learned what he had and hadn't done? He'd wanted to protect them from the sultan's wrath, but had there also been a thread of cowardice in his decision?

"At least, for most of us," Grigorii continued. "There's always someone who comes home to bad news. Do you remember poor Ljubomir? Once, he came home to a dead child. Another time, he came home to an unfaithful wife. All manner of ill luck."

Konstantin trusted Suzana. She would not betray him with another man. But childbirth was dangerous. What if she or the child were dead? Konstantin reached for the cross around his neck before remembering he was no longer worthy to ask God for anything. But he wasn't asking for himself. He was asking for his wife and child.

A new sort of guilt settled over him. He was not the only one who would pay the price for his disfavor in God's eyes. His family, too, would suffer, and they had already suffered enough.

Morale for Konstantin's men improved as they came closer and closer to home. When they crossed into Rivak, Konstantin sent Zoran ahead to let the grody know they were coming.

Soon after, Župan Dragomir and his grandson rode over to bid Konstantin farewell. "Put what happened in Anatolia behind you," Dragomir advised. "Enjoy being with your family again."

Konstantin tried to force the past from his mind. But controlling his thoughts was not as easy as controlling his expressions.

Župan Dragomir gave him a smile. "I hope to see you again soon for your baby's baptism."

Konstantin focused on that. He might be a father by now. Perhaps the sweet innocence of an infant could help him move past the evils of the campaign. If God could still give him a blessing that large, then maybe his standing before his Maker was not completely hopeless.

"Give Lidija my regards," Decimir said.

"I will."

"And thank you for saving my life."

If only Konstantin had been able to save more of Župan Dragomir's men, more of his own men and mercenaries. The Serbian vassals, all of them, were meant to store up their strength so that one day they might win their freedom. But Župan Dragomir was now significantly weaker than he'd been that spring. It would take a decade to recover, maybe longer.

The fields they rode past were nearly ready for harvest, the grain losing its green and turning to gold. Konstantin's hopes rose with each unburned field they passed. Disaster had not struck Rivak's crops in his absence. With a bounteous harvest, the merophs would be able to pay both rents and taxes and still be able to eat their fill this winter. One of the villages the brigands had burned the summer before was now rebuilt, with fresh thatch on the cottage roofs and new walls of fieldstone around the church.

Word spread among the merophs, and they gathered to greet the returning men. Some of the garrison had family in the village, so Konstantin told Grigorii to dismiss as many of them as wished to stay. With such a long campaign behind them, they had earned their leave.

A grin lit Miladin's face as he spoke with an old woman. She seemed familiar, and when Konstantin saw her tying a birthing chair onto her donkey, he recognized her as the midwife who lived in the grad. She'd probably come to the village to help one of the meroph women deliver a child. She was Rivak's only midwife, so she'd undoubtedly given Miladin good news of his wife.

Then Miladin's face sobered, and he glanced at Konstantin before looking back at the woman. Worry crept over Konstantin as he dismounted and walked to them. Neither Miladin nor the midwife met his eyes, and the worry turned ominous.

"Have you any news for me?" Konstantin dreaded the answer, but he had to know.

The woman kept her eyes on the ground. "Your child came too early, lord. The babe did not survive."

Konstantin inhaled sharply and forced his face into a mask. He would mourn later. He couldn't show weakness now. "And Dama Suzana?"

"She has recovered, lord."

That news brought some relief. Suzana lived. "When?"

"Two moons have passed."

It felt like several arrows had pierced Konstantin to the core. Two moons. About the time he'd lost his favor with God. Had the early birth been God's punishment? Grigorii had warned him that someone always came home to ill news. In the case of this campaign, it was Konstantin.

A longing and a dread to be home had followed Konstantin the entire return journey. Both grew stronger now. Suzana had suffered enough tragedy. He wished to ensure that she was recovering from the latest blow of grief. But how was Konstantin supposed to comfort her if his weakness, his failure, had caused their loss?

He mounted his palfrey again and urged Perun forward with a set of clicks. Miladin, riding Grom, quickly caught up to them. "You have my sympathy, lord. And my sincere hope that soon you will have the blessing of becoming a father."

Konstantin managed a curt nod. "You have good news of your family?"

"Yes, lord." Miladin's words seemed hesitant.

"A son or a daughter?"

"A son."

Konstantin wanted to be happy for his friend, but grief made it hard to feel anything other than sorrow. "You must spend as much time at home as you can over the next fortnight."

When Miladin didn't say anything, Konstantin turned to look at him. He seemed uncertain about something. With the exception of the campaign that had ended at Maritsa, Miladin had been near Konstantin's side every day since Konstantin's father had assigned him to be bodyguard to his heir. Konstantin's anger with Miladin for stopping the clash with Kasim had lasted only moments, but the words spoken in fury had done something to their relationship, making Miladin more cautious.

Konstantin continued. "I'm sure Magdalena will be eager to see you again."

Miladin's smile was hesitant. "Yes. And Dama Suzana will be eager to see you. You have both felt grief, but together you will find comfort."

Konstantin wasn't so sure. Before their marriage, he'd helped her smile, helped her gain confidence, helped her become stronger. But he couldn't take credit for that, not really. Konstantin had been guided by God back then. Now it was just him, and he feared he would be unequal to the task.

The miles stretched out, and the sun had just touched the western horizon when Rivakgrad came into view. It should have filled him with joy, but that emotion was overshadowed with the sorrow of broken dreams and the weight of an oppressive vassalage.

When they entered the town, Konstantin set his face, as he had so many times before. They were not greeted as victors, because their work had brought glory to the sultan, not to the Serbs. But the townspeople still thronged the streets, calling out greetings and asking for news. Miladin's wife waited with a rosy-cheeked infant in her arms on the street leading to their home, and their niece stood beside her on her tiptoes for a better view. Miladin glanced at Konstantin.

"Go." Konstantin spoke the word and motioned with his head. "Barring an emergency, there's no need to report to me for a few days at least."

"Thank you, lord."

The noise of the crowd grew faint as Perun rode up the steep length of the causeway to the grody. Fewer men traveled with him now. Just Grigorii, six men from the garrison, and Ulrich's mercenaries.

Bojan met them outside the stables. "We heard you were coming and prepared a feast. I'll take care of your horses, lord, if you wish to go inside at once."

Konstantin accepted Bojan's offer. It had been a long journey, and he wanted to see his family. Danilo was the first to appear, running down the stairs of the keep at full speed with a grin on his face.

"Kostya! You're back!" The boy flung his arms around Konstantin's waist—or perhaps a little higher than that. He'd grown taller.

Aunt Zorica followed her son. "We have prayed for your safe return, and now you are here." She smiled, but the motion was tinged with sadness.

"We saw the midwife in a village we passed. I've heard the news."

Aunt Zorica nodded. "I am relieved that I do not have to tell you myself. That is the only ill news. We've had no brigands, and the crops are promising."

That was a blessing. One he didn't deserve, but perhaps God was looking on the people of Rivak with mercy. They deserved it more than he did. "And Suzana? Is she well?"

Aunt Zorica looked over his shoulder. He turned and saw his wife coming down the stairs. Her beauty struck him with a force he hadn't expected. He'd always imagined her with an infant in her arms or a womb swollen with child when he returned, but she looked much as she had when he left. Perhaps a little frailer.

"Suzana." He took two strides toward her and closed the gap, then placed a tentative hand on her arm. "I am glad to see you well."

"And I am overjoyed to see you safely returned to us."

He had longed to see her again, but guilt and sorrow made what should have been a joyous reunion something complicated and uncertain. He couldn't decide what to say or what to do. He wanted to hold her, kiss her, cry with her over the loss of their baby. But he couldn't do any of those things in the bailey.

Ivan interrupted that decision. "Kostya!" He ran and launched himself at his brother. "You were gone for so long, and I missed you so much. Did you bring me anything?"

"Yes." Father Vlatko had remembered Konstantin's promise, even though Konstantin had forgotten, and they'd bought both boys fine leather belts in Thessaloniki. "Your gift is in one of the carts, but they haven't made it to the grody yet."

"We've been watching for you from the moment Zoran rode in. Are you hungry? I'm so hungry that my stomach is growling, and Nevena made your favorite pastries."

Konstantin took Ivan's chin gently between his fingers and examined the boy's mouth. "It looks as if you have already tasted one of them and left a bit on your face."

Ivan wiped his sleeve over his lips. "Some of them are still warm from the ovens."

Konstantin glanced at Suzana. He had so much to tell her, but now that he was home, he didn't know how to confess. She'd told him of the pain that had come from rape, and he'd stood by and let Kasim have his pillage. *Pillage*—that made it sound like the girl was property, something to be packed on an animal and carted away for whatever use its new owner wished. Kasim's crime was far more serious than the theft of treasure or household goods. If Konstantin told Suzana what had happened, she would feel that pain, and she already seemed fragile.

She took his arm, and together they walked into the keep. "I'm sure you and your men must be hungry for something other than boukellaton and dried meat. Rivak is well, so we can catch up on everything else after the meal."

Lidija greeted him when they entered the hall, throwing her arms around him. "I'm so glad you're back." She stepped away, and Konstantin inhaled with shock. She'd changed while he was gone. Her body was less angular, and her neck seemed longer. So much like the girl Kasim had taken.

"Kostya, are you all right?" Suzana asked.

Lidija seemed to have noticed, too, and she watched him with wary eyes.

"Just surprised by how you've grown." He swallowed. "Decimir sends you his regards. He has returned uninjured."

At mention of Dragomir's grandson, Lidija's wariness vanished. "May we plan a feast and invite Župan Dragomir and his family to join us?"

Had word of the dead child reached Župan Dragomir's grody, or was he still expecting an invitation to a baptism? "After harvest, perhaps. Župan Dragomir's troops were decimated during the last battle, and many in his grody will be in mourning. A celebration so soon would not be in good taste."

Lidija grew sober again. "How awful. But Zoran said our losses were light."

"Yes. We were not trapped the way his men were." Even so, responsibility for the deaths of Predislav, Akinin, and several mercenaries was a burden that had not grown easier to shoulder. He didn't want to talk about the battle or about what had followed, so he led the women to their seats.

The meal was laid out in the traditional way, with men and women at separate tables. He cared for all the women in the family, but it was easier to sit with Ivan and Danilo. Kuzman filled in Konstantin on the progress of their training, and that was a far more comfortable topic of conversation than the questions Suzana or Aunt Zorica or Lidija were likely to ask.

After the meal, he excused himself to bathe in his bedchamber. Risto assisted, and as he left, Konstantin wished the bath could have soaked away the campaign's guilt the same way it had soaked away the campaign's grime. He toweled himself dry and poured himself a cup of wine.

Soft footsteps sounded in the hallway between his room and Suzana's, and a few moments later, she stood in the doorway. Her hair was down and uncovered, cascading gently upon her shoulders and along her back. She smiled at him, an expression that showed a trust and affection he no longer deserved.

"I have missed you, my Kostya."

So many emotions pulled at him. Attraction and desire for his wife, relief that he was home, guilt over what had happened, and fear of what the truth might do to Suzana's affection for him. "I am pleased to be home."

She leaned against the wall. "You are so solemn today. I suppose I should not expect anything different. Having you return to us safely makes this the best day I've had in some time, but your grief is still new. I just missed you so much. Especially after . . ." She ran a hand over her abdomen. "I wanted a child very badly."

"So did I," he whispered. "But I am glad you recovered." God may have punished him by letting the child come too early, but at least Suzana had survived.

She walked to his bed and sat on the edge of it. "Will you tell me about the journey?" The way she looked at him—it was as if nothing had changed. As if they still had trust and love and a confidence in each other's goodness. If he told her about the campaign, would he see disgust and disappointment replace the hope and affection?

"Another time, perhaps. It's been a long day. A long summer." He sipped his wine and kept his gaze on the fire, but he could see her in his periphery.

She shifted, her expression tinged with worry now rather than hope. After the silence had stretched into awkwardness, she asked, "Would you like me to leave so you can rest?"

He wanted her to stay. He'd missed her, missed the intimacy they shared. Maybe a surge of passion would help him forget the campaign, at least for a while. But he did not think she would sleep through his nightmares. If she stayed, he would have to explain, and when she heard, she would hate him.

He still hadn't answered her question, so he nodded.

Sadness lined her recurve-bow lips as she left. She looked back once, but Konstantin pretended not to notice.

Chapter Thirty-Eight
Wine and Memory

Suzana's heart had broken when she'd lost the baby, but she had thought Konstantin would give her hope again upon his return. At the very least, give her love. Instead, he pushed her away time after time. He spent his days overseeing the harvests or visiting the families of the fallen, all away from the grody. Three nights she'd gone to his bedchamber. Three nights he'd sent her away. The sting of rejection sharpened all the broken edges of her grieving heart, making the pain more intense. She wanted to confide in him and have him confide in her, as they had before he had gone away to war. She'd lost her baby, and now it seemed she had also lost her husband's affection.

She put on a brave face when it came time for the bodyguards from Sivi Gora to journey home. Ivan rode around the bailey on Adamu's horse while the men fastened their baggage to a pair of mules. Carts were difficult in the mountains they would travel through, especially if the weather turned.

When the men finished packing, Adamu whistled to his horse, which immediately came back. Adamu could have easily plucked Ivan from the saddle and lowered him to the ground, but he allowed Ivan to dismount himself. The boy patted the horse's neck and told him to be safe. Then he clasped wrists with Adamu in a gesture of farewell.

"I will see you again at Easter time." Adamu spoke to Ivan but made sure Konstantin and the rest of the family could hear him. "And next summer, we'll continue our training in Sivi Gora."

"What's it like there?" Ivan asked.

"There's the silver mine," Adamu said. "And a town with a palisade a lot like this one." He gestured to the wall. "We don't have a grody, but we do have a palace."

"And Grandfather lives in the palace?"

"Yes." Adamu winked at Cyril. "As does a pretty young cook's assistant who Cyril is most eager to see again."

Ivan's eyes widened. "Will you marry the cook's assistant, Cyril?"

Cyril laughed, but the red in his face showed embarrassment. "I don't think she even knows my name."

"She will." Adamu turned back to Ivan. "Because Cyril has been helping to train the future župan of Sivi Gora, he'll be famous throughout town. And we will both be pleased to show you everything next summer. It's beautiful up in the mountains. And Sivi Gora is blessed with a wise župan who has a brave and determined heir."

A year ago, Ivan would have taken a family member's hand, but now he stood tall and independent as the men from Sivi Gora mounted their horses and headed home for the winter.

Half of the mercenaries, too, had collected their pay and traveled home, either for the winter or for good. The grody grew more and more empty with each day, but still, Konstantin found ways to occupy his time that did not involve Suzana, and it continued to pain her.

As the men from Sivi Gora disappeared down the causeway, Konstantin followed the pattern he'd set since his return and went into the stables. A few minutes later, he left, leading Perun behind him. He mounted and rode away from the grody, away from her.

Suzana squeezed her eyes shut. Tasks for the župan abounded everywhere, but she and Aunt Zorica had held Rivak together in his absence. None of the responsibilities he rode off to so often were more pressing than the needs of his family. She hadn't minded the previous year, when he had been busy and she had to wait for his time. But back then, she had known he loved her, that though his duties were pressing, his heart was hers. Now she had no such confidence.

She walked slowly across the bailey, following Danilo and Ivan to the archery range. She admired their friendship. They encouraged each other, knew each other's moods. She wanted that type of friendship with Konstantin. She wanted more than friendship, but since his return, it felt as if she'd lost even that. She'd trusted him the year before with her pain, and the love he'd shown her despite her past had been like a salve. He had been so pleased when they had discovered she was with child. Was his disappointment now so large that his love for her had somehow disappeared amid the grief?

"My lady?" Miladin stepped toward her. She'd not seen him since the men had returned from campaign.

She forced a smile. "I hear congratulations are in order for you and Magdalena."

"Thank you," he said. "Our condolences for your loss."

She swallowed and wasn't sure what to say. Wasn't sure which loss was most painful—her child or the love of her husband.

"How is Župan Konstantin?"

"He has been busy helping with the harvest. I'm not sure which direction he was headed when he rode off this morning."

"I didn't ask *where*. I asked *how*."

Suzana folded her arms as if her limbs could somehow brace her from the new reality she struggled against. "He no longer confides in nor wishes to spend time with me."

Miladin's face fell. He looked across the bailey, staring at nothing. "I had hoped coming home to you would help him. He . . ." Miladin paused. "Something happened on campaign. He hasn't been happy since."

Suzana processed the new information. Konstantin had been unhappy even before he'd learned of the lost babe. Perhaps the change in their relationship was not entirely due to grief for the child. "What happened? He won't tell me anything."

"I don't think it's my place to tell. He was brave in combat. You needn't worry that your husband is cowardly or unskilled—neither could be farther from the truth. But war is hard, and it can damage more than a man's body. He managed the battles well enough, but the aftermath was . . . I tried to help, but nothing I said seemed to ease his burden. And now I'm not sure how much he wants to hear from me."

Before he'd ridden away to war, Konstantin had shared everything with her. Now he wanted to share nothing with her—not his bed, not his time, not his secrets. It seemed she wasn't the only one he had distanced himself from. Did Miladin, too, feel the pain of rejection?

"He is drinking more wine than he used to." The previous summer, she'd admired his self-discipline. Drink had made her father more prone to violence of the tongue and of the fists. She didn't want to see the same thing happen to her husband. Nor did she want to be on the receiving end of a drunken wrath. She'd never seen Konstantin lose his temper before—but his change was forcing her to reevaluate everything she thought she knew about him.

"Does he still have nightmares?" Miladin asked.

Suzana felt her face burn with the heat of embarrassment. "I do not know." That was as good as admitting that she'd been rejected by her husband night after night. Perhaps all the people who had told her she was plain and stupid were right, and Konstantin now saw all her inadequacies clearly.

Miladin crossed his arms. "Our župan is a good man. The battles in Anatolia were different from anything he's ever seen before. Don't give up on him. Maybe he needs some time."

It felt as if Konstantin had given up on her, but she nodded. Some people turned inward when they struggled, but that didn't mean they didn't need help. Miladin excused himself, and she watched the boys with their bows until fatigue began affecting their aim. She clung to her memories of the love she and Konstantin had shared. That love was too precious to give up without a fight. She had to work to save it.

Since the weather was pleasant, she asked Bojan to bring the spinning wheel outside, and she spun wool into thread. The afternoon had nearly passed when Konstantin rode back into the grody. His eyes swept across the bailey, but if he saw her, no acknowledgment made it to his face. He dismounted and went into the stables.

She'd seen no one else go in or out of the stables for at least an hour, so Konstantin would be alone. He didn't wish to speak with her in his bedchamber, but perhaps he would speak with her somewhere else. She paused her spinning and followed her husband into the stables.

With one exception, she hadn't entered a stable since that day so long ago. That one exception—the day Konstantin had given her Dola—had not gone well. The stables still made her chest tighten uncomfortably, but she trusted that her love was stronger than her fear.

Inside, the musty smell of a barn assaulted her nostrils. The place was well kept, but the scent of horse and hay and manure was strong. Light sparkled against dust motes that sailed through the air on a carefree drift.

Konstantin had his back to her, grooming Perun with long strokes of the brush.

"My lord?" Her voice sounded nervous, even in her own ears. And she was nervous. Since his return, her husband had given her no reason to expect that her presence would be welcomed, and here in the stables, memory clawed at the edge of her mind.

He turned. Lowered the brush. "Suzana. I didn't expect to see you here."

Her limbs trembled. She still saw Konstantin, but she heard the man who had attacked her, heard her own muffled screams and the scrape of nervous hooves. "I . . . I'm worried about you. Can we talk?"

Konstantin glanced at his horse. "If you don't mind talking while I tend to Perun." He picked up the brush again but went to the other side of the horse. Now he faced her, but the animal was a barrier between them.

Her hands shook. She would have been nervous to talk to him anyway after the way he'd been acting, but in this location . . . she had to force her words out. "I am eager to hear about your journey."

He kept his eyes on his horse and huffed. "Journey. That makes it sound like it was something we did by choice. The campaign went well enough for the sultan. We helped him push the Karamanids out of the borderlands with the Ottomans. Glory for him. Danger and misery for us." The last two phrases were spoken with a bitterness she'd never before heard in his voice.

The sounds of memory assaulted her ears again, and the stalls seemed to shift to the darker, wider ones of her father's stable. Or maybe they weren't taller and wider, but she was smaller. "Perhaps you could tell me more outside or in the keep?" She took a step back as nausea swirled in her stomach.

"There's nothing more to tell." His voice came out flat and lifeless. Suzana squeezed her eyes shut and tried to breathe through the horrible memory that she couldn't quite push away. Her knees felt weak, but prickles along her spine told her to run. She took a step back, toward the open door, but her feet were unsteady, and she stumbled, barely catching herself against a nearby stall.

"Suzana?" Konstantin swore, then one of his arms was around her waist, pulling her outside.

She swayed. Inhaled deeply. Felt her feet grow steadier as the memory lost some of its power. But embarrassment quickly set in. She hadn't been strong enough. Konstantin released her, and she felt the loss of his support in both the literal and figurative senses.

"So many years," he whispered. "And that one act can still hurt you."

So many years. And she was still so weak.

After her visit to the stables, Konstantin had escorted Suzana back to the keep, but he'd shown no sign of thawing toward her. Before his campaign, he had given his love to her freely, as much as she was ready for, as quickly as she was ready. Now he was like a different person. But behind the barrier he had built around his thoughts and feelings, might he also be hurting? She would not give up, not yet, but she needed a strategy.

As she walked to the main hall for the evening meal, she spied Konstantin scowling at his aunt as she spoke to him earnestly in the corridor. He ended the conversation and strode away. Dama Zorica wiped a tear from her eye and did her best to compose herself. She noticed Suzana and came to greet her.

"What have I done wrong?" Suzana asked. "Why did he stop loving me?"

Dama Zorica shook her head. "It is not you, my sweet Suzana. He is pushing away all of us. But if all of us do the best we can to pull him back, eventually he will come."

During the meal, Konstantin sat with the men but didn't seem to be part of any conversation. He responded to Grigorii at times but didn't even show his customary attention to Danilo and Ivan. He did, however, give inordinate attention to his wine cup.

When the meal ended, Grigorii was quick to reach Konstantin's side. "Lord, allow me to help you." He offered Konstantin a hand for balance, but Konstantin refused it, despite being unsteady on his feet. "Perhaps some fresh air?"

Konstantin let Grigorii lead him past a dozen men from the garrison whose expressions were equally divided between concern and disapproval.

Suzana didn't follow, not immediately. Her efforts to repair the breach between her and her husband had failed miserably when she'd gone to the stables, but perhaps a different setting would bring a better result.

She left the table and approached Jasmina. "Before I came to Rivak, was the župan as fond of wine as he has been since his return from Anatolia?"

Jasmina frowned and shook her head. "No, my lady. This is a change. It's not my place to say anything, but, well, my father is worried. He heard that the župan drank himself into a stupor most nights on their return journey, and Grigorii has taken to sending some to his room each night."

Suzana swallowed a lump of emotion. Her husband wanted wine more than he wanted her, but it didn't seem to be helping him find peace or contentment. "Did you see where they went?"

"To the top of the keep, my lady."

The roof of the keep was often used as a lookout post, though the towers along the palisade wall provided better viewpoints, so the watchmen were stationed on those. There wouldn't be anyone else on the keep's roof, only her husband and the satnik to witness her humiliation if Konstantin did not follow her advice.

She climbed the spiral stairs to the top of the tower, praying that God would help her husband because he seemed utterly uninterested in help from his wife. She found Konstantin staring through one of the crenels, with his satnik by his side.

She approached her husband. "My lord? I think you ought to retire for the night. You've had far too much to drink."

Konstantin turned to face her, leaning his back against a merlon.

"Please?" she said. "You can't continue on like this. It's not good for you or for Rivak." She considered pointing out the poor example he was setting for Danilo and Ivan or the distance he was creating with his garrison, but his eyes were currently dull and unintelligent. It was better to keep her explanation simple.

He hiccuped. At least he was a sleepy drunk, not a violent drunk.

Suzana pulled at one of his hands, and he allowed himself to be led through the hatch and down the stairs, through the corridor to his bedchamber.

Risto waited. Suzana was grateful, because as much as she wanted a return to their prior state of bliss, she had no interest in helping him disrobe in his current condition. She left him to his manservant, took the flagon of wine from the table, and exited the bedchamber.

Grigorii lingered in the corridor. She approached him with caution. She had no authority to correct him, but as her husband's loyal man, surely Grigorii would want what was best for Konstantin. "I realize you are trying to help, but excess wine is not the solution to whatever haunts my husband. I ask you to stop providing it for him."

She handed him the flagon, but he crossed his arms rather than accepting it.

"You think wine is the problem?" he asked.

She had hoped he would agree with her. "I know it is most certainly not the solution. Whatever happened in Anatolia must be dealt with and dealt with soon. Rivak needs its župan to be sober."

Rather than handing the flagon to him and risk him rejecting it again, Suzana stepped past him and carried the wine down the corridor toward the lower level of the keep. When she saw Jasmina, she handed it to her. "Please put this away."

"Yes, my lady." Jasmina left.

Suzana considered following her. Perhaps in the main hall, she could find some sort of distraction. But she didn't need a distraction. She needed a plan.

Grigorii still stood outside her husband's door.

"You may leave for the night," she told him.

He straightened to his full height. "I need to discuss the watch with the župan."

"You've allowed your župan to drink himself into a state where he is not presently fit to decide such matters. I've already organized the watch. I did it all summer."

Grigorii huffed. "Župan Konstantin does not need a wife who frets over his drinking and assigns the night watch. He needs a wife who can give him an heir."

Suzana felt as if she'd been punched in the gut. She had tried to give her husband an heir, and the loss of the baby was still raw and agonizing.

Grigorii continued. "I don't know what you think happened in Anatolia, but he did well on campaign. Magnificent, even. Impressed the sultan. But when you lost his child . . ."

Suzana's face felt warm, and her breathing grew labored.

He leaned forward and lowered his voice. "I know the anguish that comes with a dead child. I lost two to camp fever. Some men drown their grief in wine. Don't blame his pain on something that happened in a distant place. If you want to know why he drinks himself to oblivion, take a look at your own reflection."

Suzana had no reply. She blinked away tears as she stumbled down the corridor to her bedchamber. When she had tried to speak with Konstantin in the stables, failure to overcome her memories had left her a burden, not a help. Now she thought of the small child she had not been able to carry to term, and the tears came in force. She shouldn't have been surprised that Konstantin no longer wanted her. He had always been so strong, and she was proving over and over again that she was not his equal; she was far too weak. If his pain was anything like hers, it was little wonder that he wanted to drown it in wine.

Chapter Thirty-Nine
Guilt and Compassion

Konstantin woke with a pounding headache. Which was harder in the morning? The punishment that came from drinking too much wine? Or the punishment that came from a night spent battling memories that left him gasping for breath and craving oblivion? Either way, he woke up tired, with pain in his head and an acute awareness that he had woken alone—again.

He glanced at the half of the bed where Suzana had slept so many times. He'd hurt her by asking her to leave over and over again, but he was doing it for her own good. Distance was the only protection he could offer her now that he'd brought God's condemnation down upon himself.

He tried to rub away the pain beneath his skull. Usually, wine sat waiting for him when he woke, but he must have forgotten to bring some into the room the night before. He couldn't remember much of the previous evening. He ought not to indulge so often and in such quantities, but the alternative was nightmares that left him drowning in a sea of guilt.

When he peeked behind the curtains, sharp sunlight revealed the late hour, and he yanked them most of the way shut again until his eyes could adjust. He'd slept longer than Suzana had when she'd been with child . . . a child lost to them as God's punishment for Konstantin's sins. It didn't seem fair that his wife and child should suffer for his mistakes, but family ties carried weight. They were bound together, to lift each other up or to drag each other down.

Regardless, he ought to rise earlier, have the entire garrison training before they broke their fasts, but he'd have to manage that another day. For what was left of the morning, he would find something to eat and then visit the stables. Horses weren't as effective as wine when it came to burying his memories, but they usually brought him calm.

Risto approached as soon as Konstantin opened the door. He must have been waiting in the corridor. "Would you like assistance, lord?"

Konstantin wore the same tunic he'd had on the day before, though it was now rumpled from sleep. He didn't need help changing his tunic. He shouldn't have needed a reminder that his tunic was dirty, but it was hard to care about things like rumpled tunics after everything that had happened on campaign. "I'll change myself."

"May I also suggest a trim for your beard?"

Konstantin felt the growth along his jaw. Aunt Zorica had told him the day before that he ought not continue on the way he'd been acting since his return. She had never gone away to war. She'd dealt with the aftermath and shouldered the long-term consequences, but she couldn't know much about guilt, because he had seen her make very few mistakes. Regardless, perhaps a more polished appearance would deflect further criticism. "Yes, I'll accept a trim."

Risto pulled the scissors from the cupboard and trimmed the hair along Konstantin's jaw and mouth. The man had never been verbose, especially not while focused on a task such as beard trimming, so Konstantin was surprised when his manservant spoke.

"If I may make another suggestion, lord?"

"You may."

"A happy marriage is an asset that should not be squandered."

Konstantin grunted. Of course his manservant would notice that the župan's bed, once clearly occupied by two people each night, was now only occupied by one. But Konstantin doubted Risto had ever done something his wife would find utterly despicable, so he couldn't understand.

"You worked very hard to earn her trust," Risto continued. "And you were both happier when you succeeded."

"Things are complicated now. I'm no longer the naive boy of last autumn."

"One does not have to be naive to be happy, lord."

Konstantin clenched his jaw, and his stern expression must have been enough of a deterrent because Risto said no more.

When Konstantin was properly groomed, he went to the hall. It was empty, save for servants going about their work. He helped himself to some bread. With his stomach no longer empty and his head no longer pounding quite so incessantly, he went to the stables. He visited Veles first because he wanted some of the reckless energy the stallion possessed. Veles didn't care about the past. Not much anyway. The horse might remember which riders were competent and might hold a grudge against anyone who treated him poorly, but Konstantin did not think the past haunted horses the way the past haunted him or Suzana or the families of Predislav and Akinin.

Konstantin pressed his forehead into Veles's neck, and both horse and man calmed. Veles had brought him home safely, but the campaign had revealed a weakness in Konstantin strong enough to shake his faith in himself. He'd struggled since his first day as župan to shoulder the heavy responsibilities. But he'd tried. And he'd tried to be a good husband, had even thought he was succeeding . . . until that day in the Karamanid camp.

"What am I going to do now?" he mumbled into his horse's neck. Surely there was a way forward, somehow. He hadn't given up when the brigands had burned his villages or when he'd almost died in the trap they'd set. But then his choice had been clear: rebuild what was destroyed, heal what was injured. Now, everything seemed muddled. He couldn't rebuild the Karamanid girl's life, couldn't heal her pain. Nor could he raise his fallen men and restore them to their families. And the small infant born too early . . . he could do nothing to save the child or repair the hole the loss had created in his and his wife's hearts.

"Will you ever smile again, Suzana?" Ivan's hazel eyes bore into hers from across the table. He and Danilo were supposed to be reviewing their Greek lessons while Konstantin and Father Vlatko visited the families of the men who had fallen on campaign, but the boys had been distracted by their dog. Aunt Zorica wasn't feeling well and had gone to lie down. Without their aunt or their tutor to keep them on task, their studies had gradually become punctuated with giggles, and Suzana was so desperate for *someone* to be happy that she hadn't had the heart to scold them.

She forced her lips to turn up. "Of course. I'm smiling now."

"But that's not a real smile." Danilo scrutinized her. "I can tell."

She'd had few reasons for happiness since her husband's return. After Grigorii's words the night before, she had little reason to expect that would change. She understood Konstantin's grief over the loss of the baby because she had felt the same misery. But for him to blame her . . . it magnified her pain, made the burden feel as though it would crush her.

She had felt that type of agony before. Time and God's grace had made it fade. Konstantin, too, had been part of her healing, but now she could neither turn to him nor completely turn away from him. With time, would his contempt for her ease? He did not love Ivan any less because the boy's health was frail. And last summer, he had not loved Suzana any less after learning of her past. He had overlooked weakness time after time. What had changed his compassion into contempt?

"Will Kostya ever smile again?" Worry wove through Ivan's voice.

"Yes." Her voice held more conviction than she felt, but the alternative . . . She could not bear it if the answer was *no.* Konstantin chafed at his role as vassal, he blamed her for the loss of their child, and lately, he had overindulged in wine, but the good man she had fallen in love with couldn't have disappeared entirely. "Yes, someday he will smile again."

"When?" Danilo's hand ran over his dog's fur, but his dark eyes studied her.

"I'm not sure, but if you are done with your lessons, I will go pray." The chapel had given her comfort before, and today, she needed some scrap of peace more than she needed anything else.

"We've been praying." Ivan wedged his elbow on the table and rested his cheek on his hand. "It doesn't seem to be working."

It hadn't been working for her either, not recently. "Prayers aren't always answered right away. That doesn't mean we stop."

The boys accompanied her to the church. They stayed for a long time, even though their dog, sitting near the entrance, whined for their attention. Perhaps an hour passed, and then the boys left for their martial lessons. Suzana's knees ached, so she stood before each of the frescos, pausing before Dama Zorica's favorite, of the Savior reaching out to a woman in need of His mercy. Suzana could easily put herself in the woman's place. She didn't have an issue of blood, but the assault and abuse from her youth had needed healing, and now her sorrow over her lost babe and changed husband begged for relief. Konstantin's blame, his rejection—the boys were right to question if she would ever really smile again.

She closed her eyes, and an image of Konstantin before the Savior, also desperate for help, appeared in her mind. Perhaps he wasn't so different from her or the woman in the fresco. He, too, needed healing, love, and forgiveness. She studied Christ in the fresco. He would give Konstantin those things, she was sure of it. And so would she, if he would only stop pushing her away.

Chapter Forty
Desperate Resolutions

The first signs of coming dawn appeared on the horizon when Konstantin pulled open the window after the night's second nightmare. Chill nocturnal air rushed past him as the screams of the Karamanid girl faded from his mind.

He squeezed his eyes shut. He had tried a night without a surfeit of wine, and it hadn't made things better. He glanced at the objects sitting atop his trunk: a cup of wine and a small knife. The wine, he had poured after the night's first dream of terror. Yet the same thing that had kept him from taking more than a single cup of watered wine at the evening meal had kept him from drinking himself into a stupor when the memories had pulled him awake: Ivan had grown wary of him. Hadn't Konstantin told his grandfather repeatedly that Ivan was better off with family in Rivak? Drunkenness seemed to prove that assertion wrong. Whatever Konstantin's failings, he did not wish to damage his brother or his cousin by setting a poor example for them.

The knife represented something darker. He had dug it from the trunk in a moment of desperation, when the weight of vassalage, a stillborn infant, and a ruined relationship with his wife had all hit him. Consciousness of all his failings and all his weaknesses had smothered his hope, but he'd languished in that desperate misery only long enough to find the knife before knowing that his family and his župa still needed him. He could not abandon his duty or abandon them, no matter how inadequate he had proven.

He looked away from the cup he had not drunk from and the knife he had not used. That night, he had shown that he was stronger than a cup of wine, stronger than the temptation to end his life rather than living with his failures. But he was not stronger than the nightmares, and since returning from campaign, he felt estranged from all who knew him. Father Vlatko had taught that God never left a person alone, but Konstantin didn't believe that, not anymore. He was completely alone, and he had only himself to blame.

Morning approached, so he would not pursue more sleep and risk a third nightmare. He put the knife away, emptied the cup of wine into the chamber pot, and went to the stables. It was early enough that the grooms had not yet woken, but Veles came to the front of his stall when Konstantin approached. It seemed his warhorse, at least, hadn't completely forsaken him.

"Come on, let's go for a ride."

As he gave Veles his head along the road to an old ruined abbey, the harvest-scented breeze seemed to clear away some of the cobwebs clinging to his mind after the unpleasant night. Aunt Zorica and Risto were right. Something had to change.

He went back to the grody and watched Father Vlatko tutoring Danilo and Ivan in Greek. He would not let either boy see him drunk again. Regardless of his other weaknesses, he would be strong enough for that.

He walked toward the strongroom to review the ledgers. Lidija met him in the corridor. Her skin and hair were a lighter color, but she looked a great deal like the Karamanid girl Kasim had taken. And that broke the small sliver of hope that Konstantin's resolutions had given him. The past would continue to haunt him because every time he saw his sister, he would be reminded of what he had been unable to prevent.

"Kostya, I've been looking everywhere for you," Lidija said.

"Oh?"

"We need to talk."

He was getting tired of the women in his family telling him that. *Talking* could not undo crimes or wipe away guilt or fix everything that felt broken inside his chest. He unlocked the strongroom and motioned Lidija inside.

"If you'd like to discuss when you can next see Decimir, the answer is not until harvest is over."

"That's not what I want to talk about. You were *drunk* the other day. I've never seen you drunk before, not even when Father died. What's going on, Kostya?"

"If you want to talk about *me*, I'm afraid it will have to wait. It's harvest time. I'm terribly busy." That wasn't entirely true. The merophs had grown good crops this year, and with their bountiful harvest came a surge of work, but they managed it largely on their own. And the grody had operated smoothly enough in his absence. Service as a vassal and production of an heir were the only tasks he couldn't delegate to others.

"Kostya, something is wrong. You're different now, and I want to know why."

"Not now, Lidija."

"But, Kostya." Hurt lined her face. "I just want to help."

He kept his emotions guarded. Nothing she said or did could help. Nothing anyone said or did could help. "Another time, Lidija. I have things to do."

She blinked over and over again, trying to hold back tears. "Please come back to us, Kostya. We need you."

Needed him for what? Was there anything he hadn't failed at? The man who had left to answer the sultan's call—the man who had at least tried to do the right thing—had died on the battlefield. All that remained was a husk of a man, and soon everyone would realize that. He turned to the window. The gray sky dimmed the color of the changing leaves and made everything feel cold. Rivak seemed as godforsaken as its župan, but there was still hope for his sister. "I'm right here, Lidija."

"No. You aren't." She turned and strode off, one shoulder stooped as the other hand wiped at her wet eyes.

Lidija didn't deserve coldness from him. He was like a wounded horse, thrashing about in pain and panic, a danger to anyone who came too close. He'd scared his brother, hurt his wife, injured his sister.

He'd make it up to Lidija someday, when her presence wasn't so painful. For now, it was easier to breathe when she wasn't nearby.

He reached for the ledger but stopped with his fingers against the leather spine when soft footsteps sounded in the corridor. It sounded like a woman's footsteps. Lidija again?

Suzana appeared in the doorway and gave him a hard stare, one that smoldered with anger. She was always beautiful, and the new emotion didn't change that. Heightened it, perhaps. "I know what I have done to earn your contempt, but what has Lidija done?"

Konstantin flinched at what could only be described as venom in Suzana's voice. He'd never heard her speak like that before. "I do not hold you or Lidija in contempt."

"Your actions say otherwise."

He turned away, away from her beauty, away from her anger, away from the fear and worry just under the surface.

"Hate me if you must." Less anger in her voice now, more hurt. "But your sister needs her older brother."

When he looked at her again, the despair he saw surprised him. "I do not hate you, Suzana."

"Don't you?" The first tears fell. "You are the first friend I ever had. You taught me what love is, what family is. We shared something beautiful together. I missed you every single moment of every single day when you were gone, and now you've come back, and it's as though I've lost you completely. You promised you would never hurt me, Konstantin. But I would rather endure a beating than your contempt."

Konstantin had never struck her and never would. He had thought distance would protect her now that he was fallen. The shock that she found his withdrawal even more painful than physical abuse made his breath catch. He had promised to love and cherish his wife, not make her cry. He'd ruined everything in Anatolia—his soul, his peace, his relationship with Suzana. "I don't hold you in contempt. Your beauty, your wisdom, and your goodness—they haunt me."

"Then why do you shut me out? We were each other's confidants before. We were friends. We were lovers. Now it is like I am invisible to you. And when I am not invisible, it seems I am an irritant. No one wanted a healthy child more than I. The grief almost drowned me, and for you to blame me for his loss—"

Konstantin shook his head. "I do not blame you for our lost child."

"Why else would you act this way? Grigorii told me of your blame, that you feel it's my fault, that grief for the child and contempt for me are the reasons behind your drinking and everything else."

Sadness engulfed him. Her grief, already heavy, had been made worse through misunderstanding. "No. Grigorii is right that I grieve our lost child. But the fault is not yours. The fault is mine." He sat on the bench and motioned for her to join him.

She still wept, and her hands trembled, but she sat beside him. "You don't blame me?"

"No, Suzana. You've always done everything right."

Emotion made her breaths erratic, but her tears seemed to contain more catharsis than anguish now. He placed a hand on her arm, and she leaned into him, and he watched some of her pain turn into relief. "But how could it be your fault?" she asked. "You weren't here."

He swallowed. "I've fallen. I brought God's punishment down upon us through my sins. I'm no longer worthy of His protection or of your love."

"I don't believe it." She wiped her tears and set her jaw.

He shook his head. "I failed Him, in Anatolia, and I no longer feel His peace or His guidance. He's abandoned me, and I fear that means He has also abandoned my family. I didn't intend to bring His wrath down on you. I was trying to do what was best for you, for my men, for Rivak, but I . . . I must have done the wrong thing, or I wouldn't still feel so much guilt."

"The God I have come to know since moving to Rivak is not a god of vengeance. Maybe you've been shutting Him out the same way you've been shutting me out."

If only it were as simple as going to the chapel, praying, and waiting for forgiveness. "No. I failed Him. And I failed you too. Do you know what it's like when an army pillages a defeated enemy's camp?"

She looked into the distance. "I can guess."

"It was awful. Like what your father's steward did to you but on a larger scale." He bent his head, staring at the floor. He would tell her everything. Then she would understand. She would hate him, but maybe hatred would be easier than the hurt he'd caused since returning to the grody. "I didn't participate. Told my men not to. But I could do nothing to stop the sultan's men. Or maybe I could have, but Miladin and Dragomir told me I'd be executed if I interfered. Told me what would happen to Ivan and Danilo, what would happen to you and Lidija, what would happen to the people I swore to lead and defend."

She reached for his forearm, but he hadn't earned her compassion. He stood and paced. "One of the women pleaded for my help. She was young. Lidija's age. The man who had her—I saved his life in battle. I told him to let her go, and he laughed at me. Miladin and Dragomir kept me from getting myself killed. But I heard her screams. Still hear them. All night long if I'm sober."

Suzana's face had turned pale as he'd spoken. She didn't say anything for several long moments, and he waited for the contempt to appear in her eyes. Or maybe it would be betrayal because he had failed to stop the crime that had hurt her so completely. But the overwhelming emotion that flooded her gaze was sorrow. "We live in a fallen world, Kostya. Sometimes we have no good choices, only ones that lead to different kinds of pain."

He shut his eyes and leaned against the table. "God has given me everything good in my life, and I failed Him when I failed to protect that young woman."

Suzana stood and approached close enough to rest a hand on his folded arms. "You could have spared her, perhaps, for the length of time it would take the Turks to execute you. Then you would have sacrificed your life and your family and your people, and I doubt she would have escaped her pain. I do not think God will condemn you for saving us when you couldn't have saved her." He stepped away, but she caught his hand. "Let me help you, Kostya. I may not understand all your hurt, but surely love will not make your troubles any worse. Don't keep sending me away, not when what I want most is to help you."

He shook his head. Distance was the only protection he could give her. "I wake up at night sometimes. On the battlefield, beside the men who followed me from Rivak and ended up buried in Anatolia. Or beside Kasim and his victim. I don't want you there when I wake up sobbing." Telling her about it was hard enough. Letting her see it would be humiliating. She said she could understand his choice—but how could she look past his feebleness?

She stepped closer, so the skirt of her dress brushed his legs, and laid a hand on his cheek. "You do not have to be invincible to have my love. And you do not have to be without sin to have God's forgiveness."

Konstantin closed his eyes. She still didn't comprehend how far he had fallen. He had neither power nor virtue. Nothing to commend himself to her. "I may bear the title of župan, but I am no more than a slave of the Ottomans. I can't even follow my conscience without their permission. I am nothing."

"You are not nothing. To me, you are everything."

Her touch still did something to him. Made his skin more alert, made him feel more at ease.

Surely all that was an illusion after what had happened, but her eyes held his, and the affection there was sincere. "How can you feel anything but hatred for someone like me?"

Her fingers moved into a caress along his jaw. "You once told me that hardship is not worse than death. Your vassalage, no matter how heavy, does not mean you can't have joy."

His chest felt tight. She was so close—and he couldn't push away how much he still loved her, how much he had lost by falling short of the husband he'd planned to be. "Joy seems very far away right now."

"Does it?" Her hand moved to his neck. "I have learned that my husband does not send me from his bed because he despises me but because he worries that his nightmares will disturb my sleep. I have learned that my husband has deep compassion, even for a people he went to war against, and deep concern for the men he leads. That is goodness, Konstantin, and it will lead to joy, even if the path winds through pain." Her fingers ended on his collarbone. "Do you still love me?"

He closed his eyes. "Yes." His answer was almost like a sob.

"And I still love you. Let us cling to that, cling to each other, and then our other problems will be easier to solve."

"Will they?" He wanted to believe her, but he couldn't see that far ahead.

She nodded. "If I know I have your love, I can face all manner of hardship. I know what it is to be haunted by the past, but, Kostya, the past does not have to hold hostage your future."

"You have my love," he whispered. "You have always had my love, since the moment I saw you in your father's garden."

Her mouth was near his, still with those perfect corners that begged to be kissed. Softly, he brushed his lips against hers. The sensation was exquisite. It was like coming home after a long journey, like finding rest after an exhausting day of battle, like drinking from a pure fountain after crossing a desert. As Suzana kissed him back, he realized she was right—love held a power to bolster against hardship, to soften regret. Love was something to be protected, relished, and used as a source of strength, even when everything else felt hard. Maybe especially then.

Sweet reconciliation quickly grew to something hungry and deep. He'd missed the passion in her kiss, missed the way her body responded to the movement of his hands.

"I missed this," he mumbled.

Suzana laughed softly through her breathlessness and put a finger to his lips. "So did I."

"Will you forgive me?" He meant for the coldness he'd shown her since his return but also for what had happened while he'd been gone.

"What do you think this is?" She glanced behind him. "You had better go bolt the door."

When Konstantin woke the next morning, his wife lay beside him. Unlike many of his recent mornings, he remembered every detail of retiring the night before, yet he still felt trepidation when Suzana began to stir. What if yesterday's forgiveness didn't keep? He'd done the wrong thing day after day upon returning home. It was only fair if she felt resentment. But as she woke, she snuggled against him and ran her fingers through his beard. Suzana's love had lasted the night. He could trust her, trust their reconciliation.

"What a fool I was not to wake up to this as many mornings as I possibly could," he whispered.

"I'm glad you've finally come to your senses." Suzana traced his mouth. "I don't remember being woken by any nightmares."

That was nothing short of a miracle. "They'll come."

"I'll be right beside you when they do."

Konstantin kissed her fingers, convincing himself that having her near would be a source of strength, not a cause for embarrassment. "I think I'll talk to Father Vlatko today. Ask for his help, ask for penance. And there are a great many people I need to apologize to." He stared at the ceiling. He wasn't sure he deserved his family's forgiveness, but Suzana had forgiven him quickly enough. Maybe the others would too. And maybe God would because Konstantin had never wanted the innocent to suffer while he campaigned. He'd been trapped in a situation that had offered hard consequences regardless of what he did.

"Shall I come with you?" she asked.

"I'd like that." He glanced at the window and studied the pale sliver of light peeking through the curtains. It was still early. He slipped an arm around his wife and pulled her into him. "But not quite yet."

Chapter Forty-One
Tokens for Vengeance

Suzana squeezed Konstantin's hand as they left the church after several hours with Father Vlatko. So much goodness lay in her husband's heart. And so much remorse over the difficult choices he'd been forced to make. But reconciliation was a potent salve for anguish, and her hope for the future was restored. Together she and Konstantin would work through all the hardships to find the joy.

They entered the keep, and he caressed her face in farewell. "I need to apologize to my aunt."

"She will forgive you quickly." Dama Zorica was still ill, but Suzana doubted she would hold a grudge.

"I think you're right." He gave her a smile—something he didn't normally do when others might see—then went toward the family's rooms.

Grigorii approached, looking after Konstantin with curiosity. Perhaps he had seen the smile. Suzana had no desire to speak with the satnik that morning, so she turned to leave.

"A moment, please, my lady."

She reluctantly turned back to him. Grigorii had been wrong when he had said Konstantin blamed her for their lost child, but Konstantin *had* blamed someone—himself—for the tragedy. Grigorii had woefully misunderstood her husband's pain, and he should have reined in Konstantin's drinking rather than enabled it, but maybe he, too, had been worried about Konstantin. His blame had wounded her like a spear, but if today was about forgiveness, she would at least listen if he had an apology.

"Bojan's been working with one of the new colts," Grigorii said. "We wanted your opinion on it before we speak with the župan."

His tone was polite and cooperative, but it wasn't an apology. "My husband knows far more about horses than I do. So do you and Bojan." Besides, the last time Suzana had gone to the stables, she'd been sucked into the past, and the day one of the new colts had been born, she'd lost her infant. Feelings about that day were still raw.

"We just want your opinion about a surprise for the župan. I'll bring the horse out—you won't have to go into the stables."

Suzana felt the heat of embarrassment along her neck. Did the entire garrison know of her aversion to the inside of the stables? And yet, despite her embarrassment, part of her softened. Konstantin found solace in horses. The pain he'd experienced would not disappear in an instant any more than the pain of her youth and childhood had. It would take time and the support of others. She wanted his support to include members of the garrison. She would look at a horse—even one in the stables—if it would be good for Konstantin. She nodded her agreement and walked with Grigorii into the sunny bailey.

A pleasant fall breeze fluttered through her hair veil. The weather was turning—the mornings and evenings growing cooler and cooler. Soon it would be time to wear thicker cloaks and build larger fires in the bedchambers at night.

"My lady." Grigorii led her to the side of the stables rather than into them. "What would you do to keep Ivan and Danilo safe?"

What a strange question. It might be easier to ask what she wouldn't do—that list would be far shorter. She glanced toward the empty archery field. She hadn't seen the boys since she went to the church with Konstantin. "Are they in danger?"

Grigorii pointed his dagger at her. "They are. And if you scream, they'll be dead."

Suzana looked from the blade to Grigorii's face and back again. Why was he threatening her? She was the župan's wife, and Grigorii was Konstantin's satnik. Indignation and shock lapped at her. "What are you doing?"

The knife didn't move. "Following orders, my lady."

"From whom?" Fear grew in her chest, especially when another man, a stranger, stepped from the shadows and looped a sash around her mouth before she could anticipate his plan. She grabbed at the cloth and tried to break free, but the tip of Grigorii's dagger pressed against her chest and an arm circled around her waist from behind, seizing her none too gently.

"Not a sound, or the boys die. You'll be safe as long as you cooperate. We'd rather not hurt you. Especially not with your father ailing. You're his only heir, so someone will want to marry you for his fortune."

The sash gagged her, so she couldn't ask what he meant. She was already married . . . unless Grigorii planned to turn against Konstantin too. She struggled against the man holding her, but his grip tightened while Grigorii wrapped ropes around her, binding her arms to her torso. Even in the open, the way they handled her, preventing any movement, brought back terror that made it hard for her to think or breathe or act.

She'd lost her brief opportunity for escape. Now she couldn't talk and couldn't move. She smashed her foot onto the man's instep, but he only grunted, then picked her up and rolled her into the back of a cart.

Grigorii looked down at her. "Like I said, we don't want to hurt you or Lidija. I think I'll go tell her that a messenger rode over from Župan Dragomir's grad with a message from Decimir."

Grigorii left, and the other man threw an old blanket over her. She kicked at it. The cart was in a lonely corner of the bailey, but surely someone would see her before too long. Except that the bailey was more quiet than usual. Grigorii's position would allow him to send most of the garrison on tasks that would keep them away from his treachery. How had someone so trusted turned on them? She might not have trusted Grigorii to keep her husband sober, but until a few moments ago, she wouldn't have suspected treason.

Konstantin—what did Grigorii intend to do with him? Konstantin would trust Grigorii even more than she had, until he was captured or killed.

She had to escape. She had to warn her husband and search for the boys. She couldn't let Grigorii destroy everything. She wriggled to the bottom of the cart and managed to get one shoe free. If she could just slide down the rest of the way and slip from the cart . . . She wouldn't be able to run, tied as she was, but maybe someone would see her. Unless the betrayal had spread beyond the satnik.

The blanket pulled back, and Grigorii's accomplice glowered at her. Then he grabbed her head and smashed in into the side of the cart. A burst of pain erupted behind her ear, and the world flashed white, and then everything went black.

Suzana awakened to a steady beat of pain and the not-so-gentle rhythm of the swaying and jerking cart. Her arms were still bound and her mouth still gagged. A cloth covered her face so she couldn't see, and ropes had been added to her ankles, making her feet numb. She tried to break free anyway, pulling at the ropes on her legs and around her arms.

The cart slowed, and the ground beneath it grew rougher. Then it pulled to a stop. Someone pulled the blanket away, and Suzana blinked in the sudden brightness. The man from the bailey pulled another cloth loose to reveal Lidija tied in the same manner as Suzana.

He left the women and flung a barrel on its side, then began rolling it to the edge of the cart.

"Careful with that." Grigorii stepped into Suzana's sight.

The other man let out a sound that was half laugh, half grunt. "Why? He just needs to stay alive long enough to keep Sivi Gora from coming to Rivak's aid."

Suzana stared at the barrel. Was Ivan inside?

Grigorii's face grew pale. "I thought he was to be released to his grandfather once everything was settled."

The other man shook his head. "Župan Teodore has no intention of letting another of Župan Miroslav's sons grow up to challenge him. Give him ten years, maybe less, and he'd start plotting revenge."

Grigorii frowned as he helped the man lower the barrel to the ground. "Keeping him alive takes effort. He's frail."

The man grunted and went for the other barrel. "This one's hardly worth the trouble. No one will stop an invasion for him. Doubt people would rally to him either, but that's hardly something we can risk."

If Grigorii was working with Župan Teodore, then that made it absolutely certain that Konstantin was in danger. So, it seemed, were Ivan and Danilo.

Grigorii tried to help Lidija, but she jerked away from his touch and scooted to the end of the cart by herself. She allowed the other man to untie her gag, and then she spat at Grigorii. "Traitor. You'll hang for this."

"Who will hang me?" he asked. "Your older brother will be dead, and your grandfather will fall in line to ensure your younger brother's survival. Župan Dragomir will fall in line to ensure your safety, at least for a time. I imagine Župan Teodore will marry you off to a man he can trust, but that will not be Župan Dragomir's grandson." Grigorii motioned to the main home of a nearby villa. The uppermost part of the wall surrounding the courtyard had partially collapsed, but the remnants of the home looked secure. "Inside for now."

Lidija flashed a look of hatred and defiance, but the man who'd been so careless with the barrels grabbed her arm and pulled her toward the home.

Grigorii twisted the top off one of the barrels and pulled Danilo out. The boy squinted and blinked, and it looked as if he'd been crying. Another man, someone she hadn't seen before, took Danilo inside while a fourth stood at the foot of the carriage and untied her feet. Suzana assumed that was so she could walk, but her feet were so numb she stumbled and had to be partially dragged.

Inside, sagging shutters covered the windows. Dim light crept through the cracks and misalignments. Lidija and Danilo had been made to sit on an old mattress with straw spilling from one corner. The hearth was empty, and a chill filled the room, though it was nothing like the chill in Suzana's heart.

They were trapped. Helpless. The same things Konstantin felt when he thought too much about his vassalage to the Turks. But the current situation had an added element of dread to it because this enemy didn't plan to simply use the family and the župa to make themselves stronger. This enemy planned to kill.

Grigorii dragged Ivan into the room. The poor boy looked disoriented, and Grigorii guided him to the mattress by his sister.

"What's going on?" Ivan asked. "You said we were going to the bakery to choose which pastries Kostya would like best."

"Grigorii is a traitor." Lidija glared at the man in question. "He's been working for Župan Teodore, and he's holding us hostage so Grandfather and Župan Dragomir don't retaliate when he kills Kostya."

"But you're Kostya's friend." Ivan's chin trembled. "You can't hurt him!"

Grigorii looked away and approached Suzana. He took out his dagger, and for a moment, she feared he was going to kill her regardless of what he'd said about her worth as a bride. She backed away but ran into the wall before she'd gone more than a pace.

He huffed. "I'm not going to hurt you." He pulled her gag free.

"Aren't you? You're planning to kill my husband. You cannot wound me any more severely than that."

He avoided her eyes but reached for her arm and cut the rope. "I don't expect you'll be here long, perhaps a day or so. You'll be locked inside. I'll have some blankets brought in." He gestured to a small table with a sack on it. "There's food there."

"Is it poisoned?"

"If we wanted you dead, we wouldn't have bothered smuggling you out of Rivakgrad."

Grigorii went to cut the others free while Suzana rubbed the indents on her arms where the ropes had held her. She didn't know where they were, had no idea how long they'd been traveling or how much longer Konstantin had. Would he be searching for them yet?

When Grigorii finished untying the others, he turned back to her. "I'll need tokens from each of you as proof that we have you. I'll take the cross your husband gave you after that botched murder attempt following the betrothal."

"Don't give it to him," Lidija said. "Don't cooperate."

Grigorii scowled at the girl, then turned back to Suzana. "You can hand it over willingly, or I'll let him take it." He motioned to one of the men standing near the door, the one who'd been so rough with the barrels. "I could never figure out what Župan Konstantin saw in you, other than your dowry, but it seems Župan Teodore's brigand and your husband share a taste for plain women. Your jewelry might not be the only thing he takes. All he needs is an excuse."

When she hesitated a moment longer, Grigorii leaned in and whispered. "We don't really need Danilo. I don't think anyone would rally around Dama Zorica should she try to take up her nephew's cause once he is dead, but should we need to control her, holding Ivan and Lidija would be sufficient leverage. Župan Teodore is ruthless. I don't want to hurt either of the boys, but I'll do what I must."

Suzana handed over the cross.

Grigorii motioned to the children. "Now, I'll need Lidija's ring and the belts Konstantin bought for the boys in Thessaloniki. Get them for me."

Suzana didn't want to obey. Cooperation might speed Grigorii's plan. Or would it hamper him?

A few days ago, Konstantin would have ridden off to work himself to exhaustion, but she didn't think he'd do that today. So, the longer she took, the greater the likelihood that he would begin the search for his missing family. Others would join the search when they were not found. If the garrison's most trusted members were all out looking for Lidija, Suzana, and the boys, who would protect Konstantin when Grigorii came to kill him?

They might already be searching. She didn't know how long she'd been unconscious. Perhaps only a while. Perhaps Kostya was only now finishing his visit with his aunt. And in that case, speed might work against Grigorii because the garrison would still be in the grody rather than dispersed into search parties.

She went to the other hostages. "We must do as he says."

Lidija shook her head. "This was my mother's ring. And he plans to use it against Kostya."

Suzana squeezed her eyes shut, trying to imagine a scenario with her husband still alive at the end of the day. But he had no reason to suspect Grigorii, and that meant Grigorii's plan was all too likely to succeed. "If we don't hand them over, he'll take them and hurt us in the process."

"They can't hurt us if they want to marry us off. And hurting Ivan will bring down my grandfather's wrath."

Suzana put a hand over Lidija's. She didn't want to scare the boys, but Lidija needed to understand their situation. "They need us alive and Ivan alive . . ." She glanced at Danilo, then back at Lidija.

Lidija's eyes widened in alarm. She handed over the silver ring, then turned to the boys. "You'll have to give up your belts, I'm afraid."

Danilo glared at Grigorii, as did Ivan, but they listened to Lidija.

Suzana gathered the belts and handed them to Grigorii along with the requested jewelry. "Please," she whispered. "Don't do this. Kostya's a good man. He hasn't done anything to deserve betrayal."

"Do you see him voluntarily giving up his župa?"

Suzana's eyes stung with tears. Konstantin considered the župa his duty, given him by his family and his God. He wouldn't relinquish it to Župan Teodore or to anyone else without a fight. And if he didn't know the fight had already commenced, didn't know who his enemy was, then he couldn't defend himself. "How can you kill someone who trusts you?"

Grigorii huffed. "It's not my fault he's too stupid to see that his own satnik is a snake." He turned from her and headed for the door.

Ivan grunted and ran at Grigorii, his fists flying into the man's back, then hip, then abdomen as Grigorii turned. Grigorii grabbed his sword and used the hilt to pummel Ivan in the face, sending the boy tumbling backward.

Suzana rushed to Ivan, as did Lidija.

Grigorii stood watching, breathing hard and rubbing his hip as the women pulled Ivan back to the straw mattress.

One of the other men laughed. "And you said the boy was frail? Looks like he got in a few good punches." He left with another laugh, and the other man followed.

"I thought you weren't going to hurt him," Suzana said as she tried to staunch the blood flowing from Ivan's nose.

"He attacked me."

"He's a boy. You're a full-grown warrior."

Grigorii checked the tokens he'd gathered and glared at the four prisoners.

"Has Konstantin ever failed to show you kindness and generosity?" Suzana asked.

"I do not fight against Župan Konstantin because he has wronged me. He saved my life in Anatolia. But someone else saved my life first. Župan Teodore, at Maritsa. I owe him everything—my life, my loyalty, my soul if needed. Even if I didn't owe him, he has leverage, so I have no choice. He wants Rivak, so I'm helping him get it."

"How long have you been planning this?"

Grigorii weighed his words carefully, as if deciding whether sharing the information would harm him. "I have served Župan Teodore since Maritsa. At first, I only passed on information. Then I was instructed to make sure Konstantin couldn't make the tribute payment. If he couldn't pay tribute, the sultan would give Rivak to someone who could. No one was supposed to die, except maybe a few merophs who'd starve if their crops burned. Then you offered Konstantin a way to fix everything. The tribute money. Mercenaries. Even the chance of an heir. You threatened all Župan Teodore's plans, so he told me to act."

Fear lapped at her chest like the waves of the river she'd been thrown into. "You paid the servant to kill me."

"It was supposed to look like suicide. Konstantin wasn't supposed to rescue you. Nor was he supposed to save you when the camp was raided." A look almost like guilt crossed his face. "It wasn't that I disliked you, but I had my orders, and you weren't even a noblewoman, and it didn't seem like anyone would really miss you all that much."

Suzana inhaled slowly, and for a moment, all the pain from her childhood of isolation swirled in her chest. But she was a different person now. She had a family who had accepted her as one of their own. She had a husband who loved her. And she had a župa to protect in any way she could. "What will you do with us?"

Grigorii shrugged. "It's not my decision. Nor will it be by my hand. After you were put in the river, I said I wouldn't kill women or children."

"But you'll deliver us to Župan Teodore so he can kill us?"

Grigorii's jaw hardened. "I doubt he will kill all of you." He lowered his voice. "Though it is a pity you reconciled with your husband. The way he was acting, a drunken accident or suicide could have been widely believed, and an estranged wife would carry nothing threatening in her womb. But you somehow ruined that, didn't you?"

Suzana's hand went to her stomach. She had no way of knowing if she was with child again, but if she was, she didn't think Župan Teodore would allow an heir of Konstantin to live long enough to make a claim.

"You'll have to excuse me now," Grigorii said. "I have one more task."

She knew what that task would be. Župan Teodore wanted Konstantin dead, and Grigorii was ideally placed to do it. "Killing him when he trusts you is a coward's way."

"It's his own fault. He could have failed, and the sultan would have given his lands to Župan Teodore. But instead, he married you and ingratiated himself with the merophs. Then he impressed the sultan with his skill in battle, enough that Župan Teodore dared not attack him while on campaign. As long as he lives, he's a threat to Župan Teodore's plans."

"But he's not a threat to you. If you stop now and take us back to him, Konstantin will show you mercy."

Grigorii gestured to Ivan's face. Though blood still dripped from his nose, the boy glared fiercely at Grigorii. He had yet to shed a single tear, despite the pain he must have felt. "He might let me live after burning his crops and picking the guide who led him and Svarog into a hunting pit, but he won't forgive me for striking his brother, poisoning his aunt, or twice hiring men to kill you."

Suzana knew Konstantin well enough to recognize truth when Grigorii spoke it. Her husband might have forgiven Grigorii had Konstantin been the one dumped in a river or attacked in the camp or injured with the hilt of Grigorii's sword, but he would feel the wrongs against his family more deeply. "And what of your soul?"

Grigorii swallowed. "I saw hell at Maritsa. Župan Teodore saved me from that."

"He can't save you from an everlasting hell if you leave us for him to murder and slay the župan you swore an oath to follow."

Grigorii raised his chin. "Župan Teodore's priest will grant me absolution. I'm just following orders, after all."

Suzana didn't know enough about theology to know if Grigorii's words were true, but her father's priest had been much the same—more loyal to his patron than to his God. Even if Grigorii were bound for hell, it wouldn't save Suzana's husband. She could almost picture it in her mind: Grigorii would find Konstantin and draw him away from anyone else. And Konstantin wouldn't suspect a thing, not until Grigorii had a knife deep in his flesh, and even then, he wouldn't know why.

She had to do something, but she couldn't fight Grigorii. Physically, she was no match. All the advantages lay with him. If only she could give Konstantin some type of warning, some hint that all was not right with his satnik.

Suzana stood and approached Grigorii. She unfastened the brooch that held her cloak in place, centered over her chest. "Will you give him this for me? Let him die with a token of my love? Because you may not care, but I have loved him deeply. And I'll never forgive you or Župan Teodore for taking him away from me."

"Perhaps." Grigorii seemed wary as she stepped closer.

She gripped the brooch in her palm and swung it toward his cheek with all her strength. Not in anger or for revenge. With purpose—an intent to mar his face, because that was the only thing she could think of to let Konstantin know that something was wrong.

Grigorii caught her hand and squeezed. She aimed with her free hand and clawed. Grigorii shouted and threw her to the floor. She landed hard on her hip and shoulder, but she'd drawn blood. More than Grigorii could hide. She said a silent prayer that the traitor would be too flustered to tell a convincing lie and that the mark and a poorly fashioned falsehood would be enough to warn her husband.

Grigorii threw the brooch at her feet. "I was going to give Konstantin a quick death with little pain. Don't expect that anymore. He'll suffer, and it will be your fault."

"I won't be the one with the knife or the rope or whatever it is you plan to use. It will not be my fault. And absolution from a corrupt priest will not save you. You'll burn for eternity."

He turned and left the room. The door slammed shut behind him, and then Grigorii ordered that the door be sealed and no one other than Župan

Teodore or his messenger be allowed in. Suzana rose to her feet as the heavy tread of guards echoed on the other side of the door.

Lidija stepped to her side, and Suzana pulled her into an embrace.

"What are we going to do?" Lidija sobbed.

Suzana scanned the small home. Only one door and that was guarded. The two windows had been boarded shut before they'd arrived. She went closer and tried to push one of the shutters out, but it wouldn't move. Nor would the other.

"Check the other window." Suzana kept her voice a whisper.

Lidija pushed, then pulled. The shutters opened inward, but nothing more than fingers could get through the cracks between the boards. They were trapped, and Suzana's family was at risk. She had to do something. Through the cracks, she saw Grigorii ride away to kill her husband. Two of the guards sat around a fire to keep themselves warm. The third, no doubt, stood closer to the door.

Danilo pulled on her sleeve. He seemed to understand the need for quiet and simply pointed at the hearth.

No fire burned inside. The chimney wasn't large, but the children were small.

"We should wait until dark so they can't see us," Danilo whispered.

Lidija shook her head. "If we wait until dark, Kostya might already be dead."

Both were right. More than anything, Suzana wanted to save her husband. But by the time the boys managed to get up the chimney and outside, Grigorii would be far ahead of them, even if they managed to steal a horse as swift as a vila.

Unless the entire garrison had turned treasonous, Grigorii would likely be cautious. He would want to commit the murder in secret, because if Miladin or Kuzman or Bojan or any of the others found out, they'd seek quick revenge. So would the mercenaries. Would his stealth make him slow? Slow enough that they could find Konstantin first if the boys escaped now?

Danilo climbed into the inner fire chamber.

"It's not dark yet," Suzana said.

"No." Danilo looked up. "But Kostya may be running out of time. Can you boost me?"

If the guards saw him, their chance of escaping through the chimney would disappear. But she suspected the guards were under orders to keep them safe for the time being. If they caught Danilo, they'd simply bring him back and tie them all up. At least that was what she hoped would happen. Might they be rougher with Danilo because he had a Turkish face and less weight as a hostage? She hated risking either of the boys. But the boys were brave, and the chimney was too small for her or Lidija.

She stepped onto the outer hearth and ducked into the fire-stained inner chamber. With Lidija's help, she boosted Danilo up as high as they could lift him. Her arms trembled under the boy's weight and under the weight of worry she felt for all of them. Danilo wedged himself inside the angled masonry and began moving upward into the vertical shaft of the chimney.

Soon Danilo was nothing more than a shadow in a dark, narrow chute. Soot trickled from his back and feet, making Suzana blink and sneeze. She heard more than saw his struggle—he grunted, and the sound of scuffling echoed down the chimney.

"It's too small." His voice, still quiet, carried desperation.

"How much too small?" Ivan asked.

Suzana heard Danilo coming down and went to help him. Covered in ashes, with his feet once again on the stones of the inner chamber, he wiped at his eyes. The tears might have been from frustration or a reaction to the soot, but they weren't from weakness. "I can't fit both my shoulders through. One or the other but not both. Even with one arm up and one arm down. I'm just too wide."

"Let me try." Ivan stepped inside the inner chamber.

He was smaller than Danilo but also less capable, and Suzana knew Konstantin would rather die than let his brother come to harm. But what if there was a way to save them both?

Much as they had done with Danilo, Suzana and Lidija lifted Ivan into the chimney. Amid sprinkles of falling ash, Danilo called out soft instructions on how to brace himself in the chute and move up. Ivan slid once, but Suzana stopped his fall, and he quickly found his grip again.

His shadow disappeared through the top of the chimney, and then his head appeared, backlit with daylight as he looked down on them. "I'm out," he whispered.

"Lidija, go watch the guards." Suzana sent her to the window. "Ivan, come down on the side of the roof away from the men. Meet me at the window."

Danilo's eyes stayed glued to the roof as if he could see his cousin's movements. Suzana listened, expecting at any moment to hear the guards shouting the alarm or to hear Ivan fall and slip down the tile roof and end up with a broken limb. All remained silent.

She went to the window, the one she hadn't been able to open. If she crouched, she could peer through a crack where the shutter didn't hang level. She waited, Danilo beside her now, and she prayed—for Konstantin and for his brother, whose courage was growing faster than his stature.

A small sound, and then Ivan's hazel eyes looked back at her. "I'm down. But I saw something from the roof. I think it's Župan Teodore's army."

"How many men?"

Ivan shook his head. "They blurred together—I could see horses, but I couldn't count the men. They're coming from the east."

East. From Župan Teodore's župa. "Along the road?" she asked.

Ivan nodded.

Suzana didn't like any of her options, but the best choice was quickly becoming obvious. If Župan Teodore was bringing his army, he would have scouts, and those scouts might catch a small boy riding to the same destination. And as much as she wanted Ivan to warn Konstantin, she suspected they were already too late for that. She had to hope that Konstantin would survive. And if he did survive, he would need help holding the grad against his hostile neighbor. In her mind, she pictured the map of Rivak. Župan Teodore's lands to the northeast, Župan Dragomir's lands to the west, and Župan Nikola's lands to the southeast. Grigorii had brought them east, closer to Župan Teodore but also closer to a potential ally. "Ivan, do you know how to get to Župan Nikola's grad?"

"Yes, but shouldn't I go warn Kostya?"

"No. Kostya is a better warrior than Grigorii. He'll beat him." Suzana could almost believe it. In a fair fight, Konstantin would win. When he thought his opponent a friend rather than a traitor, his chances were far worse. "Kostya can't defend Rivakgrad all by himself. You have to ride to Župan Nikola. Tell him what's happening—that Grigorii is a traitor and Župan Teodore is attacking Rivak. Ask for his help. And you have to be careful. You can't let any of the guards here or any of Župan Teodore's scouts see you."

"How can he leave the villa without any of the guards seeing him?" Danilo asked.

Suzana closed her eyes, trying to remember the way the villa had looked when they'd been brought in. A wall surrounded the structure, with only one entrance. The wall was damaged, but none of the crumbled sections would let a horse through. By himself, Ivan might be able to slip past the men, but without a horse, he would be far too slow, and on a horse, he would be far too visible.

She opened her eyes. Ivan was gone. She pressed her face to the crack and looked for him by the horses. All were together. Ivan crept among them and tied the lead rope of one to the stirrups of another, then the lead rope of that one to a buckle on another horse's saddle, pulling the five animals into a line.

Danilo watched from another crack in the shutters. "He's going to take them all so the guards can't follow."

Suzana glanced at Lidija. "Have the guards moved?"

Lidija turned. "No. All three are at the fire now." Lidija hunched down to watch again, then stiffened. "They've seen him."

Suzana held her breath as she looked through the crack to see Ivan scrambling onto the back of the lead horse. His feet didn't reach down to the stirrups, but a combination of noise and motion made the horse move. The guards shouted, then ran after their mounts. Ivan deftly guided the horses out of reach and made it through the gate before the men could catch him.

"He made it!" Danilo said.

Suzana allowed herself a breath of relief, but Ivan still had a long way to ride, and the guards in the villa weren't the only danger he would face.

"Now what do we do?" Lidija asked.

"Now we pray for both your brothers."

Chapter Forty-Two
THE TRAITOR AND THE ŽUPAN

Konstantin couldn't find his wife. Suzana hadn't been in the hall when he'd finished apologizing to his aunt, nor had she been in either of the bedchambers, the strongroom, or the chapel. They'd planned to go over the accounts together this afternoon, and Suzana always kept her commitments. Maybe a meroph had needed something, and she'd gone to help rather than interrupting him while he was with Aunt Zorica. He left the keep and walked across the bailey, stopping at the armory.

"Kuzman, have you seen Dama Suzanna?"

"Not since this morning, lord. Nor have I seen Danilo or Ivan. They missed their lessons."

Konstantin glanced at the training grounds. The boys were not as dependable as Suzana, but they rarely missed their lessons. They occasionally grumbled about Father Vlatko's tutoring in Slavonic and Greek, but the rare complaints he'd heard of sore muscles and bruises from their martial lessons had always come *after* their training, not before.

"I thought perhaps they were with Dama Zorica," Kuzman said.

"I was with my aunt quite recently. They weren't there."

"And how is Dama Zorica today?"

"Recovering. The worst seems to be behind her, but she'll need time." Konstantin didn't see the need to panic, but it was strange for Suzana to miss a planned meeting and equally strange for the boys to miss their training. To have both happen in the same day . . . "You haven't seen any of them ride out?"

"No, lord."

"And Lidija?" Konstantin hadn't seen his sister since he'd taken her place at their aunt's bedside.

Kuzman shook his head. "Would you like me to search for them?"

"It's probably nothing . . . but it does seem unusual for them to all disappear at the same time."

Kuzman set the sword he'd been polishing aside. "I'll ask in the stables and the kitchens if anyone has seen them."

"Thank you. I'll see if the boys have visited Father Vlatko. I can't imagine them diving into their Greek and skipping their sword work, but boys of that age can sometimes do odd things." Konstantin tried to keep his tone light. He was certain his drinking had damaged his standing with his garrison. He didn't want them to think he was panicking when no danger existed. Last summer, perhaps, worry would have been more warranted, but no one had attacked their župa for almost a year. Somewhere, no doubt, towns and villages were being burned and pillaged—he'd seen his share of it in Anatolia—but Rivak was safe. And yet something felt wrong.

He asked, but Father Vlatko hadn't seen the boys since they'd broken their fasts, and the men guarding the grody's gates hadn't seen any of his family leave or return since they'd started their shifts. Konstantin searched the stables. He didn't expect to find Suzana there, but the boys, especially Danilo, were fond of horses. Then he searched the towers without luck.

He recognized Grigorii's horse on the causeway and went to talk to his satnik. If Grigorii hadn't seen them, it was time to organize a more formal search.

When he reached the stables, Jakov was helping Grigorii with the destrier.

"Hard journey, Grigorii?" Konstantin asked. Yarilo looked as if he'd been overridden. Members of the garrison knew better than to abuse their horses without acute need, but Grigorii, no doubt, had a good reason.

"Yes, lord."

Konstantin waited for an explanation, but Grigorii was watching the horse and young groom, not his župan. "What happened to your face?"

Grigorii put his hand to the three parallel scabs on his cheek. He glanced at Konstantin, then looked away. "Trouble with a woman."

Konstantin decided against teasing Grigorii about it. Konstantin, after all, was no expert when it came to women. Grandfather had found Suzana for him, and even after being given a perfect bride, he'd almost ruined it with his stupidity. It wasn't fair for Grigorii to take his frustration out on a horse, but it was the first offense.

Konstantin looked the stallion over. "What do you think?" he asked Jakov.

"He needs a rest, but he'll be all right."

Konstantin patted the weary horse. "Have either of you seen Suzana or Lidija or the boys?"

"No, lord," Jakov said.

"I saw the boys when I rode in." Grigorii glanced to the door.

Relief relaxed the tension in Konstantin's muscles. "Good. Where have they been hiding?"

Grigorii motioned toward the bailey. "One of the towers."

"Which one? I just checked all of them."

Grigorii patted Yarilo. "If Jakov doesn't mind finishing up alone, I'll show you. I imagine they're playing one of their hiding games."

"I can see to him," Jakov said.

Konstantin thanked the groom and followed Grigorii from the stables. "I'm glad you saw them. No one else has since morning. Suzana and Lidija seem to have disappeared as well." Konstantin hoped the boys knew something, because the unsettled feeling he'd had since leaving his aunt's chamber hadn't completely left.

Grigorii led him through some of the outbuildings as they approached one of the watchtowers. He had removed his thick gauntlets while working with the horse, but he tugged one back on.

"I don't know that I've ever seen you push a horse that hard other than in battle." Konstantin would have rather said nothing, but someone had to speak up for the horse, and Jakov wouldn't feel confident enough to reprimand the satnik. Konstantin didn't want to reprimand him either, but he was curious why Grigorii had been in such a hurry.

Grigorii grunted as they reached the alley between the kitchen and the palisade wall. "I apologize if I hurt the horse." Then Grigorii stopped, pivoted, and swung his fist into Konstantin's abdomen.

It was so unexpected that Konstantin didn't believe it, even as the pain made him double forward. He barely managed to swing a hand up and block Grigorii's wrist as the knife the satnik wielded swung toward Konstantin's back.

Why was Grigorii attacking him? The question raced through Konstantin's head as he gripped Grigorii's forearm. Grigorii was his satnik, his friend, his sworn man-at-arms—not his enemy.

Grigorii struggled to free his weapon. He pulled with his hand and threw his body into Konstantin's, forcing him against the rough wood of the palisade. Grigorii was too close, blocking Konstantin from drawing his spathion.

"Guards!" Konstantin shouted, but Grigorii had struck in an isolated portion of the bailey. He wasn't sure anyone would hear him, let alone arrive in time to help. Summoning all his strength, Konstantin shoved off from the palisade, knocking back his assailant and gaining enough space to pull out his sword, even though he had to release Grigorii's wrist in the process.

Grigorii drew his sword and immediately attacked, hewing with enough force to hack off a limb. Konstantin held his ground and blocked the strike, then blocked the next one and ducked away from the third. He twisted his blade around and aimed for Grigorii's sword arm. He didn't want the man dead, not when there were so many unanswered questions.

Grigorii grunted as Konstantin's spathion sliced into his flesh. He pulled his injured limb inward and stepped back. Keeping one hand on his weapon, Grigorii raised the other to his mouth and sounded a shrill whistle.

Disbelief remained stronger than anger, so Konstantin kept his sword at the ready but hesitated to slay a man he'd considered his friend. "What's going on, Grigorii?" Surely this went beyond Konstantin's inquiry over the horse.

Grigorii didn't answer. His lips were pulled tight, and he winced as he moved.

Footsteps sounded, and when the armed stranger came into view, Konstantin's brief hope that his guards had arrived crumbled into knowledge that Grigorii's reinforcements had come first. Konstantin turned to the new assailant and moved several paces from Grigorii. Even injured, he was dangerous, especially if he attacked at the same time as his coconspirator. The stranger struck first, bringing his sword down in a quick, powerful stroke. Konstantin blocked it, but the force sent vibrations along the muscles of his arms. The next thrust from the stranger had less momentum. Konstantin evaded and sliced his blade across the man's neck.

As the enemy fell, Konstantin pointed his blade toward his injured satnik. "Drop your weapon."

Grigorii took a small step back. "No, I don't think I will."

An instant later, a sharp, snarling pain pummeled into Konstantin's back, throwing him forward, dropping him to his knees. He stayed upright only by holding the palisade, and though he gripped his spathion, it felt heavy.

When he turned, he could see the tip of a crossbow bolt protruding from his back. And he could see the man who'd shot him stalking closer. Grigorii, too, closed in.

"Shall I finish him off?" the stranger asked.

"Not quite yet. When his wife gave me this"—Grigorii pointed to the scabs on his face—"I promised her that he would suffer as a consequence."

"What have you done to Suzana?" Konstantin tried to force authority into his voice, but it came out weak and stuttering. Sweat soaked his torso and the back of his neck. Staying upright was an effort.

Grigorii stomped on the end of Konstantin's spathion. Konstantin tried to pull it free, but the effort left him gasping in pain.

"Interesting," Grigorii said. "I think this is only the second time I've seen emotion on his face. Love and pain—that's all he shows. Nothing else, not even surprise when his satnik turns traitor."

"Župan Teodore wants him dead." The stranger pulled back the string of his crossbow and reached into his quiver for a bolt.

Konstantin had to fight back. But he couldn't even yank on his sword without pain threatening to overwhelm him. A warm, wet sensation spread down his back as blood flowed from his wound. "What did you do with my wife?" he asked again.

"Nothing much, yet." Grigorii kept his toe on the end of Konstantin's sword. "We've taken her where she can be used as leverage, if needed. She, your siblings, and your cousin will remain safe as long as your grandfather, your neighbor, and your father-by-marriage all fall in line after your death."

They'd all been taken hostage. Maybe if the bolt were pulled out and Konstantin were bandaged, he could go after them. But Grigorii and his associate didn't look as if they would let him walk away from this.

He had to try something. He pulled on his sword, but Grigorii repositioned his foot for a better hold. Konstantin winced, then let that pain pull him from his knees to a seated position, where he'd have better access to the knife in his boot. But Grigorii had served with him for too long. He must have known what Konstantin was doing because he kicked first the bolt sticking from Konstantin's back, then his ribs. "Don't try anything."

Grigorii's kicks had caused an explosion of sharp misery, leaving Konstantin no longer capable of resistance. The overwhelming pain left him barely able to breathe.

"We should finish him off," the stranger's voice said. "We still have the rest of the garrison to deal with."

Grigorii stared down at him. "These are fierce times and fierce lands, Župan Konstantin. Rivak needs a leader ruthless enough to go through battle and not snivel over the fate of camp followers. In other circumstances, compassion might have made you a good župan, but now we'll never know." Grigorii gestured to the other man, who aimed his crossbow at Konstantin's face.

"No!"

The cook's voice. Not surprising since they were near the kitchens. Nevena may have been the only one close enough to hear his call, but she wouldn't be able to save him. He tried to speak, to warn her to run before they attacked her, but pain still racked him in waves, and that made speaking impossible.

Footsteps ran toward them, and Kuzman grunted and barreled into the man with the crossbow. They tumbled to the ground, and the next moment, Bojan came into view, sword drawn, pointed at Grigorii.

Konstantin was at the wrong angle to see the scuffle between Kuzman and the crossbowman, but Kuzman rose, and the other man did not.

"Shall we kill him, lord?" Kuzman motioned to Grigorii.

"No." Konstantin could barely speak. "We need to question him."

"I'll say." Bojan cuffed Grigorii soundly on the back of his head and twisted the satnik's arms around behind him.

Nevena edged closer. "I'm so sorry, lord. I ran for help as fast as I could."

"Thank you. I owe you . . . my life."

Kuzman bent over Konstantin. "I'll take you to the keep, lord." Kuzman hefted Konstantin to his shoulders with a grunt. The pain made Konstantin spasm, but Kuzman held on. The old sword master gave the cook instructions to gather more of the garrison and to fetch Miladin and Magdalena from the grad. Konstantin heard the words, but the pain was so intense it was hard for him to focus.

Only when Kuzman reached the stairs for the family's chambers did Konstantin manage to get more words out. "No. To the hall." They had much to do.

Kuzman obeyed and laid Konstantin facedown on one of the tables. He squeezed his eyes shut, hoping that the pain would fade, at least a little, now that he wasn't being moved. The tear in his back still made angry demands for his attention, but he focused and turned his head toward his men.

Bojan had tied Grigorii to one of the chairs. So many things needed to be done. If Grigorii wasn't trustworthy, Konstantin wasn't sure who was, but he couldn't do everything by himself. Especially not with a crossbow bolt in his back.

He gritted his teeth. Kuzman and Bojan had just saved his life. He could still trust them. "Grigorii is working for Župan Teodore. They've taken my family. We need to find out where. Two others attacked me. There might be more, so have the grody searched. Recall all garrison members out for rest, and have the guards at each set of gates prepare to lock out anyone hostile."

Bojan stayed to ensure Konstantin's safety. Kuzman left to carry out Konstantin's orders. One of his first stops must have been to Risto because Konstantin's manservant entered the hall with hot water and clean cloths moments before Miladin and Magdalena rushed into the room.

Miladin studied Konstantin for a long moment. "I am most relieved to see you alive, lord." Then he turned to Grigorii, still tied to a chair, and smashed his fist into his face. "You traitor!" The punch pushed Grigorii back, and the chair toppled over, causing Grigorii to strike his head on the stone floor with a loud crack. It looked painful, but Konstantin couldn't find any sympathy for his former satnik.

"Help me with this," Magdalena told her husband. She offered Konstantin a stick to bite on, and he accepted. He was too far gone to fight another flare of pain.

"It was too low to hit the heart or lungs, lord." Magdalena prodded around the bolt. Konstantin's eyes squeezed shut, and his teeth gripped the stick harder with each of her movements. He knew she was being gentle, but the pain burned. "Your armor changed the angle. Seems to have struck only muscle. Moderate blood loss. Dangerous, but it's not a death sentence. Miladin, hold him in place."

Konstantin lessened his grip on the stick to tell them he could hold still without any assistance, but then someone began tugging. Maybe it was wise to have Miladin's help after all, because the pain spiked from excruciating to unbearable. Konstantin held his breath, and the edges of his vision turned gray. He felt Magdalena's knife and the prickly head of the bolt and so much agony that he nearly screamed. He would have, had his mouth not been full of wood.

"It's out now," Magdalena said.

Konstantin began breathing again but managed only two inhalations before Magdalena doused the wound with wine. Konstantin flinched.

"That's the worst of it." Magdalena sounded apologetic. "I'll sew you up now."

After five sutures, Konstantin lost track. Pain made it hard to focus on anything else, but worry and distrust remained. So did desperation. He had to find his family . . . and he had to keep Rivak safe. Could he do both at once?

Magdalena finished and wrapped a bandage around Konstantin's injury. "I would recommend rest," she said. "If that's possible."

Rest? No, that wasn't possible, not with Suzana, Lidija, Ivan, and Danilo being held hostage.

Miladin turned to Grigorii and pulled the overturned chair upright again. "Shall I prepare a gallows for him, lord?"

"Not yet." Konstantin pushed himself up so he was sitting on the table instead of lying on it. "I need to know where he's taken my family."

Miladin grabbed Grigorii's hair and pulled his head back. "Did you hear that? You'd better start talking, or we'll use you for archery practice."

Grigorii seemed to recognize the promise behind Miladin's threat. "They're unharmed, in a villa where Župan Teodore can reach them."

Konstantin tried to read Grigorii. He could no longer trust anything the man said, but his plan had called for Konstantin's death, so he was unlikely to have planned a trap . . . A trap. Had Grigorii been involved in all the traps set last summer? "How long have you been working for Župan Teodore?"

"Since he saved my live at Maritsa."

Since Maritsa? That meant Konstantin's reign had been compromised from day one. "The bandits last summer?"

Grigorii nodded.

Bojan crossed his arms. "You burned the fields? You set the trap in the church? Then led me and the others off so our župan could burn?"

So many things had gone wrong last summer. Crops and villages destroyed. Near-death for him, for his bride. A shortfall in the treasury. "And Čučimir?" Had Grigorii been behind Rivak's financial woes too?

"Čučimir had indiscretions, and Župan Teodore knew his secrets. He promised the protovastar silence, and any money he could steal from you. That's how Teodore controls men—with threat and bribe. It worked, until we were ordered to prevent your marriage to a woman whose dowry could make you solvent again."

"You tried to kill Suzana?"

Grigorii looked away. "Only when I couldn't find another way of stopping the betrothal."

"But why?" Bojan asked. "Župan Teodore may have saved your life, but so did Župan Konstantin."

Grigorii was silent for a time. "A mix of obligation and threats." He met Konstantin's eyes for a moment. "You would do anything for your family, wouldn't you? I had no choice but to obey when Župan Teodore threatened my sister."

Konstantin understood the pull to protect a sister, but not this. "Why didn't you tell me? I would have rescued her for you."

"Why would you have shown mercy to Vasilija?" Grigorii stared at Konstantin with an eye already swelling shut from its impact with Miladin's fist. "The father of her child died at Maritsa, before they were married. I didn't want my nephew exposed as a bastard. And then . . . before your wedding, I told Župan Teodore I wouldn't attack women anymore. And that's when he threatened to kill both of them if I didn't fall in line."

"You should have come to me for help."

Grigorii shook his head. "Why would you help a fallen woman and her illegitimate son? Viktor was a member of Rivak's garrison, but they were not married, so you had no obligation to support her as a widow when he didn't return from Maritsa."

"Enough lives were ruined at that battle without me ruining any more." Konstantin recalled scores of missing faces and knew those deaths had affected everyone in Rivak. "Who am I to cast stones at someone who let passion overtake them? Look at my mistakes! I stood by while a man tortured an innocent child, and then I hurt everyone who was closest to me by pushing them away—everyone except you with your surfeit of wine that I was stupid enough to drink."

Grigorii shuddered. Pain or regret? Both? "It would have been easier if you'd been a pompous fool. Someone I could despise or condemn."

Did that mean Grigorii hadn't despised him, that maybe some of the friendship hadn't been imagined? He could never trust Grigorii again, but he could hope for some truth. "Where did you take my family? You'll have to answer for your crimes, Grigorii, but help me find my family, and I'll see that your sister and her child are cared for."

Grigorii squeezed his eyes shut. "I can tell you where I left them, though it won't matter. Župan Teodore will hold them hostage long enough to keep Župan Dragomir and your grandfather from attacking him, but he doesn't plan to let either of the boys reach manhood. And he'll marry off the women to men he can trust to control them. His allies. His family. He'll never return them to you. If you survive, he'll make sure they perish. Your resistance will kill them all."

Konstantin stood. Pain radiated from his wound, but he forced his feet forward to stand over Grigorii. "Tell me where they are."

"An old abandoned villa, but standing between you and that villa is Župan Teodore's army. It's twice as big as yours, even with the mercenaries. You might be able to hold the grad against them, but you'll never be able to defeat them in the open."

CHAPTER FORTY-THREE
PREPARATIONS FOR WAR

KONSTANTIN STARED AT THE FOOD Magdalena had encouraged him to eat. Grigorii had been bound and secured, riders had been sent to warn the villagers of an approaching army, the garrison was being assembled, and the župan was trying to recover some of his strength.

Miladin crossed his arms. "I still can't believe it. I never suspected him. I disagreed with him when he helped you drown your sorrows in wine, but I thought he was misguided, not malicious." Miladin shook his head. "That someone could fool me—all of us—so completely for so long."

"It was my failure." Konstantin had been the one to appoint Grigorii as satnik because he had been the most senior of his father's desetniks to survive Maritsa. This failure seemed more complete than most of the others—Konstantin had a sacred duty to his lands, and he'd trusted their protection to a man who had burned crops and homes. Konstantin stood from where he'd been hunched over, but that made the cut in his back burn.

Aunt Zorica's face pulled in concern. She was supposed to be convalescing, but the emerging disaster had drawn her from her chamber, despite her unsteady feet and pale face. "Perhaps you should rest."

"I could say the same thing to you, but I doubt either of us will while Župan Teodore holds most of our family hostage." Konstantin tried straightening more slowly. The pain wasn't so bad if he took his time. And he no longer felt clammy and nauseated. "The most important question is this: Do we have enough men to protect the grad and send out a rescue party?"

"We could spare a few men for a rescue party." Miladin bit his lip. "But not more than a handful if we wish to ensure Rivakgrad holds. If Župan Teodore has the hostages in the middle of his camp, it won't be enough. And if he has anyone else working for him . . ."

That nagging fear wouldn't leave. Župan Teodore had been controlling Konstantin's satnik for years. The protovastar too. Who else might the man have bribed or threatened into cooperation? Konstantin couldn't abandon his grad when it was under attack. But he had to do all he could to rescue his family.

Zoran entered the keep. "We can see the army in the distance."

Konstantin and Miladin followed Zoran to the roof. The sun was sinking, casting long shadows. In the east, a blurred dust cloud hugged the horizon.

"Won't the sultan object to one vassal taking the lands of another?" Zoran asked.

"By the time the sultan finds out, it will be too late for us." Konstantin squinted, trying to count, but the army was still too distant. "And the sultan might not care too much, as long as he's still paid his tribute and given his men when they're due. It could even be to the sultan's benefit. He'll have one less vassal to deal with, but he can demand the same duties. And I doubt Župan Teodore will get into arguments with the sultan's sipahis over their methods of pillage." Konstantin may have won the sultan's gratitude for a time, but any influence he'd gained had been lost.

"What will you do?" Zoran asked.

Konstantin looked at the men approaching the grad, measuring the distance, predicting their arrival. Nightfall. "I'll let you know when I decide."

Konstantin climbed back down the stairs and went to the chapel to pray and to think. Miladin followed, silent but present, falling back into the role of bodyguard he'd had since Konstantin's days as a boy. Back then, Miladin had always followed a little more closely whenever there had been a mishap—a fall from a horse, a rogue brigand passing too near. The attempted murder would have shaken Miladin almost as much as it had shaken Konstantin.

Konstantin knelt in the chapel, hoping that God would be as quick to forgive him as his wife and aunt had been. He begged divine protection for his family and then tried to foresee what he should do next. His wound ached, but his thoughts came together with clarity. Župan Teodore held everyone Konstantin most cared about. Despite how well Konstantin hid his emotions and feelings, Župan Teodore would know the strength of the lever he possessed. Even men who didn't love their wives or siblings would take umbrage at someone threatening a family member—there would be pride, if not affection.

Župan Teodore would make him choose. Konstantin could predict it with near certainty. He would be asked to give up Rivak or sacrifice his family.

He needed help. Sivi Gora was too far away, but Župan Dragomir would come if called. "Miladin, I want our fastest rider sent to Župan Dragomir's grad to ask for aid."

"I'll see that it's done at once."

"Wait," Konstantin called before Miladin left. "I expect Župan Teodore to issue an ultimatum. Give up the grad, or see my family slaughtered. We'll need time. Time for Župan Dragomir to come. Time to find my family and rescue them."

"He may still expect to find you dead," Miladin said. "That will buy us a little time."

"Perhaps if he thinks I am wounded too severely to make an immediate decision, he will wait before doing anything rash." That was what Konstantin needed—time enough to find his family and rescue them before he was forced to decide between a pair of choices that would crush his heart and break his soul. "Miladin, can you tell a convincing lie?"

CHAPTER FORTY-FOUR
RIDERS

"A RIDER'S COMING." DANILO STOOD at the window, looking through the crack in the dilapidated shutters.

"Does he have Ivan?" Suzana had prayed for the boy's success, but worry for him had never left.

"I can't tell yet. But now I count five."

Lidija met Suzana's eyes. "Župan Teodore's men."

Were they coming to reinforce the existing guards, or did they plan to move the hostages?

Suzana scanned the largely bare room and found only one place to hide. "Danilo, how long could you stay in the chimney without making any sound?"

Danilo glanced at the hearth, then gave her a look of confusion. "My shoulders are too big. I already tried to get through—I wouldn't have let Ivan go alone if I could have gone with him."

She knelt to be closer to his level. "I know you can't get through. But if you and Lidija were to hide inside, the soldiers might think you escaped. And then when they left, you could go to the nearest village. They could hide you, get you both to Župan Dragomir or to Sivi Gora if Rivak were no longer safe."

Lidija kept her face impassive, reminding Suzana of the girl's older brother, the man they all hoped was still alive. "What if they leave us locked in?"

"If they are gone, you can use the benches to pry the bars from the windows. We couldn't do that when there were guards who might hear, but if they leave . . ."

Lidija nodded. "Will you hide with us?"

"I don't think we will all fit, and if someone isn't here to say you've escaped, they might search hard enough to find you." One of the guards had come in after Ivan's escape, but he'd checked only the beams across the windows and growled at them as they'd sat on the straw-stuffed mattress. He hadn't checked the hearth or chimney, hadn't asked how Ivan had freed himself.

Horse hooves struck the ground outside. Suzana handed the food and blankets to Lidija—they might be hiding for a while—and helped them find ledges to balance on in the chimney. When she heard the scrape of the door opening, she rushed to one of the windows and pretended to peer through the cracks.

Two men barged in, both strangers to her.

"Where are the others?" one demanded.

She ignored him because she had yet to think of a plausible explanation. They'd been locked in. If they'd found a way out, why would she remain while the others had escaped? And she knew nothing of the guards, so she couldn't guess their intelligence or whether they might try to beat the truth out of her. She prayed they wouldn't—not here, at least, because she didn't think Danilo would stay in the chimney if he thought she was being harmed.

One strode to her and turned her around forcefully, smashing her shoulders into the wall. She bit her lip rather than letting a cry escape.

"Where are the others?"

"Mountain vila." She blurted out the first thought that came to her mind and prayed the men were superstitious. "They were rescued by vila."

The man narrowed his eyes and glanced around the room, then up at the roof. The other man stood near the doorway, his posture threatening and unbelieving. The man beside her pulled at the boards over the windows. He pulled one off—it made a tremendous amount of noise, as she'd feared, but the hole it left was almost large enough for Lidija and Danilo to crawl through. If they managed to stay hidden, they'd have an easier time escaping now, even if they were locked in.

"It doesn't matter," the other man said. "Bring her. We have the jewelry and belts. We can claim we have the others. If the assassin did his job, all will be chaos and we'll walk right in. If he didn't do his job, having her will be enough to bring the župan to his knees."

The man next to her grabbed her arm and pulled her toward the door. Suzana didn't resist and didn't look back.

Konstantin watched the figure on horseback grow ever fainter as Miladin disappeared in the distance, toward Župan Teodore's army. A pair of German mercenaries on swift horses had ridden the other direction, toward Župan Dragomir.

"We have a bit of a wait, lord." Zoran rested a hand on the watchtower's wall. "Till Miladin returns or until it's dark. And that blow to your back was no small wound. You'll be sharper tonight if you rest."

"I can try. I don't know if I'll succeed when so much is at stake."

"Try, then, lord." Zoran's eyes swept the land beyond the grad. "We'll alert you if anything changes. And I suggest you have someone you trust stand outside your door in case Grigorii had more than two accomplices."

Konstantin went to Suzana's bedchamber, with Bojan to stand watch outside. Anyone seeking to harm him would check his room first, so her room was the wiser choice. Also the more sentimental. She'd not slept in her bed the night before, but the pillows still carried her scent. He prayed they hadn't reconciled only to be lost to each other forever.

He woke when Bojan pushed the door open. "Lord? It's time."

He inhaled one last breath scented by Suzana's bedding and sat up slowly. The spot where his back had been pierced with a crossbow bolt was still tender, but he no longer felt shaky and weak. That was a relief because he would almost certainly have a fight on his hands before the night was over.

Risto and Bojan added wrappings round his wound to better brace it, then helped him into his armor. "Has Miladin made it back?"

"Not yet, lord."

Konstantin prayed Miladin would be protected. When they'd come up with their plan, they'd assumed Župan Teodore would recognize Miladin as someone important enough to treat with respect but someone who didn't hold enough authority to make decisions. And they all held the hope that he could learn something useful from the župan's camp—ideally, the location of the hostages.

When Konstantin reached the keep's main hall, he found his aunt waiting for him.

"Wisdom says you should stay." She sat near the hearth, and worry lined her face. "Rivak cannot survive if you are lost."

"Wisdom, perhaps, but my heart does not agree. Nor, I think, does yours."

Aunt Zorica blinked away a tear.

He knelt beside her. "I cannot endure the loss of my cousin, my sister, my brother, and my wife, not if I have a chance to help them. Nor can I surrender my župa. That leaves me this option."

She grasped his hand. "God go with you, Kostya."

"If I am not successful . . . Rivak will fall on your shoulders."

Her grip tightened. "You must return because I am not up to the task."

"The title of župan may have come to me, but it is your guidance that has preserved Rivak since your brother's death." Aunt Zorica was more than equal to the task, but a župan needed to be male, so if Konstantin and all the hostages were lost, she would have to find someone to marry, and there would not be time to ensure it was a marriage of love. "You'll know what to do."

Veles waited in the bailey, saddled and armored, though Konstantin did not expect to make any charges on him. He left behind enough men to protect Rivakgrad if it fell under siege, but there weren't enough men for a battle. Even if Župan Dragomir joined forces with him, they weren't guaranteed a victory over Župan Teodore, and any such confrontation was likely to cost them dearly. They'd all have trouble meeting the sultan's demands if they fell to infighting, and hope of gaining freedom from Ottoman suzerainty in their generation would be dashed.

Konstantin left Aunt Zorica in charge of Rivakgrad, with Kuzman to command the men-at-arms who remained. Earlier in the day, Grigorii had dispersed part of the garrison, but most had been called back. Konstantin hoped they could all be trusted. They'd made a careful search of the grody to ensure no additional assassins lingered in hiding, but they hadn't had time to search the lower grad, so passage between the two was limited to the garrison and few others.

As Konstantin rode down the causeway, the gates closed behind him. He kept the hood of his cloak pulled forward to obscure his face, in the hope that if Župan Teodore had spies in the grody, they wouldn't recognize him. As an added precaution, he took the road to one of the smaller gates, where he would pass fewer houses.

Kuzman had ridden ahead and waited for him there. "There's a group of riders coming. Galloping in hard."

"Not Miladin, then?" He'd left by himself, but he might bring messengers from Župan Teodore's camp.

"No, they're approaching from the west."

Konstantin dismounted and climbed the tower. The sun had set, and only the palest glow of twilight lit the horizon. Three men on horseback were highlighted against the dim backdrop. "We want Župan Teodore to think I'm on my deathbed, so unless it's someone we trust . . ."

Kuzman nodded.

The riders slowed as they drew near. One dismounted and knocked on the gate. A flash of torchlight illuminated his face, and Konstantin closed his eyes in a prayer of gratitude. Decimir. He didn't know how the messengers had reached Dragomir's grad so quickly, but he immediately called an order down to the men at the gate. "Let them in."

As the gate pulled open, Konstantin climbed from the tower. Decimir led his horse into the grad, followed by two of Župan Dragomir's men—Decimir's new bodyguards, Konstantin assumed. Konstantin embraced the young man in welcome.

Decimir looked Konstantin over. "I am glad to see you well. When we heard someone tried to kill you . . . I rode over immediately. My grandfather will come with his men, but they'll take longer. You can expect them by dawn."

"Thank you." With reinforcements from Dragomir, the garrison Konstantin left behind would be strong enough to hold the grody, even if Župan Teodore attacked. Konstantin prayed that Miladin's work would convince Župan Teodore to postpone attacking at least until daybreak. "How did you arrive so soon?"

"My grandfather and I were hunting near the border with your lands. I left from there. The messengers said something about a hostage?" Decimir swallowed. "Who was taken?"

"My sister, my brother, my cousin, and my wife."

Decimir's mouth hung open in shock. He took in Konstantin's armor and the gathering of men and horses. "You're going after them?"

"Yes."

"Let me join you."

Decimir had done well on campaign for the sultan, but he had seen only fifteen winters. He was skilled and brave, but he wasn't a full-grown man. "Your grandfather has proven himself a loyal ally again and again. I can hardly repay him by bringing his heir along on a quest with such a small chance of success."

Decimir shook his head. "Župan Konstantin, I am ready to be tested, and I am willing to risk my life for the hostages. They are like family to me."

Konstantin put a hand on Decimir's shoulder. "I need you to stay, because if I fail, Lidija will need you to rescue her. Župan Teodore will try to marry her off to someone he can control. If you can get word to my grandfather, he'll help, but Sivi Gora is far away, farther when the first snows come. You may be her only hope."

Determination lit Decimir's expression. "If I don't help rescue her now, when she's been abducted, how can I ever hope to be worthy of her hand?"

"You came, Decimir. You came when we needed you. That shows a loyalty no one in Rivak will forget, least of all Lidija."

Konstantin could tell Decimir didn't like his answer. He probably felt much as Konstantin had when his father had told him he couldn't come on campaign with him—a campaign that would have undoubtedly ended in his death, just as it had ended in death for his father and uncle and Decimir's father too. But the young man didn't argue. "Ilija and Josif are capable men. That's why Grandfather wished them to ride with me. If you need help, they will assist you."

"Thank you." They would be among the most skilled in Dragomir's garrison for the župan to trust them with his grandson, and Konstantin welcomed their help.

"Another rider." Kuzman squinted from the top of the tower. "Could be Miladin."

It was, and he made his report as soon as he rode through the gates and dismounted.

"You were right, lord. Župan Teodore has given us until tomorrow morning. He says he and his men are to be allowed into Rivakgrad, or he'll kill Danilo. And he gave me these."

From his saddlebag, Miladin took out the belts Konstantin had bought the boys in Thessaloniki, his mother's silver ring that Lidija had worn for years, and the cross he'd given Suzana that horrible night after their betrothal. He took the cross and slipped it around his neck. He would see Suzana again soon, or he would see the God who had died on that ancient crucifix.

"Did he have the hostages with him?" Konstantin asked.

"I think not. No tents had been erected, and the group traveled lightly. Two score men. No wagons. Nowhere to hide them." Miladin refastened the saddle bags. "Maybe they're still at that villa."

Could it be that simple? Konstantin cursed. He should have been riding out to the villa, not napping while he waited for darkness to mask his planned approach to Župan Teodore's camp. "I think we had better go have another chat with Grigorii." He mounted his horse and led the others back to the grody.

Rivakgrad didn't often have the need to detain its subjects. Any wrongs between merophs were dealt with quickly, with fines or restitution, or in extreme cases, with exile. Execution was a punishment Konstantin had yet to employ. In any case, the grody had no official cells, so Grigorii sat on the stone floor of the garrison, knees pulled to his chest and ropes at his wrists and ankles. A pair of guards watched him.

Konstantin looked at the man he had once trusted with his life, with his župa. The sting of betrayal was strong, and anger made it hard for Konstantin to plan his strategy. The man was a traitor, but he had information that Konstantin needed.

"You have few choices left, Grigorii," Konstantin said. "If you help me find my family, I will help your sister. That's why you did all of this, isn't it?"

"If I help you, Župan Teodore will ruin her." Grigorii squeezed his hands, then stopped. The motion would have made the ropes cut into his wrists.

Miladin crouched next to Grigorii. "Who do you think would make the better benefactor for your sister? Župan Teodore, who uses people like you to further his lust for power? Or Župan Konstantin, who has compassion for even his enemies?"

Grigorii met Miladin's gaze, then bent his head and hid his face with his knees. "I was a fool. I'm going to die, and Župan Teodore is unlikely to lift a finger for her or the boy."

Konstantin kept his voice gentle. "I keep my promises, Grigorii. If you help me, I'll see she has money to start a new life. Either here or in a place where she is a stranger. Tell me where you took my family."

Grigorii's voice was dull and defeated. "The villa lies just across the border between your župa and Teodore's."

"Might he have left them there?"

"He told me only part of his plans, but from the villa, he could move them with his army or send them back to his grad."

They would be difficult to rescue from Župan Teodore's grad, so Konstantin prayed they were still at the villa. "Help me save them, Grigorii, and you can save your sister."

Grigorii glanced up with a swollen eye and broken lips. "I can take you there. And if they aren't at the villa, I can show you the sally port in Župan Teodore's grad."

CHAPTER FORTY-FIVE
SOOT AND SHADOW

One of Župan Teodore's guards pulled Suzana from a horse and lowered her to the bailey of the unfamiliar grody. Her hands were bound so tightly that she could no longer feel her fingertips.

Dama Emilija walked onto the paved court. She glanced at Suzana with the same contempt she had shown in the days before the wedding. "Where are the others?"

"Disappeared. Escaped. But having her will be enough."

Dama Emilija sneered. "She's barely better than a meroph. Hardly worth holding hostage. She can't be all that important to her husband now that he has her dowry."

"We've been told otherwise," the guard said. "Where should we put her?"

Dama Emilija circled Suzana, eyeing her much like a cook eyed an inferior cut of meat. "She's not an honored hostage, so she won't be given one of the rooms in the keep. She's not dangerous enough to lock in the tower. And her husband withdrew hospitality—that's something I'll not forgive. Tie her up in the stables."

Not the stables. Fear tightened Suzana's chest, but a quick glance at Dama Emilija told Suzana clearly enough that a protest would earn her no mercy.

Konstantin pulled Veles to a stop and listened intently while the other horses and riders did the same. "Someone is following us."

Miladin thrust his dagger next to Grigorii's neck. "More accomplices?"

Grigorii leaned away from the blade. "You already finished off the two I smuggled into the grody, and I already told you about the ones in the lower grad."

Grigorii had given the names and locations of three of Župan Teodore's men. Two had been seized and imprisoned. The third had either escaped or been a lie. Konstantin hated his current position: he couldn't trust Grigorii, but he had to rely on him if he wanted to save his family.

The sound of hooves stopped.

Bojan turned to look behind them. "Shall I ride back and see what I find?"

Konstantin nodded. "Be careful. Enemies are out in force tonight."

The others continued onward, as it seemed whoever was following them had stopped as soon as he or she realized their quarry had paused. But they went at a slightly slower pace because if Bojan was ambushed, Konstantin wanted to be nearby to help him.

When the sounds behind them grew louder, Konstantin pulled Veles to a stop again. Bojan appeared with Decimir.

"I thought you were going to stay in the grody." Konstantin admired the boy's determination, but he owed it to Župan Dragomir to keep Decimir safe.

Decimir glanced about. Grigorii was tied, riding on a docile horse that Miladin led. Zoran was also part of their party, as was Ulrich and four of the German mercenaries. And Decimir's bodyguards, who looked displeased to discover that their charge had left the safety of the grad. Decimir lifted his chin. "Before I left, my grandfather said I was to stay with Josif and Ilija."

They were nearing the edge of Rivak's boundaries. Sending Decimir back on his own would be dangerous, but sending him back with a proper escort would weaken their group significantly, and too much was at stake to risk that.

Konstantin sighed. "Stick close to them in case there's trouble."

Grigorii pointed to a trail barely visible in the dark. "It's through there."

Zoran led the way. None of them could be completely sure Grigorii wouldn't lead them into an ambush, so they approached slowly. The rundown villa looked deserted. The dying embers of a campfire showed that someone had been there recently, but no guards remained outside. Konstantin dismounted. If the guards were gone, that meant the hostages were gone, too, but he would at least look inside. He grabbed a nearby stick and coaxed a flame out of the embers to light his way.

Miladin stayed with Grigorii, Bojan and Zoran checked some of the smaller rooms, the Germans patrolled the perimeter, and Konstantin led Decimir and his men into the main chamber. The air barely stirred. It looked like it had been used as a prison, with windows boarded up most of the way and an old mattress in one corner.

A few boards lay on the ground, with bent nails sticking from them at irregular angles. Konstantin looked for any clue that his family had been held here, but nothing appeared in the dim light to prove or disprove Grigorii's words.

Josif lifted the mattress, revealing only dirt. "He may have lied."

"That's what I'm afraid of." Konstantin held a hand toward the fire chamber, but no fire had burned there recently. It was as cold as the rest of the room.

Someone sneezed. Konstantin didn't know Župan Dragomir's men well enough to recognize their sneezes, but it sounded too childish for even Decimir, and it had echoed strangely.

Konstantin took a closer look at the hearth. When he held the burning branch next to the stones on the outer hearth, footprints appeared in the scattered ash. Footprints made by small shoes. When he looked inside the inner chamber, he saw only shadows, but an instant later, a bit of ash fell on him, something scuffled in the chimney, and Danilo dropped down.

"Kostya!" He gripped Konstantin about the waist in a fierce embrace. Konstantin caught one small arm so it wouldn't aggravate his wound. "I knew Grigorii wouldn't be able to kill you! But did you catch him? And Ivan saw Župan Teodore's army coming. Will there be a battle?"

"Yes, we caught Grigorii, and we've seen the army."

More sounds echoed from the chimney. "Kostya, will you help me down?" Lidija's voice.

Konstantin ruffled Danilo's hair—a mistake that resulted in a puff of ash and another sneeze. Konstantin chuckled and stepped inside the chamber to help his sister down from where she'd wedged herself on a ledge in the chimney.

"What on earth were you doing in the chimney?" He set her down outside the hearth and pulled her close for a sooty embrace.

"Hiding. We heard horses and thought it might be Župan Teodore's men again." Lidija stiffened. Konstantin relaxed his embrace and followed her gaze. She'd noticed Decimir and was now smoothing her hair.

"I am most pleased that you're safe, Dama Lidija." Decimir stepped forward and gallantly offered her his water bladder and a handkerchief.

Konstantin looked back at the shaft. It wasn't large enough for four people, even when two of them were small boys. "Where are Ivan and Suzana?"

"Ivan escaped through the chimney," Danilo said. "I was too big and couldn't fit, or I would have gone with him. He took all the guards' horses and rode to Župan Nikola. We wanted him to warn you, but Suzana didn't think he could outride Grigorii, and we didn't want him riding near Župan Teodore's army."

"And Suzana?"

"Župan Teodore's men took her." Lidija's voice shook with worry. "She told us to hide so we could escape later. That's what we were trying to do when we heard you—we were prying the boards from the windows because they locked us in. She saved us, and Ivan saved himself. We couldn't save her, but you will, won't you?"

Konstantin nodded, even knowing he couldn't guarantee his wife's rescue. "Where did they take her?"

"To his grody," Lidija said.

"Then I have my work cut out for me." Konstantin glanced over the group. He didn't want Danilo or Lidija to pass anywhere near Župan Teodore's encampment, and he certainly didn't plan on taking them into the enemy stronghold. Going back to Rivakgrad might be possible, but the road to Župan Nikola's lands was the safer route. Župan Teodore wouldn't attack Župan Nikola—he was too strong. And should Rivak fall, Konstantin trusted that Župan Nikola would see that his family made it to safety in Sivi Gora.

He placed his hand on Decimir's shoulder. "Can I trust you and your men to take them both to safety?"

"You can."

"Thank you. Follow Ivan's route to Župan Nikola." That would keep part of Konstantin's family safe and part of Župan Dragomir's family safe too. Decimir had disobeyed Konstantin when he'd followed him from Rivakgrad, but Konstantin didn't think Decimir would disobey him again, not when his assignment included taking Lidija to safety.

The group left the chamber, and Lidija gasped when she recognized Grigorii. Danilo picked up a rock large enough to use as a weapon and scowled.

"Don't worry," Konstantin said. "He's tied up."

"What is he doing here?" Lidija asked.

"We needed him to find you."

Lidija put her hand on his arm. "But you can't trust him."

"I know, but we've come to an understanding. I don't trust him, but I need his knowledge."

Lidija nodded slowly. "Be careful, Kostya."

Konstantin gave her another hug, hoping it wouldn't be their last. Then he whispered into her ear. "If things go wrong, take Ivan and Danilo to Sivi Gora. You'll have my blessing if you wish to marry Decimir, but not until you're older."

Her grip on him tightened. She sniffed and inhaled deeply before pulling away.

Konstantin lifted Danilo onto Josif's horse, in front of the rider. He had a feeling the boy would fall asleep before they reached safety, and he didn't want him tumbling off. Then he took Danilo's hand. "You've been brave today. You keep being brave, Danilo, and know that I'm proud of you."

"Will I see you again soon?"

"God willing."

The three horses rode away. Lidija rode behind Decimir, her arms around his waist and her head against his shoulder. No doubt she would have been mortified to know she had a smear of soot across her forehead and along her left temple.

Konstantin turned back to the remainder of his men. It was time to save his wife.

Chapter Forty-Six
THE ENEMY'S GRODY

An oil lamp burned in the stable, so it wasn't completely dark, nor was it unduly cold. The stall Suzana had been tied inside was clean, and the guards had laid down fresh straw. Still, Dama Emilija couldn't have picked a more awful place for Suzana. She would have preferred a tower or a dungeon. Neither of those locations would have given her nightmares such power.

She sat with her back against the wall and put her head on her knees, hoping that if she couldn't see her surroundings, she could convince herself she was elsewhere. She controlled each breath in, each breath out, trying to make each as full as possible to push away the fear and panic that hovered as close as her cloak. She pled with God for her husband's safety, for Ivan, for Lidija and Danilo, and for herself. She needed God's strength to be stronger than her past.

But just as threatening was the present. Konstantin might be dead. Ivan might not have made it to safety, or his efforts might have left his frail body weakened and susceptible to another illness. Župan Teodore's men might have found Danilo and Lidija. What would they do to Danilo? And who would they force Lidija to marry? Fear for her own condition swirled round her too. How long could she keep her mind clear in a place like this? And regardless of whether she kept her mind or not, what hope did she have? She had been nothing before she'd married Konstantin, or at least, that was how it had felt. If he were slain, she would feel like nothing again.

She tried to drive her present condition from her mind with memories of her loved ones. She first thought of the look of wonder and tears of joy when she and Konstantin had learned she was with child. Recalled the sensations his fingers and his lips stirred when he caressed her skin. Her mind turned to Aunt Zorica, who had cried with her when she'd lost the baby.

Lidija, teaching Suzana how to dance the kolo. Danilo, with his quick smile and arms full of wildflowers. Ivan, trying to protect her when she'd last had a run-in with Župan Teodore. Their enemies might separate her from her new family and keep her in the most nightmarish prison possible, but memory of her family's love could not be stolen or overpowered.

She shifted positions and flinched when something sharp dug into her shoulder. She scooted away from the stall's wall and looked behind her, searching for the source of pain. She couldn't see anything in the dim light, so she lifted her bound hands and felt along the rough boards. There. The end of a nail protruding from the wall, no more than the length of a knuckle.

She caught the tiniest bit of the rope binding her hands on the end of the nail and pulled. The fibers frayed and broke. Then she did it again and again. The rope was thick, and she could break only a few strands at once, but even if it took her all night, even if it did nothing more than distract her from bad memories, she would persist. Župan Teodore couldn't take away the good in her past. She didn't want him to take away the good in her future either.

Konstantin stood outside the sally port, trying to ignore the throbbing pain in his back. The gate was locked, of course. He'd need more men and a battering ram to bring it down from the outside, and he suspected Župan Teodore had left enough men in his grad to defend it against a group as small as Konstantin's. Maybe Grigorii's inside information wouldn't be so useful after all.

But Grigorii hadn't been lying about the door's location. Nor had he done anything to draw attention to the group as they waited in the shadows of the palisade wall.

"They might let me in," Grigorii said.

Miladin huffed. "So you can tell them where to strike us?"

Grigorii shook his head. "I've crossed Župan Teodore, and he'll not forgive that. My family's only hope is to rely on Župan Konstantin's mercy because Župan Teodore has none. I'll not betray you again."

Konstantin studied the wall. The stakes that made up the palisade were far taller than a man, but perhaps they could climb. "Bojan, do you think you could get a rope to lasso around the top of the stakewall?" Like the palisades in Rivakgrad, the tops were cut into jagged angles, but that didn't make them impossible to climb over.

"Aye, lord. I think I could manage." Bojan went back to the trees where they'd hidden their horses.

Miladin felt the wood and stared at the top. "I'll go."

"There's a ledge inside," Grigorii said. "The watchmen always climb to it as part of their patrol."

Miladin nodded. "I'll be sure to draw my sword quickly."

Konstantin, Miladin, and Ulrich walked back to the horses, leaving Grigorii under guard with Zoran and the other Germans.

"If they think they're under attack, they might kill her." Konstantin didn't want to turn back, but a captured wife was better than a dead wife.

"I know the stakes," Miladin said. "I'll be careful."

Ulrich glanced at one of the nearby oaks. "I'll check the view from the top of this. If we time it right, we ought to be able to slip inside without anyone sounding the alarm."

Ulrich disappeared up the tree. Bojan grabbed a rope, and Miladin grabbed a piece of mail to throw over the spikes. They returned to the wall to wait for Ulrich's signal. The time dragged out. Ulrich was no doubt observing the path of the watchmen, and that couldn't happen all at once, but the need to find Suzana was overwhelming. Finally, Ulrich signaled.

In the dark, Konstantin couldn't see the rope, but he saw the motion as Bojan threw, then saw him tug as it caught. Moments later, with the mail slung across his shoulder, Miladin accepted a leg up from Zoran and began to climb. He reached the top, then disappeared behind the palisade. Konstantin went to the sally port so he could rush in as soon as Miladin opened it.

Konstantin prayed silently, for Miladin and the rest of his men, for the group taking Lidija and Danilo to safety, and especially for Suzana. He'd wasted so much time after returning to Rivak, time he might have spent with her. She had been quick to forgive him, but he regretted the lost week, especially now, when it might have been their last.

The sally door pulled inward. Konstantin told one of the Germans to take Grigorii and go back to the horses, and then the rest of them slipped inside. Miladin's breath was still elevated from his climb, but he reported in a quiet voice. "Ulrich timed it well. I didn't see anyone."

Darkness shrouded the bailey, broken only with light from torches near the gatehouse and the main hall. Grigorii had said the tower to the northeast was the most likely place for a prisoner, so as soon as Ulrich joined them, they headed there, walking in the shadows next to the palisade wall.

The tower was made of stone, three levels high, with an entrance on the second level. The rest of the bailey appeared deserted. Either they were all sleeping, or Župan Teodore had taken more men than Konstantin had originally thought.

"If we all huddle next to the door, it will look suspicious." Konstantin didn't want to draw attention should the watchmen reappear. It might be normal for armed men to go in and out of the tower, but in ones or twos, not in larger groups. "Miladin, come with me now. The rest of you come after we've opened the door."

They strode up the wooden stairs as if they belonged in the bailey and pushed open the door with ease. Konstantin gave himself a few moments for his eyes to adjust. The tower was cold and dark. It was wide enough to shelter most of the garrison if the bailey were overtaken, but it contained few hiding places, and the entry level was abandoned. Konstantin found and lit a few oil lamps. When Ulrich and Bojan arrived, he sent them up while he and Miladin went down. The spiral staircase of stone was steep, with wide treads on the edges. The bottom level was filled with supplies but contained no cell for prisoners.

"Do you see a trap door?" he asked. There might be another level, and while he might flay the skin off anyone who put his wife in a dank dungeon, he didn't want to overlook the chance to free her.

Both of them searched, moving some of the barrels and crates. Then Konstantin's hand brushed a wooden chest that looked familiar. He stopped and stared, dumbfounded.

"What did you . . . ?" Miladin's voice trailed off, and he joined Konstantin, kneeling in front of the chest. "It looks just like your father's." Miladin felt along the wood. "I helped load it into the cart when we left for Maritsa. There was a large scratch along the side."

Konstantin remembered. "I accidently put it there when I was twelve and knocked another chest into it. He wasn't pleased."

Miladin sat back on his heels. "Then this is your father's, because the scratch is still there."

"How did it end up in Župan Teodore's tower?" Konstantin opened the chest. It was mostly empty. Armor would have been taken to the armory, coins would have been added to the treasury, and clothing would have been distributed to someone who could wear them. But a few pieces of parchment remained in the bottom of the chest, as did a small ship carved of wood. Konstantin took the toy and held it in his hand, recognizing something Ivan had loved when he'd been younger. Maybe Ivan, at five, had sent his father with a parting gift in the same way he'd sent Konstantin with an icon of the Virgin Mary. "Was Teodore pillaging from the slain Serbs?"

"Only if the Turks gave him leave," Miladin said. "And I don't see why they would have unless he had done something to earn it."

Something to earn it. Shortly after the battle, they'd learned that betrayal had played a role in the Serbs' destruction. Dragomir's younger brother, Radomir, had recalled the watch without setting a new one, allowing the Turks to surprise the sleeping Serb armies. Radomir had fled when it had become clear he wouldn't be able to take his brother's lands, so no one had ever questioned him to see if others were involved in the plot. Perhaps betrayal of that magnitude required the work of more than one traitor.

Konstantin shut the trunk. If Župan Teodore had betrayed his people at Maritsa—and been rewarded for his treachery by the sultan's pashas—Konstantin wanted the treason known to all. But first, he needed to rescue his wife. "We have to find Suzana, and I don't think she's in this tower."

They reached the main level at the same time as Bojan and Ulrich. Bojan's sword dripped with blood.

Konstantin's eyes followed the curve of the stairs leading to the upper level. "What happened?"

"Two guards. Tipsy enough to be sloppy but sober enough to fight back. We saw no prisoners."

If she wasn't in the tower, they might have put her somewhere in the keep. That would be more complicated to search, but Suzana was worth the risk.

A shout sounded from the bailey. Konstantin approached the tower's door with caution, not wanting to show himself if, by some chance, his men weren't the cause of alarm. A quick glance showed they hadn't been so lucky. Someone had spotted Zoran and the German mercenaries, and a dozen of Teodore's men were running toward them, swords drawn.

CHAPTER FORTY-SEVEN
OUTNUMBERED

SUZANA'S ARMS ACHED. EACH MOVEMENT had been small, but she'd been working on the rope for what she guessed was an hour. Finally, the frayed bits fell away from her wrists. With her hands free, she turned her attention to the knots around her ankles.

One of the nearby horses snorted, upset by something. She kicked the rope from her ankles, then stood and winced. Her feet were mostly numb, but the portion where the ropes had drawn tight burned with pain. There hadn't been any reason for the ropes to be so snug. Just Dama Emilija's scorn.

Shouts and the clank of swords met her ears. Did the commotion in the bailey mean opportunity, danger, or both? She took a few tentative steps and used the line of stalls to help her balance.

She reached the stable door and looked through the cracks between the wooden boards. A skirmish had commenced in the bailey. The men all wore armor, so she couldn't see their identities, but since some of them fought against Župan Teodore's guards, those men might be friendly to her.

She did not wish to enter the midst of a battle, but it seemed her best chance of escape. And she did not wish to turn back to the stalls. Yet a plan had formed, and that plan required her to keep her fears in check a little while longer. Walking back to the animals, she unbolted each stall. She urged one of the geldings out, and that seemed to encourage the other horses to follow. No saddles were stored in the stables, so she would have to ride bareback. She chose one of the smaller horses—one she would have an easier time mounting—and gripped the mare's lead rope. Then she wound her way back to the stable door and pushed it open.

The grody's entrance lay beyond the fighting, so she crept forward, staying in the darkest shadows next to the palisade, hoping the released horses would give the fighting men something other than her to focus on while she made her way to freedom.

A few torches placed around the bailey cast uneven light on the group. Several men lay on the ground bleeding. More rushed from the keep to join the fray. One group seemed to be coordinating a gradual retreat back to an open doorway in the wall that she'd not seen before. If this grody was anything like her husband's, there would be guards at the main gate. Hostile ones. The smaller portal the others were escaping through seemed her best option. She led the mare around and headed for the sally port.

One of the men brought his opponent down with a quick thrust of the sword. As he turned, she recognized his face, and relief almost made her sob.

"Kostya!"

Her husband still lived.

Konstantin recognized Suzana's voice at once, but it took his eyes a few long moments to find her, and by then, another of Župan Teodore's men had charged at him. The grody's garrison was too large for his small group to defeat, so he'd accepted what felt like a necessary withdrawal, even though they hadn't yet searched the keep or other buildings. But now, there was Suzana, mere paces away, if they could only get through the enemy men-at-arms.

The soldier hewed toward Konstantin with his sword. Konstantin blocked, then cut toward the man in a counterstroke. The wound in his back burned, but it hadn't yet impeded his movements. The man blocked Konstantin's first strike but not the second. The blade pierced his leather armor, and the man fell dead.

A woman screamed, and as Suzana was the only woman in the bailey, it had to be her. He sprinted toward the sound before realizing what had happened. One of Župan Teodore's men had grabbed her from behind and now held his sword across her neck.

"Drop your weapon." The man took a step back and pulled Suzana with him.

Konstantin lowered his spathion to the ground. The rest of his men pulled back from the duels they were engaged in as fighting across the bailey ceased and all turned to watch Suzana and the man who threatened her.

"She's not the one you want to kill." Konstantin spoke slowly and distinctly. "She's of much greater value alive. I'm the one your župan wants dead."

"I think Dama Emilija would prefer you both dead." The man took his eyes off Konstantin for a moment to study Suzana.

Suzana kept her gaze fixed on Konstantin. Her expression held fear but also trust.

Miladin and Bojan moved in Konstantin's periphery, their motions masked to most others by the score of horses wandering the bailey, but Konstantin kept his focus on his wife and the man holding a blade to her throat. It would take the man only a heartbeat to kill her, but if Konstantin could lengthen that time to several heartbeats, they might survive the night. "I've put down my sword. You can lower your blade. We'll trade. Her freedom in exchange for me."

"I'm certain we can have you both. You're outnumbered."

"More of my men wait outside." Not enough to make a difference in battle, but the man-at-arms didn't need to know a detail like that.

He huffed, but he also lowered his blade ever so slightly. "As does the rest of my župan's army."

Bojan let out a whistle. One of the destriers bolted across the bailey toward him. The man holding Suzana hostage followed the movement for a moment, and then he stiffened as the dagger Miladin had thrown at his back plunged into his flesh. He was still dangerous, still capable of murder, and the last time someone had held a blade to Suzana's throat, she'd frozen, but this time, she ducked away when the man's grip changed as he tried to bring his sword toward her.

Konstantin ran forward and pummeled the man in the face with his fist. Then he grabbed Suzana's hand and pulled her toward the gate. Zoran tossed him his sword, then they faced the enemy warriors who had snuck around behind them during the standoff to block their escape.

Konstantin released Suzana's hand and swung his sword into one of the guards. As the man dropped, he ran for the next guard. "Through the gate," he yelled at Suzana. "One of my men is waiting, and he'll help you. Have him bring our horses."

The moment she disappeared, Konstantin looked round the bailey. Dama Emilija had left the keep, wrapped in a cloak and surrounded by bodyguards. She was too distant for him to see her expression, but he could guess at the rage she would shower on her men at their failure to thwart the rescue mission.

He fought the next man who ran at him and the one after, then ordered more of his men through the sally port. Bojan took one of Župan Teodore's horses, leaving Konstantin and Miladin to face the enemy garrison until they, too, ducked through the doorway and ran for their horses.

Suzana sat atop Veles. Konstantin climbed on behind her, and the group galloped away from the grad.

Suzana relaxed against Konstantin's chest while his arms wrapped around her to hold Veles's reins. For a long time, neither of them spoke. They were still too near Župan Teodore's grody, and they were probably being followed. But when the group slowed their horses from gallops to canters, she thought the worst of their danger was over.

"I was afraid I'd never see you again," she said.

"You almost didn't." Konstantin shifted his grip. "Between Grigorii trying to kill me and all the men in Župan Teodore's bailey—We searched the tower, but we didn't have time or the manpower to search everywhere else."

"Dama Emilija said I wasn't high born or dangerous enough for the keep or the tower, so she had me tied and put in the stables."

"The stables . . . but . . ." He trailed off, no doubt remembering how helpless she'd always been in the stables of Rivakgrad. "Yet you escaped."

"I found a bit of a nail and used it to fray the ropes. And my memories of stables are still strong, but remembering your love helped me."

He pressed his lips to her left temple. "I was terrified I'd lose you forever."

"I had the same fear." They'd only barely overcome Grigorii's plot.

The sky to the east turned from black to gray. The new day would begin soon.

"Kostya, we have to go to the villa where Grigorii took me. Lidija and Danilo were hiding there, and if Župan Teodore's men catch them—"

"We found them. Decimir and his bodyguards are taking them to safety."

"And Ivan? Have you seen him?"

"No. I pray he arrived into Župan Nikola's care."

"And what will you do against Župan Teodore's army? He's willing to start a war."

"Župan Dragomir is riding to our aid. Maybe Župan Nikola too. And Miladin only saw two score men. I don't think he'll risk battle. His losses would be too high."

"Forty?" When Ivan first saw the army, he hadn't been able to count them. Suzana had never seen the army herself. But she'd overheard her escorts on the way to Župan Teodore's grad. "The guards who took me to the grad spoke of more. We ran into a group of a dozen out on patrol, and they claimed another patrol had gone north."

Konstantin's body stiffened, as if the danger might lurk right behind them. He urged Veles next to Miladin's horse. "How many men did you see in Župan Teodore's camp?"

"Two score, give or take a few," Miladin said.

"Suzana and her abductors ran into a dozen more on her way to his grody, and they were not the only patrol."

Suzana couldn't see Konstantin's expression, but she recognized Miladin's reaction. He'd gone from thinking they were safe to recognizing they were still in danger.

Both men slowed their horses until they were level with Bojan and the prisoner he led.

"How many men does Župan Teodore have?" Konstantin asked Grigorii.

"I don't know. Other than tonight, I haven't been to his grad in over a year."

"The sultan demanded four score," Miladin said. "They were all his men, not mercenaries. And I doubt he left his grody undefended all summer. He might have a hundred. I'd guess he left only a score with his wife—had there been more, they would have joined the fight against us."

That meant eighty men, not forty, might be laying siege to Rivakgrad and its grody. "How many men does Župan Dragomir have?" Suzana asked.

"After Anatolia?" Konstantin's voice carried a note of worry. "Perhaps fifty, but he won't bring more than thirty. We have fewer now that most of the mercenaries have gone home for the winter."

That meant they would be outnumbered. If they could make it to Rivakgrad, they could hold out against a siege. But if not . . .

"Shadows on the horizon." Ulrich stood in his stirrups to get a better look. "Horsemen . . . Hard to see how many. Maybe a dozen."

Suzana felt Konstantin's arms tighten around her. Even a dozen would present a challenge for their small group.

"We've got to get back to Rivakgrad," Konstantin said. "We'll be outnumbered here, and we're too distant for our men or Župan Dragomir to help us."

"Can your horse carry both of us?" Suzana asked.

"Veles is strong. He'll have to manage."

Suzana hoped the stallion was as strong as her husband claimed because speed might mean their salvation.

"Lord?" Bojan said.

"Yes?"

"Dama Suzana can take my horse. I took one from Župan Teodore's bailey."

Konstantin nodded, an admission that riding double would hamper their speed.

Bojan tossed the lead rope of Grigorii's horse to Ulrich and dismounted.

Konstantin dismounted as well to help Suzana down from Veles. He pressed a kiss into her check, and whispered, "I love you," before lifting her onto the other horse's back.

"There's something else, lord." Bojan pulled the spare he was to ride nearer. "I trained this horse. That's why he listened to my whistle in the bailey."

Konstantin looked more closely at the destrier. The stallion had a black coat with white socks. "My father's warhorse?"

"Yes, lord," Bojan said.

"Why did Župan Teodore have your father's horse?" Suzana asked.

"That's not the only thing he took after my father's death at Maritsa. I'll explain later; for now, we need to ride." Konstantin remounted and led the group off at a canter. Suzana hadn't slept all night. She'd slept little the night before, for entirely different reasons, but now exhaustion and fear were catching up with her. She said another prayer. They'd escaped their enemies—an enemy that dated back at least to Maritsa. Now they just needed to stay a few steps ahead of them.

Chapter Forty-Eight
When the Enemy Closes In

Konstantin shifted the group's direction yet again. Someone shadowed them—either a patrol or men following from Župan Teodore's grad. In either case, the other group wouldn't be friendly. He glanced back to ensure that Suzana remained safe. Had they not been in such a hurry, he would have kept her on Veles just to feel her against him, but they had to be prepared for a hard ride. Riding singly would allow Veles to gallop faster, and it would put less strain on Konstantin's injury.

The sun had risen fully. He could assume Župan Dragomir's men had joined Rivak's garrison at the grad by now. If Konstantin's group could get there, they'd be safe. But though they'd made good time, the horses were slowing. Horses had limits, and most had carried men all night with little rest. Ulrich's horse could barely keep up. Grigorii's, too, was slowing, but they'd purposely mounted him on an animal of unremarkable speed so he'd be easy to catch if the traitor tried to break away. They might come to regret their decision if they had to make a sudden sprint to safety.

They were so close—another few miles and Rivakgrad would come into view. They'd managed to rescue Suzana, and Konstantin had every reason to think his siblings and cousin were safe, but so much could still go wrong.

Miladin, in the lead, crested a rise and pulled his horse up. He signaled for the group to stop and led his horse back toward the others, where it wouldn't be seen from the other side of the hill. Konstantin dismounted and walked up to join him. When he saw what lay on the other side of the rise, his blood turned to ice. Župan Teodore's camp spread out below.

"They moved," Miladin said. "They were farther north yesterday when I rode out to negotiate."

"We'll have to cut to the south and hope they don't see us."

Miladin scanned the enemy camp. "With that many men, it would take a miracle. But maybe they won't recognize us."

They rode south then, trying to work their way west. Konstantin's stomach knotted with hunger and worry, and the pain in his back reminded him that he'd been nearly killed the day before.

"Župan Konstantin?" Zoran pointed behind them. One of Župan Teodore's patrols.

"We'd better see if our horses have anything left." Konstantin positioned himself near Suzana. "Ride hard to the west."

They urged their horses on, but within a quarter mile, it was clear the other group was gaining on them. And then Konstantin spotted another group to the south. Soon they would be trapped.

He scanned the surrounding land while Veles continued forward. The nearest village was some distance away, and it would offer a poor location for a battle. He pointed to a hill. "There. That's where we'll make our stand."

It wasn't ideal, but they couldn't outride the men hunting them. The elevation would at least force the enemy to come up to them. Yet even that hill—still so far from the grad—would require a hard ride that their mounts might be incapable of making with speed.

Veles obeyed Konstantin's command. Suzana's mount followed. Ulrich's horse trailed as they crossed the grassy slope, and it looked as though Župan Teodore's men would catch him. Ulrich could hold his own against any single man in the enemy's army, but not against a dozen at once.

Veles ate up the distance to the top of the hill, slowing as he approached the summit. Konstantin didn't push him. Rivakgrad was visible in the distance, with what had to be Župan Dragomir's army at the gate and Župan Teodore's army on the march toward them.

As the last of Konstantin's group reached the hill, the two patrols chasing them slowed and took up positions at the base, trapping them. He lifted Suzana from her borrowed horse.

"From this distance, will anyone at the grad be able to see what's happening?" she asked, worry evident on her face, though her voice held.

"Even if they do, Župan Teodore's men will arrive before they possibly can." Their situation was hopeless, and he could guess what that meant for him and for her. "I'm sorry, Suzana. I wanted to save you, but I don't think this will end well."

A wounded župan, seven loyal men, a traitor, and a woman. That was all they had against an army. The mercenaries could pick off anyone who came too close with their crossbows until they ran out of bolts. The others could fight off a few men at a time, but the enemy would not come in groups of one or two.

Miladin ran his hand along his horse's withers. "Don't fret, Dama Suzana. If we stall long enough to give the horses some rest, we could try to break out. They're spread about the hill evenly."

Konstantin didn't contradict his friend, even though he suspected Miladin knew as well as he did that the horses wouldn't recover before Župan Teodore's army arrived. The animals needed food and water—items in short supply on the crest of the hill. And anyone at the hill's base could see which direction they were riding and congregate at the bottom before they reached it. But maybe Miladin's words could ease Suzana's worry for a time.

She might make it out of this alive if she stayed still and kept low to the ground. The type of future that awaited her was uncertain, but Konstantin hoped she would somehow find happiness even after witnessing the slaughter of everyone else on the hill. Ultimately, that was what it would be. A slaughter.

"There's a third patrol coming," Zoran said. The group was still in the distance, but they rode hard, as if being chased. They came much more swiftly than the army did, and Konstantin counted twenty in the new group.

Suzana stood beside him, her arms folded and her shoulders hunched. He put an arm around her. He had no words that could restore her hope, but he could offer her his presence, at least until the battle began.

"I think I could hit that one there." One of the German mercenaries pointed to a man-at-arms waiting at the foot of the hill. "Shall I shoot?"

If he shot, they might fight back. Combat seemed inevitable, but it would be better to wait until the army closed. Then one of them might be able to slay Župan Teodore. With him dead, Aunt Zorica would have an easier time holding Rivakgrad.

"No. The fight will come soon enough. I'd rather them underestimate your precision with that crossbow. Surprise them when it makes more of a difference. When the time comes, you're to aim for their leaders. Regardless of what happens, Rivak has a better chance of survival if Župan Teodore is killed and his army decimated. For now, we rest."

Konstantin took his own advice, sitting in the long grasses and eating what they could find from the saddle bags. The wound in his back pulled and throbbed.

Suzana's expression sharpened. "That looked like pain. Were you injured in Župan Teodore's bailey?"

"Not in his bailey. In ours. One of Grigorii's assassins sent a crossbow bolt into my back. It's been stitched up, but it needs more rest than I've been able to give it." He didn't want to dwell on his wound. It might make hope even more elusive. He held up a piece of boukellaton. "Are you hungry enough to eat some of this?"

She accepted the hardtack, then took dainty bites.

"Lord?" Bojan squinted. "I think that's Župan Nikola."

Konstantin rose for a better view. The riders were still too distant for him to tell, but Ivan and Decimir would both have told Župan Nikola of Župan Teodore's attack. Konstantin needed another ally, and suddenly, defeat and death no longer seemed certain.

Konstantin walked to Grigorii. "Tell me what you saw at Maritsa." Konstantin suspected Župan Teodore of treason, and he wanted enough proof to convince Župan Nikola.

Grigorii's face paled. "If I have been reluctant to speak of it before, it was not merely so I could protect myself. The memory is like a nightmare."

"I need to know."

Reluctance lined his features, but Grigorii began. "I saw your father die. He struck down five Turks before a group attacked him. He'd been sleeping, so he wore no armor. He blocked one scimitar with his shield and one with his spathion, but he couldn't stop the third blade that went beneath the shield. Darras rushed to save him, but after Miroslav fell, I fled. Like most everyone, I ended up in the swollen waters of the river. I was swept away." He paused and swallowed. "I was bruised. I had lost my weapons. But I pulled myself to shore again. The Turks found me the next morning. They would have killed me, but Župan Teodore asked that my life be spared."

"And the Ottomans listened to him?"

"Yes."

"Why?"

Grigorii shook his head. "When a man has found reprieve after being threatened with impalement, he does not ask why. I assumed the župan had already sworn fealty to the sultan."

"They allowed him to swear vassalage, then let him plead for prisoners, but they spoke of impaling you? Why would they not offer you the same?"

Grigorii shrugged. "He's a noble. He had some standing with them, and all I could do was be grateful. He told me that someday I would repay him. At first, he just wanted information about Rivak and its ruler." Grigorii shook his head. "But the demands grew to burning crops, then to arranging deaths. When I balked, he threatened my sister."

"Župan Teodore's arrangement with the Turks," Konstantin began. "Might it have been struck before the battle?"

"His arrangement with the Turks is different from yours. That is all I know."

Konstantin stopped his questions, fairly certain what Grigorii's story and the lost items from his family in Teodore's grody meant. Either before the battle or in its immediate aftermath, Župan Teodore had come to terms with the Turks to give him an advantage over his neighbors.

The newest group of riders grew closer, and their identities became more certain. Župan Nikola rode with his best men, and they would arrive at nearly the same time as the advance portion of Župan Teodore's army. Konstantin met Suzana's eyes and wondered if there was any way they would both survive the morning.

When both groups arrived, Župan Nikola spoke with Župan Teodore. One of Župan Nikola's men climbed the hill to suggest a temporary truce and invite Župan Konstantin to the negotiations.

Konstantin squeezed Suzana's hand in farewell. "Stay here for now. I would ask for your prayers."

She clung to his hand for an extra moment and looked as if she were trying not to cry.

Miladin joined Konstantin without asking permission to do so, but Konstantin didn't turn him away. Both other contingents included subordinates.

Župan Teodore glared first at Konstantin, then at Miladin. "Yesterday, you told me Župan Konstantin was on his death bed."

"I am young, and I recover quickly." Konstantin returned Župan Teodore's hard look. Then he turned his gaze on Župan Nikola, hoping to find some of the same common purpose he'd found while they'd campaigned together in Anatolia. "Several of my family members fled to you for refuge. Did they arrive safely?"

Župan Nikola's expression held sympathy. "Yes, and I will ensure their continued safety. If their tale is to be believed, Župan Teodore has committed treachery of the worst sort. We are župans. We do not attempt to murder our neighbors or abduct their families. You will leave at once, Župan Teodore, and perhaps we can forgive what you have done."

Župan Teodore gave them both a cold smile. "My army commands the field. I can wipe out both of you before noon, so I think I shall be the one to make demands."

Župan Nikola ran his eyes along the men assembled behind Župan Teodore, then to the men on the hill and Rivakgrad in the distance. "Your men may outnumber my current contingent, but the rest of my army could crush yours, especially if the men now manning Župan Konstantin's grad joined us, as they most certainly would should you stoop to such base perfidy. You might win the morning, but you would not win the war, and you would lose everything. Yet even now, you can step back, Župan Teodore. If we fight each other, we will all pay a heavy price in blood. Let not Serb blood be spilled here by brother Serbs. We need unity if we are ever to regain the strength and liberty we lost at Maritsa."

"Why would I back down when Rivak is mine for the taking?" Župan Teodore sneered.

"Rivak belongs to Miroslav's son, not to you. Take it, and it will cost you dearly. I doubt you'll have the men the sultan requires when next he makes his demands."

Župan Teodore looked to his men again, then back to the other župans. "The sultan will be forgiving should my contingent be slightly smaller than his demands."

"Yes," Konstantin broke in. "Because you betrayed your brother Serbs at Maritsa and let the sultan's army slaughter them."

"Lies!" Župan Teodore's hand went to the hilt of his sword. "Do not tell lies that impinge my honor!"

"They aren't lies." Konstantin's hand also rested on the hilt of his sword. "I found my father's wooden chest in your tower and his warhorse in your stables. An Ottoman pasha who leads soldiers paid in pillage would not have given such things to an enemy. Only to an ally."

"You had no right to trespass in my grody!"

"You had no right to abduct my wife! Had you left her alone, your guilt would have remained secret. Was that your plan, even before Maritsa? To let the sultan weaken all your neighbors so that you could take their lands?"

Red crept up Župan Teodore's face. Župan Nikola watched him closely. Župan Teodore turned from Konstantin and spoke only with Župan Nikola. "You are right. A war between us weakens us all. And despite Rivak's lies, I am a Serb in the truest sense. I would not have bloodshed between your people and mine. I would even spare the people of Rivak, should they recognize their župan as the liar he is. He, however"—Župan Teodore raised a finger and pointed it at Konstantin—"he has insulted my honor and my good name, and I will not allow that crime to go unpunished."

Župan Nikola crossed his arms and raised his chin. "So you would avoid war if your honor could be satisfied?"

"Yes."

Župan Nikola looked over Konstantin, then turned back to Župan Teodore. "Perhaps a fight between the two of you. You claim he has lied about your role at Maritsa. He claims you conspired with the Turks. The victor will be vindicated. The loser will be dead."

Miladin spoke quietly but forcefully to Župan Nikola. "It wouldn't be a fair fight. My župan is recovering from a serious wound given him by one of Župan Teodore's assassins, and he has been up all night trying to rescue his family."

Župan Teodore spoke over Miladin. "I agree to the duel. And should I win, you, Župan Nikola, will leave the field of battle. Rivak will need a župan, and you'll not stop me should I prove the best man for the job."

Župan Nikola nodded. "Should you win, I will leave the field, with my men and with anyone who wishes my protection." He glanced up the hill. "I imagine that will include Dama Suzana. Do you agree, Župan Konstantin?"

Miladin shook his head. "Ask for a delay."

"Now," Župan Teodore said. "Or we let our men fight it out, no matter how much blood is shed."

Konstantin tried to picture the consequences if he said yes, the consequences if he said no. In the end, there was only one choice he could accept. "I agree."

Chapter Forty-Nine
A Duel to the Death

After they agreed to the duel, Župan Nikola told Župans Teodore and Konstantin to instruct their men to leave the field of battle should their župan be defeated. Miladin followed Konstantin as he walked back up the hill to do precisely that.

"Lord, are you sure this is wise?" Miladin asked.

Konstantin thought of Suzana's words. *Sometimes we have no good choices, only ones that lead to different kinds of pain.* "It is not a good choice, but it is the best I can make. If we fight his army, we will all die. This way, perhaps it will just be me."

"But what of Rivak, lord?"

"My aunt will need your help defending the grad. But first you must take Suzana somewhere safe. No matter what else happens, I need you to protect her."

"I will."

"And, Miladin?"

"Yes, lord?"

"Thank you. I've always been able to depend on you."

"As you will for many years in the future, lord. You are a fine warrior."

Konstantin glanced at Župan Teodore fussing over his warhorse. "I am wounded and exhausted, and I have drunk too much wine and spent too little time in the practice fields since returning to Rivak. But I am in the right. Perhaps God will be merciful, if not for my sake, then for the sake of those who depend on me."

Miladin put a hand on Konstantin's shoulder. "Take a moment to rest. I'll have everyone else come down to you."

Konstantin closed his eyes and said a prayer for help, one short on words but filled with sincerity. His small group gathered around him. Suzana came to his side, and he took her hand in his as he spoke. "We've agreed to a duel. If I win, Župan Teodore will never be able to harm us again. His army is to quit the field, but I suggest caution—his men will still outnumber us, and I am not sure how quickly they will comply. There is strength in numbers, so we will stay near Župan Nikola's group." He paused, then said what he had to say. "If I do not win, the agreement allows those who seek refuge protection with Župan Nikola. That includes my family, and I charge you to serve my wife, aunt, and siblings as you have served me."

The men put on brave faces. Konstantin purposely did not look at Suzana, but he felt the tension in her hand.

"Shall I check your wound, lord?" Bojan asked. "Wrap it again so it is less of a hindrance?"

Grigorii spoke before Konstantin could answer. "Župan Teodore will always go for a man's weakness. If he knows where you are injured, he will attack it. I suggest you keep the wound's location secret."

The advice had come from a liar, but it felt true. Župan Teodore had taken advantage of his small garrison by burning croplands. He'd manipulated Konstantin's ready trust by thrusting a traitor into his midst, and when he'd attacked the family, he'd gone after its youngest and most vulnerable members.

Bojan waited for his answer.

"Not at present," Konstantin said. "Stand with Župan Nikola's men in case things do not work out as we all pray they will."

Most of the men left, but he kept hold of Suzana's hand, and Miladin waited to the side, already fulfilling his new role as Suzana's bodyguard.

Konstantin finally turned to her. He wiped away the tears that ran down her cheeks and pulled her into an embrace. "Whatever happens, my Suzana, remember that I have loved you with my whole soul."

"I've had only a year of your love, Kostya. I need more."

He placed a gentle kiss on her lips. "There is nothing I want more than to spend a great many more years with you. God willing, we'll be home together for supper. But if not . . . you know what to do."

He couldn't bear a more drawn-out farewell, so he grabbed Veles's lead rope and took his horse down the hillside to join the other župans.

Župan Nikola studied Konstantin, then Župan Teodore. He spoke with a loud voice so all could hear. "As champions for your given župas, your victory or defeat will determine what happens this day. Should any of your men interfere, your cause will be forfeit. Just man, horse, and any weapons of your choosing."

Župan Nikola led Konstantin one way, and his satnik led Župan Teodore the other. Their fight was to be much like the jousts favored by men of the west.

"I wish it had not come to his, Župan Konstantin. I promise to do all I can for your family. But I must also do what I can to preserve the strength of our people. If we wage war with each other, we will never break free from the Turks."

"I understand, and I am grateful. This offers me a better chance than war against his army does."

Župan Nikola watched as Konstantin mounted Veles and checked that his spathion slid easily from its sheath. "God gave David victory over Goliath. I hope He will also give you victory over Župan Teodore. Your wife and kin will be protected regardless, but your people need you to win."

Konstantin threaded his arm through the leather thong of the kontarion lance and grasped the long wooden shaft. He settled his helmet in its place and inhaled and exhaled, seeking calm, seeking confidence, seeking victory.

One hundred paces away, Župan Teodore slammed his heels into the flanks of his stallion, sending him bolting toward Konstantin and Veles. Konstantin followed suit, though Veles didn't need a swift kick, just a shake of the reins and the right sounds as signal. As the two rode toward each other, all the noise and sights of their surroundings faded from Konstantin's view, leaving only Konstantin, Veles, and the enemy.

At stake were all his hopes for his family, all his hopes for his lands, all his hopes for his future. Before him rode a man who had contributed to his father's and uncle's deaths, the decimation of the Rivak garrison, the burning of fields and villages, and threat after threat to Suzana and the rest of Konstantin's family.

The horses closed, and Konstantin deflected Župan Teodore's lance with his shield. His own lance rammed past the edge of Župan Teodore's shield and then glanced off the armor of his shoulder. He would have felt the blow, but it drew no blood.

Konstantin slowed Veles and turned him around for another charge. Despite the long ride of the night before, Veles remained strong. That was Konstantin's one advantage—the mighty horse Suzana had sacrificed for. The two charged again, and this time, Konstantin aimed for Župan

Teodore's mount. The iron blade sank into horseflesh, and the stallion fell, throwing off Župan Teodore's aim. Konstantin blocked the shaft easily with his shield as Župan Teodore tumbled to the ground. But Konstantin lost his lance when it went down with the horse.

He drew his sword and steered Veles with his knees, charging back toward his opponent. Župan Teodore had found his feet and his lance. He held it with one end against the ground and the tip toward Konstantin, who swerved away rather than risk impaling Veles.

Mounted, Konstantin had the advantage, but it was not so large, given the longer weapon Župan Teodore held. He could sacrifice Veles—and he would, if necessary. He loved the horse, but he loved the people of Rivak more. But if there was another way to win, he would seek it.

He charged again, changing his direction at the last moment to throw off Župan Teodore's aim and using his sword to knock the long shaft from the man's hand. Then Konstantin brought Veles around to trample the enemy.

But Veles cooperated only for a moment, then reared so Konstantin could barely stay in his saddle. When he caught his balance, he saw the blade sticking from Veles's shoulder. An injury like that would make a horse difficult to control, so Konstantin dismounted and took a moment to send Veles toward Bojan. Better a stab than a broken leg. If they didn't have to gallop off in a hurry, the horse might recover.

Now both men fought on the ground, and that gave Župan Teodore the advantage because he wasn't injured. Župan Teodore waited, sword in one hand and shield in the other. Konstantin raised his own shield and ran at his enemy, hoping speed would aid him.

The two crashed together, and the sounds of their grappling shields echoed across the field. Konstantin hewed with one arm and blocked with the other. The wound in his back pulled with pain, but he dared not slow his attack. He aimed high, and when Župan Teodore raised his blade and his shield, Konstantin cut low, striking flesh.

Župan Teodore fell to the ground. From his low position, he swiped at Konstantin's feet and knocked him, too, into the dirt.

The fall wouldn't have been so awful if Konstantin hadn't landed on his wound. The pain went from a steady throb to a howling burst that made the edges of his vision blur.

Župan Teodore dove onto him, shieldless now but armed with a sword as vicious as his intent. Konstantin blocked one stroke with his blade and held it, his muscles burning with the strain. Župan Teodore hewed again, and again, Konstantin stopped the blade with his own and managed to hold. Then another swing, and Konstantin knocked it to the side and swung his shield into Teodore's right temple. The man's head snapped back, and Konstantin thrust his blade into his opponent's neck.

As his enemy's body collapsed and bled, Konstantin inhaled relief. He stumbled to his feet and kicked Župan Teodore onto his back. A blow like that ought to kill someone, but with an entire army waiting nearby, Konstantin would leave no doubt. He raised his sword, then brought it down with all his remaining might, sundering Župan Teodore's head from his shoulders.

He stepped away from the corpse. The slain župan's men watched. He saw surprise or anger in most faces. Then one face met Konstantin's gaze for a moment, lifted a crossbow, and aimed. Konstantin threw his shield up, knowing he would be too late, but the bolt hadn't been aimed at him.

Grigorii had been standing nearby to watch the duel. He slumped forward and, with his hands still tied, wasn't able to catch himself. Miladin bent beside him, but even from a distance, Konstantin could tell that the wound was mortal.

Men from all three župas drew out swords and took up defensive postures, but no one else raised a crossbow or stepped from their ranks, other than Župan Nikola, who strode forward with several of his men. "What is the meaning of this? Your champion is dead. According to the agreement made by your late župan, you are to march back to your grad and cause no disorder on your return."

Župan Teodore's satnik stepped forward and bowed with respect to Župan Nikola. "We will withdraw now."

"You slew one of Rivak's men and breached your agreement."

The satnik glanced at the ranks of men from his župa. "My župan's last request was that the spy not leave the field alive. Grigorii knew too many secrets. We will withdraw now, and I ask for your clemency. We do not wish a battle. We only wanted to fulfill our župan's command."

Župan Nikola looked to Konstantin, who nodded. "They may leave." Only a day ago, he would not have been so forgiving. But Grigorii's actions had earned him an execution Konstantin hadn't wanted to carry out. Now justice had been served, in a way.

Župan Nikola motioned for Župan Teodore's men to leave, and as the tension eased, Suzana rushed to Konstantin's side.

"I'm covered in blood," he warned her.

"I don't care." She threw her arms around him, and he dropped his sword to embrace her. That was something he had feared he would never do again, but now he held her quivering body while Župan Teodore's men retrieved the pieces of their leader's remains and withdrew from the field, heading east on the road back to their župa.

Exhaustion pulled at Konstantin, but so did relief and gratitude. For so long, he had struggled against invisible foes, and it had felt as if he would never be the župan he wished to be. Now he would have an opportunity to rebuild and make his people strong again. He kissed Suzana's forehead. Now he would have another chance with her too.

Suzana stood in the doorway between her room and her husband's as Magdalena examined the bruises along Konstantin's body and checked the stitches from the day before.

They were safe now, all of them. The German mercenaries had journeyed with Župan Nikola to his grad, then returned with Lidija, Ivan, Danilo, Decimir, and Decimir's bodyguards. The group had made it to Rivakgrad as the late afternoon sun had warmed the bailey. Danilo and Ivan had been quick to climb from the horse they'd shared so they could run to Dama Zorica, then to Kostya, then to her. Lidija, riding behind Decimir, had been more leisurely in her dismount, lingering near Decimir as long as she could.

Magdalena tsked as she examined Konstantin's back while Miladin looked on. "This wound needs rest if it is to heal."

Konstantin nodded. "Now that everyone is safe, I can give it the rest it needs."

"I'll come again tomorrow." Magdalena gathered her supplies, took her husband's hand, and left.

Konstantin turned to Suzana and smiled. She recognized the love there, and the weariness.

"Shall I leave, so you can rest?" she asked.

He held a hand out to her. "I expect I will be very sedate company, but I'd rather you stay."

She climbed into his bed, and he snuggled next to her and closed his eyes.

"I was afraid Župan Teodore's army wouldn't leave," she said. "They still outnumbered us. They could have killed us all. They would have had a war on their hands, but emotion had to be high, for them to see their župan killed."

"I think with him dead, they had no choice but to follow his last orders. He ruled completely. With him gone, there was no one else to follow."

Konstantin, too, was a župan, and he held authority, but he didn't command it so much as earn it with the concern he gave his men and the care he gave his people. Suzana did not think any of the garrison, other than Grigorii, would have calmly take up Konstantin's body and left the field when the numbers had favored them, had the situation been reversed.

"What do you think Dama Emilija will do?" Suzana asked. The woman had disparaged Suzana for her birth, and now she would hate Konstantin, too, because he had slain her husband.

"We will wait and see, but she can't hope to beat us when we have strong allies and she's lost her husband's spy."

"Everything will be easier now, won't it?"

Konstantin open his eyes. "I hope so. But I am still a vassal to the sultan, and I do not wish to die a slave to the Turks."

"You defeated Župan Teodore. Perhaps in time, you can defeat the sultan as well."

He let out a heavy breath. "Prying myself loose from the sultan's grasp will be more difficult than defeating a fellow župan. But if we garner our strength and gather allies . . ."

"We've time now. To build. To grow. To prepare. You ensured that today."

"I hope so. Then I will be a vassal only to my wife."

Suzana chuckled as he ran his hands along her back. "Will you?"

"Yes. I am yours to command."

She pushed herself onto an elbow and leaned over him. "Then I humbly ask you to accept this kiss and then sleep and return it in the morning."

She kissed him softly on the mouth, intending to make the kiss gentle and short, given his injuries. Yet the way he kissed her back quickly convinced her that there was no hurry to end the gesture. Cords of relief, joy, and love wove together, almost tangible enough to grasp in her hands. For themselves, they had trust, friendship, love, and passion. And now for their lands, they had time and the hope of coming freedom.

Epilogue

1378

Konstantin looked on as Decimir handed Lidija a ripe red apple and a golden ring. Lidija beamed as she accepted the betrothal gifts. She looked radiant. A girl grown into a woman. It was time for her to marry, but the moment was bittersweet for Konstantin.

Suzana nudged him gently with her elbow. “You are allowed to smile on the day of your sister’s betrothal.”

“Perhaps, but I’m not sure if I want to smile or cry.” He pulled his eyes from his sister to his wife, remembering how shy she’d been at their betrothal. Lidija, in contrast, showed no reservations. “I’m going to miss her, but I don’t think a župan is allowed to shed tears because his sister is marrying a man she loves and moving a half day’s ride away.”

Suzana’s lips pulled up in amusement. “A župan beloved by his people, his garrison, and his family is allowed to do a great many things.”

They stood outside the main church in Župan Dragomir’s largest grad. Four years had passed since Konstantin had defeated Župan Teodore. He remained a vassal of the sultan, but they’d made progress toward their goal of freedom. Harvests had been plentiful the last several seasons, and new men had joined the garrison. Suzana had inherited her father’s business upon his death two years ago. His trade had grown smaller during his illness, but between a new steward and Suzana’s oversight, it now brought in enough to pay the sultan’s tribute and hire mercenaries when needed. Rivak was no longer so weak.

As the ceremony ended, the crowds pressed toward Župan Dragomir’s grody. Konstantin walked with Suzana on one side and his grandfather on the other. Župan Đurad Lukarević had accompanied Ivan back to Rivak after his latest summer in Sivi Gora so they could both be present for the betrothal and for the marriage ceremony set to take place the following day.

Ivan walked on the other side of Grandfather with Danilo. The boys, young men now, had been nearly inseparable since Ivan's return a week before. Both had grown over the summer, in height and in confidence. Ivan had promised Konstantin that when the time came to rebel from the Turks, Sivi Gora would stand with Rivak. Ivan had yet to see his thirteenth winter, so years would pass before he could fight by his brother's side, but someday, Konstantin would be glad to have him as an ally.

People lined the main road, cheering their župan's heir and his soon-to-be bride. Konstantin recognized a few members of Dragomir's garrison, and Grigorii's sister. She had married one of the German mercenaries, and they'd made their home in Dragomir's grad, where fewer people knew her past. The townspeople would follow the family into the grody for feasting, then do the same thing after Decimir and Lidija were married.

After the week's festivities, Konstantin would meet with the other local župans to discuss their goal of throwing off Ottoman rule. Župans Dragomir and Nikola were his firm allies, and the cousin who had taken over rule of Teodore's župa was married to one of Nikola's kinswomen. He focused all his efforts on planning a rebellion against the Turks rather than encroaching on his neighbor's lands. Rebuilding a people after the disaster at Maritsa and the constant cost of campaigns for the sultan was a task not yet complete for any of them, but the hunger for liberty remained strong.

Konstantin would have to answer the sultan's summons and feign loyalty for several years more. He already had three times since his first journey to Anatolia. He hadn't repeated the feats that had made him, briefly, one of the sultan's favorites. Now he did what was required and conserved the strength of his men. He had learned to campaign with efficiency and leave the horrors of war behind when he returned to his family. He didn't enjoy his service to the sultan, but there would be an end of it, of that he was sure.

Suzana pressed his arm to catch his attention. That morning she had shared her suspicion that she was with child again, and the still-secret joy seemed to light her face. "They look happy."

Konstantin watched his sister and Decimir. They did look happy. Their love was already strong, and now it would grow, just as his love for Suzana had grown from a tiny trickle of promise in the small garden of her father's villa into a vast sea that stretched beyond the limits of his vision. "I pray they will be as happy as we have been, because I can think of no better fate."

Author's Note

The Battle of Maritsa (also spelled Marica, or called the Battle of Cernomen/Chernomen) is shrouded in legend. Though this battle is less famous than the 1389 Battle of Kosovo, some historians argue that the 1371 Battle of Maritsa was more devastating to the Serb warrior class. As portrayed in this novel, the Turks attacked the Serbs while they were camped and soundly defeated them. The roles of Župan Dragomir's brother and Župan Teodore are, like the characters, fictional. Betrayal is a strong theme in Serb legends, but its inclusion in the Battle of Maritsa is added for storytelling purposes. Most historians agree that Maritsa left the Serbs without a king of their own and made them instead vassals of Sultan Murad, with the accompanying tribute and military service.

I have tried to depict the overall political atmosphere as accurately as possible. The Serbian Empire was in decline during the late fourteenth century and the Ottoman Empire on the rise, though still some distance from its apex of power. Most accounts of Serbian and Turkish history were recorded some generations after the events. As might be expected, many of my sources contradicted each other. In my research for this series, I took notes from over sixty books and read many of them cover to cover, but that doesn't mean I got everything right. If I've made any errors, I offer sincere apologies.

Serbs in the late fourteenth century spoke a language that originated as Old Church Slavonic but was in the process of transforming into Early South Slavic. Contemporaries wouldn't have been familiar with either name; they would have called their language Slavonic or Slavic.

At the time of the story, the Ottomans would have been reluctant to refer to themselves as Turks, considering that term more appropriate for rival, less civilized Turkish tribes in Anatolia. Their Christian opponents wouldn't have placed much of a distinction between Turk and Ottoman.

I've done my best to describe clothing, weapons, and buildings as they are most likely to have been at the time. I have also tried to portray the religious and cultural beliefs and attitudes with accuracy to the time period.

If you enjoyed this book, I would be very grateful for your review on websites where books are sold or discussed or for your recommendation to other readers in person or via social media.

Special thanks to Ron Machado, Tina Peacock, Kathi Oram Peterson, Charissa Stastny, and Bev Walkling for their insightful test reads. I also wish to thank the teams at both Covenant Communications and Shadow Mountain. This series includes pieces of history that I've wanted to tell for a long time, and I'm grateful for their help in bringing this book to readers. I especially wish to thank my editor, Samantha Millburn, for believing in and improving this project.

Enjoy this sneak peek of

BEYOND THE CRESCENT SKY

THE BALKAN LEGENDS

Chapter One
Off to Wander

The Balkans, 1383

Ivan lifted his three-year-old nephew from the back of a dappled gray pony. The hem of Marko's short tunic fluttered around his small trousers as Ivan placed him on the straw-strewn floor of the stable. "We'd like to take you with us, but if we took you away for an entire fortnight, your mother would kill us."

"And if your mother kills us, there will be no one to help you snitch pastries from the kitchen." Danilo, Ivan's cousin, winked, then plucked the boy up, tossed him in the air, and caught him again.

Marko squealed in delight and patted Danilo's beard. It was dark and full, and Ivan, a year younger than his cousin, tried very hard not to be envious of it. "But you'll be away too long!" Marko stuck out his bottom lip.

Ivan took the saddle off the pony and put it on a post. "It will be shorter than my last trip. You'll remember me when we return, won't you?" Ivan had been gone most of the summer, off to his grandfather's lands, where he was heir. But it was here in Rivak where he'd grown up and where the people most dear to him lived. It had taken little Marko dozens of pony rides, a score of stolen pastries, and a full week to grow comfortable with Ivan again upon his return. Leaving so soon meant he might fade from Marko's memory again.

Marko squirmed in Danilo's arms. "But I want to see my father again."

"So do I." Ivan pulled a few pieces of dry grass from the pony's coat, then set about doing a thorough brushing despite their hurry. Based on the news they'd received from a passing monk, the army Ivan's brother led was somewhere in Macedonia, still some distance from Rivak, but Konstantin's brotherly lectures over the years had stuck in Ivan's head—there were no shortcuts in the care of horses or ponies. Ivan and Danilo had taken Marko out for a ride, so it was their responsibility to care for the animal afterward.

"We'll make sure your father comes home safely." Danilo set Marko down and saddled two coursers. Though kinsman, Ivan and Danilo looked nothing alike. His aunt said Ivan took after her brother, the former župan of Rivak, and Danilo took after her husband, the Turkish refugee who'd served Župan Miroslav until their deaths at the Battle of Maritsa. Ivan had to take her word for it because the battle was twelve years in the past. Ivan had been five. He remembered his father only a little and his uncle even less.

"Why are you taking so many swords?" Marko poked at Ivan's sheaths as he fastened them to the saddle.

"The saber is for fighting on horseback. The spathion is for fighting on foot." Ivan took the swords out to show the boy. "See how the saber has a curved blade so it's less likely to get stuck? And the spathion is sharp on both sides. But we won't need either. Your father leads a mighty army. And we'll be in friendly lands all the way there."

"Mostly friendly." Danilo's lips twisted into a half smile.

Ivan adjusted his horse's bit. "Mostly friendly." Travel in the remnants of the Serb and Roman Empires always involved risk. The monk had made it unmolested, but few brigands would see him as a tempting target. Men traveling with warhorses and pack mules might not be so lucky. Ivan should have known better than to tempt fate. He'd seen illness, death, and other disasters befall his family often enough that caution should have been his constant companion. Yet standing in the familiar stables, warmed by the early autumn sun, it was hard to feel anything other than excitement at the prospect of a journey with his cousin.

Danilo took his horse's reins in one hand and Marko's fingers in the other. "Come on, we best turn you over to your mother before we ride off."

Ivan expected to find Suzana in the chapel or in the keep, but she stood just outside the stables, arms crossed as she studied the two laden mules Ivan and Danilo had left near the palisade wall of Rivakgrad's fortified grody.

"Where are you two going?" Her brown eyes hadn't lost their normal warmth, but now they narrowed in suspicion.

"To find your husband." Ivan glanced around the bailey to make sure his aunt wasn't nearby. He didn't think they would get away with leaving if both women were set against it.

"Your brother isn't lost. And you're needed here—you can't ride off during harvest. It's bad enough that Kostya and most of the garrison are gone."

Ivan checked the ropes on his pack mule. "The merophs will manage the crops, as they always do. We'll be back in time to help with everything else."

Suzana frowned, probably because Ivan was right. There was work for them if they stayed but nothing that couldn't wait until their return.

"Don't be angry, Suzana." Danilo's lips made a charming sort of pout. "We'll pester him with tales of your sweetness and beauty and speed his return to you."

"Kostya will do what is most practical for the army, regardless of his wishes to see me again." Her voice was stern, but the frown had softened.

"Marko was saying how much he'd like to ride with us. You'll let him come, won't you?" Ivan knew the answer would be no, but if they agreed to leave Marko behind, Suzana might feel that she'd won a concession from them.

She took Marko's hand and pulled him to her side. "That's not funny, Ivan. Marko isn't going, and you aren't either. There may be brigands or ghazis, and there are only two of you. It's simply not safe."

"I'll keep my bow strung just in case we run into trouble." Danilo pulled his bow out and wedged it between his feet to string it.

Ivan suspected he would unstring it again as soon as they were out of sight, because Danilo was meticulous with his bows, and leaving it strung would put too much wear on the string and limbs.

"You're still boys. You may not go," Suzana said.

Ivan mounted his horse. "Nearly eighteen is hardly a boy. And Danilo is nineteen. We should have gone with the army in the spring."

Suzana walked to Ivan's horse. "Kostya had you stay because he wanted you safe."

"And I need to see that he is safe." Ivan and Konstantin had lost both their parents and all three of their sisters over the years. They still had Aunt Zorica and Danilo and Suzana and Marko, but as much as Ivan loved each of them, no one could replace his brother.

Suzana glanced at Danilo. "What did your mother say?"

Danilo fiddled with his horse's bridle. "I wrote her a loving letter explaining our intentions and asked one of the grooms to deliver it." Ivan had overheard his cousin tell the groom not to deliver it until they were out of Rivakgrad, but neither of them told Suzana that.

"I really think you should stay." Suzana crossed her arms again.

Danilo finished adjusting the straps. "I think you're jealous. You want to come. I'll saddle your mare for you."

Suzana sighed. "I know my place. It is here, managing my husband's lands when his overlord calls him away to war."

"And our place is at our župan's side," Ivan said.

"Kostya won't be your župan for long, Ivan. You know your place."

"Which is why I must go to Kostya now. It's one of my last chances to show him my loyalty." Come spring, Ivan would live with his grandfather in Sivi Gora permanently, and then he would see his brother but seldom. "Our days together are numbered. Can you blame me for wanting an extra week with him?"

"I understand why you wish to go." Suzana ran her fingers through Marko's fluffy brown hair. "But what if something happens to you?"

"We're armed. I'll sleep in my armor, if it will ease your worry." Ivan hoped she wouldn't make the request, because the mail hauberk was heavy and uncomfortable. He intended to leave it on the pack mule unless they spotted bandits.

Suzana shook her head. "Don't be too proud of your skill with the sword. It can't protect you from everything, and it's easy to outnumber a party of two."

"But Danilo has his bow, and he's the best archer in all of Rivak. It's unlikely he'll let anyone get close enough for me to test my blade, should we encounter anyone hostile, which we won't."

Suzana looked over their equipment. They both had bows, quivers, multiple swords and daggers, lances, and maces. "I've sent enough people off to war this year, haven't I? Will you make me send you off as well?"

"You're not sending us to war. The weapons are mostly for hunting. We're bound to grow tired of salted fish and biscuits." Danilo managed to say everything with a straight face. Ivan had to reach down and pretend to adjust his stirrup to hide threatening laughter. He supposed it was possible to hunt wild boars with a mace, but he couldn't see why anyone would try. He and Danilo intended to ride, not hunt. The weapons were for defense should they be attacked.

"Please, Suzana?" Ivan asked when laughter was no longer imminent. "You can't blame us for loving Kostya."

She groaned in frustration. "You'll keep arguing with me until I agree, won't you? Or ride off the moment I'm distracted?"

Ivan and Danilo both nodded.

Suzana looked to the eastern horizon, then back at them. "It seems I can't really stop you, but do try to stay out of trouble."

"Danilo excels at keeping me out of trouble."

"He also excels at getting you into trouble." Suzana chuckled. "God speed you on your way. And give my love to Kostya."

Danilo gave Marko a final goodbye and then tossed Ivan the lead ropes for the pack mules. He mounted, and the two of them left before Suzana could change her mind.